Samuel M. Peto

The Resources and Prospects of America

ascertained during a visit to the States in the autumn of 1865

Samuel M. Peto

The Resources and Prospects of America
ascertained during a visit to the States in the autumn of 1865

ISBN/EAN: 9783337368104

Printed in Europe, USA, Canada, Australia, Japan

Cover: Foto ©Andreas Hilbeck / pixelio.de

More available books at **www.hansebooks.com**

THE

RESOURCES

AND

PROSPECTS OF AMERICA

ASCERTAINED DURING A VISIT TO THE STATES

IN THE AUTUMN OF 1865.

BY

SIR S. MORTON PETO, BART.

M.P. FOR BRISTOL.

LONDON:
R. CLAY, SON, AND TAYLOR, PRINTERS,
BREAD STREET HILL.

TO

MY AMERICAN FRIENDS

WHO RECEIVED ME WITH SO MUCH KINDNESS AND

HOSPITALITY DURING MY RECENT VISIT

This Work

ON THE RESOURCES AND FUTURE OF THEIR COUNTRY

IS

RESPECTFULLY DEDICATED.

PREFACE.

DURING my visit to America in 1865, a large number
of volumes and other documents, abounding in statistical information relating to the resources and progress
of the United States, were placed in my hands by
members of several departments of the Government
and other authorities. Some time after my return to
England I was asked to read a paper on America to
the Statistical Society of London; and having recourse
to my books and papers with a view to such a compilation, I found that I had been placed in possession
of a mass of information not generally accessible to
the British public, and which appeared to afford valuable subjects for reflection.

It was thus that the present volume arose. In its
compilation I have received much assistance from
American friends thoroughly acquainted with the
various topics I have undertaken to treat, and whose

corrections and suggestions have been extremely valuable.

It will be observed, that I have carefully confined myself to my subject—the " RESOURCES AND PRO-SPECTS OF AMERICA." As far as possible, I have avoided all political allusions; and I have not attempted any descriptions of the country, or of the manners and habits of the people, which have been rendered familiar to us by far abler writers than myself. That which I have been anxious to afford my fellow-countrymen is an opportunity of forming a more correct judgment than that at which many have hitherto arrived, of the progress, means, and probable future of the great nation on the other side of the Atlantic, with which, by every tie of fraternity, we ought to be so closely allied.

In portions of this work I have drawn largely upon the several volumes of " Reports issued by the Commissioners of the Census of the United States, 1860." At the commencement of my task I resorted to those Reports merely as books of reference, but I soon found that, on many points, they were of far higher value and importance. For the greater part of my statistical information I am indebted to those Reports, and I have followed the calculations of the Census even where I have found its figures liable to be disputed.

Let me add, however, that in arriving at conclusions with reference to those statistics, I have by no means permitted myself to be led blindly by the Census Reports, or by the feeling prevailing in America which in many cases they reflect. On the contrary, it will be observed that, on several very important topics, I have recorded my entire dissent from the conclusions arrived at by the Commissioners, and especially from those relating to the manufacturing industry and commerce of the country.

My book bristles with figures, and I fear will scarcely commend itself to those who think that there was wisdom in the emphatic enunciation of the Eastern Pacha, who is reported to have declared to some one making inquiries relating to his Government, that he was sixty years old, and had governed a province for five-and-thirty years, but had never even thought of counting the tiles upon the roofs of the houses or the number of donkeys within his pachalik. It may, possibly, be thought by some who do not fully appreciate the force and value of statistics, that I have made unnecessary use of them : in reply, I have only to observe that I have written principally for those who do find in figures a source of valuable information.

In submitting the volume to criticism, not only

on the European but on the American side of the Atlantic, I will only ask leave to make one claim. However my conclusions may be judged of in America, I do claim that I have written with a friendly feeling towards a people from whom, during my visit to them, I received nothing but attention, hospitality, and kindness. I should be very ungrateful, indeed, did I not entirely reciprocate the feeling shown towards me by all classes in America ; and, however much my views may differ from those of many persons in the States, I trust they will find in no single observation I have made a ground on which to charge me with a want of due sense of their kind consideration.

13, KENSINGTON PALACE GARDENS,
London, 15th March, 1866.

CONTENTS.

✦

SECTION II.

AGRICULTURE.

SECTION III.

MANUFACTURES.

Section IV.

M I N E R A L S.

Section V.

C O M M E R C E.

—

Section VI.

RAILROADS.

CHAPTER I.

CHAPTER II.

CHAPTER III.

Section VII.

THE SOUTH.

CHAPTER I.

CHAPTER II.

CHAPTER III.

Section VIII.
FINANCE.

CHAPTER I.

CHAPTER II.

Section IX.

SECTION I.

POPULATION.

AMERICAN RESOURCES,

&c.

SECTION I.—POPULATION.

CHAPTER I.

PRELIMINARY.

WHEN I visited the United States in The Civil War. the autumn of last year (1865), the Civil War — a war of unparalleled magnitude and severity—had only just been brought to a termination. The position of the country gave rise to considerations of unequalled interest. To what extent had it suffered? how long was it likely to languish under the effects of war?

It was a happy circumstance, that, throughout this Condition in which it has left America. unequalled civil contest, peace was preserved with every foreign nation. Internal order also was maintained throughout the North :—the laws had been respected and obeyed. Although a million of the population had been withdrawn from their industrial occupations to assume arms, the progress of peaceful industry had not been arrested. In the words of the late President of the United States :—

" The axe has enlarged the borders of our settle-
" ments, and the mines, as well of iron and coal, as of
" the precious metals, have [during the war] yielded
" more abundantly than before. Population has
" steadily increased, notwithstanding the waste that
" has been made in the camp, the siege, and in the
" battle-field. The country, now rejoicing in the con-
" sciousness of augmented strength and vigour, is
" permitted to expect continuance of years with large
" increase of prosperity and freedom."

To this may be added the most remarkable feature of the Civil War in the United States,—namely, the marvellous sustentation of credit in the North, throughout the whole period of the rebellion.

On the European side of the Atlantic, the enquiry was constantly repeated, " When will the finances of America collapse ?" Speculations were made in the money markets on the assumption that the American resources must inevitably fail. Yet on the American side, not only was there no idea of failure, but, despite the increase of debt, which accumulated with a rapidity absolutely unknown in any previous history, the pressure of taxation was unflinchingly borne, and the payment of interest was regularly made. Nor was this all. Although the country might have been expected to have been drained both of men and stores, to supply the immense armies which were sustained, the requirements of the entire population were met without any increase of prices beyond that which resulted from a depreciation of the currency. Throughout the war the nation gave evidence of rapidly increasing wealth.

Probably, the parallel of this is not to be found in the world's history. All records, of whatsoever period, show, that during fierce and desolating struggles, the populations engaged in them have suffered fearful privations and miseries, and that protracted periods have elapsed before they have been able to recover from their effects. America, which in so many respects has shown herself superior to ordinary rules, has, in regard to the effects of war, shown that the heaviest and most costly civil conflict can be borne not only without exhaustion, but even with an increase of national prosperity.

Historically unexampled,

If I am asked to account for this, I can only do so by attributing it to the wonderful elasticity of the RESOURCES OF THE UNITED STATES.

and attributable to the RESOURCES of AMERICA.

In my travel through the United States in the autumn of last year, the abundant resources of the country was the feature which struck me most forcibly. It appeared the key to everything else. I saw wild territories, both of forest and prairie, being cleared and populated: I saw villages springing into towns, and towns into cities, with a rapidity so marvellous, that one's first idea was to attribute it all to the work of some powerful magician: I passed through whole regions where every description of grain seemed to spring up spontaneously: I went over lines of railway seemingly constructed for the express purpose of conveying this produce to ports from which it could be shipped to countries where there was a superabundant

Abundance of those resources.

population to consume it: I passed down immense rivers, swarming with steamboats and other vessels, filled with produce: I was brought into communication with the merchants who conducted the varied commerce to which all this gave rise: and, looking at all I met with, I could not fail to be struck, as a practical man, with the extraordinary and wonderful character of American resources, surpassing, by far, anything of which we have the slightest experience in the old world, great as are our own products, and remarkable as is the industry of our teeming population.

The National Debt.

It is mainly with the desire to draw the attention of my fellow-countrymen to this remarkable feature of America, that I have undertaken the task entailed on me by this publication. But, before I enter upon any details respecting American resources, I must offer some particulars relating to the debt. Commercial men and others, who are abou to embark in the great trade which America will speedily open up, will naturally desire to look, in the first instance, at the Dr. side of the account, and examine the extent of the indebtedness, before they proceed to consider the means the nation has at its disposal of meeting its liabilities.

Its enormous Total.

The debt incurred by the war amounts to an enormous item, as expressed in arithmetical figures. On the 31st of May, 1865, at which date the war may be taken to have ceased, the public debt of the United States was officially declared by Mr. McCulloch, now Secretary of the Treasury, to amount to $2,635,205,753, equal, at the ordinary rate of five dollars to the pound, to upwards of £527,000,000 of English money. The interest upon this debt was computed at $124,638,874, equal to £24,927,775 of our money. Besides the interest-bearing debt there were, in circulation, nearly 660 millions of dollars of "Legal Tender Notes" (better known here by the title of "Green Backs"), which were legally receivable for all dues to the nation, except Customs. Adding to the debt of £527,000,000, the provision which must be made on account of these and other liabilities, we have a total indebtedness on the part of the Government of the United States, in round numbers, of $3,000,000,000 (Three Thousand Million Dollars), or £600,000,000 (Six Hundred Millions) of our money.*

At the commencement of the war, the National Debt of the United States amounted to only $65,000,000, or £13,000,000 sterling. The official statements show its increase as follows:— Its rapid increase.

25 April, 1862	$523,299,945
10 „ 1863	939,497,359
26 „ 1864	1,656,815,105
31 March, 1865	2,366,955,077

It will be seen, from these figures, that the increase of the debt was by far the greatest during the last year of the war. Between 1862 and 1863 the debt increased

---

* Since this chapter was written, the "Report of the Secretary of the Treasury on the state of the Finances" for the year 1865 has been presented to Congress. It substantially confirms these estimates. The debt on the 31st October, 1865, including the United States or Legal Tender Notes, was declared to be $2,808,549,437 ; and the Secretary says, "when all our liabilities shall be ascertained, it seems safe to estimate it at *Three Thousand Million* Dollars." [*Vide post. Sec. Finance.*]

at the rate of $1,189,135 a day; but between 1864 and 1865 it increased at the rate of $2,094,808 a day! Nothing can show more forcibly than such statistics the efforts which were capable of being made by a country which many persons considered must have already exhausted its resources.

Rate of Interest at which it was incurred.

It is a very remarkable fact, that all this accumulation of debt was incurred at rates of interest absolutely lower than those which prevailed prior to the commencement of the war. In 1860 the current rate of interest upon the national securities was 6 per cent.; and it is said that the then Secretary of the Treasury was borrowing money at nearly double that rate of interest. In 1863, however, the average rate of interest on the greatly increased debt was only 3·89 per cent., and the highest rate (for a comparatively small sum) was only 7·30 per cent. At the close of the war, the average rate of interest on the whole debt is actually less than it was at the commencement of the war, being only 5·55 per cent. 276 millions were at 5 per cent., 1,117 millions at 6 per cent., 156½ millions (or the compound interest notes) at 6·46 per cent., and 301 millions at 7·30 per cent. The two last items of the debt were convertible into 6 per cent. stock in August 1867 and 1868. This appears, undoubtedly, to show a skilful administration of financial affairs.

Almost the whole debt held by American citizens.

It is another noticeable fact that almost the entirety of this debt is held by Citizens of the Republic. During the War, the financiers of the United States were not, indeed, in a position to negotiate their securities out of the country, except at excessive and unreasonable sacrifices. The whole of the debt incurred had, therefore, to be raised within the territory. It is insisted by those who have turned their attention to the question in America, that this was effected by Mr. Chase with great skill and judgment, and by the adoption of a system which tended to place the financial position of the country on a peculiarly sound and satisfactory basis. This part of the question, however, is mainly of local interest. The principal means employed was the authorization of National or United States Banks (instead of separate State Banks), as Banks of Issue; the circulation of such new Banks being secured to the public not only by private Capital, but by adequate deposits of United States Stocks with the Government. The new arrangement, which materially interfered with vested interests, was, in the first instance, greatly opposed, and after a Session of eight months in 1861, Congress failed to adopt it. But when the State Banks in 1861-2, found it necessary to suspend specie payments, the country came round to Mr. Chase's plan, and adopted "An Act to provide a National Currency, secured by a pledge of United States Stocks, and to provide for the circulation and redemption thereof," upon the basis of which enactment the whole financial system of the country has since been conducted.

Mr. Chase's financial policy.

In Great Britain, where our Debt is £800,000,000 and the Annual Interest payable upon it £26,000,000, we have been accustomed to hear constant complaints of "the burden of the debt," without one syllable ever being uttered, that I can remember, respecting its liquidation. Nothing struck me more forcibly in America than the different tone of the population

Resolve of the Americans to liquidate the debt.

respecting their liabilities. With a debt of £600,000,000, involving an Annual Interest of (say) £25,000,000 (nearly as heavy a payment as our own), the cry of the whole population is that "The Debt MUST be paid, "and CAN be paid." "The faith of our Nation is "pledged for its discharge," is cried on one side. "We "are financially able to pay," proclaims another party. I was referred by several parties to the past experience of the nation. They told me that the debt entailed by the War of 1812, was wholly discharged, from the ordinary sources of revenue, in a period of nineteen years ; and that practically the burden of that debt had never been felt by anybody, though, considering the difference in the numerical population, the capital wealth and the future prospects of the country, it was almost as great a debt, in proportion, as the present. In fact, from the President at Washington, down to the humblest agriculturalist in the far West, I found but one prevailing feeling respecting the debt. Emphatically the whole population said—"It *must* be paid : "it *can* be paid : it *shall* be paid : and it *will* be paid." Everybody seems to have his own scheme for effecting the object : in fact, the Americans are just now almost as great financiers as the Birmingham people used to be in the days of Mr. Thomas Attwood. In almost every town there is some Stock-broker or Banker, or Financial Agent, who has made and published his calculations on the subject. The most sanguine calculate the payment of the amount to cover a period of twenty years : others estimate that twenty-five or even thirty years will be needed. The President of the United States in his Message to Congress, and the

Period assigned for its redemption.

Secretary of the Treasury in his last Annual Report, assume that "the whole will be liquidated within a "period not exceeding *thirty* years." But, whatever the period assigned for the total redemption of the liability, there is but one feeling as to the necessity of liquidating it, and there seems to be but one faith in the capability of accomplishing the object.

I own that, without being sanguine at the outset, I at length brought my own mind to a conclusion equally strong with that of all the Americans I encountered, that the Nation could well bear all her liabilities, and was quite equal to the payment of them within a reasonable period, if necessary.

The Nation able to bear the liability.

To this conclusion I was brought, more especially, by an examination and estimate of the Resources of the United States: the subject which I propose to treat.

CHAPTER II

THE POPULATION.

THE population of the United States has increased in the following rapid ratio :—

1800	....	5,305,925
1810	....	7,239,815
1820	....	9,638,121
1830	....	12,866,020
1840	....	17,069,453
1850	....	23,191,876
1860	....	31,429,891

There is nothing in the old world to equal this rate of progress. The population of Great Britain and Ireland in 1800 was 16 millions, and in 1861 was under 30 millions. Since 1830 the population of the United States has increased 19 millions, whilst that of our kingdom has increased less than 6 millions.

The cause of this great increase of population in America is attributable to immigration,—a cause which does not appertain to any of the older European nations. Whilst the increase of the population in Great Britain represents almost exclusively the natural increase of a populous and thriving country, the increase in the population of the United States represents an entirely different element.

It has been mathematically demonstrated that if the to which one-third of the present population is due. United States since the year 1800 had been in the same circumstances as Great Britain—that is, if there had been no immigration, and the increase of her population had arisen from natural causes only—the free white and coloured people of the United States would, at the present time, have only numbered 10,463,000, or one-third of the whole present population. In fact, it is estimated that, of the whole population in 1863, the immigrants of the present century, and their descendants, number more than 21,000,000, or two-thirds of the whole.

Prior to 1820, no returns were taken of the number Statistics of Immigration from 1800 to 1860. of aliens landing in the United States. It is estimated that there were about 70,000 arrivals between 1800 and 1810, and about 114,000 between 1810 and 1820. From 1820 there are official records of the number of immigrants, and I think it may be interesting to give the details, as showing how the country has been gradually built up.

Year.	Immigrants.	Year.	Immigrants.
1820	8,385	1833	58,640
1821	9,127	1834	65,365
1822	6,911	1835	45,374
1823	6,354	1836	76,242
1824	7,912	1837	79,340
1825	10,199	1838	38,914
1826	10,837	1839	68,069
1827	18,875	1840	84,066
1828	27,382	1841	80,289
1829	22,520	1842	104,565
1830	23,322	1843	52,496
1831	22,633	1844	78,615
1832	60,482	1845	114,371

Year.	Immigrants.	Year.	Immigrants.
1846	154,416	1855	200,877
1847	234,968	1856	200,436
1848	226,527	1857	251,306
1849	297,024	1858	123,126
1850	369,980	1859	121,282
1851	379,466	1860	153,640
1852	371,603		
1853	368,645	Total ...	5,062,414
1854	427,833		

Proportion of Sexes.

Of this total there were—

Males	2,977,603
Females	2,035,536
Sex not stated	49,275
Total	5,062,414

This disproportion of sexes amongst the immigrants maintains itself in the United States generally. At the census of 1860 there was an excess of 730,000 males over the females; just the reverse of the case in Great Britain and Ireland, where, with about the same population, the females outnumber the males by 877,000. This is a curious fact, as showing how wisely and accurately Providence has proportioned the sexes in different parts of the globe : our disproportion being obviously the result of emigration to America and Australia, whilst the obverse disproportion in both those countries is due to their immigration of European males.

Decennial proportions.

Classifying this immigration in decennial periods, we find that it has increased in the following proportions :—

	Immigrants.
In the 10 years ending 1829	128,502
In ,, ,, 1839	538,381
In ,, ,, 1849	1,427,337
In the 11 years ,, 1860	2,968,194
	5,062,414

It is of great advantage to the United States that by far the greater proportion of the immigrants are of the age at which they are best fitted for labour. The records shew that upwards of 50 per cent of the whole were between 15 and 30 years of age. Only 10 per cent. were above 40, and only about 8 per cent. under 5. *Ages of Immigrants.*

Great Britain and Ireland have contributed most largely to this immigration. Our own emigration returns show that, between 1814 and 1860, no less than 4,244,727 persons have emigrated to the United States and Canada. Of these the United States officials claim to have received directly 2,759,874, or, with those who came through Canada, about 3,250,000. It is certainly a fact that excites some wonder as regards our own country, that we should have been able to spare such immense masses of our population (comprehending upwards of 5,046,000) as have gone forth, not only to people the United States and Canada, but Australia, New Zealand, the Cape of Good Hope, and the numerous other possessions of Great Britain. That we should have been able to people the world in this way, and yet have made such unequalled strides in the acquisition of material wealth at home, remarkably illustrates the force of our manufacturing power and of our commerce, as well as the industry and enterprise of the British people. *Countries which have contributed to the population.*

Statistics.

But it is not Great Britain alone which has contributed to the population of America. It will be seen from the following table, that more or less of the population of almost every European country have been attracted to the shores of the United States.

IMMIGRATION, 1820–1860.

Great Britain and Ireland	2,750,874
Germany	1,486,044
France	208,063
Prussia	60,432
China	41,443
West Indies	40,487
Switzerland	37,733
Norway and Sweden	36,129
Holland	21,579
Mexico	17,766
Spain	16,248
Italy	11,202
Belgium	9,862
South America	6,201
Denmark	5,540
Azores	3,242
Portugal	2,614
Sardinia	2,030
Poland	1,659
Russia	1,374

Wealth introduced by the Immigrants.

It has been calculated, though on very imperfect data, that each immigrant who lands in America brings with him an average sum of 68 dollars, or (say) £13 12s. sterling. But these returns were obtained from amongst the poorest class of immigrants. Among cabin passengers the average amount would evidently be much higher; and from returns made to the Governments of Prussia and Bavaria, for seven years, by emigrants who left those countries with official permission, it appears that they each carried to America an average amount of 180 dollars, or £36 of our money. The United States officials calculate that the immigrants have brought into the United States not less than 400,000,000 of cash dollars or (say) £80,000,000 sterling, besides the much superior values represented by their physical, intellectual, and moral powers.

The causes which have led to the great emigration from Europe to the United States are very various. We all know that the early settlers in America were impelled to seek a refuge there from religious bigotry and political exclusion at home. Those causes are not now generally operative. It is probable that the tide of emigration to America which commenced to set in strongly about 1825, was occasioned by the opening out of the north-western States in that year, and by the prospect afforded of obtaining land in the country at exceedingly low rates. It will be observed that a great and sudden rise in the immigration occurred in 1832. This may have been occasioned both by the success of the settlers of the seven previous years, and by the unsettled condition of Europe at that time. Another accelerated movement, attributed to the loss of the potato crop in Ireland, began in 1847 ; and for several years from that period the immigration was swollen by the continental revolutions of 1848, and the discovery of gold in California. After the year 1854, the emigration from Europe declined, which is ascribed to the Crimean war, and afterwards to the outbreak of the Indian mutiny, absorbing large numbers in European armies. Subsequently the construction of new rail-

Side notes:
Causes of the large Emigration from Europe to America.

Religious and political exclusions.

Low prices of Land.

The Potato famine.

The Gold discoveries.

The recent decline of Immigration accounted for.

roads created a remunerative demand for labour at home. And after 1860 the civil war in the United States, and the effects it occasioned, greatly affected the immigration.

Occupations of the Immigrants. It is to be regretted that the occupations of immigrants have not been very perfectly registered in America. Out of five millions of immigrants, the occupations of three millions are not stated. Most of these, no doubt, were women and children, but it is also possible that a considerable number, being prepared to turn their hands to anything, considered it undesirable to define that they followed any particular occupation. Of the 3,000,000 whose occupations are stated, we find the following registration :—

OCCUPATIONS OF IMMIGRANTS.

Labourers	872,317
Farmers	764,837
Mechanics	407,524
Merchants	231,852
Servants	49,494
Miners	39,967
Mariners	29,484
Weavers and Spinners	11,557
Seamstresses and Milliners	5,246
Physicians	7,109
Clergymen	4,326
Clerks	3,882
Tailors	3,634
Shoemakers	3,474
Manufacturers	3,120
Lawyers	2,676
Artists	2,490
Masons	2,310
Engineers	2,016
Teachers	1,528

Bakers	1,272
Butchers	945
Musicians	729
Printers	705
Painters	647
Millers	631
Actors	588

Throughout the entire period of immigration, New York has been the principal port for the reception of immigrants, and continues to be so to this day. This is to be accounted for by the superior facilities of transit to and from that great commercial emporium. Out of the 8,300 immigrants in 1820, New York received 3,834; and out of 153,640 in 1860, she received 131,565. Their ultimate destination is, no doubt, very materially affected by the port at which they arrive. We are not, therefore, to be surprised at finding that 8 to 1 settle in the Northern States, and that of these 8 to 1 a very large proportion settle in the districts most adjacent to the place of landing. Until recently the State of New York itself contained the largest percentage of English and Irish in comparison with the native population. But, recently, the proportions have altered. California, and the great agricultural territories of Wisconsin and Minnesota, are now the principal resorts of foreigners. Wisconsin has been developed by English and Irish, Minnesota by Germans, California by the introduction of Chinese. The following table will show the proportions of native and foreign populations in sixteen of the principal States of the Union :—

Districts to which the Immigrants principally resort.

Proportions of the Foreign population,

PERCENTAGE OF NATIVE AND FOREIGN POPULATIONS ACCORDING TO CENSUS 1860.

STATE.	Native.		Foreign.
California	52.02	....	47.98
Wisconsin	64.31	....	35.69
Minnesota	66.22	....	33.78
New York	74.27	....	25.73
Rhode Island	78.58	....	21.42
Massachusetts	78.87	....	21.13
Michigan	80.09	....	19.91
Illinois	81.03	....	18.97
Virginia	97.81	....	2.19
South Carolina	98.58	....	1.42
Tennessee	98.09	....	1.91
Alabama	98.72	....	1.28
Georgia	98.90	....	1.10
Mississippi	98.92	....	1.08
Arkansas	99.14	....	0.86
North Carolina	99.67	....	0.33

in the Northern,

and in the Southern States.

This table shows how largely the tide of immigration has spread in the Northern in comparison with the Southern States. But for the purpose of this argument, let me show how it has spread in the most flourishing cities of the States. I take some of the most populous—those numbering over 40,000 inhabitants :—

Proportion of Foreign population

CITY.	Total Population.	Foreign.	Percentage of Foreign.
New York	805,651	383,717	47.62
Philadelphia	585,529	169,430	28.93
Brooklyn (*N.Y.*)	266,661	104,589	39.22
Baltimore	212,418	52,497	24.71
Boston	177,812	63,791	35.88
New Orleans	168,675	64,621	38.31
Cincinnati	161,044	73,614	45.71
St. Louis	160,773	96,086	59.76

the great Cities.

CITY.	Total Population.	Foreign.	Percentage of Foreign.
Chicago	109,260	54,624	49.99
Buffalo (*N.Y.*)	81,129	37,684	46.44
Newark (*New Jersey*)	71,914	26,625	37.02
Louisville (*Kentucky*)	68,033	22,948	33.73
Albany (*N.Y.*)	62,367	21,619	34.66
Washington	61,122	10,765	17.61
San Francisco	56,802	28,454	50.09
Providence(*Rhode Island*)	50,666	12,570	24.80
Pittsburg (*Pa.*)	49,217	18,063	36.70
Rochester (*N.Y.*)	48,204	18,897	39.20
Detroit (*Michigan*)	45,619	21,349	46.79
Milwaukie (*Wisconsin*).	45,246	22,848	50.49
Cleveland (*Ohio*)	43,417	19,437	44.76
Charleston	40,578	6,311	15.55

Thus we see that whilst the newly settled cities of the North and North-West, such as Chicago, Milwaukie, and Buffalo, have the largest *proportion* of foreign settlers, and whilst New York itself and the cities in that State have the largest *number* of such residents, the City of Charleston, though situated on the sea-board and a great port of commerce, has by far the smallest resident foreign population of all the cities in the United States numbering over 40,000 inhabitants, and consequently has increased in population in the smallest ratio.

Increase of Population in the North and South contrasted.

This fact is very suggestive. I shall have to deal with the subject more at length when I come to speak especially of the Southern States. In the meantime, I may observe that I have not thought it necessary in this chapter to consider, at length, the disproportions between the various races in the United States, or the variations in their respective rates of increase. As the information, however, is not altogether foreign

The Coloured races.

Their proportion of increase.

to the subject, it may be stated that, in 1860, the FREE COLOURED population of the United States numbered 482,122, and their then SLAVE population 3,953,587. The whites, between 1850 and 1860, increased 38 per cent.; the slaves 23 per cent.; and the free coloured somewhat less than 11 per cent. These statistics still further sustain the position that it is to immigration that America owes the rapid increase of her population.

Improvement of the Immigrants' position.

The great mass of the immigrants to the United States are known to have changed their circumstances for the better. This is shewn by the very large amounts of money remitted, annually, from America to Europe. Between 1850 and 1860 no less than £10,000,000 of money is *known** to have been remitted through the agency of the Banks and large Mercantile houses, by settlers in North America to their friends in Europe. A large proportion of this amount has, doubtless, been destined to assist relatives and friends to emigrate: but for whatever purpose sent, the amount shews the extent to which the immigrants themselves profited by their settlement in the new world of their adoption.

States chiefly selected for settlement by different nations.

The largest number of *foreigners* reside in the following States in the order named: New York, Pennsylvania, Ohio, Illinois, Wisconsin, and Massachusetts: the smallest number reside in North Carolina, Florida, Arkansas, Oregon, Mississippi and Delaware.

The English.

The greatest number of *English* reside in the States of New York, Pennsylvania, Illinois, Ohio, Wisconsin

---

* " How much sent through private hands is not known."

and Michigan : the least in Florida, Arkansas, Oregon, North Carolina, South Carolina, and Mississippi.

The greatest number of *Irish* reside in New York, Pennsylvania, Massachusetts, Illinois, Ohio and New Jersey : the smallest reside in Florida, North Carolina, Oregon, Arkansas, Texas and Kansas. Irish.

The greatest number of *Germans* reside in New York, Ohio, Pennsylvania, Illinois, Wisconsin and Missouri : the smallest number in Vermont, Maine, New Hampshire, Florida, North Carolina, and Rhode Island. Germans,

Thus we see that it is no distinction of Nationality or Religion that makes any difference in the settlement of the country. Objects sought to be attained by the Immigrants.

What, then, do the people seek ?

Obviously, the opportunity of settling themselves in districts where land can be obtained which they can cultivate with profit, and where the reward of industry is, consequently, certain.

CHAPTER III.

DIFFUSION OF THE POPULATION.

Area of the
United
States.

INCLUDING lakes and rivers, the area of the United States is 3,250,000 square miles, an extent of surface larger than all Europe. Deducting lakes and rivers, the land-surface of the country is 3,010,370 square miles, giving 1,926,686,800 acres of land.* This territory is compact and contiguous. For the most part it is united by lines of communication, which consist of lakes, rivers, canals, railroads, and telegraphs. By the settlement of California and Oregon the country has now the immense advantage of fronting the two great oceans—the Atlantic and Pacific.

Varieties of
Climate.

As regards climate, the whole of the United States is within the temperate zone. The settler, however, in selecting his residence, can have any temperature he chooses from St. Petersburgh to Canton. He may settle in a cold or warm climate, according to his health, his habits, his predilections, or the object which he seeks : whether he desires to farm, to fish, to hunt, to graze cattle, to cultivate garden lands, or to propagate the vine. He can select the shores of the lakes or of the ocean ; live on the tidal waters or above the

* *Vide* " Report of Secretary of Interior to Congress," 1860.

tidal waters of magnificent rivers ; and have his choice
of mountain or of valley.

Of the 3,250,000 square miles, which constitute the   The Soil.
territory of the United States, the public lands embrace
an area of 2,265,625 square miles, or 1,450,000,000
acres.   This domain embraces soil capable of yielding
the richest and most varied productions in the
greatest abundance.   Nearly one-third of this land
(say 441,000,000 acres) has been surveyed, and about
395,000,000 acres disposed of by sales and grants.*
The lands are surveyed by the Government : divided   Government
into townships of six miles square : subdivided into   divisions of
                                                       the Lands,
sections, and these into quarter sections of 160 acres
each, which are set apart for homesteads.   The system
of "squares," by which every section and quarter
section is divided by lines running due north and
south, east and west, precludes all disputes as to boundary or title.   As the country is filled up and settled
new surveys are made, and undoubtedly one of the
great attractions of the United States is, that there is
so boundless an expanse of territory that the price of
land is not likely to be unduly raised by an immigration however great, or by other means than the
application of industry to the cultivation of the soil.

There is no description of produce, European or   Productions,
tropical, which may not be raised in this territory.
Every part of the country produces wealth.   The
Western, North-Western, and Pacific States afford
abundant crops of the two great cereals, wheat and
Indian corn, with the additional advantage that the

* Report of " Commissioner of the Land Office," 1860.

first of these is gathered in the summer and the other in the fall, thus affording a double harvest to the farmer. The Southern and South-Western States grow sugar, cotton, rice, tobacco, corn, and the grape. Other parts of the territory afford immense mineral resources : and on the plains of Kansas, Texas, and other States, are the widest grazing grounds, and the finest herds of cattle in the world.

Settlement of Immigrants according to their Nationalities. The settler in the United States has an opportunity of selecting a locality peopled, to a great extent, by his own countrymen. He can have either an Irish, a German, Scotch, English, Welsh, Swiss, Norwegian, or American neighbourhood. He can be near a church of his own denomination. Freedom of conscience is complete. He pays no tithes or church-rate, except voluntarily.

The "Homestead Law." If he is the head of a family, or twenty-one years old, and intends to settle and become a citizen of the United States, he can receive at the hands of the Government, substantially as a free gift, a "homestead," consisting of a quarter section of a square, or 160 acres of land. Each of his children, reaching twenty-one years of age, receives the like advantage : and it is not to be despised. If, instead of taking **Wages.** up his homestead in a distant district, the immigrant chooses to pursue his profession, trade, or business in any of the large cities or towns, or in the country parts of the more densely-peopled States, he ordinarily finds the wages of unskilled labour at least twice as large as those he had in Europe, with, for the most part, cheaper prices of the necessaries of life.

The low price of Land. The price of land is generally so reasonable in

America that it little exceeds the rent payable in England. A farmer here cultivates the land of others, and lives in constant remembrance of the rent-day. In the United States, he works his own freehold without fear of eviction. In Europe the labourer has little to hope for but severe toil, perpetual poverty, and, as a last refuge, the union workhouse : in America, he is certain that he can raise more than he can consume, and he can look forward with cheering hope to competence, accompanied with the security of a provision for each member of his family.

Having regard to all these advantages and temptations, the immense extent of the immigration from Europe becomes the less surprising. That immigration, however, could only be made profitable by the constant addition of new territories, embracing fertile lands, into the field for settlement. Between 1850 and 1860, three new States,—California, Oregon, and Minnesota, were added to the Union. The name of the last, perhaps, has scarcely even yet reached the ears of many people in Great Britain. Yet Minnesota, during the decade, 1850—60, was one of the most flourishing of all the districts of America. *New States added to the Union since 1860.*

Minnesota was organized as a territory of the United States on the 1st of July, 1849, at which period it contained but little over 4,000 inhabitants. The tide of population set in rapidly. In 1860, the census numbered more than 172,000, and in 1864 the population was estimated at 350,000. The number of acres of ploughed land in the State, in 1850, was 1,900 and in 1860, 433,276 ; and the produce of grain and potatoes was nearly 15,000,000 bushels. St. Paul, the principal *Minnesota.* *Rapid increase of this State.*

town, numbered 10,401 inhabitants in 1860, and may be now taken to contain nearly 17,000. Minnesota was admitted into the Union as a State in 1858, and, despite an incursion of Sioux Indians into her territory, who committed great ravages and had to be repelled by force of arms in 1862, she was able to contribute no less than 15,000 men to the armies of the United States during the War.

WISCONSIN.

The adjacent State of Wisconsin is another example of the most surprising development. In 1830 this State only contained 5,318 inhabitants. In 1840, the population had only risen to 6,100 ; but in 1850 it was 305,391, and in 1860, 775,881. The City of

The Cities of America.

Milwaukie, on Lake Michigan, which had scarcely an existence a few years ago, now numbers 45,000 inhabitants, and does the second largest corn and flour shipping trade of any city in America.

Cincinnati. Chicago.

Cincinnati, in Ohio, had a population, in 1860, of 161,044 ; Chicago, in Illinois, numbered, at the same period, 109,260. These comparatively new places are the two most thriving and increasing cities of the West. I shall refer to them hereafter. But let me first speak of a place perhaps not yet heard of in Europe,

"Fort Wayne."

—a town called Fort Wayne, in Indiana. On the 11th of last October (1865), Secretary M'Culloch delivered a speech to his fellow-citizens at Fort Wayne. I extract the following passages from his graphic references to that hitherto almost unheard-of place.

Secretary M'Culloch's description of Fort Wayne.

"No place," said the Financial Secretary (or Chancellor of the Exchequer) of the United States, "will " ever be so dear to me as Fort Wayne. No friendships " will ever be so strong as those I have formed here.

" I am, as you know, one of the pioneers of this beauti-
" ful city. When I crossed the St. Mary, swimming my
" horse by the side of a canoe, on the 23rd June, 1833,
" Fort Wayne was a mere hamlet. It contained a few
" hundred souls. It was a mere Indian trading fort,—
" a mere dot of civilization in the heart of the wilder-
" ness. Under my own eye, as it were, it became a city
" of nearly 20,000 people,—a city full of vigour and
" enterprize ; the second city of our State. I am
" proud of Fort Wayne, and of the noble State of
" Indiana—a State second to none in the Union in
" her devotion to the Government, and in the gallantry
" with which her sons have defended it. I am thank-
" ful that when I crossed the mountains to seek my
" fortune, my feet were directed to Indiana, and
" especially to this place."

Indiana is, indeed, a remarkable illustration of
American progress :—

The State of
Indiana

In 1800 her population was	....	4,875
1810	,,	....	24,520
1820	,,	....	147,178
1830	,,	....	343,031
1840	,,	....	685,866
1850	,,	....	988,416
1860	,,	....	1,350,428

And I must here observe that when Secretary
M'Culloch alludes especially to the increased population and prosperity of Fort Wayne, he only speaks
for the whole State of Indiana. There are in that
State upwards of 1,060 cities, towns, and villages :
of which more than 600 have a population exceeding
1,000 each. Indiana, be it remembered, is a perfectly

an illustra-
tion generally
of the rapid
growth of
America.

free State : settled within a period of little more than thirty years. I say nothing here, at present, of its extent or of its various productions, but I content myself with asking where, in the whole face of this globe, is there (except in America) a corresponding advancement to be found ?—where can you show an extent of territory so rapidly settled : so rapid a growth of towns and cities and civilization : such a conversion of mere pauperism into absolute wealth : such a contribution to the resources of an empire ?

Despite the largest con- tributions of men and money to the War,

Indiana, first incorporated into the Union in 1816, when she numbered a total population of less than 100,000, contributed to the armies of the United States no less than 125,000 soldiers during the war, besides a large amount of treasure raised by taxation and voluntary contributions ! Where, again, I ask, is such a record to be found ? And yet, at this time, the very country of which I speak, was, and throughout the war she continued to remain, one of the most thriving of the States. She stands sixth of all the States

Indiana progressed rapidly,

in her production of wheat, growing nearly 10,000,000 bushels ; and fifth in the production of Indian corn, growing upwards of 70,000,000 bushels. During the

and was able to repel inva- sion.

summer of 1863 this State was exposed to a Confede- rate raid under General John Morgan, who mustered 5,100 cavalry, with five pieces of artillery, to invade the best part of the province. Within four-and-twenty hours no less than 60,000 volunteers offered their services to drive the invaders from the State ; and of these 13,500 were accepted, organized, and equipped. In addition, large bodies of militia and minute men were placed in the field to defend their farms and homesteads, composed chiefly of squads of squirrel hunters, who turned out, armed with their own rifles. The enemy retreated and escaped, but the people of Indiana boast that, independently of the force they contributed to the regular army, not less than 20,000 armed inhabitants were prepared to drive the invaders from their soil.

Such facts as these require no comment. But they raise serious considerations, especially amongst ourselves at home. Without depreciating the exertions we could make, were we called upon to do so, in defence of our hearths and homes, let us regard these facts for our own benefit. We have made immense progress here in England during the last thirty years : not, perhaps, in the way in which progress has been made in America, but even in modes more conducive to wealth, and to individual, if not to general, prosperity. Yet, in our most populous districts, where can we find the progress and the energy exhibited, in so few years, in any one part of the United States ? Take Lancashire, with a population nearly double that of Indiana, and with productions and resources, no doubt, many times greater—what should we expect Lancashire to do under circumstances of war ? Besides enormous taxation for national expenditure, could we hope to raise in Lancashire 120,000 men for external, and 20,000 men for internal warfare, or anything like that number ? I fear not. We boast, and with reason, of the numbers who have joined our volunteer force, but at the highest estimate that force could never count above 160,000 riflemen. And if not in Lancashire, where there is every encouragement and induce-

[side note:] Considerations suggested by the exertions of the population of Indiana.

ment to exertion in periods of difficulty—where the greatest exertions were made for the support of the population when all the cotton mills were stopped recently—where else, I ask again? Take the peoples of Hungary or Poland, where the whole populations have been fighting for their liberties: what analogy .can they afford to this devotion exhibited by one small fraction of the United States? If either of those countries could have sent 100,000 armed men into the field, besides keeping 20,000 men at home to defend their families, where would have been the invader? It seems to me that facts like these demonstrate, in a remarkable manner, the resources of America, which seem to grow and increase with the emergency.

Attempt to
trace the
cause of
their ex-
ertions.

To what are we to trace all this: to what shall we attribute it? First, of all, I must think, to the absence of pauperism in the United States. There every man has something to defend. There may be dependency, but it is not the dependency arising from want. In Indiana, for example, there are 132,000 farms, averaging 124 acres each. There are more than 8,000,000 acres of improved, and the same number of unimproved, but enclosed lands; giving a total of 16,000,000 acres to about 1,250,000 of population,—that is to say, 60 acres at least, to every head of a family. Where settlements are thus universal, and where pauperism may be said to be impossible, it is obvious that a very different state of feeling must exist from that which prevails in any country where the population does not exist in circumstances of independence. The independent feeling of the Citizen of the United States is, it cannot be doubted, at the root of all his nationality. The desire to achieve liberty is great : but the determination to maintain it is still more effective. Probably had the people of Indiana been as depressed in circumstances as the people of Hungary or Poland, they would have been as liable to be over-run by invaders. It was their resources, and their determination to protect and preserve them, which drew forth their extraordinary exertions : not indeed proportionately more extraordinary than those of other States of the Union, but exertions which, whether we consider them individually or collectively, tend to exhibit in a surprising point of view, what can be done, in a moment of apparent difficulty, throughout America.

And the exertions which have been made to bring the War to a close, are, I apprehend, only indications of those which will be made to wipe out every relic of it : from which I argue that the resources and energies of the United States are more than ample to redeem her liabilities readily, speedily, and without undue difficulty.

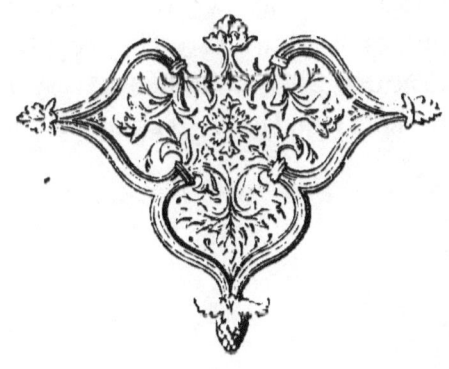

CHAPTER IV

OCCUPATIONS OF THE PEOPLE.

The United States THE United States is an agricultural, a commercial, and a manufacturing country, but it is by no means equally agricultural, commercial, and manufacturing. I hope I shall not wound the national esteem of my American friends when I say that I regard their essentially Agricultural, country as essentially agricultural, and by no means essentially commercial or manufacturing. But I think their own records establish my position. Of about 8,217,000 heads of families and other individuals, whose occupations were recorded at the period of the Census of 1860, it appears that upwards of 3,000,000, as shown by the occupations of the people. or more than one-third, were directly occupied in the tillage of the soil. 2,423,895 entered themselves as "farmers"; 795,679 as "farm-labourers." Besides these there were 85,561 entered as "planters": but, I take no account of these, as I am not dealing with the Slave States in the present argument.

On the other hand, the number of "merchants" Numbers engaged in various pursuits. and "clerks" in America, are only 300,000; ["merchants 123,378," "clerks 184,485,"] and of the clerks we must assume that a certain proportion are engaged in retail establishments. The population engaged in manufactures do not assume a very large proportion to the whole population. Taking all the "occupations" of the population in businesses which number over 100,000 each, I find the account to stand as follows :—

Farmers	2,423,895	Shoemakers	164,608
Farm Labourers	795,679	Merchants	123,378
		Miners	147,750
	3,219,574	Blacksmiths	112,357
Labourers	969,301	Teachers	110,469
Servants	559,908	Tailors and Tailoresses.	101,868
Carpenters	242,958		
Clerks	184,485		6,037,256

Here are more than 6,000,000 of the 8,217,000 heads of families accounted for; and the account appears very clearly to show the great preponderance of agricultural over other employment in the States.

This fact developes itself the more forcibly when we come to consider the number of persons engaged in the principal professional and business occupations. It will be found that they are classified as follows :—

Numbers engaged in professions and trades.

Judges and Lawyers	33,980	Coopers	43,624
Clergymen	37,529	Drivers	19,521
Physicians and Surgeons	55,055	Druggists	11,031
Civil Engineers	27,437	Gardeners	21,323
Public Officers	24,693	Grocers	40,070
Students	49,993	Harness-makers	12,728
		Hatters	11,647
Apprentices	55,326	Innkeepers	22,818
Bakers	19,001	Jewellers	10,175
Barbers	11,140	Laundresses	38,633
Barkeepers	13,263	Lumbermen	15,929
Boarding-house keepers.	12,148	Mantua-makers	35,165
Bricklayers	14,311	Masons	48,925
Brickmakers	13,736	Millers	37,281
Butchers	30,103	Milliners	25,722
Coachmakers	19,180	Overseers	37,883
Cabinet-makers	29,223	Peddlers	16,594
Carters	21,640	Painters and Varnishers	51,695

Plasterers	13,116	Stonecutters	19,825
Printers	23,106	Tanners	10,491
Railroad men	36,567	Teamsters	34,824
Saddlers	12,756	Tinsmiths	17,412
Sawyers	15,000	Tobacconists	21,413
Seamstresses	90,198	Wheelwrights	32,693

Seven-eighths of the population

Some of these businesses are closely associated with agricultural employment, and all of them must be more or less dependent on the ruling trade of the community. And here we have upwards of another million heads of families engaged in these employments; so that, exclusive of those engaged in seafaring occupations, such as—

(exclusive of mariners, &c.)

Boatmen	numbering	23,816
Fishermen	„	21,905
Mariners	„	67,360
Ship Carpenters	„	13,392

dependent on agricultural pursuits.

(or, in the whole, more than 126,000), we find upwards of *seven-eighths* of the entire population of the United States engaged in agricultural pursuits, or in the various professions and trades materially dependent thereupon.

Important bearing of this fact on the national policy.

I dwell the more emphatically upon this, because the consideration seems to me of the greatest importance in regard to those questions of revenue, taxation, &c., with which I shall hereafter have to deal. Amongst some parties in the country there is a cry in favour of high rates of Import Duties for the protection of native manufactures. But if it appears that the manufacturing industry of the country, however important in itself, really represents so inconsiderable a proportion of the industry of America, I apprehend it will be admitted that the cry for protection for native manufactures loses a large proportion of its force.

During my visit to America, I was less impressed with the manufactures of the country than with its agriculture. The people of the United States are taught to think and speak of themselves as a great manufacturing community; but this appears to me to be a mistake. The "stranger" is told of the vast aggregate of the annual products of their manufacturing industry. He is assured that in 1860 they amounted to the enormous sum of 2,000,000,000 dollars or £400,000,000. It is to be borne in mind, however, that this aggregate includes a vast deal that would not be included in what we call "manufactures." For example, one of the principal products of American manufacturing industry is "flour and meal"; of which the annual product is put down at $224,000,000. On this side the Atlantic we should never think of including the product of flour-mills in an estimate of our national manufactures. Nor is this the only fallacy involved in the estimate : for, inasmuch as the corn ground at the mill had already been included in the statistical estimates as a "product of agriculture,"—to reckon its value, a second time, in the form of flour and meal, as a product of manufacturing industry, obviously gives an erroneous view of the real value of the productions of the country.

In the same way with very many other items included in the national computations, as "products of the leading manufactures of the United States." Thus, we find "lumber," or the products of the saw-

The American estimate of the importance of their manufactures,

considered.

" Flour and meal,"

" Lumber,"

mills, put down at $96,000,000 : whereas, of course, only the increased value of the sawn or planed wood over that of the log, tree, or stick, ought to be estimated. We find not only $60,500,000 put down as the value of "wool" produced, which is, no doubt, correct enough, but we find the value of a large proportion of the raw material included in a computation of "woollen goods" which are set down at $69,000,000, and reproduced a third time in the

"Clothing," form of "clothing"—*i.e.* the products of sewing machines and the industry of tailors and tailoresses,— which are set down at $70,000,000. In the same way with leather. We have not only the value of the hides and skins of animals included in the computation of the value of agricultural productions under the head of "animals slaughtered" ($212,871,000), but we have "leather manufactures" computed at $72,000,000, and again given to us in the form of

"Boots" and "boots and shoes manufactured," $90,000,000. In
"Shoes," none of these cases should we have included the articles computed in an estimate of our manufacturing productions. And so with a vast number of other items which the Americans include in the list of their national manufactures. They estimate the value of

"Spirits, barley and hops amongst their agricultural products, and then give us the value of their malt, and afterwards of their beer and spirits, as "manufactured

"Malt produce," under the respective heads of "spirituous
liquors," liquors" and "malt liquors." In a still more glaring instance, they give us "paper" $17,500,000 and re-

"Printing" produce it in the form of "printing" $42,000,000.
and They also include in their manufactures the annual

value of all their "fisheries." According to our ideas,
therefore, of what should be included under the head
of manufactured products, it is clear that the American computation of 2,000 million dollars per annum
is swollen very far beyond the legitimate estimate, and
that we must very largely discount that item in order
to arrive at a correct view of the value of the manufactures of the United States.

We are told in the "Preliminary Report of the
Eighth Census," that "the production of the immense
" aggregate above stated gave employment to above
" 1,100,000 men and 285,000 women, or 1,385,000
" persons. Each of these, on an average, maintained
" 2½ other individuals, making the whole number sup-
" ported by manufactures 4,847,500, or nearly one-
" sixth of the whole population. This," it is added,
" was exclusive of the number engaged in the produc-
" tion of many of the raw materials ; in the distribution
" of their products, such as merchants, clerks, dray-
" men, mariners, the employés of railroads, expresses,
" and steamboats ; of capitalists, various artistic and
" professional classes, as well as carpenters, bricklayers,
" painters, and the members of the industrial arts, not
" classed as manufacturers. It is safe to assume, then,
" that *one-third of the whole population* is supported,
" directly or indirectly, by manufacturing industry."

It is obvious that this is a most exaggerated view.
If such a mode of estimate was correct, it might,
indeed, be far more truthfully and properly said,
not that *one-third*, but that *the whole* population is
supported, directly or indirectly, by manufacturing
industry. For, according to this American view, there

is, I suppose, no article of produce which, in some form
or other, does not enter into manufactures. If the
flour-miller is to be classed as a manufacturer, why not
the baker and the pastry-vendor; if the painter, why
not the cattle-dealer, the butcher, and the cook? But
the idea is obviously carried to the point of absurdity.
"The employés of railroads, expresses, and steamboats" are regarded as quasi-manufacturers because
they are engaged in "the distribution of manufactured
products." But, inasmuch as the tonnage of agricultural and raw products on railroads, in steamboats, &c.
is, at least, I suppose, 20 to 1 of the tonnage of manufactured goods, upon the same principle all these
should be classed as agriculturists.

The numbers
asssumed to
be " main-
tained " by
manufac-
turing in-
dustry
"4,847,500 persons, or nearly one-sixth of the whole
population" is claimed as being *directly* supported
by manufacturing industry, because, it is said, "each
of the workers in manufactures maintains, on an average, two and a half other individuals." Now, I venture
to doubt this altogether. It is not averred, nor, as
the Americans express it, is it even "claimed," that
the individuals directly employed in manufacturing industry are all " heads of families." On the contrary,
we know very well that a very large proportion of
those who are engaged in manufactures, especially in
the manufacture of textile fabrics, are very young
persons,—members, and not heads of families,—and
that their weekly earnings are, in a vast majority of
e qually erro-
neous.
cases, only sufficient for their own support. But,
besides this, we know that the entire population of the
United States which is able to work is fully employed.
It is, therefore, a fallacy and error to put down " *two*

and a half other individuals," as "MAINTAINED" by the wages of each manufacturing labourer. I venture to believe that nothing of the sort obtains in the United States. Where heads of families are exclusively employed in manufacturing industry, no doubt they do support, and perhaps principally maintain, two and a half other persons, or even more. But this does not and cannot apply to the whole of the persons so employed, and hence the calculation embodies, in my opinion, a complete error.

I cannot, indeed, understand upon what principle even 1,385,000 persons are computed as directly engaged in manufacturing industry in the United States. It is only by including all the fishermen, blacksmiths, carpenters, tailors, shoemakers, mantua-makers, seamstresses, painters, varnishers, printers, hatters, masons, mariners, millers, sawyers, lumbermen, and handicraftsmen of every sort in the community, that anything like that aggregate can be arrived at. If we take the Census-tables, and regard the numbers stated to be engaged in what may be properly regarded as manufacturing industry, we shall find that they fall very far short of any such calculation. The following are the principal figures, as far as I can gather them:—

Real proportion of the population engaged in manufacturing industry.

Miners	147,750
Factory hands	87,289
Machinists	43,824
Weavers	36,178
Moulders	17,077
Manufacturers	11,283
Jewellers	10,175

I doubt whether I ought to include the last-mentioned any more than ship-carpenters, shoemakers, or wheel-

wrights; but as jewelery is at the present time claimed
to be a very considerable item of American manufacturing production, I put down the number engaged
in that business. But, even including this class, we
find that the total population engaged in manufactures
(*including Mining*), instead of being one million three
hundred and eighty-five thousand (1,385,000), as stated
in the "Preliminary Report," is, in reality, less than
three hundred and fifty-four thousand (354,000).
And of this number by far the largest proportion is
engaged in *Mining*, and not in *Manufacturing* industry, properly so called.

Principal
manufactures
of the United
States.

Many branches of manufacturing industry in
America are, at the present time, very little developed. The manufactures of which they chiefly speak
are those of agricultural implements and sewing
machines (of both of which they are justly proud); of
cotton and woollen goods (in the production of which
they have been making very rapid advances); of furniture, clocks, jewelery, and musical instruments (with
which they now mainly supply themselves), and clothing
and boots and shoes, which a quarter of a century ago
were almost all imported, and which are now almost
entirely home-made.

Manufac-
tured articles
which they
import.

But there are other articles ot European manufacture, which the people of the United States almost
exclusively import. Their iron and steel wares are
almost wholly taken from England: so is their earthenware and glass. They draw large quantities of silk manufactures from Great Britain and France. We supply
them also with the better classes of machines, although
they manufacture the inferior instruments very largely.

Judging from the small number of instrument-makers, twine-makers, shot-manufacturers, paint-manufacturers, chandelier-manufacturers, and such-like trades, I should apprehend that by far the larger proportion of the articles produced in those branches of manufacture were imported from Europe : and, indeed, it will be found, if our own list of exports is carefully examined, that Great Britain has been accustomed to export to the United States large and increasing quantities of manufactured articles,* not only of those descriptions which are not, but of those which are included in the largest items of her home productions.

With regard to American manufactures, we have to bear in mind that, so far as regards one-half of the territory of the United States, manufacturing industry has been hitherto entirely unknown to it. Some of the Northern States are "manufacturing ;" but (in our sense of the word) the South is totally devoid of manufactures. The South, indeed, has hitherto been absolutely dependent upon New York and the North for its supply of the commonest articles of use. One traveller in America reports, and I can well believe him, that in the considerable city of Mobile he was

No manufactures in the South.

---

* My friend Mr. C. Capper, in his valuable work upon the " Port and Trade of London," shows the declared value of exports to the United States from Great Britain and Ireland to have increased as follows up to the year before the war :—

Year.	Amount.
1840	£5,283,020
1845	7,742,839
1850	14,362,976
1855	17,318,086
1860	22,907,681

unable to find a working hatter. I think all this very likely to be corrected, now that slavery is abolished. I believe that manufacturing industry is likely to find as fair a field in the South as in the North, now that the country is about to be opened to free settlers and a free population.

General progress of American manufactures. But this is anticipating. I will, therefore, only further observe here that I must not be misunderstood as depreciating, in any way, the manufacturing enterprize, industry, or progress of the people of the United States. Such is very far from my intention : indeed, when I come to speak more especially of the progress of the manufacturing industry of the Americans, it will be seen that I thoroughly appreciate the vast stride their industry has made. What I have been desirous of effecting in this chapter is to clear the ground. I would not have my friends in the United States believe that I was flattering them ; nor would I have my friends at home believe that I was misleading them. It is my opinion that the public statistics of the values and products of manufacturing industry in the United States, and of the amount of population engaged in them, are based on erroneous calculations, and I frankly state my opinion and endeavour to establish my position. The country has made progress enough in this respect, and it is unnecessary that it should delude itself or allow others to be misled by exaggerations, or by calculations based upon erroneous premises.

SECTION II.

AGRICULTURE.

SECTION II.—AGRICULTURE.

CHAPTER I.

AGRICULTURAL DEVELOPMENT.

ALTHOUGH the civil war in the Republic extended over so great a breadth of territory, and although more than a million of men were withdrawn from the producing classes for employment in military service, yet the yield of the great staples of agriculture continued to increase, and never were greater than in the last year of the war !

Increased production throughout the War.

This is a most surprising fact. It can only be accounted for by the immense area of the country, the remarkable fertility of its soil, and the earnestness and industry with which the population apply themselves to agricultural improvements. One fact alone will illustrate the last position. In 1850 the cash value of the farms under actual cultivation in the United States was $3,271,575,000 :—in 1860 it had risen to $6,645,045,000, being an increase of no less than 103 per cent. in those ten years. In 1865, at the close of the war, the value of the investments in land was known to have increased.

Increased investments in Land.

It is unquestionably upon the agriculture of the
United States that the progress of the country
mainly depends. Considering America as the granary
of Europe, agriculture takes its place as the most
important interest of the country. It is, therefore, of
the first consequence to consider what is the condition
of the agriculture of the United States, and what are
the prospects of her being able to compete successfully
with other countries in the supply of grain to the
European markets.

Fortunately, on this subject, the most complete
statistics are at hand. The census returns of 1860
give the fullest details concerning every class of farming operations and agricultural productions. We derive
from them, in the first place, the important fact that
the agricultural area of the country was in that year—

Improved Land in Farms	163,110,720	Acres.
Unimproved Land enclosed in Farms......	244,101,818	,,
Uncultivated Territory, fertile and waste .	1,466,969,862	,,

Thus we see that for every two acres of improved
land there were three acres, connected therewith, not
as yet brought under cultivation, whilst the gross aggregate of land remaining to be brought into cultivation
is sufficient to prevent the possibility of any rise in
the price of the cultivated lands.

But whilst land is cheap, labour is dear in the
United States. This accounts for the character of the
cultivation. "American agriculture," it is said, "is
half a century behind that of Great Britain." No
doubt this is true as regards the drainage, manuring,
farming, and fencing of the lands. But, on the other
hand, says the Superintendent of the Census, "we can,

and we do, *produce a bushel of wheat* at much less
cost than the most scientific farmer of England can,
by the most approved method of cultivation, *even if
he paid no rent.*"

The following figures show the increase in the
number of farms in the enclosed acreage of the country
between 1850 and 1860 :—

but the produce superior.

Nature of the holdings in America.

Acreage in Farms.	1850.	1860.
Number of Farms of 3 acres and upwards	1,449,073	2,044,077
Acres of Improved Land in Farms	113,027,514	163,110,720
„ Unimproved Land „	180,528,000	244,101,818
Average No. of Acres to each	203	194

Size of the Farms

The farms in the United States are chiefly of from
20 to 100 acres. There are not above a fifth of the
whole number which exceed 100 acres, and there are
only about 25,500 which exceed 500 acres. The
largest properties were held in the slave States, especially in Virginia, South Carolina, North Carolina,
Louisiana, Georgia, and Alabama. The greatest proportion of small properties, as might be expected, are
to be found in the more densely-peopled States, such
as New York, Pennsylvania, Maine, Connecticut, Rhode
Island, and Massachusetts. In these States the average
number of acres to each farm does not much exceed,
even if it reaches, 100. In the State of New York the
average is 106 acres—in Massachusetts only 94. In
these States a very large proportion of market-garden
and dairy-produce is cultivated.

The State of New York contains the largest number
of farm properties, and the greatest average of improved

The Western States out-

E

stripping the Eastern.

lands. It has over 197,000 distinct properties on which 14,358,400 acres of land have been improved. In respect of improved land New York stands at the head of all the States; but during the next ten years it may be expected that, in this respect, she will be outstripped, the State of Illinois having, between 1850 and 1860, thriven so remarkably as to tread very closely indeed on the heels of the Empire State. The advance of Illinois is most surprising, and I cannot better exemplify it than by placing in contrast the statistics of New York, one of the oldest, and Illinois, one of the youngest, States of the Union :—

	1850.		1860.	
	New York.	Illinois.	New York.	Illinois.
Number of Farms . .	170,621	76,208	196,990	143,310
Acres of Land Improved	12,408,964	5,039,545	14,358,403	13,096,374
Ditto Unimproved . .	6,710,120	6,997,867	6,616,555	7,815,615

Illinois the largest Wheat producing State in the Union.

But this is not all. Illinois between 1850 and 1860 grew into the largest WHEAT-producing district of the United States. Pennsylvania stood at the head of the wheat-growing States in 1850, her produce being fifteen million bushels of wheat, whilst Illinois only produced 9,500,000 bushels. In 1860, however, Illinois produced no less than 23,000,000 bushels, or more wheat than the States of Pennsylvania and New York put together.

Great progress of the Western States in Wheat growing.

As wheat-producing countries, the Western States made, indeed, the most remarkable progress during the decade. What can be more wonderful than the details shown in the following table :—

WHEAT PRODUCE OF WESTERN STATES (in Bushels).		
	1850.	1860.
Illinois	9,414,575	23,837,023
Indiana	6,214,458	16,848,267
Wisconsin	4,286,131	15,657,458
Iowa.....................	1,530,581	8,449,403
Michigan	4,925,889	8,336,368
California...............	17,228	5,928,470
Minnesota	1,401	2,186,993

The produce of 1850 and 1860 contrasted.

In 1850, the ten States classed as Western States, with a population of 6,370,000, produced 46 million bushels, or 7¼ to each inhabitant : in 1860, with a population of 10,219,000, they produced 102 million bushels, or 10 to each inhabitant. The increase of produce, therefore, largely exceeded the increase of population, though the population had increased more than 50 per cent. We shall see, hereafter, that greatly as the means of transport had increased, those facilities were far from keeping pace with the increase of production, and the consequent requirements of the country.

Increased production largely in excess of increase of population, and means of transport.

The prices obtained for corn by the wheat-growers in the Western States materially depend upon the demand for corn in the European markets. An unfavourable crop in Europe naturally occasions a rise in price in America. Prior to the outbreak of the Civil War, complaints were beginning to be made that the growth of Wheat was comparatively unremunerative : but the large demand occasioned by the War, and the high prices consequent thereon, naturally abated those complaints. In point of fact, the Western farmer has been receiving prices for his produce, during the last

The price of Wheat increased by the War,

E 2

few years, which he cannot expect to be wholly maintained, now that the War has ceased, and that the
country is about to return to specie payments. It was
the same, it will be recollected, with our own Agriculturalists, who revelled in high prices during the war
at the early part of the present century, and made
extraordinary profits until the introduction of Sir
Robert Peel's Currency Act of 1819 put an end to the
inflated currency previously existing.

*and the state
of the
currency.*

But there is one circumstance in favour of the
Western farmer. Improved railway communications
will greatly reduce the rates of freight for his produce,
and he will, probably, receive net prices in gold equal
to what he has lately received in paper ; the saving
in freights counterbalancing the depreciation of prices
in the Eastern markets.

It is a favourable feature, moreover, for the Western
farmer, that whilst his own produce increases so far
above the ratio of his home population, the reverse is the
case in many of the Middle and Eastern States. New
England is becoming almost entirely dependent upon the
Western States for breadstuffs ; and the Middle States
(New York, Pennsylvania, New Jersey, Maryland and
Delaware) produced only 30 million bushels of wheat
in 1860, to 35 millions produced in 1850, although
the population of those States had increased nearly two
millions in the interval. The decline in the wheat-
production of these States is to be attributed primarily
to the employment of portions of the population and
the use of portions of the soil to greater profit.
There can be no doubt that with a rapidly increasing
population, employed in the Eastern and Middle States

*Increased
demand for
Wheat to
supply the
Eastern
States.*

in more profitable occupations than wheat-growing, the demand for corn from the Western States will continue to increase, and thereby prices will be assisted.

The extent to which the population relies upon the Western States for wheat, can be best shewn by the statistics of shipments of grain from the West. Let us take Chicago : which is now one of the greatest grain markets in the world. Prior to 1838, only 17 years ago, there was no shipment of corn from Chicago. In that year 78 bushels of wheat were exported from that town. The trade has increased as follows :— *Immensely increased shipments of Wheat from the West,*

SHIPMENTS OF WHEAT FROM CHICAGO.			
Year.	Bushels.	Year.	Bushels.
1838	78	1847 ..(estimated)	2,000,000
1839	3,678	1853	1,689,798
1840	10,000	1855	7,110,270
1841	40,000	1857	10,783,292
1842	586,907	1860	16,054,379
1845... (estimated)	1,000,000	1862	22,902,765

The largest proportion of this enormous movement of wheat was for the accommodation and supply of the consumers in the Eastern and Middle States. The quantity of wheat destined for export mainly depends, as before observed, upon the character of the crops in Europe, and the consequent condition of the European Markets. During the period when famine prevailed in Ireland, the quantity of wheat shipped from Chicago was even greater than it was six or seven years afterwards. In 1859, however, the total shipment of wheat to Great Britain only amounted *for the supply of Eastern consumers.*

Shipments to Great Britain.

to 295,248 bushels. In 1860, it rose to nearly 12,000,000 bushels: and in 1861 and 1862, to 20,061,000 and 29,798,000 bushels respectively, falling in 1863 to 16,000,000 bushels.

Unlimited capacity of the Western States to supply the demand for Wheat.

The Superintendent of the Census of 1860, in his able papers upon the agriculture of the country, discusses the question "Whether the Western States are capable of supplying the increased demand and growing deficiency of the New England and Middle States, besides supplying the rapidly increasing home demand, and have a surplus to export to foreign countries." He appears to arrive at a conclusion that they cannot: but in this I must venture entirely to differ from him. From all that I observed in the United States, and from the statistics and accounts before me, I believe the supply of wheat to be obtained from the Western States to be absolutely unlimited. I believe that those States will always be able to produce more than sufficient for every home demand, and will always have a surplus to export.

Prices regulated by European demand.

In such case, the price which rules for wheat in Europe, must materially affect the price of the whole of the American markets, and thus wheat will continue to be grown at a profit in the Western States, which it certainly would not were it to be solely governed by the home demand. The dearest market in the world, wherever it may be, must rule the prices of the markets generally; and the market which, through facility of communication, is nearest to that which is the dearest, will reap the earliest advantage, whilst that which is most distant will have to struggle, in the competition, weighted with the cost of freight.

And this leads to the conclusion that there is
nothing so desirable for the interests of the great
West as to obtain every possible facility for reaching
the European markets. The great element of the
cost of everything is cost of transport : and although
it may be said that the cost of transport must eventually fall on the consumer, yet it is obvious that
it must affect the producer also, for if the prime cost
of the article and the cost of transport put together
should exceed the value of the article in the market
in which it is delivered, it is obvious that the shipment becomes unprofitable, and that the demand for it
abates and ultimately ceases.

Consequent importance of facility of transport

Let the Western States, however, have the freest
and fullest access to the European markets, which
means the lowest possible price for carriage, together
with absolute certainty of speedy transport, and I
believe they will be able to grow their wheat at
a profit, and that the production of it will, in consequence, be so much stimulated that the supply will
be practically unlimited.

*as a stimu-
lant to
production.*

CHAPTER II.

THE EXPORT GRAIN TRADE.

The Export of Breadstuffs, a slowly increasing trade,

COMMENCING at an early period with the scant products of the Atlantic States, the grain trade of America was gradually pushed up the Hudson river, and ultimately by means of the Erie Canal was carried to the great Lakes. Then the vast territory of the West was opened, and became the great scene of agricultural enterprize.

The following Official table shews the ratio of increase in the value of the grain exported from the United States for a period of 40 years :—

Years.	Aggregate Value of Exports of Grain.	Percentage of Increase.
1823 to 1833	$67,842,211	—
1833 to 1843	73,303,440	8.0
1843 to 1853	198,594,871	170.9
1853 to 1863	512,380,514	158.0

greatly stimulated by the Repeal of the British Corn Laws.

The repeal of the Corn Laws of Great Britain in 1846 gave the greatest encouragement to the exportation of American corn. During the years 1862 and 1863 the total exports of grain, flour and meal, from the United States were of greater value, in either year, than the aggregate value of the whole corn trade of America for the ten years 1833 to 1843.

Year.	Bushels.	Value.
1862	76,309,425	.... $83,692,812
1863	77,396,082	 88,597,064

The years during which this very great supply of food was exported were, it should be remembered, years of Civil War. Of the total amount of the export, nearly two-thirds were shipped to Great Britain and Ireland. The proportion sent to us is represented as follows :—

Year.	Bushels.	Value.
1862	34,102,735	.... $47,916,266
1863	47,082,026	 56,059,360

The supply of wheat from the United States to England and Ireland during the years 1861–62, and 63, was estimated to amount to $37\frac{1}{2}$ per cent. of our whole import. Of the imports of Flour into Great Britain, 58.3 per cent. were from the United States.

It has been estimated by the *Mark Lane Express*, a paper of authority on Agricultural matters, that the average consumption of wheat in Great Britain is six bushels per head per annum; and as our population amounts, in round numbers, to thirty millions, this gives a total annual consumption of 180,000,000 bushels. For the seven years prior to 1864, the average importation was 56,000,000 bushels: and deducting this amount from the estimated consumption, there remains for home production 124,000,000 bushels. On this data the general importation of corn and flour would be *one-third,* and the home production about *two-thirds*, of the total consumption of wheat in Great Britain. Of this deficiency of one-third, America may be taken to supply us with about one-half.

History of the American Grain Trade.

Early Records.

The United States, it may be observed, has always been a grain-exporting country. As early in her history as 1790 there are records of exports of Wheat, Indian Corn, Flour, Meal, Rye and Oats, the growth of the different States on the shores of the Atlantic. The Southern States at that time sent a considerable quantity of Indian Corn to the West Indies, and there were exports of corn to both Spain and Portugal—countries which, so far as climate and soil are concerned, ought themselves to be amongst the best grain-producing nations of the world.

Development of the Grain Trade consequent on opening the Erie Canal.

It was not, however, until after 1825 that the importance of the export grain trade began to be appreciated. Previous to that period the Mississippi river was the only outlet to the ocean from the north-west. But in 1825, the opening of a canal which placed the Hudson river in communication with Lake Erie, inaugurated a new era in the trade of the United States. The shores of the great lakes were brought by this line of communication into connexion with the Atlantic, by a navigable water-course through the entire State of New York. "This grand avenue," says an American writer, "developed a new world to the pioneer, the agriculturalist, and the merchant."

Settlement of Ohio and

The growth of the trade was, however, slow. A very large portion of the territory had in fact to be settled. The counties, in Ohio, bordering on Lake Erie, were the first to become populated and cultivated, and as late as 1835, that State was the only grain-

exporting territory in the West. Michigan soon fol- Michigan.
lowed. The first shipment of grain on the lakes of
which there is any record, was made in the year 1836, First Ship-ment from the Lakes.
when the brig *John H. McKenzie* shipped, at Grand
Haven, Michigan, 3,000 bushels of wheat for the port
of Buffalo.

It was mentioned in the last chapter, that the first Chicago and
shipment of grain from Chicago, consisting of 78
bushels of wheat in 39 sacks, was made in 1838. The
first shipments from the State of Wisconsin were made
three years later, in 1841. These shipments consisted
of about 4,000 bushels of wheat, purchased at Mil- Milwaukie.
waukie on Canadian account. Milwaukie, which was
scarcely inhabited five-and-twenty years ago, now
ranks as the second largest grain-shipping port in
America. It is interesting to note the rapid rise and
progress of that city, as shown by the following account
of the shipments of grain and flour :—

Grain and Flour shipped from Milwaukie, Wis.	
1841	4,000 bushels.
1845	143,260 ,,
1850	820,033 ,,
1852	1,772,753 ,,
1855	3,758,900 ,,
1860	9,995,000 ,,
1862	18,712,380 ,,

Rapid in-crease of Shipments from Mil-waukie.

In 1848 the Illinois and Michigan canal was com- Development of Illinois.
pleted, opening up another great field of cultivation
in the State of Illinois. In 1849 the era of railroad
communication was inaugurated by the opening of the
Chicago and Galena Union Railroad, traversing a widely

cultivated district. This line of railroad led to a great and rapid development of the country which it traversed. In 1863, nearly *eleven and a half million* bushels of grain were carried over this line.

Shipments of Grain from ports on Lake Michigan.

The total shipments of grain and flour from ports on Lake Michigan up to the most recent accounts are shown by the following table. The great bulk of these shipments have, no doubt, been from Chicago, the great export port of Illinois, but some other ports contribute to the total.

SHIPMENTS EASTWARDS FROM MICHIGAN PORTS.		
1858	27,879,293	bushels.
1859	25,829,753	„
1860	43,211,448	„
1861	69,489,113	„
1862	78,214,675	„
1863	74,710,664	„

Such a record of progress is probably unparalleled.

The productions of these States

The production of grain in the North Western States of America is estimated to have increased from 218,463,583 bushels in 1840, to 642,120,366 bushels in 1860. The eight food-producing States west of the lakes, embrace an area of 262,549,000 acres, of which only 52,000,000 acres were under cultivation in 1860. Having regard to the rapid progress of cultivation, and

can be sustained and increased

the immense extent of territory remaining to be tilled, I think it is not to be questioned that there is ample room and scope for increased production. In fact, I look upon the exportation of grain from these States as only to be limited by want of facilities for transportation. Some American writers appear to fancy that the supply of corn from the Western States will not, presently, equal the demand. I am only anxious that the supply should not be checked by want of a sufficient demand. If there is a sufficient demand, and if there are facilities of transport to meet that demand, the resources of these States are such, that for the next century at least there need be no apprehension of insufficiency of supply, except from some blight or scourge of nature.

to meet any demand.

Prior to the opening of the Erie Canal, the only outlet to the ocean from the North Western territory was by the river Mississippi. During the progress of the Erie Canal it was predicted that "it would never pay," for that "the trade would follow the rivers," and was not likely to be diverted across the continent. It has turned out, however, that the artificial channels of trade, the canals and railroads, have completely diverted the course of the traffic. There are various causes for this. The principal, no doubt, is the increase of the corn-consuming population in the States of the Atlantic. Other causes are to be found in the uncertainty of river navigation during the summer months ; the greater speed and security of transport by railway ; the superior advantages of New York to New Orleans as a place of trade ; and the greater risk of damage to corn and flour by "heating" in the southern latitudes of the Gulf of Mexico. Thus it comes that New Orleans has almost entirely ceased to be a shipping port for grain, although her trade in cotton, sugar, and tobacco has largely increased.

Facilities of transport.

Diversion of the trade from the rivers.

Causes of this change.

One of the most remarkable transitions in the grain

The Grain Trade of California.

trade has, however, occurred in California. When the first rush to the gold diggings occurred, the entire population of that country was dependant upon import for breadstuffs. Riches, other than gold, have, however, been found upon this soil, and California has now

California a wheat export-ing country.

actually become a wheat-exporting country! Almost every mail from the Pacific conveys intelligence of one or more ships laden with wheat having sailed from San Francisco. In 1861, the export of wheat from San Francisco amounted to 2,379,617 bushels, valued at $2,550,820; and the export of flour to 186,455 barrels, valued at $1,001,894. The cereal exports of California are therefore yielding her a revenue of at least £700,000 a year; a most remarkable fact in the history of so young a State. It is probable

The future granary of the Pacific.

that at no distant period, California will prove to be the great granary of the Pacific Ocean. In 1863, California is estimated to have produced 11,664,000 bushels of wheat, and 5,293,000 bushels of barley, besides 1,057,000 bushels of oats, and other grain. It will, therefore, be seen that the quantity she exported was limited in proportion to her produce.

Exportation in proportion to produc-tion,

And this, it will be found on examination, is true not only of California, but of the United States at large. The entire export of grain from the United States, at the present time, does not equal the total product of any single State in the Union. For instance, in 1860, the single State of Illinois produced 23,837,023 bushels of wheat; whilst the whole export of wheat from the United States to foreign countries, (including flour reduced from wheat) was only 17,213,133 bushels. Of Indian corn Illinois produced in the same

year 115,174,777 bushels, whilst the whole export of
that description of grain from the United States
amounted to only 15,448,507 bushels,—a mere fraction very frac-
tional.
of the product of one State.

The following table will more completely demonstrate
this position :—

AMERICAN WHEAT (in Bushels).		
Year.	Produced.	Exported.
1850	100,485,944	7,535,901
1860	173,104,924	17,213,133
INDIAN CORN.		
1850	592,071,104	6,595,092
1860	838,792,740	15,448,507

Looking at these figures it is obvious that, large as is
the export trade of the United States, it is a mere
nothing compared with her production. She exports
less than 40 millions of bushels of corn, out of a product of *upwards of* 1,000 *millions!*

Yet it is a fact that the price of wheat in Prices in
America
England governs, to a very great extent, the price of
wheat in America. The farmer, naturally, looks to
the best market, and the price he can obtain in that
market regulates the price at which he offers his
product in any other. Thus it comes that, throughout
the United States, the aspect of the weather in England,
and the prices of wheat at the corn-market in Mark governed by
" Mark
Lane."
Lane, are quite as much objects of anxiety as the con-
dition of the weather at home, or the prices of grain
in New York or Chicago. Almost every American
publication connected with agriculture, gives the last

items of Mark Lane information ; just as Mr. Reüter's telegrams from India and China invariably record, to the wonderment of a large proportion of our population, the last prices for "Grey Shirtings," in Canton and Calcutta.

What gives such fertility to American soil ?

But, it may be asked, what is it that gives that peculiar fertility to the American soil, which enables the people to produce every description of grain with so much more ease than we can ? The soil itself, it will be said, cannot be so much more fertile ; its cultivation, admittedly, is far less skilfully conducted ; the crops are not better husbanded ; the operation of harvesting is even more costly, and by no means so well performed as our own. What is it, then, beyond the cheapness of land, which gives America so great a superiority as a grain-producing country ?

Sunshine.

I answer, "Sunshine." No high farming will supply the absence of the sun. High quality combined with great quantity in wheat, can only be obtained where there is sufficient summer heat. In England, the best wheat years are the driest and the hottest. In California, where they can hardly be said to have commenced the wheat cultivation, some of the valleys are yielding sixty bushels to the acre. The wheat in America, well protected by the deep snow-fall in the severe winter months, comes forward rapidly in the cool weather of the spring, and is just sufficiently advanced and full of sap when the dry, hot summer months commence, in which it perfectly matures. It is seldom, indeed, that America has not sufficient sun to mature the heaviest crops, to elaborate the juices of the plant, and to give the grain the highest quality.

Not that it is intended to be argued that the quality of American wheat is all superior. Very far from it. What Nature has provided is too frequently lost by man. In many parts of the United States, the harvesting is very slovenly and much more care is required in threshing and cleaning the wheat. Too little attention, moreover, is paid to the quality of the seed: and, as far as the cultivation is concerned, it has already been observed that the growth is almost spontaneous. In point of fact, labour in these grain-growing districts is so costly, that the farmer has only himself and his family to rely on ; which goes very largely to account for the smallness of the holdings.

CHAPTER III.

GENERAL PRODUCE.

General List of the Agricultural Products of the United States. BESIDES Wheat, there are various agricultural productions of the United States, which almost wholly enter into home consumption. The following list of the products of the country may not be unacceptable.

AGRICULTURAL PRODUCE OF THE UNITED STATES.—1860.

CEREALS.

Wheat	Bushels.	173,104,924
Indian Corn	"	838,792,740
Oats	"	172,643,185
Barley	"	15,825,898
Buck Wheat	"	17,571,818
Peas and Beans	"	15,061,995
Rye	"	21,101,380

ROOTS.

Potatoes	Bushels.	111,148,867
Sweet Potatoes	"	42,095,026

OTHER PRODUCE.

Orchard Produce. Value	Dollars.	20,000,000
Market ditto "	"	16,159,498
Wine	Gallons.	1,627,242
Wool	lbs.	60,264,913
Butter	"	460,000,000
Cheese	"	103,663,927
Hay	Tons.	19,083,896
Clover Seed	Bushels.	956,188
Grass Seed	"	900,040
Hops	lbs.	10,991,996
Hemp	Tons.	74,493

Flax	lbs.	4,720,145
Flax Seed	Bushels.	566,867

SOUTHERN PRODUCE.

Tobacco	lbs.	434,209,461
Rice	„	187,167,032
Ginned Cotton	Bales of 400 lbs. each.	5,387,052*
Silk Cocoons	lbs.	11,944

SUCCADES.

Maple Sugar	lbs.	40,120,205
Cane Sugar	Hhds. of 1,000 lbs. each.	230,982
Cane Molasses	Gallons.	15,000,000
Maple ditto	„	1,597,000
Sorghum ditto	„	6,749,123
Honey	lbs.	23,366,357
Beeswax	„	1,322,787

ANIMALS.

Value of Animals Slaughtered	Dollars.	213,618,692

HOME MANUFACTURES.

Value of Home-made Manufactures	Dollars.	24,546,876

It will be seen that the production of INDIAN CORN was no less than 838 millions of bushels. This was more than double the aggregate of the wheat, rye, oats, barley, buck-wheat, peas and beans; and was nearly five times the amount of the wheat alone. Illinois stands at the head of the Indian corn, as it stands at the head of the wheat-producing, States. The Western States, indeed, produce nearly one-half of all the Indian corn grown in America, although the late slave-owning States produced large quantities of Indian corn for the supply of their dependent population.

The culture of Indian corn, throughout the United States, fully keeps pace with the increase of popu-

INDIAN CORN.

Its production

keeps pace with the increase of population.

---

* This quantity is questioned, but I give it according to the official returns. *Vide* "Eighth Census of the United States," p. 185.

lation, which is not the case with other varieties of
produce.   One cause of this is the ease with which it
is grown : its cultivation involving the smallest expen-

Ease with
which it is
grown.

diture of trouble, time, or money.   A loose, moist,
and not wet, but fertile soil, with abundance of sunshine, is solely needed for the growth of this cereal ;
and, says the Agricultural Commissioner, "there are
millions of vacant acres that seem as though they
were absolutely formed for its production."   The

Extent to
which it is
used.

extent to which Indian corn is used throughout the
United States as food for every description of animal,
including swine, as well as for domestic poultry, gives
immense importance to this production.   In the South
the coloured population subsist to a very great extent
on Indian corn ; indeed, throughout the war, "Hom-
iny" made of this cereal formed a most important
item of subsistence for the entire people.   In many
cases, we are told, that even the higher classes of the
Southern population were frequently unable to obtain
any better provision during the progress of the war.

Its larger use
in England re-
commended.

The army was also very largely fed with Indian corn.
I confess to some surprise, that this product does
not enter more largely into consumption in Great
Britain and Ireland.   Much of the comparatively small
quantity imported is worked up by parties who sell it
as farinaceous food for children, for pastry-making, &c.
In this form Indian corn is a comparatively costly
article.   It is in the cheaper forms in which it is
used throughout America that it seems to me it might
be much more generally introduced into consumption
here.*

---

* There are various ways of dressing Indian Corn. Boiled,

The cheapness of Indian Corn accounts for the comparatively little attention which is given in some of the States to the production of OATS :—Indian Corn being considered a more nourishing food for stock. The increase of the Oat production between 1850 and 1860 was far less than that of wheat, and in the Slave States the large decrease in the growth of Oats was said to be singularly curious. The Western States, too, comparatively disregard this crop. Whilst they produce over forty-five bushels of Indian corn to each inhabitant, they only produce six-and-a-half bushels of Oats. In the Middle and New England States some lands, which have gone out of wheat culti-vation, have been laid down in Oats, and in these States alone does the cultivation at all increase.

Oats comparatively neglected.

BARLEY also occupies a subordinate position in American agriculture : indeed, the climate generally is too dry for its production. But with the rapid increase of a foreign population, there has been latterly an annually increased demand for barley for malting pur-poses, and the price for it is said to have advanced more rapidly than that of any ordinary grain crop. At the present time, wonderful to narrate, California raises the largest barley crop of any State in the Union : a sandy soil having been found favourable to its produc-tion. It is sown just before the November rains. Owing to the general dryness of the climate, the grain dries rapidly as it approaches maturity, and in harvesting

Barley.

used for malt-ing purposes.

Growth of Barley in California.

in its green state, it is a most delicious vegetable. There is no reason why it should not be introduced into this country. It is cheap enough in America, and it bears the voyage here. I have it frequently at my own table, where it is much approved.

it "shatters out some." This sprouts, and again taking root in a rainy season, yields a crop which is called the "volunteer crop," and which is well worth harvesting. In some instances a second "volunteer crop" is produced by the same process, which affords a fair average. Thus, even without the trouble of sowing seed, hundreds of thousands of bushels of barley are grown in California.

The "Volunteer" crop.

RYE is not largely cultivated in the West. It is grown principally on light sandy soils of the Middle States, in Pennsylvania especially, not so much for the grain as for the straw. BUCK-WHEAT is grown extensively in the Middle and Eastern States as an article of food for sheep in winter, and it is said that there are few crops which produce a better profit. "Buckwheat cakes" are also a popular item of human dietary.

Rye.

Buck-wheat.

PEAS and BEANS are raised very largely in the State of New York, and also in the Southern States—especially in the Carolinas, Georgia, Alabama, and Mississippi. In the rest of the United States these crops are not much attended to. It is to be regretted that there is no separate return of peas and beans, for they are cultivated and used in the United States for very different purposes. The bean is used principally as food for man, whilst the pea is principally used as food for animals on the farms, or for ploughing under as a green crop for manure. In the South, what is called the "cowpea," is of great importance to the agriculturalist. It occupies in the rotation of crops the place which the turnip occupies in British agriculture. It grows very luxuriantly, is largely consumed

Peas and Beans.

The Cowpea.

by the cattle, and is also ploughed into the land as manure, for which purpose it is highly valued, on account of the high percentage of nitrogen contained in it. The "cowpea" does not flourish north of Virginia; it is, however, largely extending itself in California.

The cultivation of POTATOES is a very important item   Potatoes. of American agriculture. In the North, the "Irish potato," as it is there called, is the most largely grown, whilst the sweet potato is principally cultivated in the South. The produce of both is very large: in some cases quite excessive. The State of Maine in 1860 raised ten bushels of potatoes for every inhabitant, and the new State of Minnesota actually produced nearly *fifteen* bushels for each of its population.

The Dairy Produce of the United States is very   Dairy great, and between 1850 and 1860, it showed an   Produce. increase, in butter alone, of nearly 50 per cent. The principal butter and cheese producing States are those   Butter. most largely settled, as New York, Pennsylvania, Ohio, &c. New York makes nearly one-fourth of all the butter made in the United States, and more than one-third the cheese.

Whilst the butter product has so largely increased,   Cheese. the cheese product of the United States has, until very recently, been decreasing. Cheese is said not to enter largely into the dietary of the people of the United States; and the quantity produced not only meets the demand, but leaves a considerable surplus for exportation. The New England States used to produce nearly 10 lb. of cheese for each individual, it being estimated that not one-fourth of that quantity was consumed at home. The cheese exported from these States was not found, however, to meet the tastes of European customers, and consequently the manufacture languished. Very recently a "cheese factory" system has been established in the great dairy districts of the State of New York and parts adjacent. Each farmer sends his milk to the dairy, and is credited for the quantity supplied. Skilled persons are employed at the factories, to make the cheese; and it has been found that these factories turn out an article of far better quality than used to be made in private dairies. Pains have also been taken to suit the requirements of the European market, and the result has been such high rates of profit to the farmers and manufacturers, as have very greatly stimulated the business.* At the time I visited the United States, this stimulus was still further excited by the accounts received there of the prevalence of the Cattle Plague in England, which, it was thought, would occasion a still greater advance in the prices of American dairy produce.

In a recent article on "Cheese as a Staple Article of Export," written by the Secretary of the Maine Board

---

* Messrs. J. and E. Corderoy and Co., who are amongst our largest provision-merchants, state in their circular, under date London, 6th January, 1866:—"We cannot but be impressed with the increasing appreciation of American Cheese on the part of consumers, and the high range of price for the best sorts. The finest "factory dairies" are equal to almost anything that can be made in England, and now that the prejudices of the public are swept away, we may expect that they will successfully compete with other descriptions, quality now being the test of the value of Cheese, without reference to the place of its production."

of Agriculture, I find the following curious facts adduced to support an argument that "*cheese is as good as gold.*"

"The export demand governs the price of cheese. In June, 1862, prime cheese was bringing in Herkimer County, N.Y., 8 cents per lb. But as soon as specie payments were suspended and gold bore a premium, the price of cheese advanced with even step. When gold fell, the price of cheese receded: when gold rose, the price of cheese advanced: and all the while just in proportion to the current rate of exchange.

"This proves, conclusively, that to cancel indebtedness, or to pay for goods purchased in England, cheese was as good as gold, and answered the same purpose exactly.

"With a market," he adds, "of such great capacity open to us, it seems as certain as anything in this uncertain world can be, that the manufacture of cheese will increase annually; and I see no reason why all farmers who possess really good grazing land may not share in the profits."

I quote these passages the more readily as they illustrate the sort of enthusiastic feeling which appears to enter into every enterprise an American embarks in. On this side of the Atlantic it is difficult to realize the sort of feeling which induces an American to treat such a product as cheese as a substitute for "gold" in commercial transactions. Yet it is this sort of enterprising calculation which drives forward the United States. They try to make everything—even cheese—as "GOOD AS GOLD."

I have not much to say as to the other products of the Northern States. ROOT CROPS are neglected—a great mistake, which the more experienced and scientific agriculturalists of America are striving to correct.

Root crops.

Hops.

The growth of Hops is principally confined to a very limited area, in the State of New York. The increase in the cultivation has been very large, in consequence of the increasing demand in America for beer, which, by the way, is for the most part extremely badly manufactured by brewers who emulate the German lager beer production.

Wool.

Sheep have not generally been fed in the United States for the sake of Wool; but of course there is a certain production of that article. It has not, however, hitherto been a very rapidly increasing product. Ohio stands at the head of the wool-producing States; but California is likely, at no distant period, to take a very high place in respect of wool produce. California is reported to have had, in 1863, as many as 3,000,000 sheep; and Ex-governor Downey has declared that at the next Census "his State will show a wool product equal to that of the whole of the United States at present."

Flax and Hemp.

The cultivation of Flax and Hemp has received some attention in Kentucky and some of the Western States, and has been stimulated in the North since the outbreak of the civil war, with a view to test the practicability of the preparation of those articles in lieu of cotton. By a law of 1863, a commission was appointed to make investigations and conduct experiments; and a sum of 20,000 dollars was placed at their disposal for the purpose. Their report is expected to be made in the course of 1866. Now that peace is restored, I do not look, however, for any great results from these experiments. The production of flax could only be stimulated by the high price of cotton; and as long as

cotton can be cheaply produced, cotton will continue
to be " King."

The last product that need be referred to is WINE. Wine.
The grape is indigenous to America, and wine is
reported to have been made in Florida as far back as
1564. There is no evidence, however, that any quantity of wine has ever been produced until the present
century. The enterprise of agriculturalists in different
States, has, at different times and especially of late years,
led to the culture of the vine with a view to wine production; and some varieties of American wine have obtained
considerable local reputation. It is contended, and no
doubt with truth, that America is as well adapted for
wine-making as any other country; that she has in
various parts the requisite soil and climate, and even,
in the German vine-dressers, the requisite skilled
labour for the manufacture of wine. Admitting it all, Prospect of
it does not seem to me that the United States is likely American
Vintages
to compete successfully with other nations in respect competing
with those
of wines, or, in other words, to become an exporter of of other
the article. The tastes for wines are so much influenced nations.
by circumstances of climate, habit, fashion, price, celebrity, and a variety of personal, local, and commercial
considerations, that it is one of the most difficult
things in the world to introduce a new wine into
general consumption. Since the reduction of our
wine duties, the attempt to introduce into English
consumption the Hungarian, Greek, and Italian wines,
and some of the vintages of France, not previously
known here, has met with little success. I apprehend it will take a long time to bring up American
vintages to the standard of any of these European

wines ; and they certainly cannot be produced at less prices. My own experience of the American wine is not favourable. I confess frankly, that I think their wines, even including the famed Catawba, altogether inferior. However, there is scope enough for a domestic wine trade in the United States, if the product of the vintage is improved ; and in California, where the culture of the vine is extending itself with extreme rapidity, the people appear to be enraptured with their produce, and to be great consumers of it.

CHAPTER IV.

THE PROVISION TRADE.

In treating of the agricultural products of the United States we must not forget their stock. The stock of the country is not only important as regards home supply, but the extent to which beef and pork are exported, renders this business important in considering the subject of national resources.

Importance of the stock, in America.

The total value of the LIVE STOCK in the United States in 1860, was estimated at $1,089,329,915 : equal to £217,865,983. The total number of animals was estimated at 87,000,483 ; thus giving an average of about £2 10s. for each animal. The animals were classed as follows :

Number and value of the cattle.

LIVE STOCK OF THE UNITED STATES, 1860.		
Horses .... No.	6,249,174
Asses and Mules .... „	1,151,148
Milch Cows.................... „	8,581,735
Working Oxen	„	2,254,911
Other Cattle .... „	14,779,373
Sheep .... „	22,471,275
Swine .... „	33,512,867

These, it should be stated, are only the stock on farms and plantations. Those in the cities and towns

on farms and plantations.

are not enumerated; and, of course, increase the aggregate. It serves to shew the prosperity of the United States that, excluding sheep and swine, we find in this enumeration of horses, asses, and neat cattle, at least one animal for every inhabitant.

Neat cattle. It is computed in the United States, that every 100 people require 80 NEAT CATTLE : that 8 of those cattle should be working oxen, and 28 milch cows. It is remarkable that for the past 30 years these proportions have been maintained in the United States. Although the population has so greatly increased, the

Proportion to population. number of neat cattle has kept pace with it, as the following table shows :

Year.	Population.	No. of Neat Cattle.	Proportion per cent.
1840	17,069,453	14,971,586	0·87
1850	23,191,876	18,378,857	0·79
1860	31,417,331	25,640,337	0·81

This increase is, of course, quite irrespective of the animals slaughtered. No return that I know of distinguishes the neat cattle in the general account of animals killed; but we know that the total annual value of these amounted in 1860 to $213,600,000, or nearly £43,000,000 sterling.

Horses, Ohio has more than 625,000 HORSES—considerably more than any other State; horses being largely used there for agricultural and general purposes. In the

in the West, Western States generally, in 1850, there was a team of 5 horses to every family of 5 persons. In consequence of the vast increase of population, this proportion was greatly diminished in 1860 ; but even then there were 2 horses to every 7 persons. The horses in California increased from 21,719 in 1850, to 160,610 in 1860.

in California.

Highly bred horses are, however, admittedly very rare in America, and there appears to be nothing in the country that compares in any way with European studs. The breeding of horses has not been sufficiently regarded, and consequently the race is comparatively inferior. It is complained that the best trotting horses, which a few years ago were the most prized of all American steeds, are, after all, " only the highest type of the mongrel," that they get lame with half the work of an English racer, and that, "if it were not for a dash of superior blood in their veins, it would be found that after a trot they, literally and metaphorically, have not a leg to stand upon."* The " Conestoga horse," is, however, as a beast of burden, a very highly prized animal. He derives his name from a valley in Pennsylvania, to which State the original stock is supposed to have been introduced by some of its earliest settlers. The " Conestoga " combines great strength, with lightness and agility. The Philadelphia and Pittsburg mail was formerly horsed almost exclusively with this animal, and, although " young America" is said now to require a swifter horse, it is believed that there is no surer, safer, or more lasting one.

Inferiority of the breed.

" Trotters."

The " Conestoga."

---

* *Vide* " Report on Cavalry Horses in America," in appendix to " Report of the Commission of Agriculture presented to the House of Representatives, 1863."

Mules and
Asses

In the Southern and Pacific States, MULES and
ASSES are largely bred as substitutes for horses. The
mule is hardier than the horse; subject to fewer
diseases; more patient; better adapted for travelling
over rugged and trackless surfaces; less fastidious
as to food; much less costly in feeding. He requires
less grooming and attention, and usually lives and
works to double the age of the horse. A mule is
also more muscular in proportion to weight; and
as a troop of mules will follow their leader, if that
leader is only provided with a bell, they require
on a journey much less attendance than a troop

much used
in New
Mexico, &c.

of horses. Hence, in many parts of the United
States, mules are largely used as beasts of burden;
their power of endurance and determined persever-
ance enabling them to overcome difficulties which are
peculiar to that class of service.

Advantages
of using
mules.

The Census Report tells us, that, in America—

" A good, well-bred mule will do as much work as a horse,
whilst it can be kept at one-third the expense. Mules are
liable to fewer diseases than horses, and will bear ill-treat-
ment better. For careless hands they are more profitable than
horses. They require less than half the expense for shoeing;
and it is claimed that an average lot of mules can be
disposed of more readily and at better prices than an average
lot of horses; and that, as they cost less to feed, and can be
worked a year earlier, they are a more profitable stock to
raise."

All this appears to be conclusive testimony in
favour of the use of the mule, especially in the
Southern and less populated parts of the country, and
it also accounts for the fact that the number of mules

and asses increased, in the United States, upwards of 100 per cent. between 1850 and 1860.

WORKING OXEN increased in a much smaller ratio. The whole increase throughout the States was only 32 per cent. : in the Eastern States, indeed, and also in Ohio, there was a decrease in the number of working oxen. This is to be expected; inasmuch as in districts which become more densely peopled and consequently more civilized, and (in the case of the United States) more wealthy, horses supersede oxen in agricultural and other operations. Oxen, in fact, are more useful in a new country than where a higher system of agriculture is adopted : and hence we find them in larger use in such States as Missouri, Mississippi, Wisconsin, Texas, and New Mexico than in such States as Pennsylvania, or Maryland, where, indeed, working oxen are not increased in number, whilst horses and mules are largely increased. The use of improved agricultural implements also diminishes the force required from working oxen, and consequently diminishes their use, as such implements come to be introduced. Thus it, no doubt, occurred that in such States as Iowa, Illinois, and Michigan, the proportion of working oxen to population showed a considerable diminution.

The number of MILCH COWS largely increases in those States which are turning their attention to dairy produce : and also in Texas, where the wild cattle appear to be increasingly domesticated. In the Pacific States there are more than two milch cows to every family of five persons : showing the extent to which those States are becoming breeders of stock.

It has been observed that, in proportion to the number of milch cows in the United States, the quantity of butter and cheese brought to market is singularly small : but I think this is to be easily accounted for by the large consumption of milk amongst the population in the prairie districts, by the large number of " other cattle " reared, and by the great waste ; it being deemed unnecessary, as in countries where milk is more valuable, to keep calves from the cow at their earlier ages.*

The movement of neat cattle in the United States is a subject that involves considerations of some importance. It appears, from the official statistics, that at every period the great herds of cattle have been found gathered around the pioneers of civilization in their march towards the West : in other words that, with few exceptions, the inhabitants of the most Western States possess the largest quantities of cattle in proportion to population. Thus, in 1860, such States as New York, Pennsylvania, New Jersey, and Massachusetts were extremely deficient in cattle in proportion to population, whilst the States of Missouri, Mississippi, Georgia, Indiana, Illinois, Alabama, and

The movement of cattle,

with the population, towards the West,

---

* A breed of short-horned cattle, originally imported from the Valley of the Tees, appears to be amongst the most highly-appreciated of any breed of cattle now in the United States. The Americans boast that they have considerably improved on this nock, and that Samuel Thorne, of Thorndale (New York), "has shipped to admiring purchasers in England the descendants of former importations." Colonel Pennant, M.P. is stated to have been the purchaser of one of these cattle at a high figure. "Ayrshires " are much prized in Massachusetts, and have passed in some numbers into Michigan and the North-Western States.

Ohio, had large excesses. It is inferred from this, involves the movement of capital to the West also. that as the deficit of the Eastern States is constantly increasing, the Western States must be increasingly drawn upon to make up the deficiency : and hence *capital must move westward* to bring cattle eastward, in order to supply the increasing demand and abate the increasing prices amongst the eastern populations. This is an important consideration in estimating the prospects of America.

SHEEP, as mentioned in a preceding chapter, have Sheep, not been generally reared in the United States, either for their wool or for any other purpose than for the supply of mutton to the home population. Hence the sheep feeding in the more closely peopled States has not kept pace with the population : indeed, their decrease in proportion to population. between 1850 and 1860, the number of sheep decreased throughout the United States from 93 to 71 per cent. of the inhabitants : the total number being 22,471,275 in 1860 against 21,723,220 in 1850 : an increase of only 748,055.

Except in the cases of fancy properties in the The breed. Eastern States, and in those districts of the Western States where large runs of sheep-feeding lands have presented themselves, very little attention has comparatively been paid either to the quality or the The Vermont Merinoes take the prizes at the Hamburg Exhibition. number of the sheep produced. Nevertheless (and I regard this fact as very remarkable) a pen of twelve Merino ewes, bred by a gentleman named Campbell, of Westminster, in the States of Vermont, carried off the two first premiums and another high class prize at the Great International Agricultural Exhibition, held at Hamburg, in 1863, against all the best breeds

Character of
the competi-
tion and of
the awards.

of Saxony, Prussia, and Silesia.　One of the first prizes
was taken for length of staple : the other for weight
of fleece.　There were 1771 sheep shown, and eighty-
six prizes were awarded.　England competed with
Southdowns, Leicesters, and Cotswolds : the Emperor
of the French sent sheep from France　America had
no other sheep or other animals in the Exhibition ; Mr.
Campbell being the only feeder who dared to carry
stock over the Atlantic and German Oceans.　It is
said that nothing excited greater surprise than the
fact that the American sheep received the highest
awards ; but the decision remained uncontested.*

Report of the
U.S. Com-
missioner on
these facts.

* As the result of this Show was so very remarkable, I think
I ought to quote the report of the Commissioner sent from the
United States to attend it.　He says, respecting the sheep,—

"All the best breeds of Europe were represented.　Here were
merinoes from Prussia, Saxony, France, Silesia, and the United
States : merinoes with broad backs, full bosoms, and buttocks :
with round bodies and short, thick heads and necks : with short
legs, wide apart, straight and strong : merinoes with heavy folds
and wrinkles, with wide dew-laps, plaited or smooth ; merinoes
with heavy folds on the neck, and thick, even wool ; merinoes
with short staple and uneven, with a combination of thickness
and length, with wool low down on their knees and hocks : merinoes of all sizes and weights, from pens of little Mecklenburghers
to pens of tall, heavy French, weighing more than 200 pounds.
Every variety of merino was there, and as we laid open the fleeces
of sheep after sheep in this class, and noticed the difference in size,
weight, and form, and in length, thickness, and quality of staple,
we wondered if it was possible that this great variety had sprung
from the same stock.　Beyond, were pens of Southdowns, Leicesters,
and Cotswolds, from Great Britain and many continental countries,
with longer and closer wool ; some of them of enormous size, too
heavy to stand, and too indolent to indicate, either by motion of
head or tail, their dislike of the uninterrupted personal examination, of the visitors.　The small quantity of hay and grain fed

After the Exhibition these twelve sheep were sold by Mr. Campbell to Count Shen-Thors, *of Silesia*, for $5,000 (£84 each); thus confirming the conclusion that America had produced the most valuable stock of ewes that could be shown in Europe. These Vermont sheep were bred from a stock of true Spanish merinoes, the importation many years back of Messrs. Jarvis and Humphreys. Mr. Campbell states that, in 1839, he purchased twenty of Mr. Humphrey's sheep, direct descendants of his original importation, and that he has no doubt these prize sheep were all direct descendants from this original stock. I think these facts very significant as showing that, with care and attention, the breed of sheep does not degenerate on American soil or in American climate, although the Americans aver that even so great an European authority as Buffon gave his opinion to the contrary.[*]

Prices realized for the Vermont prize sheep.

out to these fat sheep was quite surprising. The shepherds from England were very intelligent in matters appertaining to the breeding and blood of sheep, but beyond their occupation had little knowledge of the world." Afterwards, he observes, " the moral influence of our triumph was very great. The thousands who had flocked round the pens of sheep on exhibition from the flocks of Louis Napoleon, deserted the pens of the Emperor, and gathered in equal, if not greater numbers, around the Vermont merinoes. That the result of the Exhibition will be to give America a great trade in Vermont merinoes, and make her one of the leading sources of the world for fine-woolled sheep, I cannot doubt."

I may add that at this International Exhibition a Suffolk bull took the first prize of 200 thalers in his class, and a Suffolk cow the first prize of 100 thalers, and a Yorkshire cow the second prize of 50 thalers in their class.

[*] In justice to Count Buffon, I am bound to say that I am unacquainted with the authority on which the Americans rest

A great loss of sheep from dogs is complained of in the United States. In Ohio, alone, the average of ascertained damage from this source is stated at $111,548 per annum, at a period when sheep were very low in price:—in 1863 the ascertained loss was $144,658. The Secretary of the New York Agricultural Society estimates the loss in that State in 1862 at 50,000 sheep, worth $175,000—£35,000. Higher proportional estimates have been made for Maine. The Western States are still more exposed to the ravages of dogs, and it has passed into a proverb that "Dogs are the great drawbacks to the full-range system." This is another illustration of the extent to which the United States suffer from the want of labour. Where labour is abundant there are plenty of shepherds to protect the flocks against the ravages of dogs, or even wolves. But it is cheaper in the States to sacrifice a proportion of sheep to dogs than to keep and maintain an efficient staff of shepherds.

---

this dictum. So far as my own knowledge goes of "Buffon's Natural History" I have no recollection of his having laid down any such position; and I have been at the pains to have an edition of his works examined, to ascertain what he may have said upon the subject. In his special article on "The Sheep" he makes no mention whatever of sheep in America; and in his article on "The Ox" he speaks, generally, of "European cattle" as having multiplied in an astonishing manner in South America, "although," he says, "the Coast of Brazil produces very indifferent cattle, small and with flesh of a bad flavour, most probably owing to the bad quality of their pasturage." It would, therefore, seem that some misapprehension exists in America as to Count Buffon's opinions; and I shall be glad if this note tends in any way to correct it.

Upon the whole, however, there is reason to believe that an increasing degree of attention is being paid to sheep-feeding throughout America. Railways have promoted this. It is found that where access to good city markets is rapid and cheap, improved " Mutton Sheep" afford profitable returns to the farmer. The mutton-breeds which find most favour are stated to be Leicesters, Cotswolds, and New Oxfordshires : together with the Down sheep, for which, however, it is more difficult to find suitable up-down pasturage. Some French merinoes, imported within the last twenty years, are proclaimed " Mongrels," unsuited to the country, and incapable of sustaining themselves. They have quite gone out of favour. As the rearing of sheep comes to be more general, lambing and the various complaints of the flock, as well as the best modes of feeding sheep, are better understood; and the summer, fall, and winter management of this class of stock is attended to with increased interest. I have already referred to the amazing increase of sheep in California, where they counted upwards of 1,000,000 sheep in 1860, and boast that they possess more than 3,000,000 at the present time. A large number of sheep have been brought to California from Australia.

Sheep-feeding for home consumption.

Sheep-feeding becoming better understood.

I now come to speak of the animal by which the Americans have hitherto probably made their largest profits, though it may be doubted, from the increasing demand for beef and mutton in the United States, whether this will continue long to be the case. The raising of Swine has proved to be so well adapted to the varied phases of agriculture in the United

Swine.

States, that there is no district in which it is not carried on, although it is only of comparatively recent years, that the pork trade has become one of commercial importance.

The climate and produce of America peculiarly adapted to swine.

The growth of this trade has been coeval with the development of the Western States. And this is to be mainly accounted for by natural causes. Although the hog, it is said, will live on anything and everything, yet to bring him to maturity rapidly, and therefore profitably, some special natural circumstances are required. First, the animal flourishes best in a temperate climate ; secondly, the country in which he is reared should be peculiarly productive of the most fattening descriptions of food ; and thirdly, in order to effect the processes of cure, with the least expense and the greatest certainty, the climate should admit of a somewhat severe winter.

All these conditions are realized in the Western States more perfectly than elsewhere. They have a temperate climate in summer,—a soil which produces in the utmost abundance Indian corn, which proves to be the best of all possible foods for the hog ; and a winter temperature well suited to every process requisite to the curing, packing, and export of meat. Thus it comes that such immense numbers of swine are bred, fed and annually converted into CORN-FED PORK in the Western States, and that cities like Cincinnati (or as it is ironically called, " Porkopolis ") have risen into such importance, and flourish so greatly on this trade.

Number of swine in America.

The number of swine in the United States in 1860 was taken, as we have seen, at upwards of 33,500,000:

certainly an immense number. But, large as this
number is, strange to say it is by no means so large as
it ought to be. In 1850, there were 30,300,000 swine :
so that in 10 years, this most prolific animal had
only increased throughout the United States to the
extent of about 10 per cent. or 1 per cent. per annum.
The decrease of swine in proportion to population in
all the States (except those in the Pacific) between
1850 and 1860, was very remarkable. It is shewn
in the following table, which is otherwise interesting
as shewing the very large extent to which Swine are
bred in some parts of America.

States.	Swine to each 100 inhabitants.	
	1850.	1860.
New England States ...	13	10
Middle ,, ...	41	31
Western ,, ...	181	149
Southern ,, ...	215	175
Pacific ,, ...	23	101

Decrease of swine to population.

The falling off in the number of swine, in proportion to population, is attributed to the increased facilities for the transport of grain, and its consequent
relative advance in price. When grain is cheap in
New York it is more profitable for the Western farmer
to feed pigs with it, than to send it to market, because
the carriage of a pig is relatively much less than the
carriage of the quantity of food which he consumes.
Proportionately, the pork may be as cheap as the corn ;

Causes of this decrease.

and, most probably, when the price of grain is low, the price of pork is low. But under the best system of feeding, it requires seven bushels of corn to make a cwt. of pork, and as the freight is much less on a cwt. of pork, than it is on seven bushels (or say 420 lb.) of corn, it is evidently less costly to the farmer to send his pig to market than to send his corn. And we must remember how largely the cost of transit enters into the cost of every article sent from the Mississippi or Lake Michigan to New York or to England.

Number of "swine used in the packing business."

The number of hogs annually killed, or as it is more politely expressed in a work of authority in the United States, "used in the regular commercial packing business of the nation," can only be approximated. It is believed, however, that in 1859-60, the number reached about 3,000,000, or about 10 per cent. of the stock of pigs.

Annual value of the "produce."

The value of these animals (on an average of 2 cwt. to a pig) is computed at \$35,000,000 or £7,000,000; about £2. 10s. per pig. The cost of packing and transport is stated at nearly \$15,000,000, (or £3,000,000 sterling) more, giving a total of ten millions sterling annually employed in this trade. This amount, however, would raise the price of each pig, without profit to the vendor or merchant, to an average of £3 10s. per pig, which I take to be excessive. It is admitted however, by the authors of these figures, that "fair averages are difficult to arrive at, and that those engaged in the business find the most extensive experience furnishes but few data for reliable precedents." The fact, I take to be, that the pork and bacon trade fluctuates largely with the supply and demand, the state of the seasons, and a number of other circumstances over which the producer has no control.*

I have mentioned the enormous extent of this trade at Cincinnati: a city on the banks of the Ohio, erected on a site which, within the memory of man, was a forest, but which now boasts of 250,000 people. Cincinnati kills and exports 400,000 hogs per annum. But recently Cincinnati has been quite surpassed as a pork-exporting town by the comparatively new city of Chicago.

Chicago, on Lake Michigan, in the State of Illinois, was a site acquired from the Indians by treaty only at the close of the last century. A wooden fort or stockade, called Fort Dearborn, was constructed on the site of Chicago in 1804: alongside of which, in a wooden house, lived the first settler on the spot, one John Kinzie (probably McKenzie), a trader with the Indians. The place continued to be a mere Indian trading station until 1830, when a town was planned

---

* A very recent monthly report of the "Agricultural Department of the United States," refers to a comparative scarcity of hogs at the present time. "The cause of this decrease," it says, "is obvious enough. The high price of corn has induced farmers to sell it rather than to feed hogs." The prospects of the "pork crop" of 1866 are much discussed in this publication. It was anticipated in many quarters, that as the harvest of 1865 would give a superabundance of corn, therefore there would be a large pork crop; but the departmental officers represented it to be fallacious to assume that "the abundance of corn would make an abundance of hogs, when hogs were very scarce." According to the latest accounts, there appeared to be a struggle going on in the West between the hog-growers, and the pork-packers,—the one seeking to raise and the other to lower the price of hogs.

and laid out, the site being regarded as suitable for commercial development. When, soon after, the tide of emigration began to set towards the West, Chicago became the key of the position. So lately as 1840, however, it numbered only 4,479 inhabitants. But

Rapid rise of Chicago.

from that it took a spring. The population of Chicago was :—

In 1845	12,088
„ 1850	28,269
„ 1855	80,023
„ 1860	169,963
„ 1865 (estimated)..................	180,000

Nor is it only in population that this wonderful city has thus developed itself. It has become the great

Its market.

centre of the Northern Railroads. I was taken, when I was visiting Chicago, to see the new market-place just constructed there. It covers a span of 500 acres! Every railway that enters the City has a cattle-station in the market, so that the animals may be brought into and, if necessary, taken from it without passing through the city. There are 40 or 50 acres devoted to pens for cattle, and every single pen is lighted, drained, and supplied with water. Even our fine cattle-market at Islington is inferior to it; in fact, I never saw so fine a market. All the public works at Chicago, it should be recollected, have been going on during the war; another illustration of the small extent to which the North has been affected by it. The Chicago people are also building an University.

The future of Chicago is scarcely to be foreseen : let me confine myself to what she is at present.

Chicago has grown to be the largest market in the world for corn, timber, and pork; the three great exports of North America. So recently as 1835, a Mr. Clyburn opened the pork trade at Chicago, by packing for export about 300 hogs. The trade developed itself slowly at first, but during the last 12 years it has increased as follows :—

Extent of the trade of Chicago.

HOGS PACKED AT CHICAGO.	
Year.	Number.
1853	52,849
1854	72,694
1855	80,380
1856	74,600
1857	99,262
1858	185,000
1859	167,968
1860	231,335
1861	511,118
1862	970,264
1863	904,159

The average yield of lard and weight of hogs packed during the year 1863 is stated at

The average weight of hogs.

Yield of Lard .... 34 lbs.
Average weight of Hogs .... 192 „

A friend who accompanied me in my journey through the States has described the process of pig-killing :—

The process of killing and curing.

" At Chicago," he says, " a million pigs die every year for the benefit of the public. They are all killed by machinery in the quickest and most scientific way. Within twenty minutes of the time of your hearing the pig squeak, he is killed, cut up, packed in barrels and on his way to Europe."

The process is not quite so rapid as is implied by this description, for after they are killed, the hogs are hung in the curing-room for two days, that all animal heat may be gone before they are cut up. Every operation as to curing and dressing the meat is performed in the most scientific manner. The English *Packing.* meats are usually packed in boxes; the more ordinary meats in barrels. Every market requires its own description of pork, and the animals are cut up variously, in order to suit the demand. The tongues are packed separately in barrels. The feet formerly *The feet.* went to the glue-makers, but during the late war great numbers of them were sent to the army sutttlers, who found a large sale for them amongst the soldiers. Another mode of preparing the feet is by thoroughly cooking them and pickling them in vinegar. As *Bacon and* regards the bacon and hams, everything depends upon *hams.* the mode of curing previously to smoking. The greatest attention, therefore, is given to the character of the curing-house, and the temperature maintained in it. Out-of-doors the temperature should not be above 50°, or in-doors above 65° or 70°, during the process.

The collateral Without going into the details of this trade further *trade.* than they are likely to be interesting and instructive, I may say that every item of the animal is turned to account. Not a particle is wasted, and the collateral trade in bristles, lard, oil, stearine, grease, skins, &c., has grown to be scarcely less important than the original trade in meat. Even the very offal is bought up for the manufacture of manure; and there is a firm in Chicago which collects all the bones it can obtain for the manufacture of animal charcoal. Thus the West not only feeds the people of the Eastern States, but feeds their lands.

Rapid as has been the development of this trade, its future promises a growth at even an increasing ratio. In quest of cheap food, the people of Europe are learning more and more rapidly to appreciate provisions of American cure; and upon the increasing demand, and increased competition, follows marked improvements in the breed of hogs, their mode of feeding, and their preparation for the market. At the present time, as recent letters inform me, a large increase in our demand is anticipated by the Pork-packers of Western America, in consequence of the increased prices of provisions in England occasioned by the Cattle-plague; a fact which shews the mutuality of the interests of England and the great West.

The aggregate value of the live stock in the United States was estimated—

In 1850 at $545,180,516
In 1860   1,089,329,915

being an increase over 100 per cent. In the new Pacific States the increase was no less than 576 per cent.! But I think enough has been said to establish the enormous resources of the United States as a food-producing country.

One word as to the benefit we derive from her export of salted and cured provisions. We have seen how infinitesimal is the proportion of corn we take in England from America, in proportion to her own annual production and consumption. With respect to the value of the stock, we see that the live stock on her farms is estimated at $1,089,329,915, or £218,000,000 sterling; whilst the value of animals annually **Its small rela-** slaughtered is computed at $213,000,000, or nearly **tive amount.** £43,000,000 sterling. Now, the imports into Great Britain from the United States, which bore any reference to this production were as follows, in 1860 :—

Articles.	Estimated Value.
Bacon	£424,566
Beef (Salted)	347,345
Pork (Salted)	108,584
Hides	183,584
Wool	92,211
Hams	55,300
	£1,211,590

Why is not this trade larger? Thus we see the amount exported is as nothing to the production. It certainly cannot be said that this is because Europeans do not want American food, or because the Americans cannot supply the quantity we require, or because we cannot pay for larger supplies. What is the reason that this trade is not infinitely larger? I fear we must look to the United States for a reply. They have not yet followed our example, in adopting that system of unrestricted interchange which we designate FREE TRADE.

SECTION III.

MANUFACTURES.

SECTION III.–MANUFACTURES.

CHAPTER I.

AGRICULTURAL IMPLEMENTS.

THE AGRICULTURAL IMPLEMENT manufacture is in many respects the most important branch of the manufacturing industry of America. It is not, indeed, the largest branch, for the value of the Agricultural Implements produced in 1860 was only $17,800,000, whilst the value of cotton goods, boots and shoes, &c. were taken at much larger amounts. But the superior importance of this branch of business, is attested by the fact that the manufacture of Agricultural Implements was the manufacture which exhibited the greatest increase between 1850 and 1860, the quantities produced being—

Superior importance of the Agricultural Implement Manufacture.

In 1850 .... $6,842,611
„ 1860 17,802,514

Or an increase of no less than 160 per cent. !

As an agricultural country, deficient of labour,

It could scarcely, in fact, be otherwise. America is an agricultural country. It is an agricultural country suffering under a grievous deficiency in the supply of agricultural labour. The high rate of wages, and indeed I may say the absolute absence, in many cases, of workpeople to take wages, has stimulated invention. Mechanical contrivances of every sort are produced to supply the want of human hands. Thus we find America producing a machine even to peel apples; another to beat eggs; a third to clean knives; a fourth to wring clothes; in fact, there is scarcely a purpose for which human hands have been ordinarily employed, for which some ingenious attempt is not made to find a substitute in a cheap and efficient labour-saving machine. Many of these machines have been brought to Europe, and some of them are appreciated and largely used in our own country. But we do not appreciate them as the Americans appreciate them, because they are not of the same value to us. They do not save us, that is to say, the same amount of expenditure in wages, for the simple reason that our wages are not so high.

the supply of labour-saving machines is greatly stimulated in America.

Number of patented agricultural implements.

As America is pre-eminently agricultural, it follows that the most numerous attempts to produce labour-saving implements have been directed to facilitate the labours of the farm. Every succeeding year produces new inventions for saving muscular labour in the farm and household. Up to 1848 the number of patented inventions in the United States belonging to the class of agriculture was 2,043; but since that year they must have more than doubled, for there were no less than 350 applications for new patents for Agricultural Implements in 1861, a number which had increased to 502 in 1863. The withdrawal of nearly a million of agriculturists from their ordinary pursuits to engage in military service, seems to have greatly stimulated this class of invention—as was, indeed, not unnatural.

It must be admitted that throughout the world the implements of husbandry have remained in a very rude, and in many cases, a very primitive condition. The hoe, the spade, and even the ploughshare, are really almost barbarous contrivances.*   As far back as 1660, our Royal Society felt the importance of improved agriculture, and endeavoured to awaken the public mind to the value of mechanical aids in farming. Agricultural Societies in America appear to have been established, in 1785, in South Carolina and Pennsylvania, with the object of " affording encouragement to the making of engines for the propagation of the staples of the colony." The Massachusetts Society for

Early efforts to improve instruments of Agriculture.

---

* There was a little book, published some years ago, by a gentleman who has since obtained some celebrity as an agriculturalist, Mr. Chandos Wren Hoskyns, which brought this fact, as I remember, very forcibly home to my conviction. It was called " TALPA, or, the Chronicles of a Clay Farm," and one of the writer's principal objects was to show the difficulty of working on certain soils with a plough, and to recommend the substitution of some machine for creating the seed-bed such as the mole (Talpa) was provided with. This little volume, so eminently instructive, and, at the same time, so agreeably amusing, I recommend to the perusal of all my American friends, and especially to those interested in the production of agricultural implements. I should not despair of seeing a steam soil cultivator and pulverizer of an efficient character produced upon the principles recommended by Mr. Hoskyns in his " Talpa," if some ingenious mind would turn attention to the best mode of superseding the plough.

Promoting Agriculture made efforts in the same direction in 1792; but the principal result of all these exertions was improvement in the form and finish of ordinary farm-tools.

"The Hussey harvester."

In 1833, as we are told, the harvesting of corn by machinery was effected near Cincinnati by a gentleman named Obed Hussey, "who cradled wheat as fast as eight persons could bind it." About the same time State and County Agricultural Societies began to spring up in the United States, and a system of annual fairs and exhibitions instituted by those Societies, powerfully stimulated invention, and made the farmers familiar with the best forms of Agricultural Implements in use.

The Great Exhibition in Hyde Park.

Still, however, inventors in America were without the opportunity of comparing their machines with others in use in the Old World, and mechanics in Europe were comparatively unacquainted with the American implements. It was not until our Great Exhibition of 1851 that an opportunity was offered of comparing ideas on the subject of mechanics as applied to agriculture. "That exhibition," the Americans officially report, " exercised a vast influence on this subject, as it did upon all the branches of art."

Its effects on Implement Manufacture.

"Although the number of implements of each kind exhibited by the United States was small, the variety was considerable. The general excellence of American ploughs, reapers, churns, scythes, axes, forks, and other implements was acknowledged by the public admission of disinterested judges, and the particular merits of many by the medals awarded, and by the number of orders received at the time by the manufacturers. The triumph of the "American Reapers" worked a new era in agriculture and gave a strong impulse to the inventive genius of Europe and America. The emulation awakened among manufacturers by the London Exhibition was still further stimulated by the Exhibition in New York in 1853-4 when more than 100 manufacturers competed in this department of mechanics."

The Report adds that the influence of these exhibitions, in furnishing American mechanics with a standard of comparison by which to measure their own implements with those of the world at large, can scarcely be over-rated.

The magnitude of the profits resulting from the production of new labour-saving implements of husbandry in America must be a great spur to inventors and mechanics. It is stated that a slight improvement in "Straw-cutters" enabled the inventor, in a western tour of eight months, with only a model instrument, to realize $40,000. Another inventor sold a machine for "threshing and cleaning" grain for $60,000. The "M'Cormick Reaper" yields its inventor a princely income. A single manufacturer has paid a patentee $117,000 in a single year for the use of a patent-right on an agricultural machine, which others, at the same time, were engaged in making by contract with the owner, and which, therefore, he did not obtain exclusively.

Large profits resulting from the American inventions.

The American machines are generally exceedingly light and simple. Many of our own implement-makers regard them, I believe, with some disdain in consequence, and make frequent endeavours to "improve" upon them by strengthening and elaborating them. But it has to be considered that the great merit and advantage of a machine in America is its simplicity

Peculiar characteristics of the American machines.

and lightness. If it were a cumbersome machine it
could not be, to the same extent, a labour-saving
machine; if it were a complicated machine, it could
not be used, to the same extent, in those regions which
are far distant from the cities where alone the frequent
reparations consequent on complications can efficiently
be made. Above all, a cumbersome and complicated
machine would be unsuited to America, because such
a machine must necessarily be an expensive machine;
and where the average size of farms is less than 200
acres, it is evident that the great bulk of the agriculturists could not afford, even if they required, a
highly expensive implement. Lightness, simplicity,
and comparative cheapness are absolutely essential to
the perfection of an instrument in America, even
although those qualities may be obtained at the cost, as
some of our implement-makers consider, of strength,
comprehensiveness, and elaboration.

It is gratifying to find that the production of agricultural implements in America follows the path of
the population. The New England States, and the
States of New York and Pennsylvania, may be
regarded, generally, as the great manufacturing States
of America; but although the production of agricultural implements was greatly multiplied in these
States during the years between 1850 and 1860, yet
it was in the Western States that the great advance
was made. In those States the value of agricultural
implements produced was augmented as follows:—

1850 .... $1,923,927 | 1860 .... $8,707,194

or no less than 352 per cent. The total production of

implements in these States was nearly one-half of that of the whole Union ; and nearly equalled the total manufacture of the United States in 1850.

One illustration to show how naturally this trade adapts itself to the wants of the population. We should say, probably, that Ohio, as the wealthiest, and Illinois as the most productive, agricultural States of the Union, were those in which agricultural implements would be most employed, and in which their manufacture would consequently be most extended. We find, accordingly, that the largest manufacture of these implements in any one district of the United States was in Stark county, Ohio, where fifteen establishments produced $900,480 worth, the largest part consisting of mowers and reapers, threshing-machines and separators. We find, also, that the next largest production was at Chicago (Illinois), where upwards of 4,000 mowers and reapers were made, in one year, by a single establishment, the largest of its sort in America. Thus we see, that in the most recently settled districts of the United States, the number of agricultural implements in use is the largest: an indication of the increased extent to which machinery is likely to be employed hereafter in farming operations.

The value of the agricultural implements and machinery in use on farms in the United States amounted, in 1860, to $246,118,141, say £50,000,000. This was an increase of more than 63 per cent. over the estimate for 1850. It is obvious from this, that an immense increment of productive power accrued to the United States between 1850 and 1860, *in the mechanical appliances of agriculture alone*, a fact of

Their extensive manufacture

in Ohio

and Illinois.

Increase of productive power arising from the use of these implements.

great significance and importance in considering the resources and prospects of the country.[*]

" Improved inventions" still demanded.

It is a curious fact that, with all their labour-saving implements, many of which have never found their way into use on this side of the Atlantic, the Americans are continually calling out for improved inventions. "The farmer," says a recent writer of authority,[†] " must be relieved from the drudgery of hard and " continuous muscular exertion, such as mowing by " hand and cutting the grain with the sickle; other- " wise his sons will betake themselves to the mechanic " arts, where steam does all the heavy work. The " contrast between the labour of the field and that of " the shop, without a corresponding advance in the " mechanic arts applied to the field, will become so " great, that no labourers will be obtained without " greatly increased wages, and the agriculturist will soon " find himself among the pariahs of the social scale."

American ploughs.

The great object of the American at the present time appears to be to obtain a new form of instrument in lieu of the plough. This is a fact which shows, as I think, the remarkable advance in the science and enterprize of the people of the United States. For we must bear in mind that the Americans are celebrated for their ploughs, and have always been improving on them. Jefferson himself exercised his mechanical tastes and ingenuity on ploughs as far back

---

[*] I should observe that, in the estimate of the value of " Agricultural Implements and Machinery," such articles as cotton gins, scythes, hoes, shovels, spades and forks, are not included. Neither are wagons, carts, or wheelbarrows, the value of which amounted to $11,796,941.

[†] The Hon. M. L. Dunlap, of Champaign, Illinois.

as 1798.   In 1815 Judge Peters, then President of the
Philadelphia Society of Agriculture, sent to Mr. Robert
Barclay, of Bury Hill, near Dorking, two American
ploughs, " of great simplicity, lightness of draught,
neatness, and cheapness," which, when tried against
the best English ploughs, were found to do the work
quite as well with two horses as ours did with four.
At the plough trial, at Hounslow, during our Great
Exhibition of 1851, the American ploughs were
approved for the same characteristics—" extraordinary cheapness and lightness of draught."   It is,
curious, therefore, to find the Americans, above all
things, anxious to supersede their plough by some new
and labour-saving invention.

In 1858, the Illinois Central Railway Company, Their opinion
desiring, no doubt, to fall in with the popular feeling, of steam
offered a prize of $3,000 for the best steam-plough ploughs.
of American manufacture.   Three ploughs were tried,
but all failed.   They were all drawn by traction
engines.   One of them employed knives instead of
ploughshares to slice the earth horizontally.   The conclusions to which the best judges arrived respecting
steam-ploughs from these trials, were, no doubt, correct.
They reported—

"First : That the machine cannot pass over soft land, as
the soil yields to the motion of the drum, or driving wheels,
and, instead of carrying the plough forwards, merely exca-
vates for itself a hole into which it sinks beyond its own
power of rescue.
"Second : When loaded with half a day's fuel and water,
the machine is incapable of drawing the ploughs.
"Third : It cannot rise the ordinary grades of the rolling
prairie with the plough at work.

"Fourth : On level land it cannot do the work as cheaply, under the most favourable conditions of water and fuel, as animal power."

Different conditions of England and America as regards steam-ploughing.

The Americans draw a distinction between the use of the steam-plough in Europe and America. They say the condition of everything in England is different. The soil in England is, generally, a stiff clay, that requires three or four horses to turn a furrow. The dampness of the climate, the tenacity of the soil, and the retention of moisture, make it imperative to have perfect drainage and thorough aeration to produce good crops. In America the soil is less tenacious, is easily moved by the plough, and, as the climate is warm and dry, is naturally well aerated. Consequently, in America, deep-ploughing and under-draining is not so essential. American farms, moreover, are small. They are chiefly worked by the owner and his sons. A farmer of 200 acres could not invest in a steam-plough costing $3,500. Besides, they doubt the economy of using the steam-plough.

The "Rotary Spader."

The plough which at the present time excites most attention in America, is an implement called the "rotary spader." The rotary spader, with four horses, spades the earth 8 inches deep and 3 feet wide, at the rate of five or six acres a day. It is thus a very labour-saving machine, but its heavy cost ($200) is against it. The Hon. Mr. Dunlap, who I have already quoted, says : "Should this mode of stirring the soil ultimately become popular, it can only be by slow degrees. Nothing short of the most decided testimony will induce farmers to change an implement costing

10 or 15 dollars for one costing 200, to do the same
work. The advantage must be largely in its favour to
accomplish this."

What the Americans principally appear to aim at,
at present, is the construction of a "Sulky Plough," The "Sulky
that is to say, a plough with all the modern improve- Plough."
ments ; but having a seat for the driver on the top of
it, instead of a man following its furrows and pressing
it down by handles. " A large amount of ploughing,"
it is said, "is done by farmers' sons of the age of 14
" and upwards. To follow the plough in the furrow,
" day after day, is very tiresome work, and gives the
" boy a heavy, awkward gait, by stiffening the lower
" limbs—a condition from which he seldom recovers.
" To remedy this, the plough must be made to give the
" driver a sulky seat on which to ride. This can be
" done without extra power to move it. A plough
" thus rigged can be run by a class of persons who
" cannot manage the common plough, either from being
" lame or from want of muscular ability to stand the
" hard labour of travel over the rough ground, and the
" handling of the plough and team."

A "Two-horse Cultivator," and what is called a The "Two-
"Double-shovel Plough," appear to be popular im- horse Culti-
plements in America, on account of the facilities vator."
they afford for easy working. "A boy who is too
slender to handle the shovel-plough on foot ; a lame
person, who cannot walk to advantage ; an invalid
partially recovered from sickness ; or a young lady
fond of driving, and who wishes to assist her father or
brother in their farming, can do a full day's work with
this new and valuable implement."

Thus we see the aims and objects of the American inventor.

Difficulty attending the Sulky Plough.

Several patents appear to have been taken out for sulky ploughs, but none of them have hitherto proved practicable. This, no doubt, arises from the use of gig-wheels, which sink into the earth and impede the progress of the plough, as in the case of traction engines. The great object seems to be to overcome this difficulty, and it appears to be thought that it will be speedily attained.

Reaping and mowing machines.

It serves to illustrate the different conditions of the two countries, and the consequent aptitude of the one to embrace the opportunity which is rejected by the other, that the American REAPING and MOWING machines, which are now being largely used in England, are, in reality, English inventions.

Their extensive use in America.

In one of our Patent Office publications it has been shown that, of 69 examples of Reapers, 60 were of English invention, and 9 of American. Yet the value of these machines never came to be understood or appreciated amongst us until after 1851, when the American machines were exhibited at our Great Exhibition. These machines are now universal in America; indeed, the harvest could not be gathered without them. The Census Report of 1860 says, " their usefulness is now universally acknowledged; but in our own land, where labour is so high, and where the season is so short, they are *indispensable.*"

" The nature of our climate, the character of our crops, the scarcity of labour, and the extent of our agricultural operations, all conspire to increase the introduction and use of these and all other implements and machines that will expedite the labours of the farm."

The extent to which these machines are used is described as "enormous." It is estimated that there are not less than 250,000 in use in the United States, each of which will cut an average of 10 acres in a day of 12 hours.

Yet the Americans are far from being content with this machine. They want one which will "cut, gather, and bind up the grain at one operation;" and they expect to get it. On the large grain fields of the west the binding is now done with wire, and a separate machine has been invented for performing that part of the labour. The Americans have also asked for an improved threshing machine, and this they appear to have obtained in the form of a machine which not only separates the grain from the chaff, but carries the straw up to the stack, and puts the corn into the sack, after clearing it. "This simple apparatus," it is said, "attracts no notice, except from the English or Continental visitor, to whom it is a novelty. The English "threshing machines, especially those drawn (*i. e.* "worked) by steam, have a much more finished appearance, but for simplicity and efficiency, they are in "no way superior to those of American manufacture. "In fact, wherever the American machines have come "into direct competition with those of British and "European construction, the American machines have "proved superior." *Improvements in reaping and threshing machines.*

English contrasted with American threshers.

In many of the minor implements of agriculture the Americans have made substantial improvements. Their shovels, spades, hoes, and forks, all present some advantage over those in common use. A firm in Philadelphia has lately been manufacturing axes, hoes, *Minor implements.*

picks, and shovels, on an entirely new principle. Each instrument is made solid, but the handle with which it is to be worked has upon its end an iron socket, through which the pick or other instrument to be worked, is put and fastened by an iron wedge. The advantage of this new form of instrument is, that the handle, which will answer for any number of tools of the same size, does not become loose, and the blow made by the pick, hoe, axe, or shovel, is consequently more effectual. These tools appear to be especially adapted for miners: and many of them have been sent to California, where they are reported to be highly prized.

Inasmuch as the Americans claim to manufacture these implements cheaper and better than other people, it appears absurd and anomalous that they should levy an import duty upon such articles, or upon any of the materials of which they are made. It must be for the benefit of the American farmer that he should get all his implements of the best description and at the lowest price; and it is obviously detrimental to the largest class of producers in the country to tax, in any form, the instruments they use in producing those supplies which so materially contribute to the wealth of the community. Every tax that tends to prevent the farmer from obtaining the best form of agricultural implement at the lowest price, ought to be removed, in the interest of every class, including the agricultural implement maker himself.

CHAPTER II.

TEXTILE MANUFACTURES.

IF it were not for the want of labour which affects, generally, all the occupations of the United States, it might, certainly, be anticipated that a nation which possesses Cotton as a principal product of its own soil, would increase, beyond precedent, in the production of that class of fabric, which now enters the most largely into human consumption, and which holds the highest rank in the industrial occupations of the world. *The Cotton Manufacture of America,*

Labour, however, enters more considerably than anything, except machinery, into the cost price of cotton manufactures; and it is, therefore, not surprising to find that, in comparison with other countries in which labour and the necessary machinery are both cheaper, the cotton manufacture of the United States has not progressed in an equal ratio with those countries. *does not progress in an equal ratio with that of England.*

The cotton woven in America in the year 1860 was 422,000,000lb. valued at about $56,000,000, or say £11,000,000; but I cannot regard this as a very large quantity. In the year 1860, we imported into England from the United States alone, very nearly 2,000,000,000lb. (two thousand million pounds) of *Cotton woven in America and England.*

I

Cotton, or five times the amount which was manufactured in the United States; and, considering the quantity of the raw material obtained from other nations, I think it probable that the quantity we produce may be taken at *ten* times that of the Americans.

Estimates of Values fallacious.

Owing to the variation in the price of cotton at different periods, and to the differences in the cost of labour in different countries, as well as to the differences in the quality and style of products, the relative prices which they bear according to the requirements of different nations, and the appreciation in which those nations hold them, it is not easy to form an estimate of the *value* of the cotton goods produced either in America or England. There can, however, be no doubt that, owing to the cost of labour in America, the value put upon their goods, at the mill, very much exceeds the value put upon the same classes of goods in Great Britain.

The estimated value of the goods produced in America, in 1860, was taken at $115,137,926 = £23,027,585.*

The Exports of British cottons.

So far back as the year 1833, Great Britain was estimated to have produced cotton goods valued at £31,338,693; and, in 1860, the declared value of our

---

* I think it ought to be observed that this total includes the values of every description of cotton produce : not only of the cloth produced, but of the yarn spun and also of the raw material. I doubt, indeed, if the yarn and thread spun is not estimated twice over in this estimate ; once as a manufacture from the raw material, and a second time as a raw material for the manufacture of cloth. I have already observed, in a previous chapter, upon the mode in which these estimates of " values of manufactured products " are sometimes swollen. [*Vide ante*, p. 38].

exported cotton alone amounted to £40,346,342. Our British exports, therefore, nearly doubled the value of the entire manufactured productions of the United States. And this, it should be observed, is without reference to a class of goods which we do not consider (though the Americans do estimate them) as "cotton manufactures," and the export of which from England amounted to nearly £10,000,000 additional.*

But let us judge of the cotton productions of the United States by the number of spindles in that in comparison with other countries. I take the following statistics from a return laid before Parliament, from papers read before the Statistical Society in 1863, and from the returns contained in the United States Census :—

Number of spindles in the Cotton manufactures.

YEAR, 1860.	No. of Cotton Spindles.
Great Britain	30,387,267
United States	5,235,727
France	4,000,000
Germany	2,000,000
Russia	2,000,000
Austria	1,500,000
Switzerland	1,300,000
Italy	500,000
Belgium	500,000
Spain	300,000

* This was exclusive of cotton yarn, cotton thread for sewing, counterpanes, cotton stockings, and cotton nets, which amounted to nearly £10,000,000 more. I take 1860 as the year before the civil war in America, and the year with which comparison is best instituted. It is to be observed that the declared value of our British exports is always under-rated.

Number of hands employed.

The greatest number of hands claimed to be employed in the cotton factories (of whatsoever description) in America in 1860 was 122,028 : in England, our operatives in cotton factories numbered in the same year, according to Parliamentary returns, 405,256. It therefore appears that Great Britain has more than *six times* the number of spindles, and nearly four times the number of hands, employed in cotton-spinning in the United States.

Progress of the Cotton manufacture in America.

At the same time, we must not allow ourselves to undervalue the *progress* of the cotton manufacture in America. The increase between 1850 and 1860 was very great, although by no means so proportionately great as in our own country. The qualities of the raw material used in America were computed as follows :—

Year.	Raw Material Used.
1850	272,527,000 lb.
1860	422,704,975 „

The increase is very large, though very much below our own. The British *imports* of cotton from the United States alone were, in

1840	487,856,504 lb.
1849	634,504,050 „
1860	1,955,982,800 „

So that in twenty years we more than quadrupled our imports of the raw material.

Conclusion as to this manufacture.

What I gather from all this is that the United States gains a vast deal more by exporting the raw material than she does by attempting to manufacture it.

Low description of the American cotton fabrics.

This position is strengthened by a consideration of the descriptions of cotton goods chiefly manufactured in America. I find the quantity of cotton spun into yarn and thread, batting, wicking, and wadding, largely in excess of other classes of fabrics. "Cotton cordage," "cotton bags," "seamless bags," and "packing cloths" (chiefly used for packing the raw cotton) formed also a large proportion of the manufacture. The Southern States have been largely in the habit of manufacturing this material for themselves, and probably many persons will scarcely be prepared for a fact which appears in the United States official returns, that in 1860 the Southern States produced nearly *one-third* of the whole quantity of yarn spun in the Union.

The cotton manufactures of the United States, even with the advantage of a protective duty in their favour, cannot compete with those of other countries even in their own market. Cotton fabrics are peculiarly adapted for apparel in the warmer climates of America—in fact, every one in the country at some period of the year wears clothing the greater part of which is made of cotton. This description of clothing, moreover, recommends itself to a large proportion of the population by the comparative cheapness of its cost.

The cotton manufactures of America cannot compete with the European manufactures in American markets.

But the United States do not produce anything approaching the quantity of cotton goods they require for their own consumption. From 1821 to 1839, the average annual value of foreign cotton goods imported amounted to $10,624,687. From 1840 to 1856, it amounted to $16,795,418. From 1856 to 1860, to $28,811,966. These imports consisted chiefly of piece goods from Great Britain,

Vast importation of cotton goods from Europe.

estimated, of course, at the lowest possible values, in order that they might pay the lowest possible amount of duty in America. Of plain white British calicoes alone, the importation increased from 10,000,000 yards in 1846, to 85,000,000 yards in 1856 : of printed and dyed calicoes from 13,500,000 yards in the former year, to 97,000,000 yards in the latter ! In 1860, Great Britain sent to the United States no less than 226,776,939 yards of cotton goods, or more than *one-fourth* of the number of yards of sheetings, shirtings, printing cloths, &c. which America manufactured for herself.

Absurdity of attempting to protect this manufacture.

With such facts in view, it appears an act of the greatest improvidence to attempt to foster the cotton manufacture of the United States by protective duties. Not only are the Americans thereby unnaturally raising the price of an article of the largest consumption amongst every class of their own community, but they are actually raising this price at their own expense as growers and exporters of the raw material from which these articles are made. And all this for the protection of an interest which cannot compete with its rivals in its own market, and cannot produce anything like the quantity required for the use of its own population !

American WOOLLEN products.

The position here laid down, is, I think, still further illustrated, when we come to regard the WOOLLEN products of the United States. $68,865,963 (or say £14,000,000) is the declared value of the produce

Their small value,

of all the woollen stuffs (including carding, fulling, and mixed goods) manufactured in the United States in 1860. Now, in that year, the British

exports of wool and woollen goods alone, was as
follows :—

BRITISH EXPORTS OF WOOL AND WOOLLEN GOODS, 1860.	
Wool	£877,082
Woollen Cloths	2,996,091
Mixed Stuffs (Flannels, Blankets, and Carpets)	4,401,936
Stockings	657,053
Worsted Stuffs..................................	4,101,918
Total	£13,034,080

compared
with the
British pro-
ductions and
exports of
woollen
cloths.

or little less than the entire production (as estimated)
of the United States.   I may add that of this quantity
upwards of *one-third* was taken by the United States,
showing that the Americans stood in the greatest
want of the very articles they are struggling to
manufacture.

Thirty-five millions and a half of dollars, or upwards
of £7,000,000, of Capital, are taken to be invested in
the woollen manufacturing trade of the United States,
but I question very much whether this capital might
not be better employed.   Indeed, the official reports
tell us that "in Ohio, which, in 1850, produced a
" greater value of woollens than all the other Western
" States, there was a decrease on the product in 1860,
" *owing to the shipments of wool to Europe, which, in*
" *1857, was found to be the most profitable disposition*
" *of the rapidly increasing wool crop of the State.*"

Better to ship
the wool than
to make the
cloth.

Here again, then, we find the Americans standing in
their own light as producers of the raw material by
levying duties, and thereby raising the prices and
consequently diminishing the consumption of that

very raw material when converted into useful articles. Why should the immensely increasing wool production of California be sacrificed to the comparatively limited manufacturing interest of New England?

As in the cotton manufacture, so in that of woollen goods, I apprehend that the produce of America for the most part consists of an inferior article. The official report speaks of the use in this manufacture of very large quantities of "wool flocks," "waste," and "shoddy," which form the basis of "the manufacture of army and navy clothes and blankets in the United States."

"This article consists of cast-off woollen clothes, rags, stockings, carpets, and all soft woollen and worsted articles, reduced by powerful machinery to their original flocculent state to be respun and woven, either alone or mixed with new wool, into a variety of fabrics. Hard or superfine cloths, mechanically reduced to filament in the same way, produce what is called 'mungo,' which means a better class of goods. 'Shoddy' was originally only used for padding; but for some years past has been used for the manufacture of pilot and Petersham overcoats, table and piano-covers, army clothes, &c. White 'shoddy' enters into light-coloured goods, blankets, &c., and the dark-coloured into carpets and close cloths of all kinds, which are dyed to cover the original colours. 'Mungo' is extensively used in the production of the cheap Yorkshire broadcloths, which in finish and appearance when new, are little distinguishable from the best West of England cloths. These shoddy cloths, on account of their cheapness and deceptive appearance, have been much used in the United States to the injury of our cloth manufacturers. Being, in some respects, better adapted to produce a close, short nap than American wool, this material has entered into our domestic manufactures of late years. Machines for reducing rags to shoddy are also in use here. About the beginning of the current century a machine was patented by a Philadelphia manufacturer for that purpose. There are shoddy mills in several States at this time."*

It would appear from this that the claim to the honours and emoluments of "shoddy" is disputed between Yorkshire and Pennsylvania. I think the Americans might do better than to stimulate this trade at all, especially seeing the cost at which they do so. It is officially stated that "the gross profits of the woollen manufacture of the United States, after deducting the cost of materials and labour, was upwards of 50 *per cent.* upon the capital employed, to cover the interest on capital, the wear and tear of machinery, and other incidental expenses." This 50 per cent. profit comes solely out of the pockets of the American people: who are thus made to pay an enormous percentage beyond what they ought to pay for every article of wearing apparel,—cotton or woollen—which enters into their consumption.

Large profits abstracted from the people by this trade.

The remarks which I have made on the woollen cloth manufacture of the United States, apply equally to the other branches of their woollen trade. The manufacture of WORSTED Goods, including delaines, bareges, Cashmeres, alpacas, &c. for ladies' dresses, is limited to three establishments. The manufacture of HOSIERY is not considerable, though it is reported as increasing, which it certainly ought to be considering that foreign stockings are taxed to the extent of no less than 35 per cent. *ad valorem!* The CARPET manufactories number upwards of 200. Carpets of all sorts are in large and increasing demand in the

WORSTED goods.

Hosiery,

Carpets.

* Report of the Commissioner of Census on Manufactures, 1860.

United States, but hitherto all the better class of carpets have been imported : indeed, there are only six American manufactories capable of producing the finer class of carpetings required in the best houses. But the author of the Census Report on Manufactures, writing last year, says : "*As the present tariff is nearly* PRO-"HIBITORY, *we may soon expect to find the market* "*entirely supplied with carpetings of our own domes-* "*tic manufacture !*"

LINEN.

It is admitted that the manufacture of LINEN goods has made but little progress in the United States. "A "few mills, chiefly in Massachusetts, made some coarse "fabrics, the two largest producing six million yards "of linen cloth in 1860. Others are engaged in "making twines, shoe, and other threads." But it is admitted that farmers have grown flax merely for the seed, and thrown out the fibre as valueless—shewing that there is no demand for it in America for any manufacturing purpose. "With the exception of cord-

Cordage.

"age," says the Census Report, "our manufactures of "hemp and flax have never been general or extensive. "They are at present confined, chiefly, to two States, and to the production of a very limited number of

Sewing Twine.

products. Shoe-thread and sewing-twine seem to be the principal fabrics. In a country where cotton abounds, linen, except for peculiar purposes, cannot be expected to be an increasing manufacture.

"Cotton bagging"

I ought, perhaps, to mention "cotton bagging" amongst the fabrics in this class. It is a coarse stuff, made of hemp, sometimes mixed with cotton, for the bagging of raw cotton, and it is manufactured in con-siderable quantities in Kentucky and Missouri. I believe, however, that even in this cheap production our British manufacturers are successfully competing with the Americans in their own market, large quantities of coarse sacking, manufactured from jute at Dundee, having been exported to the States, for the purpose, as I am told, of packing the cotton of the South.

There is a limited manufacture of sewing SILKS in America, and there are a few ribbon and silk-trimming manufacturers in New York and Philadelphia; but almost the whole of the silk goods consumed in the United States are imported from Europe.

SILKS.

We thus see the extent of the manufacture of woven fabrics in the United States. In comparison either with the requirements of the country, or the productions of other nations, this branch of industry assumes comparatively small proportions. I have been the more anxious to dissect this branch of manufacturing industry, because I have been especially desirous neither to be misled myself, nor to mislead others respecting it. Papers are issued and published from time to time, which shew something most astounding as the result of the manufacturing products of the United States. I think these documents are illusory, and I much fear many of them are issued for party and political purposes.

The extent of the manufacture of woven fabrics in America

One of the last documents submitted to me gave the value of the products of manufacturing industry in America in 1860, at nearly £400,000,000 per annum. I do not doubt that this paper was fairly compiled, according to American notions of "manufactures,"—namely, that all the corn that

largely over estimated.

is ground at the mill, all the trees that are sawn
and planed, all the fish that are caught out of
the seas and rivers, all the boots and shoes that are
made out of leather, all the pianofortes that are tuned,
all the spirituous liquors that are distilled, all the beer
that is brewed, all the dress-coats and trowsers that
are made up, and all the printing, all the gas, all the
furniture, jewellery and silverware, soap and candles
in America, in addition to all the products of the
mines, the coal raised, the iron smelted, the machines
erected, and the salt and other minerals produced,
are "manufactured articles." In this point of view,
£400,000,000 is, I think, a very moderate estimate of
the products of the manufacturing interest of the
United States. But on this side of the Atlantic, we
are not accustomed to regard "manufactures" in this
point of view. And having regard to textile manufactures only, I very much doubt if it can be shewn
that the United States produces more than £40,000,000
per annum (or one-tenth of what is claimed as the
product of her manufacturing industry) in this form:
indeed, I think that that estimate is rather in excess
than otherwise, of the real figures. And how small
this gross amount must be to the European total, the
preceding figures shew conclusively.

Recent in-
crease of the
manufacture

During the civil war in the United States, the
production of textile manufactures, as I understand,
considerably increased. This is to be accounted for
by two circumstances: first, in Europe, we were
deprived of our supply of cotton, which occasioned a
great increase of price in all our fabrics, cotton, woollen
and linen:—secondly, very heavy additional duties

were laid by the United States government upon all accounted for by protective duties. imported articles of manufacture, thereby stimulating home production. The first cause will speedily abate. From America herself, or, if not, from other portions of the world, the great manufacturing interests of Europe will be speedily supplied with all, or nearly all, the raw material they want. The second cause must depend on the action of the Americans themselves. If they like to pay half as much again, or in some cases double the money needful to be paid, for a The advantage of such duties considered. cotton, woollen, or linen fabric, simply because it is of " home manufacture," they are, of course, entirely at liberty to make that sacrifice. We, in England, were oppressed in that sort of way, and made to pay twice as much as we ought to have paid, for a great number of years after the Continental War, under the pretext that it was necessary to protect our agriculture. We English experience of them. found out the enormity of that abuse : we raised our voices against that injustice, and against all the influences of our aristocratic country, we put it down. If the Americans choose it, they may suffer, under the extortions of their manufacturers, just as we suffered under the extortions of our agriculturists. But I do not believe they will. I believe that they will demand FREE TRADE, as we demanded it : and they will do so with equal prospects of advancement to themselves and others. England demanded free trade as a manufacturing country anxious to sell the commodities she produced in the best markets, and to import, in lieu of those commodities, what were to her the luxuries of human existence, such as corn, flour, pork, and beef. America will demand free trade as an agricultural country, anxious to sell the commodities she produces, in the best markets, and to import, in lieu of those commodities, what are to her the luxuries of existence, cotton-goods, linens, silks, and woollens.

The increased traffic of England under Free Trade,

The cry, in England, some years ago, was "Who wants all your cotton-prints? If you get free trade, you will never be able to export your products." But under the free-trade system, the exports of England have increased ten-fold. And so will those of the United States. Europe requires American corn, bacon,

And what may be the traffic of America.

timber, cotton; her rice, her tobacco, her cheese, and everything in the shape of produce she can send us. And Europe can send her in return abundant supplies of commodities which she cannot produce so well for herself.

The people of America believed not to be oblivious to such advantages.

On our side, such are the advantages free trade has produced, that there is no party—I may say, scarcely an individual, in Great Britain—who doubts the advantage of the system: I am sure there is not one who would desire that this country should revert to the days of so-called "protection." I do not believe that the people of America are behind ourselves in estimating the advantage and value of a commercial policy which has done so much for every European nation that has adopted it. Some amongst them may be misled, as, for an interval, many were amongst ourselves, by fears and apprehensions, by the conflict of interests, and the natural desire to retain a state of things by which certain parties seem to profit. But the time must come, and that at a very early date, when all delusions respecting a tariff for the protection of native industry must, assuredly, be swept away, and when the people of the United States, with one accord will acknowledge the immense advantages which result from the adoption of the great principle that nations, like individuals, should "sell in the dearest, and purchase in the cheapest market."

CHAPTER III.

MACHINERY.

American appreciation of English Machinery.

OUR American cousins are not generally credited with too large a share of generosity when speaking of the productions of others in contrast with their own. But here is a passage from the Report of Mr. Edward Riddle, the Commissioner sent by the United States Government to England, to report upon the Great Exhibition of 1851, in which full credit is given to English machinery :—

Commissioner Riddle's report.

"The genius of Great Britain is mechanism. More than in any country on the globe, mechanism is there, extending its dominion over the whole empire of labour. In textile fabrics, in fashioning iron like wood to the most exact proportions, in working the printing-press and navigating the ocean, in all agricultural pursuits, everywhere, in everything, lightening the burden of toil and rescuing human life from dangerous pursuits, mechanism reigns supreme. Beyond this the genius of Great Britain has not gone. Ornament in all her productions is inseparably wedded to usefulness. The creation of the beautiful, with her artisans, rests only in the adaptability of mechanism. It is said that a better and purer style of national industry is beginning to be observable in England; but however this may be, her best productions, when placed beside similar productions from the Continent, show violation of harmony in colour and design, and evidences of neglected taste to the most casual observer. But in mechanism—in its highest and noblest ends, in its

tendencies to relieve labour of its drudgery, and to delegate
to iron, to steam, and to other powers of the inanimate
world the burden of toil—Great Britain must be acknowledged to be in advance of all the world."

Most of us remember the disappointment which was
occasioned at the opening of the first Great Exhibition
by the barrenness of the spaces (and they were by no
means inconsiderable) which had been assigned to
Russia and America, at the extreme west end of the
nave.   It was not for many weeks that the American
compartment filled ; and it was not until late in the
summer that the magnificent specimens of Russian
malachite and other natural productions of that extensive empire arrived for exhibition.   How deep was
the interest then derived from those compartments !
They attracted all.   But I cannot do better than let
Mr. Riddle himself report the effect which they produced.   Here is his own account of it :—

*Our first
Exhibition.*

"Perhaps the industrial products of no two countries which
ever existed presented so many points of strong contrast as
did those of Russia and the United States at the Exhibition.
In the one case, everything which was shown was costly ; in
the other, cheap.   The compartments of Russia, splendidly
fitted up and appointed, were attractive from the princely
magnificence of the articles displayed.   The compartments
of the United States, on the contrary, decorated with great
plainness, drew admiration from those who visited them by
the adaptability of everything they contained for the purposes for which they were intended.   Thousands never ceased
to gaze with wonder on jewels, embroidery, velvet, silks, and
furs contributed from the various imperial establishments of
St. Petersburgh and Moscow.   There were others, however—
and they, too, were counted by thousands before the Exhibition closed—who found—in the water-pails, made by
machinery, and furnished at one-quarter the usual price ;

*The Russian
and American
compart-
ments.*

K

in the pegged boots and shoes, between the upper leather
and soles of which not a waxed end was drawn; in the
improved household, barn, garden, and field implements; in
the bell telegraphs, and spring chairs, and cooking ranges,
and hot-air furnaces, and camp bedsteads—a degree of intelligent interest excited by the display in no other part of the
building. The Russian exhibition was a proof of the wealth,
power, enterprise, and intelligence of Nicholas; that of the
United States an evidence of the ingenuity, industry, and
capacity of a free and educated people. The one was the
ukase of an Emperor to the notabilities of Europe; the other
the epistle of a people to the working-men of the world."

Value and
importance of
American
machinery.

There can be no question that a very strong impression was made upon all of us by the ingenious
and simple machines which the Americans exhibited
on the occasion in question. But we must go beyond
that Exhibition, if we would rightly judge of the value
and importance of American machinery. It is to be
borne in mind that the first thing an American usually
looks for, in making his settlement, is a "water-

Hydraulic
Machinery.

privilege." To turn this water-privilege to advantage
he must have hydraulic machinery; and hence, I suppose, of all the countries in the world, America possesses
the largest number of water-mills. In almost every
section of the United States the water-power is so vast
as to be practically unlimited. When they come to
Europe, the Americans look with astonishment at the
enormous quantity of water-power which we allow to
run to waste; and it is, indeed, a remarkable fact how
little comparative use we make of hydraulic machines
in this country. The Americans, on the contrary, use
them everywhere, and especially for sawing timber,
grinding flour, working cotton-mills, &c. I do not

think that they have yet brought hydraulic machinery into use for those larger objects for which it has been employed, on this side of the Atlantic, since the construction of the Britannia-bridge, but a very large amount of capital is invested in the more ordinary description of hydraulic machinery, and there can be very little doubt but that the use of this machinery is largely on the increase.

Next to the hydraulic machinery of America, the American PRINTING PRESS may be considered to rank in importance ; and here, I must say, that, as it appears to me, every European nation has been excelled by the American inventions. Their machines, no doubt, work with far greater expedition, facility, and economy than any we have been able to produce. Comparing one of our best English drum-machines with one of the American horizontal instruments, I think there can be no question of their relative advantages. It was the American machine which facilitated the production of the cheap newspaper ; for without facilities for printing, and the consequent production of large quantities of newspapers within a very limited period of time, cheap newspapers could never pay. Nor is it only the rapidity with which papers can be produced that is of importance. When a machine can be worked smoothly, there is less wear and tear, not only of the instrument itself, but of the paper. Consequently, a thinner, and therefore, a cheaper paper can be used in the American machine than in the English : a consideration of the highest importance in relation to the profit upon the issue of a cheap paper.

The Printing Press of the United States is, relatively,

American PRINTING Presses.

Their special advantages.

Their general adaptability.

so cheap that it can find its way into the most distant districts of the country. I apprehend there are few provincial towns in England to which a first class printing machine has penetrated. Yet this is essential to the issue of a first-class daily paper. In America, owing to the lightness, compactness, and cheapness of their machine, there is scarcely a town in which there is not a daily press. There are nearly 400 daily news-papers issued in the United States, and no less than 3,266 daily, weekly, bi-weekly, and monthly. Nearly 10,000,000 copies of these papers are in circulation : or one daily and weekly paper to every third person in the whole population. The number appears prodigious. But I only refer to it here, for the purpose of illustrating the character and extent of the machinery which is employed in its production.

PAPER.

The production of PAPER for printing purposes has fully kept pace in America with the improvements in the printing-machine. The annual value of the paper now produced is estimated at $17,500,000 or £3,500,000 : nearly as large a product, I should imagine, as our own.

British and American production of paper.

The paper manufactured in Great Britain, in 1858, amounted in weight to 187,500,000 lb. The manu-facture of printing and stationery papers in America, in 1860, was 153,776,000 lb. The stationery we exported, in 1860, was valued at £759,391, the printed books at £100,000 more. In 1858, the gross revenue derived in Great Britain from paper, under the then re-duced duties, was £1,244,722. This indicates a very large production of paper. At that time we had about 400 mills at work ; but the number of mills is no criterion of the produce, as some are so much larger than others.

No doubt the paper manufacture of the United States has thriven, whilst our own trade has been suffering under the burdens imposed, until very recent years, by the Excise Duty upon paper. The clamours of the English paper-makers have made us all conscious how much, since the repeal of the duties, they have suffered from a deficiency in the supply of the raw material. In respect of raw material, America possesses, or ought to possess, a far greater affluence than ourselves. I do not affect to know of what all their paper is made, but there are other fibres in the country besides cotton, which ought to supply the place of rags.* I may observe that few things, in respect of American manufactures, struck me more forcibly during my visit than the very great improvements effected in the printed productions of the country. It is not many years since American publications were of the commonest and coarsest quality, the sole object aimed at being cheapness. Specimens of the year 1835, and perhaps of more recent date, will show that nothing could be worse

The British production depressed by the duty,

And by deficiency of raw material.

---

* Since the above was written I am more fully informed as to this point. The materials used for paper-making in America are stated to be "not only cotton and linen rags, the waste of cotton, flax and hemp mills and of rope and cordage manufacturies, coir and jute and other fibres (either crude, fibrilized, or in the shape of worn-out bagging, cable-rope, &c.), but also straw, hay, and *stable refuse*, various kinds of wood, hemlock, &c., corn-husks, mulberry leaves and bark, and canes and reeds." It is evident that in the list of refuse, from which the Americans make their paper, there are some articles that could only enter into the construction of the lowest qualities.

than the quality of the paper, the character of
the typography, and the nature of the binding of books
in the United States. They would not, at that date,
bear any comparison with even the common form of
novels then produced in England, which were very
indifferent. But all this has undergone a complete
change. On the table before me, as I write, I have
an enormous pile of American books, of every variety
of size, form, and cost—pamphlets, duodecimos, quarto
volumes, publications of Congress, books got up at
cheap rates, and volumes on the production of which
no labour, trouble, care, or cost whatever has been
spared. Select whichever class of books you will, it will
be found to bear comparison with, if not in some respects
to excel, our English publications of the same class.
The qualities of paper in use are most admirable ; in
most cases the type is perfect ; the work of the printer
appears to be done with the greatest skill and excellence ; and in many instances the specimens of binding
rival those of the famous Mr. Hayday. I select from
the books before me a work got up, not for presenta-
tion or special service, but for general sale and circulation throughout the United States. It is called the
" TRIBUTE BOOK," and is a " record of the munificence,
self-sacrifice, and patriotism of the American people
during the war for the Union." I do not think I have
ever seen a book superior to this as regards paper, letter-
press, and binding. I do not know what is the price
of the volume, for it was kindly given to me by an
American friend ; but its preface suggests that the
cost of its production has been very large. One of
the proprietors of the *New York Times* appears to

have been the projector of this elaborate work, and to be responsible for its cost. And it is admittedly published with a view to profit.

It ought to be observed that Printing in the United States is very largely done by female compositors. In New York one in six of the average number employed in printing productions are women and girls. To a certain extent this is due to the use of machines for setting and distributing the types. These machines are much more used in the United States than in Europe. I apprehend the cause to be, that they are found to be labour-saving in a branch of industry in which wages are much higher than with ourselves. In Great Britain our principal master printers have set themselves, for a number of years, very decidedly in opposition to all typographical instruments. Major Beniowski's type-setting machine and the various adaptations of it have been, it may be said, universally ignored. In the same way the employment of female labour in the typographical art has been rejected. And I confess that, looking at the question as one of economy, I have seen no reason, hitherto, to doubt the correctness of the conclusions on this subject which our master printers have arrived at. But I am informed, on good authority, that a time may speedily arrive when these views will have to be reconsidered. The state of the printing trade in England is, at the present time, by no means satisfactory. On the subject of wages, hours of labour, &c., the compositors and the master printers in our country appear to be very rapidly diverging. The masters complain that they are too much controlled by the trade associations in

American printing.

labour,

And typographical machinery.

which the compositors are united. As I have only a general knowledge of the subject, I do not profess to offer an opinion upon the merits of a very delicate question. But I do know, from personal experience, that the public suffer from these differences, and I would strongly recommend both parties to come to a speedy conclusion with respect to them. We find, at the present time, that many of our principal London publishers are transferring a considerable portion of their printing business to the provinces, to Scotland, and even to the United States. We all know that this must be as inconvenient for authors and publishers as it must be injurious to master printers and compositors. If the disputes which lead to such consequences are not speedily terminated, it may happen that the London printers may find it expedient in many cases to use type-setting machines and female work-people, as is done in the United States. This would tend still further to reduce the wages of compositors. At the present time, I do not think that they are under-paid, considering the intelligence, the skill, the time, and the labour required in this magnificent branch of art. But the printers must consider their position.

The sewing-machine is another instrument for which we are entirely indebted to American ingenuity and enterprise ; and which, already, within the space of ten years, has recommended itself to all the world. This machine, as the Census Commissioners of the United States have put it, is unquestionably a "revolutionary instrument" in the arts. "It has opened avenues to profitable and healthful industry for thousands of in-

(margin note: Our own Printing business.)

(margin note: Sewing Machinery.)

dustrious females, to whom the labour of the needle had become wholly unremunerative and injurious. Like all automatic powers, the sewing-machine has enhanced the comforts of every class, by cheapening the process of manufactures, without permanently subtracting from the average means of support of any class of the community."

The manufacture of these machines has become one of considerable magnitude since 1850. In the year 1860, 116,330 sewing-machines were made in the United States, the estimated value of which exceeded $5,600,000.

Their general use.

The sewing-machine was eminently calculated for such a population as that of the United States, in which all of the mending and very much of the manufacture of wearing apparel and of articles of household use had to be executed by the female members of each family. But the machine has outgrown the use for which it was designed. It is not only found to be an indispensable appendage to every considerable household, but it is found a substitute for labour in large manufactories. It has come to be applied to an immense variety of materials, and in a number of different operations, far beyond those originally contemplated. Improvements are constantly made in it to suit the various purposes for which it is now required; and it may be anticipated, that this useful instrument will be made of still further general applicability.*

Their adaptibility to the United States.

---

* Although, from the greater abundance of female labour in England, the sewing machine is not so necessary to ourselves as it is to our cousins in America, and our children in Australia,

Revolution
they have
effected in the
supply of
clothing.

One very remarkable result appears to have followed the introduction of the sewing-machine into America. Twenty years ago nearly all the clothing worn in the country was imported; and, indeed, judging from the export of "apparel and slops" to the United States, from England, still valued at nearly a million and a half (pounds) per annum, a considerable proportion of ready-made clothes must be still sent to New York from the East End of London, for consumption, probably, in the South and West, as well as amongst the maritime population. Nothing, at one time, was more expensive than clothing, especially cloth clothing, in the United States. But the sewing-machine, if it has not greatly moderated prices, has, at any rate, largely operated throughout the Union upon the production of articles of wearing apparel of almost every descrip-

Clothing
manufac-
tures.

tion (stockings, perhaps, excepted). A number of clothing manufactories have been started, in which articles of various descriptions are now produced, wholesale, by this machine. The increase of this manufacture, we are told, has been general throughout the Union. Naturally, it has been largest in the great towns. In the four cities of New York, Philadelphia, Cincinnati, and Boston, this manufacture, in 1860, amounted to nearly $40,250,000 (or more than

───────────────────────────

(where women are in a still larger minority,) yet I do not think it can be said that we are indifferent to the advantages of this domestic friend. Whilst penning these pages I happened to come across an advertisement of a "Furnished house to Let" in one of our metropolitan suburbs, amongst the inducements to take which are enumerated, not only a garden, and a conservatory, but "a billiard-table, two pianos, *and a sewing machine.*"

£8,000,000). " The manufacture of gentlemen's shirts Cloaks and Mantillas.
and collars, and of ladies' cloaks and mantillas (a new
branch, which has received its principal impulse during
the last ten years), and of ladies' and gentlemen's
furnishing goods generally, form very large items in
the general aggregate of this business." In Troy (State
of New York) the value of the shirt collars annually
manufactured alone approximates to $800,000.*

There are 2,800 establishments engaged in the
United States in the manufacturing of men's and
women's clothing, employing nearly 90,000 hands.
We have already seen that the " tailors and tailoresses "
in the United States are numbered at upwards of
100,000.

The engineering manufactures of the United States Engineering manufactures.
have also become of great magnitude. The great
majority, if not all, of the locomotive and stationary
steam-engines, of the engines used in mines, factories,
mills, forges, &c., are now made at home. A certain
proportion of machinery is still imported — equal,
perhaps, to about £50,000 a year; but I apprehend
that these machines are those only of the finer description.

In the manufacture of Iron goods, however, the Iron goods
United States does not appear to make such great
progress, as in some other branches of manufacturing
industry. The value of the production of her iron-
foundries in 1860, is calculated at $27,970,193, or chiefly im-ported.

---

* Troy appears devoting itself to the paper collar manufacture.
I have before me accounts of two manufactories in that city,
one of which turns out 100,000 and the other 30,000 paper collars
a day.

say, £5,400,000. But in that year, the United States imported from Great Britain alone, "iron" to the *Hardwares.* extent of £3,136,000, "hardwares" to the extent of £1,055,000, and "iron in bars" to the extent of £34,400 ; or, making allowances for the differences in prices and calculations on either side, a quantity probably not far short of her production. Many of the lighter articles of hardware we know that America *Revolvers.* is making for herself to great advantage. "Colt's *Locks.* revolvers," and "Hobbs's locks," are now institutions *Stoves.* in England as well as in America. Stoves are now extensively manufactured in the country, where coal is beginning to be more commonly employed than *Edge Tools.* it once was for domestic purposes. Some edge-tool manufactories are also established, and I have before *Files.* me the particulars of some file-manufactories that are said to be returning considerable profits. In respect, however, to most iron goods, and especially those of the heavier descriptions, I apprehend that England can supply them very much cheaper, at the present time, than Americans can produce them : and this especially *Railroad Iron.* applies to railroad-iron, which must inevitably form, for many years to come, so large a proportion of the iron used in the United States.

Steam Engines. The entire value of the steam-engines and other machinery produced in America (exclusive of sewing-machines) was estimated, in 1860, at $47,000,000, or (say) £9,400,000 sterling. This is an increase of more than 60 per cent. upon their production of 1850. But I cannot regard the total as a large one, especially considering all the articles included in the enumeration. The supply of steam-engines alone for such a progressive country as America ought not, I apprehend, to fall short of this amount. But we must regard the manufacture of steam-machinery in America as, to a great extent, still in its infancy.

It is observable from the official returns, that the States which made the largest progress in the production of machinery between 1850 and 1860, were the distant States of Iowa, Mississippi, California, and Wisconsin. I infer that the articles classed as "machinery," include some very simple instruments, because it is not to be imagined that a very high class of "steam machinery" could be produced in any of these States : certainly not in the two last, which were settled before the commencement of the decade. Such instruments as butter-churns, cheese-presses, washing-machines, wringing-machines, and mangles, enter, no doubt, very largely into the computation of "machinery" made in the far West. Nor are these machines to be despised. They are all adapted to the one great end of economizing labour; and many of them do so most effectually. It is complained of the American washing-machines, that they very rapidly destroy the linen; but it is to be recollected, that in primitive countries, the ordinary mode of washing is to beat the clothes between two large stones in a flowing-stream : a process which, I apprehend, must be even more destructive. I am told that the American wringing-machines and mangles, do not, according to the notions of our washerwomen, give a sufficient "gloss" to the clothes. But they are cheaper and more effective instruments than our heavy box-mangles : and the "gloss" required in Illinois and Minnesota,

Character of the machinery generally made in the West.

Washing machines.

Mangles.

is probably not so great as in Piccadilly or the Phœnix Park.

Advantages America might derive from developing this trade. It is, however, greatly to be desired, that the invention, ingenuity, and skill of the Americans should receive the fullest opportunities for development, whether at home or abroad. Every nation in the world is interested in the improvement of machinery; and when we reflect on the advantages afforded by such an instrument as the sewing-machine, it is impossible not to desire that machines which save so much labour, and afford such largely-increased employment, may be abundantly multiplied. England is above all countries interested in the improvement of machinery. With her manufacturing skill, her capital, her cheap supplies of iron and fuel, and her abundant labour, it is impossible but that she must maintain a superiority in the production of machinery where other circumstances are equal. It is for our interest to turn to the utmost advantage every improvement that may reach us from whatsoever source. If this is admitted in America, it will be also admitted that it adds to the strength of the argument with which I have concluded each of the chapters under this section. America may export her cheap machinery to Europe:— Europe cannot but be glad to have it, in whatever form it may arrive. But in order to receive it, and to use it with advantage, America must consent to take back what we can produce from it with advantage to herself. We shall not ask her, nor would it be consistent with common sense, to ask her to receive any produce of that machinery which, by its means, or by any other means whatever, she can produce more cheaply for herself. But, so long as she cannot convert her own raw materials, by the aid of her own machinery, as cheaply as they can be converted into manufactured articles in other countries, it is obvious that she is only imposing a penalty upon herself, and upon every one of her own citizens, by the imposition of duties which preclude the use of her own raw materials and machinery to the greatest advantage in other countries.

CHAPTER IV.

GENERAL MANUFACTURES.

Effects of the sewing machine IN the preceding chapter I have mentioned the sewing-machine, and referred to some of the effects that that purely American instrument has had upon American manufactures. I should not do justice, however, to this invaluable invention, if I did not refer more at length to some of the results it has produced.

on American manufacturing enterprise and industry. It has been observed that the production of men and women's made-up clothing is one of the most remarkable of the recent developments of America. But I must mention one important article not yet referred to, which the sewing-machine has most materially assisted to develop in America. A quarter of a century ago, the Americans were large importers of all sorts of manufactured leather articles, and especially of boots and shoes. A new era has dawned

Boot and shoe manufactories, upon the country. America now not only manufactures her own leather, but makes for herself all her own boots and shoes, and, indeed, is an exporter of them to the extent of little less than a million and a half of dollars a year. The tanning and currying establishments of the United States produced leather in 1860 to the extent of $63,000,000 (£12,600,000). The value of the boots and shoes manufactured from this leather, amounted to nearly $90,000,000 (£18,000,000). This branch of trade nearly doubled itself between 1850 and 1860 in the New England and Western States. It has attained its popularity and success entirely by the employment of machinery. The manufacture of *worked by steam power.* shoes and boots is chiefly carried on in large mills, some of which are worked by steam power, and employ large numbers of hands. Five establishments belonging to the same proprietors in Massachussetts produced, in 1860, over a million pairs of boots and shoes, valued at $1,300,000, or an average of about 5s. 6d. per pair.

It is not to be forgotten, that the late Sir Mark *Sir Isambard Brunel's* Isambard Brunel, as far back as 1810, invented a *inventions,* series of machines for the manufacture of boots and shoes, which, until the close of the European war in 1815, were employed for the purpose of supplying shoes to the British army. His ingenious inventions, probably on account of the cheapness of manual labour in England, never came into common use in this country, and Sir Isambard is reported to have been a considerable loser by them. *said to be used in* I believe it is claimed by the family of Brunel and *America.* their many friends in England, that the machinery now so commonly in use in America for the manufacture of boots and shoes, is based upon Sir Isambard's inventions, and I think this very probable. But, at the same time, we must not forget that steam machinery has *but steam-power and* been applied to many of the processes now in use in *the sewing-* the United States, for the production of boots and *machine give such inven-* shoes, and that the "SEWING-MACHINE," as has justly *tions their practical* been observed, "is the crowning invention which has *value.*

supplemented and given practical value to this production."

Details of the boot and shoe machinery.

As parts of the machinery employed in the boot and shoe manufacture of America, I may mention a lathe for turning lasts, which are now made to every size, with perfect facility and cheapness. Steam peg

Peg machines.

machines, for the production of wooden pegs for boots and shoes, have also been introduced, and they turn out pegs by the bushel. Another instrument for cutting and blocking boots is found of practical utility;

Cutting machines.

and a sole-cutting machine, which produces any number of soles required in an infinitely short space of time, is growing into general use. With all these labour-saving appliances, boot and shoe-making in the States is undergoing a complete revolution, and is becoming

State of the trade.

a steam factory business, instead of a handicraft. A very large amount of money is invested in the business, and as preceding statistics have shewn, the boot and shoe trade employs as large an amount of labour as any occupation, except farming, in the United States.

In the face of such facts as these, it is quite time that our cordwainers at Stafford, Norwich, and Northampton, should look about them. Although we have no duty on leather, the price of boots and shoes in England is continually advancing. I am not recommending pegged boots, or asserting the superior durability of boots and shoes which are made by machinery, but it is certain that the element of price

The element of price will control the market.

will largely control the market in regard to this, as well as in regard to other articles, and that we shall lose the Australian market for our wrought leather goods, unless our prices can be reduced. America has no doubt an advantage in regard to the supply of hides, which she is able to get in large quantities from her own territories, as well as from more Southern parts of the American continent. But a reduction of the price of the manufacture must be even a still more important element in ruling the price of these articles. America is now proving that every class of boots and shoes can be cheaply and efficiently made by machinery, and it is quite necessary that we should not disregard the lesson.

Caution to boot and shoe makers.

I have already spoken of the articles of clothing in the manufacture of which the sewing-machine is applied. I must not, however, pass over its special application to every description of ladies' clothing, including "corsets," "hoop-skirts," (as they are called in America) and "millinery." All these branches are largely assisted by the sewing-machine, which is also applied to the manufacture of straw goods of every sort, and especially to that of straw hats and bonnets. The palm leaf or palmetto hat trade is a branch of business of some importance in Massachusetts, and Connecticut, and the Americans are now exporting these hats to some parts of Europe.

Ladies' clothing made by machinery.

Straw bonnets.

Palmetto hats.

Practically, I believe that we are indebted to America for the general use of another class of goods, which, in consequence of the humidity of our climate, are even of more practical value with us than even with the Americans themselves. I refer to those India-rubber goods, which have of late years been presented to us in such various and useful forms. In England we are accustomed to regard these articles as of

INDIA RUB-BER GOODS.

American origin, and I own that for some time I
thought they were so. But Mr. Mackintosh, to whom
the waterproof outer clothing owes its name, was,
as I am informed, a Glasgow manufacturer, who,
under the instruction of Professor Syme, of Edinburgh,
dissolved caoutchouc in naphtha from native petroleum
or mineral tar, and applied the solution as a varnish
to cloth surfaces. His invention was first established
in Great Britain as far back as 1825; though we
appear to owe the general development of this important business of waterproofing to American enterprise. I am afraid, however, that I shall be trespassing
on very debatable and delicate ground if I go into
this. The number of patents which have been taken
out for this invention, and the extent of litigation
consequent upon real or assumed infringements, is
sufficient to overwhelm any one, except, perhaps, a
patent agent. Let me, therefore, confine myself to
the development of the trade in America itself, where
the manufacture of India-rubber articles is very
large.

These goods are chiefly made in the States of New
York, New Jersey, Connecticut and Massachusetts; and
in 1860, the trade was calculated to produce to the
extent of \$5,799,900, or £1,145,920 per annum. There
are about 30 establishments engaged in this manufacture, and nearly 3,000 hands are employed in it.
At one period a very large amount of India rubber
goods was sent to England from America, but I apprehend that we are now manufacturing the greater
proportion of these articles for ourselves. Our importation of raw caoutchouc or gutta percha has for

Marginal notes:
Mr. Mackintosh's inventions.
Waterproofing generally.
Extent of the waterproofing trade.
British manufacture of India-rubber goods.

many years been a largely increasing quantity. It rose in the year 1861 to nearly 60,000 cwts., of which the real value was given in our official returns at nearly £500,000. Of this quantity, nearly one-fifth was sent us by the United States. Only a small proportion of caoutchouc enters into the value of the majority of the articles produced from it.

Another important business which the people of the United States are now doing for themselves is that of CABINET FURNITURE manufacturing. The furniture produced in the United States in 1860 was valued at $22,701,000 (£4,540,000). America, which used to import so largely of these articles, has not only ceased to do so to any extent, but actually exports much more largely than she imports them. The cabinet furniture manufactured in the United States is for the most part plain, but with the growth of wealth and luxury it will, no doubt, presently assume a more costly character. It is complained in America that the house-decorator, the cabinet-maker and the upholsterer, have hitherto been without training in ornamentation, and England has been railed at as affording them no guides. Our schools of design will, probably, help before long to induce a better taste than, it must be confessed, we have hitherto exhibited in some of the decorative arts. In the meantime, I may say that many of the houses I visited in New York were as elegantly furnished, and as elaborately decorated as any I ever met with.

Sam Slick made us all acquainted with American CLOCKS, and such large numbers of them have been brought over to Europe as entirely to have superseded

FURNITURE

exported from the United States.

Character of American furniture.

American CLOCKS

the Dutch clocks which, in former days, were in such general use in England. The American clock exemplifies the general character of the mechanism of the people,—their "mission" to invent inexpensive machines of general applicability and utility. But though we know something of American clocks, there are not many amongst us who know much of American and WATCHES. A watch manufacturing trade, commenced, however, within the last ten or twelve years at Boston, has proved eminently successful, and has spread so rapidly as to make watches quite an item in the list of American productions. Most of the movements are made by made by machinery, so that the American watches are, to some extent, of a very similar character. The cases are stamped out in the same way. Inasmuch as machinery has for some time been largely employed in producing many portions of the works of watches, both in Switzerland and England, I apprehend that there is not much novelty in this; though there may probably be some new or some additional applications. But, however this may be, the manufacture is progressing, and it may have the effect of diminishing the importation of foreign watches.

JEWELRY. JEWELRY presents a large item in the list of the manufactures of the country. Not only are the Americans, at the present time, manufacturing their own silver, plated and Britannia ware, but they are manufacturers of their own jewelry, and carry on the business very largely in New York, New Jersey, Pennsylvania, Rhode Island, and Massachusetts. The rapid growth of wealth, and the demand for articles of luxury, has greatly stimulated this trade; and the use

(marginal notes: and WATCHES; made by machinery.; JEWELRY.)

of cheap jewelry, facilitated by the improvements in electro-metallurgy, appears much to have assisted its development. About $16,000,000 of silver plate and Extent jewelry (exclusive of watches and watch cases) was manufactured in the United States in 1860; and, although the patterns appear generally to be adapted from those most in request in London and Paris, yet the workmanship does not appear to be inferior to that of the and character general run of jewelry in either city. As to prices it is impossible to speak. Plate and jewelry are articles which always fetch a certain value, the increase of this manu-facture. upon which depends on fashion, taste, the means at the command of purchasers, &c. In regard to jewelry, more than perhaps to any other article, the old adage holds good, that "the price of a thing is what it will bring," and this prevails, I suppose, all the world over.

The manufacture of MUSICAL INSTRUMENTS is an- MUSICAL INSTRU-MENTS. other branch which the Americans have developed for themselves, and in which a considerable number of mechanics are employed, in New York especially. It Organs and pianofortes. is "claimed" that the organs and pianofortes manufactured in America "are better suited to the climate, and in other respects fully equal to those which come from the most celebrated establishments in Europe." The ladies say so, and therefore, the fact is indisputable. But what I believe to be equally indisputable is, that there is a certain class of instruments, peculiarly adapted for the settlers in distant districts, to the production of which the Americans have applied themselves with much success, and no small commercial advantage. We can easily conceive the demand for such instruments as seraphines, concertinas, Concertinas

melodions, harmoniums, accordeons, clarionets, and
flutes. Banjos and India rubber flutes are probably
peculiarly American productions. Besides these, they
make considerable quantities of drums, tambourines,
guitars, bugles, sax-horns, and other instruments of
brass and German silver. It is very probable that the
large immigration from Germany has stimulated the
production of those musical instruments which are in
common use amongst the German population.

I shall not go through the other branches of manufactured articles which are produced in the United
States. It is easily to be understood, that with so
largely an increasing population the production of
such articles as SOAP and CANDLES would be greatly
increased, especially in a nation where so much tallow
is rendered from the fat of animals. The Americans
include the product of their FISHERIES among their
manufactured products, and so far as relates to their
whale fishery—no inconsiderable proportion of the
whole—train oil may be fairly so considered. But the
fish of the coasts,—the codfish, the mackerel, the shad
(answering to our herring), the bass, the white fish,
and the salmon (the latter chiefly caught in the rivers
which empty themselves into the Pacific Ocean), or
the oyster, of which there are such very fine varieties
in the Bay of New York,—I think that these can
scarcely be regarded as " manufactured products."
Amongst the products of their industry, the Americans likewise include GAS, of which the annual product is estimated at the value of $11,225,000. One
is pleased to see the cities of the United States well
illuminated by gaseous products of their own manu-

Banjos,

and other
instruments.

Other manu-
factures.

Fish.

Gas.

facture; but, although it undoubtedly exhibits great advance in civilizing arts, it does not strike us in Europe as necessary to treat Gas as one of the manufactured products of a nation.

The manufacture of SPIRITUOUS LIQUORS is another product of the United States which has vastly increased; but it will probably be admitted that this is not to be regarded with unmingled satisfaction. In 1864 they produced 88,000,000 gallons of spirits, principally whisky, "high wines," and alcohol, from 1,138 distilleries, chiefly in the Middle and Western States. Where corn of every sort is so abundant, it is obvious that the opportunity of manufacturing spirituous liquors must be excessive; but it is obviously not desirable, except, it may be, for purposes of revenue, to stimulate this production.

Eighty-eight millions of gallons of spirits in one year, for a population of 32,000,000 of people, seems a very excessive produce.* In Great Britain, the number of gallons charged to duty in 1860 was only 20,000,000 gallons: and that was sufficient to produce a revenue (under an equalized system of duties, generally approved) of nearly £10,000,000 per annum. The product of distillation in America is of a low class; but this makes it all the worse.

The various and enticing modes in which spirits are drunk in the United States is not to be over-

Spirits.

Excessive production of Spirits in America.

Enticing beverages.

---

* The quantity produced in 1864 was considerably in excess of the average, in consequence of an anticipated increase of duty; but the average consumption of Spirits in the United States is more than double the whole quantity produced in Great Britain and Ireland.

looked. The most ardent advocate of temperance cannot be indifferent to the forms in which "Cocktails," "Juleps," "Slings," and "Twists," are presented, whether as summer or as winter beverages. All this, however, only makes the general result the more unsatisfactory. The Americans are, by no means, an intemperate people: but they are induced to consume very large quantities of highly intemperate liquids under an engaging form. I believe that, under another system, a class of beverages better adapted to their climate, and consequently to their general health, might be secured to them.

"High Wines."

Ohio, Illinois, and California have recently been distilling immensely increased quantities of "high wines." In such climates, such spirits cannot but be most deleterious. Some years ago, the rural population of Norway was one of the largest spirit-consuming populations of Europe. They drank a deleterious compound distilled from their own grain, and popularly known as "Finkle." The authorities, the clergy, the whole of the better class of the people, saw the necessity of checking the consumption of finkle, and they effected it by opening up the light wines of France, and beer manufactured by German brewers, to the whole interior population. The result has been most satisfactory. In the same way, some years ago, nothing was to be had in Ireland in the shape of a beverage, but whisky and water. The excellent Father Mathew and his coadjutors denounced strong drinks; and the consequence has been an immensely increased consumption of tea in Ireland, together with the establishment of numerous breweries,

Norwegian Finkle,

and Irish Whisky,

which supply the population with admirable ales.
Norway and Ireland are two of the most humid
climates of the globe, and consequently the very
climates in which spirituous liquors might be deemed
the most necessary for the population.   But if the
people of those countries do not find strong spirits,   ill-adapted
like finkle and whisky, necessary for their consumption,   for the population of
how much less necessary must they be to the popula-   America.
tions of countries like Ohio, Illinois, and California,
where the atmosphere is dry and the temperature,
during the greater portion of the year, extremely high.
In Europe, we do not find that the populations of
Spain or Italy desire "high wines."

MALT LIQUORS have been introduced into the United   LAGER BEER,
States chiefly to suit the palates of the Germans, who
form so considerable a proportion of the population.
The number of brewing establishments in 1860 was
970, and they produced 3,239,000 barrels of beer.   I
believe that this is a larger proportionate increase
of consumption even than in the case of spirits.   It
would, probably, be larger still, if the beer brewed   its quality and
was superior in quality and cheaper in price.   I am   price.
sorry to say that I believe the malt productions of the
United States to be, for the most part, dear and bad.
Let us hope that great improvements will be speedily
effected in them.   The supply of a really pure, strengthening, and agreeable beverage to a nation is an object
of the first moral and social, and therefore of the first
political importance.

I think I ought not to pass over the great con-   ICE.
sumption of ICE in America.   Though it scarcely
ranges under the head of a manufacture, ice is one

of the most valuable articles of commerce in the States. You find it everywhere, and applied to everything: and those who do not know what the heats of summer are, even in the most northern latitudes of the American Continent, will be utterly unable to realize the importance and the luxury of this production.

Its universal use.

Export of ice. It has been reserved to the Americans to show the value of ice, and the extent to which it can be carried as an article of commerce. They not only send their ice to all the southern ports of the Union, but to the Spanish Main, South America, the West Indies, the East Indies, China, and Japan. Numerous companies and large amounts of tonnage are engaged in this trade. The ice is taken from fresh-water ponds situated at a great elevation above the sea. It is usually cut into blocks of about a foot thick, and is beautifully transparent and free from air-cells. It is conveyed from the lakes to storehouses by railway carriage. The storage and export is managed in such a way as to avoid waste, and the ice usually arrives at its destination in almost as solid a condition as when it was cut from its native pond.

Nature of the trade.

The English ignorant of the use of ice. In England, we have not the remotest idea of the ice trade; and we seem to have the faintest glimmer of the value of ice. The particles which we get at first-rate dinner-tables in London and Paris afford but a faint indication of the profusion with which ice is served in every house in America, and of its addition to the luxurious enjoyment of a feast. The prevalent moisture, and the excessive variations of temperature in our climate, no doubt, have much to do with our general disregard of ice ; but even as a means of preserving articles of consumption, it is extraordinary that it is not more generally employed. The luxurious manner in which the single item of "butter" is served at every table in America, between transparent cakes of ice, occasions those who have visited the country to regard with disrespect the product of an English dairy.

In treating this part of my subject I have been anxious to *discriminate.* I am impressed, beyond measure, with the *progress* America has made in the useful arts. I regard many of her manufactures as most original, as eminently adapted to the requirements of the people and of the country, and, in many cases, as valuable to the world at large. But I think that the Americans pride themselves far too much upon their production of fabrics, which they cannot produce either so cheaply or so well as other nations, and which a section amongst them is endeavouring to foster by enactments which, in their consequences, must be most pernicious to the national prosperity.

American progress in manufacturing industry.

If the influence of my name or of my experience could for a moment avail in a country where I am comparatively so little known, I would endeavour, above everything else, to use it for the purpose of deprecating the delusion of "protection," as it is called, for national industry. The experience of every nation shows the fallacy of that. We tried it in England, and restricted our commerce.

Caution against the delusion of Protection.

At the present moment, Spain, the most backward country in all Europe, is suffering from so-called protection of manufacturing industry to an extent which reduces her to a position of contempt amongst the nations.　For such a country as the United States, the system is, of all others, the *least* adapted.　The very basis of republican institutions is the principle of the general good,—which involves the principle of buying in the cheapest and selling in the dearest markets.　I may be told that, on this side the Atlantic, we want the trade of America opened for our own purposes.　Let me, once for all, deny the injurious imputation.　We want trade opened, *not for our own*, but for THE WORLD'S purposes: for we have discovered that which all Americans ought to appreciate, that no nation can prosper which isolates herself from the world.　If we have found protection *insufferable* in the OLD WORLD, how much more must it prove so in the NEW.

SECTION IV.

MINERALS.

SECTION IV.—MINERALS.

CHAPTER I.

THE PRECIOUS METALS.

THE mineral wealth of the United States is more largely diffused than is generally known. Gold has been found in Virginia; and at an early period of the present century, North and South Carolina, and the State of Georgia contributed gold so considerably to the Mint of the United States, that it was deemed desirable to institute branch mints for the deposit of gold, and the manufacture of coinage at New Orleans, Charlotte (N. C.), and Dahlonega* (Georgia). At these three branches gold has been deposited at different periods to the value of upwards of $33,000,000. Since the discovery of the far more productive gold fields of California, the search for gold in the Atlantic States

General diffusion of Mineral Wealth throughout America.

---

* Dahlonega is situated 141 miles N.N.W. of Milledgeville. The gold mines in its neighbourhood are very rich, but the hills have been completely riddled by the miners. The gold was first obtained from the alluvion of the streams; afterwards from veins embedded in pyrites of quartz rock. The Indian name of this place, "Tau-lau-ne-ca," signifies "yellow money."

appears to have been neglected. Of recent years the attention of the Americans has been almost exclusively directed to their Pacific gold field.

Mr. Chase's description of the Pacific Gold Fields.

The Pacific gold fields were described as follows by Mr. Chase, the then Secretary of the Treasury of the United States, in his Official Report for 1862 :—

"The gold-bearing region of the United States stretches through near eighteen degrees of latitude, from British Columbia on the north to Mexico on the south, and through more than twenty degrees of longitude, from the eastern declination of the Rocky Mountains to the Pacific Ocean. It includes two States, California and Oregon ; four entire Territories, Utah, Nevada, New Mexico, and Dacotah.* It forms an area of more than *a million of square miles*, the whole of which, with comparatively unimportant exceptions, is the property of the nation. It is rich not only in gold, but in silver, copper, iron, lead, and many other valuable minerals. Its product of gold and silver during the current year, 1862, will not probably fall very much, if at all, short of $100,000,000, and it must long continue gradually yet rapidly to increase."

The Gold-producing regions of America.

A great portion of the region described by Mr. Chase is as yet unworked ; but enough is known of its general characteristics to establish the correctness of his description. From every one of the districts above mentioned, more or less of the precious metals have indeed been produced. Utah, New Mexico, Nevada, Dacotah, Colorado, Idaho, Arizona, and the Washington Territories on the Pacific, have all sent large quantities to the United States Mints. In

Establishments of Branch Mints,

addition to a branch Mint, which was established

---

* Under the recent apportionment of the territorial domain of the United States, Washington, Colorado, Idaho, Montana, and Arizona must be added.

at San Francisco in 1852, and which has contributed 165 million dollars, or more than £33,000,000 to the coinage of the country, branch Mints at Denver, in the Colorado territory, and at Carson city, in the Nevada territory, were established respectively in 1862 and 1863, the produce of those districts being considered sufficient to render such a measure necessary.

at Denver and Carson City.

In a previous chapter, I have referred to the extraordinary progress of California as an agricultural country. The development of her soil attests not only the fruitfulness, but the population and prosperity of the region : for it is to be recollected that the production of corn and stock and wine was undertaken to supply a country in which, previously to 1848, nothing whatever was produced, and where the white population did not then exceed 10,000. What agriculture has done for California is amazing. In proportion to population (it now numbers nearly 400,000) no country in the world produces a more abundant supply of food. Every description of farm, orchard, and garden produce is cultivated ; every variety of animal and of domestic poultry is reared ; every description of fruit is grown. The wine product of California alone would be a source of wealth to any country. In 1855 California did not number one million vines ; in 1862 she had under cultivation upwards of 10,500,000, and in 1863 she produced 350,000 gallons of wine and brandy, which was estimated in 1865 to be increased to 1,000,000 gallons.*

Agricultural progress of California.

---

* An account I have just received from America estimates the

Gold-mining
in California.
But it is to the mineral produce of California that I have here to direct attention. She commenced gold mining in 1848, and from that period to the end of 1864, sixteen years, she produced $816,500,000, or £163,300,000. Of this aggregate upwards of $555,000,000 has gone into the United States mints for coinage, so that in 16 years, California has contributed nearly £112,000,000 of gold to the coinage of Lands mined. the nation. It is said that about 10,000,000 acres of land have been "mined;" but it is remarkable that these very acres, if no longer productive of gold in its natural form, are rendered peculiarly prolific of it in another form. The lands dug for gold lie principally along the foot of the Nevada, and other ranges of Their cultivation. mountains. They have a most delightful climate : and the "pick" of the miner in his search for gold has just disturbed the surfaces sufficiently to render the soil peculiarly adapted for the planting of the vine and other fruits, all of which are so prolific in California.

Prospects of
California.
Gold mining in California has suffered little during the five years of the civil war. Now that the war has terminated, the population of the country will largely increase, and with its increase gold will undoubtedly be proportionately developed. As I was leaving the Bay of New York in November, in Migration to
the district. the Scotia, for Liverpool, the "United States Mail Packet," "H. L. Chauncey," carrying passengers from New York to Aspinwall, passing them by railroad from Aspinwall to Panama, and conveying them by steamer of "the Pacific Mail Steam Ship

---

vintage of 1865, in Los Angelos, at 350,000 galls., the Sonora district at 350,000, and in the rest of California at 300,000.

Company" from Panama to San Francisco, (all at one rate of passage) was departing for her destination. This one vessel had no less than *a thousand passengers for California*, and her way bill amounted to $300,000, or £60,000 ! How strong is the stream of population to California which this fact illustrates, and how large must be the resources of a community which requires the supply of such quantities of first-class goods !

It may be interesting to record in this place the quantities of gold, the produce of the United States, deposited in the United States Mint, and its several branches up to 1863. The official reports give the following particulars as the total produce of the Pacific States.

Production of Gold and Silver in America.

GOLD RECEIVED INTO THE UNITED STATES MINT UP TO THE YEAR 1864.	
State.	Quantity.
From California	$541,674,400
„ Colorado....................	7,646,386
„ Oregon	3,980,285
„ Utah	78,559
„ Nevada	65,199
„ New Mexico	63,023
„ Washington	31,451
„ Arizona	25,761
„ Dacotah..................	7.958
„ Idaho	1,816

Native Gold received for Coinage.

This return shows the large yield of California, and indicates the other districts of the United States in which the precious metals have been found. I am

Export of the precious metals in bars, &c.

assured, however, that the figures do not at all express the extent of the Gold Yield of America. The Director of the United States Mint himself reports that "these returns do not assume to give the amount of the entire production of the precious metals." It is stated that considerable quantities of Gold, and still larger quantities of Silver, are run into bars, and exported in that state both to Europe and to China without passing through the Mint or any of its branches.* And the diggers also carry away some quantities in the raw state.

It may be interesting to look at the position and progress of the auriferous localities.

COLORADO.

COLORADO, which has produced the second largest quantity of gold of any of the new divisions of America, is situated immediately west of the State of Kansas, and between that and Utah. This country was first explored by Zebulon Pike, at the head of an

Its position.

expedition sent out in the year 1802. He discovered a range of mountains, to which he gave his name, and which culminated in a peak, called "PIKE's PEAK." The knowledge of this region remained very meagre until 1858. In the summer of that year a few adventurers and explorers from Kansas and Georgia, under the leadership of Greene Russell, an old Georgian and Californian miner, followed up the Arkansas river,

---

* A fact which is reported in the papers of the "United States Army Sanitary Commission" goes to confirm this statement. The people of Storey county, Nevada, made a collection for that Commission, which amounted to the sum of $20,226. This contribution was transmitted to the Commissioners "in eight massive silver bars, five of which weighed 111 lb. each." A friend I had the pleasure of making in New York, Mr. W. B. Ogden, received his dividends from mines in Nevada in the shape of *a ton* of Silver bars.

and explored the country at and around Pike's Peak, and Discovery of Gold northward along the mountain range to the Cherokee pass in the Rocky Mountains. In the bars and banks of the Arkansas river, 250 miles away from the mountains, they found certain indications of gold. These indications increased as they approached the range, and, ultimately, to the north of Pike's Peak, near the at Pike's Peak. eastern base of the mountains, they found a very superior quality of washed gold in paying quantities. Close to the spot where this discovery was made, has sprung up the town of Denver, already mentioned, now the capital of Colorado.

In May of the following year (1859) the Gregory The Gregory Mines. mines were discovered by an old Georgian miner of that name. Quartz mills were put in operation, and a large emigration soon began to set in to this El Dorado. Last year a further discovery was made of silver mines Silver mines. in this territory, which are reported to be prolific. The yield of the precious metals has, indeed, largely increased in Colorado. In 1863, the district sent The yield of Colorado. $2,893,336 into the United States Mint; and it is said that, in 1864, the yield was very much larger. It is difficult, however, to arrive at any entirely satisfactory account of the yield of this territory, in consequence of the gambling speculations which are going on in the shares of many of the gold mines, and the consequently very unreliable character of many of the state- Quartz-crushing machinery ments published respecting them. One thing, however, is certain. There is an immense quantity of machinery being made for and exported to this district. The gold presents itself in Colorado in large masses of quartz, and it has been generally complained that being largely supplied.

there were no stamping or crushing machines in the locality of sufficient power to extract it. These are now being supplied from St. Louis and Chicago. The whole population of Colorado was only 52,000 in 1860. As the steam engines and crushing machines advance into the territory, they will no doubt be attended and followed by large numbers of gold-seekers, and it may consequently be expected that in a year or two the abundant mining field of Colorado will be much more fully explored and developed than it is at present.*

Oregon.

The State of OREGON, the third most productive gold State of America, lies on the Pacific, immediately to the north of California. The district was organised in 1848, and admitted into the Union as a State in 1859. It had, in 1860, only about the same population as Colorado. Near the Southern and on the Eastern borders of this State, extensive and rich gold fields have been discovered. Father de Smet, a Jesuit missionary to the Indians, who has traversed the country, and whose name carries, and with justice,

* As I write this, an article in a New York paper of the month of January, 1866, affords information as to the "Great Overland Stage Route," which undertakes the carriage of passengers from Nebraska city on the borders of the State of Iowa to Denver city in Colorado. The system seems complete. The journal in question, speaking of the State of Colorado, writes, "No one, who has observingly traversed her steep sides and narrow valleys, and noted the profusion of their mineral veins, can doubt that they contain more gold than is to-day in possession of the civilized portion of mankind; and the progress of discovery and the invention of machinery, aided by that of the Pacific Railroad, must very soon render the reduction and separation of the rock and mineral abundantly and extensively profitable."

great authority, gives the most glowing account of the Cœur d'Alène gold fields, and of the district in which they are located. The whole country is said to be auriferous.

The Cœur d'Alène Gold Fields.

Utah, the territory in which the Mormons made their settlement after their expulsion from the State of Illinois, is a part of the district ceded by Mexico to the United States in 1848. It is far more a pastoral than a mining country; yet gold and silver are found in it, and some mines are worked with advantage, at a place called Egan Canon, on the Overland Mail route, about 200 miles to the west of the Great Salt Lake.

Utah.

The Egan Canon mines.

Nevada, the territory lying immediately west of Utah, and situated between that and California, has proved to be a most prolific territory. This district is said to have been actually untraversed before 1859. In the spring of that year it was explored by Mr. Horace Greely, and in the month of September following by a party of young men from Illinois, who traversed the district on their way to California. Both parties gave a most uninviting report of the district. In the spring of the following year (1860), a discovery was made of an immense mine of silver, now known as the " Comstock Lode," of which it is said that " no description can give an idea of its wonderful wealth." " The deeper the mine is worked, the richer and wider is the vein. The lode has been traced for a distance of two miles or more, and is believed to extend much further." It is owned for the distance spoken of by nearly one hundred different Companies, whose claims vary from 25 feet to 2,000 feet each of the lode, each company being entitled to the whole depth and width

Nevada.

The Comstock Silver mine.

of the vein, whatever that may prove to be. A fine city, called Virginia City, has sprung up in close proximity to these mines. The explorations are extending themselves to other parts of the country, and Star City, Humboldt City, Austen City, and Aurora are represented to be all flourishing towns. Austin City has a population of between 5,000 and 6,000; Virginia City of more than 10,000. Indeed the whole of Nevada is most rapidly increasing in population, and according to the most recent accounts new silver mines are being opened in different localities.

New Mexico and Arizona.
New Mexico and Arizona, which fill up the space between the State of Texas and the Southern part of California, both belonged to Mexico until 1848, when this district was acquired by the United States. Though at present thinly inhabited, they are both old settled territories; and, in New Mexico especially, mines have long been worked with a view to the production of precious metals. But it is said that some of the most promising districts, especially of Arizona, have not been prospected at all, and others only in the most superficial manner. The " Report of the Commission of the General Land Office," transmitted to Congress in 1863, states that " Arizona is believed to be stocked with mineral wealth beyond that of any territory of equal extent." "The richest mines are yet unfound." New Mexico is most easily reached from New Orleans; Arizona from San Francisco.

Washington.
The Territory of Washington is the most northwesterly of the United States. It lies between the British boundary and the State of Oregon, and borders

on the Pacific. "Puget Sound," as this district has been heretofore called, taking its name from the water instead of the land, has been chiefly known as a lumbering district and fishing station, but it is indisputable that of late years a large and increasing quantity of gold has been discovered in this locality, which will perhaps be regarded as the less extraordinary when we consider its proximity to British Columbia. The population of this district is at present very small, only numbering 15,000.

IDAHO, another of the new territories, organised so recently as 1863, lies immediately to the east of the Washington district. It is, therefore, as yet only three years old, and a large portion of the territory is unexplored. The miners, however, have discovered three sets of gold fields, called respectively the "Barncock," "Centreville," and "Salmon River" mines, which are all said to be productive, together with the "Owhyhee" silver mines, which lie in the south-east corner of this territory. These mines are said to have produced, in 1864, as much as $6,000,000. There can be no doubt that the mineral discoveries in this district within the last two years have largely attracted the attention of capitalists and miners, despite all the difficulty of reaching so distant a location. I extract from the United States National Almanack of 1864 the following account of this locality :—

IDAHO.

"The gold mining regions of Idaho Territory are but the prolongation to the northward of the mineral regions of California and Nevada. Until within the last three years, what is now Idaho was uninhabited, except by Indian tribes. It owes its present activity and rapid progress of settlement to the discovery of the gold mines in the British Possessions north of its boundary. This discovery drew from the gold fields of California thousands of adventurers, who, in search for new fields of wealth, discovered the places of Eastern Oregon and Western Idaho. Since then the exploration of this new region has been constantly and rapidly pressed; flourishing settlements and towns have sprung into existence, roads have been opened, rivers navigated, mail-routes established, and farm improvements commenced; and, besides all this, the Territory has attracted the attention of the monetary and commercial world."

The new territory of MONTANA was recently separated from Idaho. Although only three years old it is reputed to have produced over twenty million dollars of gold and silver.

DACOTAH.

DACOTAH, an entirely new territory, is much nearer home. It is the district immediately to the west of Minnesota, and although at present quite unsettled, population will probably flow into it as Minnesota becomes populated. The Missouri river waters a large part of this territory, and gold, together with other mineral products, has been found in the Black Hills, about 300 miles west of the south-eastern boundary. The district is at present wholly uncultivated, but if its mineral products prove equal to their promise, it is not unlikely, from the comparative ease with which it can be reached from Iowa and Minnesota, that this territory will speedily "settle up."

Insufficiency of our information respecting the auriferous territories of America.

I have been anxious to give this outline of the localities in which gold is found in the United States, not only because they are important indications of the resources and prospects of the country, but because I believe a large proportion of my fellow-countrymen are entirely unacquainted with the districts I have

referred to, and in many cases even with their names.
If the general idea which prevails in England respecting California does insufficient justice to the character
of that highly civilized and most productive State, how
much less appreciative are many amongst us likely to
be of territories so comparatively new and remote as
Colorado, Nevada, and Idaho.   Yet a day is probably
not far distant when the stream of emigration will set
towards these and the other gold-producing territories
of the United States, in not far less proportion than it
has heretofore set to California.   The mineral wealth
of these districts only requires working.   In order that
the gold fields may be worked, populations must flow
into them.   The war in America has, for the last five
years, diverted the attention of the bulk of her population from other to military pursuits; but now that
the struggle is over, the migration for which the
Americans are so famous, will unquestionably speedily
people territories which afford such abundant promise.

Probability of large Emi-gration to these districts.

We should not be unmindful that the discovery of
gold in California has been one of the great causes
of the recent development of the United States.   It
has been said by a philosopher that " wherever gold
pours in, an increased abundance, labour, and industry gain life; the merchant becomes more enterprising, the manufacturer more diligent, the mechanic
more skilful, and even the farmer follows his plough
with the more alacrity, as he feels that his crops will
produce good prices."   An influx of money invigorates
industry; and this must be more peculiarly the case in
a country where almost every man is his own freeholder,
and where the fixed charges on industry are, therefore,

The Gold discoveries a main cause of the recent development and progress of the United States.

comparatively light. I do not mean to say that the skill and industry of the United States would not have made considerable strides even had no gold been discovered in her territories; but that skill and industry has, no doubt, been excessively stimulated by the constant and continued influx of gold, and the great accession to wealth thereby occasioned. Vast fortunes have been made in New York by trade with San Francisco, and large proportions of those fortunes are expended in articles of luxury, which never would have been required, and consequently which would not have been produced, had the trade with California not existed. Hence, therefore, we must attribute very mainly to the discovery of gold on the shores of the Pacific the vast development of the States of the Atlantic.

Official estimate of the yield and value of these products.

The "Secretary of the Interior," in a report to Congress, has estimated that when a railroad to the Pacific is completed, traversing Nevada and other mineral regions, "*the annual yield*" from the mines will amount to $150,000,000 or £30,000,000 sterling. It is to be remembered that the mines of the precious metals in America are nearly all on the public lands of the United States. Writing on the resources of America, my friend, Governor Walker, who has himself been Secretary of the Treasury of the United States, has publicly declared,—"They are the property of the Federal Government, *and their intrinsic value exceeds our public debt.*"

CHAPTER II.

IRON, &c.

IRON ORE is widely distributed through the United States, but it is only in the old States of Pennsylvania and New Jersey that it is, at present, largely worked. On that field there are about 130 establishments for mining Iron Ore, which give a produce of about 700,000 tons per annum. More than half the capital invested in Iron mining in America is employed in this region. It does not appear that the trade is very profitable. It is admitted that, "it hardly holds its own, in spite of its admirable location, in the present condition of the manufacture, owing to the proximity of the district to sea-ports which are glutted with foreign Iron." I apprehend this to mean that iron can be imported into the United States at cheaper rates than it can be produced there. And having regard to the enormous quantities and comparatively low prices of iron produced, during many years, in England, Wales, and Scotland, this is not a circumstance calculated to excite surprise.

Iron-mining in Pennsylvania

not very profitable.

The quantity of Iron Ore raised in America is, however, less to my present purpose than the extent of the field in which this mineral is located. Besides the several iron-fields of Pennsylvania, iron is raised and

Extent of the Iron Fields of America.

worked in different parts of the States of New York, New Hampshire, Massachusetts, Connecticut, Maryland, and Ohio. In the South there is an old iron-producing district in Virginia, and both the Carolinas have a considerable number of forges and furnaces at work. In northern Georgia, passing into Alabama, along the line of the river Chattahoochie (so celebrated in the great march of General Sherman) there is a district which is officially represented to " possess incalculable, inexhaustible abundance of the richest ores, though its production of iron still remains at a minimum." We shall probably hear more of this district at a future date.

Iron in the Southern States.

Missouri.

But the State which presents the greatest field for Iron Mining is the State of Missouri. This district appears to possess an inexhaustible supply of the very best ores. Iron in Missouri is represented not to be found, as with us, far below the surface of the earth, but in immense masses, or " mountains," towering above the ground. " Iron Mountain " is the largest mass. It is composed exclusively of iron ore in its purest form. The height of this mountain is 228 feet, and its base covers an area of 500 acres; which is calculated to give 1,655,280,000 cubic feet, or 230,187,375 tons of ore. There is every geological reason to believe that this deposit extends downwards, enlarging as it descends; but, on the supposition that the base is not extended, every foot of descent below the surface will give 3,000,000 tons of ore. " Pilot Knob," distant about six miles from " Iron Mountain," is another of these stupendous masses. It rises 581 feet out of the valley in which it stands, and

Its iron mountains.

Pilot Knob.

covers an area of 360 acres with almost a solid mass of iron. There are several other "Mountains" in this region, and it is computed that there is iron ore enough in Missouri to furnish 1,000,000 tons per annum of manufactured iron for the next two hundred years.

This district has naturally attracted the attention of capitalists and miners, and during the last decade several furnaces were put in blast. Unfortunately, however, it is deficient in its local supply of suitable coal, and the railway-system of Missouri has been too incomplete to enable coal to be brought into it.*

> Difficulty attending iron-mining in Missouri.

A considerable amount of capital has been invested during the last ten years in iron-mining in MICHIGAN, which raised, in 1860, 130,000 tons of ore, or more than any other State in the Union excepting Pennsylvania and New Jersey. The business in this State is quite in its infancy, but the quantity of ore already produced shows what may be anticipated on the shores of Lake Superior, where minerals are said to abound, not alone in the American States which touch it, but, more especially, in the British territory. At the present time the bulk of the ore of Michigan and Lake Superior is brought as ballast to the port of Cleveland, on Lake Erie, from whence it is carried by the Atlantic and Great Western Railway to Pittsburg to be smelted. This ore is pure, of good quality, and

> MICHIGAN.

> The minerals of Lake Superior.

> Their superiority.

---

* I hear that the "St. Louis and Iron Mountain Railway" is now open. If it is not already, it is intended to be, carried on to "Pilot Knob," a distance altogether of eighty-seven miles. It has twenty-seven stations including its termini, and one branch to Potosi, another mineral district. Although it is said to have been opened, I have not as yet seen its time bill in the American Railway Guides.

is largely worked at Pittsburg. It contains 90 per cent. of iron, and is quite free from sulphur. I may mention that from this iron the Pittsburg manufacturers have been able to make that description of ordnance which has been found to withstand the greatest pressure.

Quantity of ore raised in America.

The total quantity of ore mined in America in 1860 amounted to 908,000 tons, valued at about $2,000,000 (say £400,000)—not a very large quantity compared with our own.* It is claimed that "many of the large iron-foundries of the country either own or farm mineral lands, and raise their own ore," and that the quantities thus raised (said to exceed 2,000,000 tons) ought to be added to the quantity regularly mined. But there does not appear any very good foundation for this assumption, and from the fact that, in 1860 the export of iron from Great Britain to the United States was valued at upwards of £3,000,000 sterling ($15,000,000)—an immense excess over the production of the United States—I prefer to believe that the bulk of the iron used up in American manufactures is British iron; the more especially, as we are told on

Import of iron from Great Britain.

---

* The great increase in the Iron production of Great Britain is shown in the following table:—

Year.	No. of Furnaces.	Tons of Iron Produced.
1825	354	615,236
1840	490	1,395,900
1848	623	2,008,200
1857	823	3,659,447
1864	—	4,767,951

The iron ore mined in 1864 was estimated at 10,064,000 tons. In 1857 the declared value of the export of iron was £13,603,337.

authority that the iron-mining trade of Pennsylvania is unproductive, in consequence of the glut of foreign iron in the seaports.

But, however this may be, it is not the less a fact that the people of the United States, as manufacturers, are prepared to use, at the present time, almost any amount of iron with which they can be supplied. They produce very considerable quantities of bar and railroad-iron, of boiler-plates, and nail-plates, of sheet-iron, and wire-rods. They forge their own anchors, and their own axles for railway carriages, and they also make their own wheels for railway purposes, which, by their excellent process of chilling iron, endure longer than any others that are known. They have a large number of factories for iron-castings of every sort, including stoves, cooking-ranges, hot-air furnaces, and iron railings. These foundries are diffused throughout the Union; although the largest are reported to be in the State of New York. During my visit, I examined several locomotive-engine manufactories, and found their work, as a rule, quite equal to that in our country. Those factories, which are 19 in number, are principally in New Jersey, Massachusetts, and New Hampshire. In the aggregate they turn out between 450 and 500 engines a year, valued at about $10,000 or £2,500 each. Besides all this, the sewing-machine, and fire-arm manufactories of America, the tool-manufactories, spring-manufactories, nail-works, and blacksmiths' establishments, all consume large quantities of iron.

The production of pig-iron as returned by the census of 1860, was 884,474 tons, valued at $19,487,800, or

Extent to which the Americans are able to use iron.

Their iron manufactures.

Large quantities of iron required

for American uses. (say) £4,000,000. The production of bar and rolled iron amounted to 406,298 tons, of the value of $22,250,000. These large quantities shew the extent to which the United States is capable of using up the raw material. Iron is now required in America "in civil and military architecture, and all the engineering arts; in the construction of railroads and telegraphs, which have spread like a net all over the country; of steam-engines, and locomotives; of various descriptions of machinery, and in the manufacture of numerous articles of luxury and convenience in the household, the field, and the factory." The statistics shew the largely increasing extent to which it is being employed. The several branches of iron-manufacture are estimated to have yielded altogether, in 1860, a product of $205,879,510 (say) £41,000,000. And that this is not a very excessive estimate, appears to be shewn by the amount of the direct taxes paid on "iron and manufactures thereof," at rates varying from $1.50 to $3 per cent. ad valorem, and which produced to the revenue in that year, $3,694,178 :— "manufactures of iron" contributing fully one-half of the amount.

COPPER is found in considerable quantities in Michigan and on both sides of Lake Superior. There are, also, a number of valuable copper mines in New Mexico, some of which have been profitably worked for many years by Spaniards and Mexicans. The Hanover mines, the Santa Rita mines, the San José mines, and the Juarez copper-mines, are all within reach of civilization. Since the district has been taken possession of by the Americans, specimens of the ores, some of which I inspected personally, have been sent to New York for examination, and are favourably reported on.

LEAD is worked in Missouri, Wisconsin, and Iowa, to the extent of about $900,000 per annum. The mineral region of Iowa (which is mainly an agricultural State) is in the neighbourhood of Dubuque, on the borders of Illinois. It is said that these mines are sufficient, if they were properly worked, to afford profitable employment to 10,000 miners. Missouri, however, stands at the head, at present, of the lead-producing States. She produces upwards of 4,000 tons a year, and it is calculated that her lead mines extend over a much larger surface than I can well credit. The mines in this State have been worked for many years. None of them are exhausted, and many are worked now with greater success than at any previous period.

QUICKSILVER appears to have been found in some quantities in California; but, in consequence, it is said, of the ignorance of the parties engaged in working it, and also of the superior attractions of the gold-fields, the claims which have been located and worked, have not, in all cases, proved remunerative.[*] Mining engineers, however, report that the production is rich, and that the mines, if properly developed, would pay. Quicksilver is so largely used in gold-mining,

LEAD in Iowa and Missouri.

QUICKSILVER in California.

---

[*] In Mr. Chase's Report on "Foreign and Domestic Commerce," 1863, I find it stated that the exports of quicksilver from San Francisco amounted, in 1861, to 36,000, and, in 1862, to 33,790 flasks. It is stated that the "annual supplies of this metal have increased, but only to a small extent compared with gold."

that the production of it on the spot is of the utmost value.

The deficient supply of iron and other ores,

It will be evident from the foregoing, that the United States can be abundantly supplied from her own resources, with most of the more important minerals. It will be also evident, that she possesses the skill and the machinery required for all the more important branches of their manufacture. At the present time I do not believe that iron or copper are produced or manufactured in America at so low a rate as

attributable to the deficient supply of labour.

that at which they are produced and manufactured in Europe; but this is not owing to absence of quantity, or to inferiority in quality, or to want of skill, but solely to the difference in the price of labour. Where so much money can be made in other and far easier and more agreeable occupations, it is not to be expected that any large proportion of the population would employ themselves in mining iron or copper ores, except under the stimulus of high rates of wages. And hence not only the disproportion between the quantities produced in America and other countries, but the disproportion in the prices of the articles. As America increases in population, and as railways become more available for the transport of freight, the metallic wealth of the country will, no doubt, be more and more developed, and the cheaper probably will be the cost of her productions.

CHAPTER III.

COAL.

"COAL, next to gold, is the most important mining interest in the United States." So say the official reports. It may be doubted whether, properly worked, and properly employed, coal would not be even a more important interest to the United States than gold itself. But in the run after the other elements of material prosperity, including the far more tempting one of gold, it would seem that the production of coal has hitherto been comparatively neglected.

COAL.

Its production too much neglected.

I think I am justified in saying that, thirty years ago, there was little or no coal used in the United States, except in a certain class of manufactories. The anthracite coal of Pennsylvania was, at that time, the only coal offered for consumption ; but its cost was so high, first from the expense of mining it, and secondly from the cost of transit, that even in the city of Philadelphia it was only very sparingly used. This coal was first employed at a forge in the Wyoming Valley, close to the scene of its production, by a blacksmith, in 1775. In 1788 a nailer in the same place is known to have employed it in his factory, and " *twenty years after* (*i.e.* in 1808) he contrived a grate for burning it as fuel in his house." It was not until 1829 that any extensive mining operations were com-

Some account of the American coal-trade.

First use of anthracite.

menced at that most appropriately named village, " Carbondale," which about 1832 began to send regular supplies of coals to Philadelphia.

Its supply to the towns.

The construction of railroads, the increase of population, and the consequent increase in the price of other articles of fuel, soon, however, stimulated this supply of coal ; and about 1839 the general supply of coal to the population of towns began sensibly to increase. Even, however, at that period, coal was imported into the United States from England and Wales, as it is to this day, for the supply of the New York and other gas works. The fires of the engines on the railways and in the river steam-boats were fed then, as they are still to a very great extent, with firewood.

First use of bituminous coal.

The first cargo of bituminous coal which reached Philadelphia, from inland, appears to have been mined so recently as 1845. Even up to 1850, I imagine that the quantity of these coals sent to market was very limited.

Quantity of bituminous coal raised in 1860.

The total quantity of bituminous coal, mined in the United States in 1860, was 6,218,080 tons : about the entire annual supply of the city of London. These coals were developed in sixteen States, and the following table shows the produce in each * :—

---

* An official account has just been published of the discovery of coal in the immediate neighbourhood of Denver City, Colorado, by Professor Hodge, the geologist of the Union Pacific Railway, in course of construction through that district. Specimens which he has sent to New York have been submitted to Professor Torrey, who reports that " in calorific power this rocky mountain coal may be placed between dry wood and bituminous coal, and therefore it is a most valuable fuel. It may be used for smelting iron and other ores. For locomotives it could be employed to advantage."

| BITUMINOUS COAL PRODUCED 1860. ||
States.	Tons.
Pennsylvania	2,690,786
Ohio...............................	1,265,600
Illinois...........................	728,400
Virginia	473,360
Maryland........................	438,000
Kentucky	285,765
Tennessee.......................	165,300
Indiana	101,280
Iowa..............................	41,920
Alabama	10,200
Washington......................	5,374
Missouri	3,880
Rhode Island	3,800
Michigan	2,320
Georgia	1,900
Arkansas	200

To this has to be added the quantity of anthracite coal raised in Pennsylvania. It amounted to 8,115,842 tons, making a total of all the coals raised in the United States in 1860 of 14,333,992 tons.

It must be allowed that, for household purposes, there is not the same use for coal in America that there is in England. A very large proportion of the population live in a climate so warm, even in the winter months of the year, that fuel, except for culinary uses, is scarcely needed. The supply of wood, moreover, in many of the States, and especially in those north-western districts where fuel is more peculiarly needed, is so abundant and so cheap, that the want of a supply of coal is not yet much felt.* Moreover, it is to be re-

Substitutes
for coal in
America.

* I am sorry to say that I have recently met with an account of

collected that the water-power of America is employed with sufficient effect in working a very large proportion of its stationary machinery. The grist and flour mills, the lumber and saw mills, and very many other of those "establishments," as they are called, which are included in the returns of "manufactories," are exclusively driven by water-power. A great saving in fuel is hereby effected.

The coal pro-
duce of
America sin-
gularly small,

But with all this the mining of coal in the United States is carried on to a far less extent than might be expected in a country claiming so much manufacturing progress, and in which there has been, of recent years, such great development. I have been rather surprised at the small quantity of coal raised—only 14,000,000 of tons. The best authorities in England gave the Americans credit for raising at least one-third more—21,000,000 tons. Undoubtedly, the supply of 1860 exhibited a very considerable increase—an increase, it is said, of as much as 182 per cent.—upon the produce of 1850,

---

another, and to the world a much more precious article, used in the Western States as a substitute for coal. The following appears in a New York paper. Perhaps I should observe that it applies to *Indian* corn.

CORN AS FUEL.—"The last corn crop in Iowa was very large—far above the demand for home use ; so that the super-abundance of this 'staff of life' is being converted to the useful purposes of fuel. It is said that a bushel of corn will produce as much heat as a bushel of coal ; and those who have tried the experiment affirm that corn in the ear gives considerably more heat than the same bulk of wood. Ears of corn can be bought at ten cents. per bushel, and seventy bushels will measure a cord. Wood, including sawing, costs nine dollars and fifty cents per cord, which is two dollars and fifty cents more than the cost of a cord of corn, besides the fact that the corn produces more heat. There is a mill in Muscatine, Iowa, which has for some time been using this kind of fuel, and it is found to be superior to and cheaper than any other."

ten years preceding; but still 14,000,000 tons of coal, looking at the population and manufactures of America, appears singularly small.

In order to form a due estimate of this, we must look at the coal supply of other countries. No great reliance is to be placed on estimates of our own coal-mining earlier than 1854, when the "Mineral Statistics of Great Britain," collected by Mr. R. Hunt, were first published. The following, however, is believed to have been the produce in that and several succeeding years :— *in comparison with that of Great Britain.*

Coal Produce of Great Britain.	
Year.	Tons.
1854............................	64,661,401
1855............................	64,453,070
1856............................	66,645,450
1857............................	65,376,706
1858............................	66,109,603
1859............................	71,979,765

The total produce of the various countries of the world may be taken as follows :—

Coal Produce of the World.	
Countries.	Tons.
Great Britain .... (1859)	71,979,765
United States .... (1860)	14,333,922
Prussia, Saxony, and Hanover. „	12,000,000
Belgium .... „	8,900,000
France	7,900,000
Spain	3,000,000
Japan, China, Borneo, Australia	2,000,000
British Possessions, North America ...	1,500,000
Austrian Empire	1,162,900
Russian Empire	1,500,000

Coal produce of the world.

giving a grand total of about 121,000,000 tons as the coal produce of the world.

Now, when we consider that the coal-fields of North America are computed to be thirty-six times the size of those of Great Britain and Ireland, and that they are equivalent, as the official reports state, "to " nearly three-fourths of the coal-areas of the principal " coal-producing countries of the world," 14,000,000 tons appears an absurdly small produce. The Americans speak very much of the extent of their coal-fields. "The relative amplitude of the coal-seams of " our own and other countries may be made more " appreciable by taking the amount of workable coal " in Belgium as our unit : then that of the Britannic " isles becomes rather more than 5 : then that of all " Europe, $8\frac{3}{4}$; and that of North America, 111." But what is the use of this 111 if they do not work it?

No one who has visited America can doubt the coal-producing capabilities of the country. Surface indications of coal meet the eye almost everywhere. Its existence on the Illinois river was reported, as early as 1679, by a French Jesuit missionary, Father Hennepin, who visited the country to convert the Indians. In 1763, Colonel Coghlan, a British officer, sent on an expedition to the natives, noticed on the south side of the Wabash river, "a high bank in which are several fine coal-mines." In the map of

Captain Hutchins, published in London, fourteen years later (1777), coal-beds were marked as existing on the western side of the Ohio river, and bituminous coal-seams were noticed as existing in the great basin of the Ohio. The great coal-field, extending on both sides the James river from Petersburg to a distance of fifteen or twenty miles above Richmond (Virginia), was first discovered by a boy whilst digging for cray-fish. In fact, in travelling through the country it is scarcely possible, in a day's journey, not to come upon some spot where there are indications of coal. From the earliest period, almost' every observant traveller has noticed them. in Virginia.

The great Pittsburg (Pennsylvania) coal-seam, which has been the main stimulus to the manufacturing prosperity of that city, was first purchased as a tract of land from the Indians in 1736 by the family of PENN. The extent of the bituminous coal-field around Pittsburg has been estimated at 8,600,000 acres. The upper seam alone of this area is estimated to contain 53,516,000,000 tons of coal. The Pittsburg coal-seam.

About one-sixth of our coal in England is supposed to be blown away in generating steam-power. But this steam-power is said to be equivalent to the power of fifty-five millions of men. This is far more than doubling the power of the population of our country; and, having regard to the fact that the whole population of America is employed, it is singular that they should not employ their coal in larger proportions, especially considering how much greater profit they ought to be able to derive from the use of it.

The States in which the coal is worked in America number, at present, only sixteen. But there is every reason to believe that the mineral is to be found in several other States, where it may be worked with advantage. I can have no doubt that a profitable Profitable field for capital in American coal-mining.

field for capital exists in various parts of America in connexion with coal mining.

Improved machinery required. Improved machinery might be introduced with advantage, especially in below-ground mines, which are comparatively little understood. Prior to 1836, indeed, few if any of the mines in the United States were below water level, nor were steam-engines applied to them until nearly ten years later. A system of cheap and simple machinery by which coal could be raised to the pit's mouth and put into the truck ready for delivery by one process would insure fortune in America to its inventor.

CHAPTER IV.

PETROLEUM.

THE discovery of "Petroleum," or rock oil, in Penn- <inline type="margin-note">PETROLEUM.</inline>
sylvania, is of such recent date, that to many persons
some particulars respecting it may be novel. Rock oil is
said to have been known to the ancients, and it is stated <inline type="margin-note">Its general diffusion.</inline>
that in Sicily, especially, it was used at a very early
period instead of fish oil. There is said to be an oil-
spring, still flowing, in the island of Zante; and it is
also said that the Persians use petroleum obtained
from the shores of the Caspian. On the banks of
the Irrawaddy, in the Rangoon district, oils are derived
from the rocks, with which the Burmese largely supply
themselves; and our own colony of Trinidad has been
long known to contain pitch lakes, which, at various
times, efforts have been made to develop,—and once,
notably, by the late enterprising Earl of Dundonald.

It remained, however, for the Americans to show <inline type="margin-note">Used by the Indians medicinally.</inline>
the way to the profitable application of rock-oil. The
existence of the product in Pennsylvania was known
to the Indians, who employed it for medicinal purposes.
There are evidences in the "Oil Creek Valley," of
pits having been dug to obtain it. In 1791 an
article in the "Massachusetts Magazine," described

the oil-springs in that valley, and stated that a body of American soldiers, in marching that way, had stopped at the springs and collected the oil, which they had found good for rheumatism, and also as a gentle purgative.

Its first practical employment.

A Mr. Paterson, of Pennsylvania, appears to have been the first person who turned petroleum to a practical purpose. In the year 1845, he took a sample in a bottle to a cotton factory at Pittsburgh, and the manager of the spinning department having pronounced that it was as good a lubricator for machinery as the best sperm-oil (which cost nearly a dollar and a half a gallon), the proprietors of the factory determined to use it, and contracted with Mr. Paterson to supply them with two barrels per week, which was for a long time used in their establishment without the difference being discovered.

The Rock Oil Company.

Twelve or thirteen years ago some attention was directed, in different parts of the world, to the subject of rock-oil, and "Oil Creek" became the object of examination. A Company was formed in New York, under the style of the "Pennsylvanian Rock Oil Company," Professor Silliman being at its head. The operations of this Company were, however, limited to collecting the surface oil, until, in 1858, a Colonel

The first oil-well.

Drake visited the valley, and set about sinking a well. After one unsuccessful attempt, his drill struck an oil cavity at a depth of 71 feet; and, on the tools being withdrawn, oil rose to within five inches of the surface. This well yielded at once four hundred and afterwards a thousand gallons a day.

I take the following account of what followed, from

a very useful little work on the Petroleum wells, Flowing wells tapped.
written by Mr. J. H. A. Bone, and published by
Messrs. J. B. Lippincott and Co., of Philadelphia :—

"The excitement was very great. Every one who held
land in the vicinity of the 'Drake' well made preparations
for sinking wells on his own account, or leased to others
a right to sink them, on payment of a royalty. Some of the
wells were successful, but by far the larger proportion sunk
contained no oil at all, or in such small quantities as to be
unremunerative. Still several of the adventurers were making
fair wages ; when, suddenly, the whole business was revolu-
tionized by the discovery of—*flowing wells.*

" The first flowing well ever struck was on the McElhinny The Funk Well.
or Funk Farm, and was known as the 'Funk Well.' Funk
was a poor man when the well was sunk. It was struck
June, 1861, and commenced flowing, to the astonishment of
all the oil borers in the neighbourhood, at the rate of two
hundred and fifty barrels a day. Such a prodigal supply
upset all calculation, but it was confidently predicted that it
would soon cease. The oil, however, continued flowing, with
but little variation, for fifteen months, and then stopped, but
not before Funk became a very rich man. Long before the
Funk Well had given out, there were new sensations—the
Tarr Farm, yielding two thousand barrels daily, and the
Empire Well, yielding three thousand barrels daily."

The discovery of the Empire Well caused, in the The Empire Well.
first instance, a glut in the oil market. The supply
was already in advance of the demand ; which had, to
a large extent, to be created. The price of oil fell to
20 cents a barrel, then to 15, then to 10. Great diffi- Difficulties arising from the flow of oil.
culty arose from the want of barrels, which could not
be made fast enough. The owners of the wells tried
to stop the flow of oil, but the wells would not cease
to flow. "Oil Creek" became literally what its name
imported, for the oil was necessarily allowed to run to

waste into the stream, the surface of which was covered with oil for miles.

Want of means of transport.

Besides all this, there was great difficulty as to conveyance. No railway, at that time, had penetrated the locality. The oil-casks were obliged to be floated down the creek to the river Alleghany, and thence shipped by steamer or flat boats to Pittsburg. The supply of flat boats was far from meeting the requirements of the trade. In some cases, to mitigate the deficiency of barrels, the flat boats were made oil-tight, and the oil was conveyed in them in bulk. But this practice proved to be attended with much danger : the oil, in several cases, having taken fire, and burnt everything around.*

---

* The great danger arising from fire in this district is forcibly illustrated in *The Times'* Commissioner's account of the "United States" well at Pithole. He says :—

"The 'United States' pipe pours oil into its tanks with immense force, for about thirty seconds, and then has a thirty seconds' pause, during which it only pours forth gas of the most terribly inflammable nature. So bad is this vapour even for Pithole, that the tanks of this well are covered with huge wooden lids, each having a wooden spire-shaped chimney rising from its centre to take off the gas as high as possible. I have spent many hours in great powder magazines, yet, on the whole, I would rather pass a month in them than a day by the great wells in Pithole, which are simply as dangerous as any powder stores without one of their precautions. It is true that at every turn one meets the warning notices, 'No smoking,' 'Beware of smoking,' 'Smokers will be lynched,' &c. Yet, in spite of everything, smoking does go on on the sly, when teamsters and others can slip into the brushwood and furtively light their pipes, even though, like miners who do the same in fiery pits, they know that they do so at the risk of their own lives and those of all around them."

A melancholy story is told of the loss sustained by the widow of one of the original owners of the soil at Oil Creek in consequence of a fire :—

In the spring of 1862 another great flowing well The Sherman
Well. was found. A Mr. Sherman, the owner of the land, had commenced to sink it with very limited means. He was unable himself to procure an engine, and obliged to admit to shares in the enterprise two men who possessed one. Soon after, the funds of the united speculators were exhausted, and they offered a sixteenth share in the well for $100. No one would purchase it at the price; and it was ultimately disposed of for $60 and an old gun. A horse became necessary for the work, and another share was disposed of for that animal. At length, their means being exhausted, the enterprise was about to be abandoned, when, suddenly, oil was struck, and commenced flowing at the rate of 1,500 barrels a day. An immense fortune was realized.

The next flowing well discovered was in May 1863. The Farell
Well. This was on the land of a poor man named Farrell, engaged in hauling oil-casks. The Farrell well commenced flowing at the rate of 2,000 barrels daily. The column of oil from it spouted up 50 feet high, with a tremendous roar. At first the oil all ran to waste, but, as soon as its first flow was spent, a

"Close by this farm is that of the Widow M'Clintock. Her wretched, half-scratched land was valuable enough for oil. She got a very large sum for it, which, with the characteristic business habits of a poor old country widow, she would receive in nothing but greenbacks, which were accordingly paid to her in a bundle as big as a bolster. She hoarded them, still living amid the noise of derricks and the gas of wells in the shingle-hut in which she had for years been accustomed to dwell, till one night her petroleum lamps exploded, lighting her and her wooden house at once, and from the sudden fire neither she nor her greenbacks were saved; nothing, in fact, but some $80,000 which she had been persuaded to invest in United States' securities. All Petrolia is full of anecdotes like these."

stop-cock was applied, and the stream was reduced to controllable dimensions.

Enhanced value of land near the wells.

All this naturally caused great excitement. The land, not only in the immediate vicinity of the wells, but throughout the district, began to be bought up at sometimes fabulous prices. Those prices were the more swollen because a very small portion of land was required whereon to sink a well. Properties, therefore, were capable of being extensively sub-divided; and, if they were near a flowing well, each section had a considerable value.

Companies formed to sink wells.

Numberless Companies were formed to sink wells, and wells began to be sunk in every direction. Nothing was heard throughout the valley but the working of engines; and cities soon began to spring up in the vicinity of the wells, some of which have already become populous and important places.

Cities spring up in the forest.

But I am saved the trouble of describing these cities, by an admirably summarized account of them which appeared last October in one of the letters of the able correspondent sent by *The Times* to the Oil Region. He writes as follows:—

"I am within the mark when I say that within a circuit of thirty miles round this Oil City there are more so-called cities and towns now existing than there were villages, or even farms, four years ago. Take one instance.

Corry.

Corry, four years ago, was a poor farm where the thinly scratched soil of cold clay land yielded so little that the whole place, buildings and all, might easily have been purchased at $8 or $10 an acre. It was a mere halting-place for sportsmen *en route* to shoot deer in the now manufacturing regions of Petrolia. I was at Corry the other night. It is a fine rough city of about 10,000 inhabitants. The Atlantic and Great Western Railway, which has opened it up, has its great depôt there, and has made it the central exchange of petroleum. It has nearly twenty banks, two newspapers, and the city is now building a large opera-house. The quotations made in the oil-exchange at Corry, whether of oil, gold, or breadstuffs, influence Wall Street, and have infinitely greater weight on the trade of the country than anything done at Philadelphia, or indeed throughout all Pennsylvania. Yet all this has been done within four years, and the site of a city which now transacts business to the amount of £3,000,000 sterling annually, and where the land sells almost as dear as in Cheapside, could all have been bought four years ago for less than £5,000.

"But Corry is only one sample out of many. Its position as the arbiter and ruler of prices between the oil regions and New York and Europe gives it, of course, great importance, though in reality the city is not larger than many others of Petrolia, which are much younger. Rouseville, Plummer, Titusville, Franklin, are all the juniors of Corry by a couple of years, yet some of these are almost as important as Corry itself and nearly as large. The city from which I write (Oil City) can scarcely be counted as more than three years old, yet even after what I have seen of the sudden rise and sudden wealth of oildom, its extent, its squalid wealth, and dirty evidences of incessant activity, its population, and its resources, all make it a phenomenon even in this land of hurried wonders. Oil City claims to dispute pre-eminence even with Corry, though I am told that its rise, its wealth, and business energy are things of every-day occurrence compared with the new light which has risen further up the hills, the now universal beacon of attraction in the rush for speculation—Pithole City. Pithole City is only four months old. It is only four months since the first trees of the forest amid which it stands were felled; yet a city, both in size and population, it is admitted to be—a city which is now, in influence and excitement, second to none in all Petrolia."

It was to be expected, however, that all this success would be accompanied with some amount of disappointment. The multitude of wells sunk could not all be expected to produce oil; and many, of course, produced

[marginal notes] Oil City. Pithole City.

less than others. *The Times'* correspondent tells us of a whole district where the borings resulted in disappointment :—

Plummer.

"Plummer," he writes, "is one of the 'dreadful examples' of the uncertainty of oil wells. Its natural position, above Cherry Run, its geographical and geological formation, all pointed it out as likely to be one of the best-paying regions in Pennsylvania. Oil was found over all its brooks and under its stones; the air smelt strongly of gas, and brine was said to be abundant between its strata of sandstone. Plummer, therefore, at once became the Promised Land of Oildom. Its acres of uncleared forest sold at fabulous prices, a town was built, hundreds of derricks were erected, hundreds of wells put down in all directions, millions and millions of dollars spent lavishly, and the result was absolutely *nil.* Not a 'red cent,' as they say here, was obtained in return for all this enormous expenditure of capital and industry. Of all the wells sunk, not a single one found as much oil as would have greased its machinery. Here in the valley the derricks are as thick as trees, as new and unstained by oil as the day they were first erected. Here all the agencies and offices are closed, all the machinery idle, all the huge vats as clean and as empty as when the coopers finished them. Plummer is not much talked of here. Its mention, in fact, is avoided by general consent, as its very name is not unnaturally thought to exercise a depressing influence on would-be oil speculators."

The uncertainty attending this enterprise.

The uncertainty attending the production of the Oil Wells is, indeed, one of the great disadvantages of the enterprise. There is no certainty as to what an oil well will produce, or how long it will last. The freaks of the wells are very curious. In some, the flow of oil will cease altogether for many hours, and will then commence again with increased vigour. In very many the flow is intermittent. Some flow at half-hour intervals, some at three, and others at twelve. Some

Intermittent supplies of oil.

wells only flow at night, others only in the day. Some
only evolve gaseous vapours, others only pour forth
quantities of brine. One well will supply its owner
with a small quantity of oil, then with an abundant
yield of salt water ; then it will stop altogether, and
just when its proprietor has abandoned himself to
despair, it will, as if to encourage him, fill all his tanks
with oil, and then stop again.

" The Wild Cat Well is sulky for 40 minutes at a time ; it
then spits forth a few drops of the precious liquid, then sulks
for 20 minutes, foams and spurts again, and then gives forth
the petroleum freely for about ten minutes, and again goes
her round of sulks and sullenness as before. The Wild Cat
accompanies its yield of oil by a succession of sharp reports,
as though the supply were sent up from the earth from the
barrel of a small field-piece. The majority of the wells are
quiet in their work, but many of them hiss and spurt as they
discharge the oily fluid. Each well has its own peculiar
characteristics, which are perfectly known to the attendants,
and it is usual to apply to them terms such as would be used
in describing the qualities of a horse or a dog. A well is
' skittish,' or ' sulky ;' it is sometimes ' fond,' and often
' clever ;' it is ' liberal,' and sometimes ' elegant,' and not unfrequently ' real nice,'—a phrase which in America appears to
combine everything that is good and desirable in this planet."

An illus-
tration.

Another peculiarity of the wells is their susceptibility
to external temperature. The rise or fall of the mercury
in the thermometer or in the barometer does not indicate
more accurately the changes in the temperature or in
the condition of the coming weather than does the rate
of supply of petroleum from the oil wells. Twenty-
four hours before or after a cold night or a snowstorm,
the oil well is sensibly affected. The column of petroleum in the tube seems, in fact, to feel the atmospheric

Suscepti-
bility of oil-
wells to
external
temperature.

pressure in the same manner as the mercury. One well which in summer will yield 100 barrels, will only produce 20 in the winter; in another, the decrease is from 85 to 10 barrels; in a third, from 300 to an average of 50. The cause of a diminished supply of oil with a falling temperature is not satisfactorily explained. It was at one time thought, by some, that the tubes got clogged with paraffine during cold weather; that the deficiency, in fact, was not due to the well, but to the instrument by which the oil was raised to the surface. Measures were accordingly taken to prevent obstructions in the tubes, and in some cases new tubing was supplied, but the results remained the same; and it now appears to be generally recognised that the oil wells are extremely sensitive to meteorological influences.[*]

Limited existence of the wells.

Another uncertainty respecting the wells, is the period of their existence. Some last for years, others only for months, and some flow only for a few weeks. The Funk well, referred to a few pages back, as the first flowing well, is now dry and silent. The Empire well, for two years, yielded nearly 3,000 barrels of oil daily; its flow then stopped, but, on the application of a pump, it yielded about a hundred barrels daily. Then it stopped for some time, but by the gentle persuasion of an air-pump (or "blower") it is now sending up about the same quantity. The fact seems to be, that

---

[*] *The Times'* correspondent observes that, "the generally received idea of the temperature of the earth increasing in certain ratio with the depth is not supported by the experience of Petrolia, inasmuch as the oil brought up from the greatest depths has a lower temperature than that obtained nearer to the surface."

the oil lies deposited in holes, some of which are large, and some small; and it depends upon the size of the hole, and the quantity of oil deposited in it whether the well is a "flowing" or a "pumping" well, and whether it produces oil for a month or for a year.

But there is no probability of any deficiency in the supply of oil. Far richer deposits than those first discovered at Oil Creek, have since been reached not only in different parts of the same district, but in various other parts of the United States. At present, "Pithole" is the principal scene of enterprize, the "Cherry Run oil-field," which, during 1864, had an amazing reputation, having, according to the prevailing impression, almost been "pumped out." In a short time, no doubt, there will be other fields discovered, equally productive with the "Oil Creek," "Cherry Run," and "Pithole" districts. Oil has recently been struck in other parts of Pennsylvania; indeed, all the western portion of the State is conjectured to have more or less oil beneath its surface. The Virginians have got a district which they call "the great oil belt," and in which some small flowing wells were struck antecedently to the outbreak of the Civil War. In Ohio there are several oil-fields which are coming into notice, and in Kentucky there are four localities which produce oil. Indications of oil are also reported in different parts of the States of New York, Illinois, Iowa, Missouri, and Michigan; also in Oregon, Utah, and California. In Canada it has been produced for 3 or 4 years. Indeed, now that Petroleum has acquired a commercial value, there can be no doubt that it will be eagerly sought for and abundantly found.

Deposits of oil in other districts

of Pennsylvania,

Virginia,

Ohio,

Kentucky,

and other States.

I am not aware that there are any statistics of this production; in fact, so much oil has been allowed to flow to waste, and has been lost by fire and water, and in the course of transit, that it would be very difficult to estimate the production of the wells. Hereafter, as the trade becomes more steady and better conducted, we may hope that this deficiency may be supplied. In the meantime we must content ourselves with the official accounts of the EXPORTS OF OIL from the United States. In 1861 the exports were small, and no account appears to have been kept of them. In the three following years they amounted to the following quantities :—

Statistics of
the supply.

The exports
of petroleum

EXPORT OF PETROLEUM FROM THE UNITED STATES.	
Year 1862......................	10,887,701 Galls.
„ 1863......................	28,250,721 „
„ 1864......................	31,792,972 „
„ 1865......	42,273,508 „

in very small
proportion to
its yield.
But this is a very small proportion to the yield of the district. It was estimated last year that the entire oil district of Pennsylvania yielded from 80,000 to 90,000 barrels per week; equal, at the lower figure, to, say, 4,000,000 barrels per annum. The quantity forwarded from the stations of the Atlantic and Great Western Railway was 533,000 barrels in 1863, and 675,028 barrels in 1864.

Prices of
petroleum,
The average prices show a heavy rise, despite the largely increased production.

PRICES OF PETROLEUM IN NEW YORK (PER GALLON).		
Description.	1860.	1864.
Crude	28 Cents.	41 Cents.
Refined	28 ,,	39 ,,
Ditto, in bond.........	44 ,,	65 ,,
Ditto, free	51 ,,	74 ,,

1860-1864.

The present duty levied on this article is $1 a Duty.
barrel. The great difficulty which has hitherto at- Difficulties
tended the oil trade has been transport. It was easy of transport.
enough to produce oil, but far more difficult to convey
it to the consumer. The roads in the oil region are
execrable; in fact, there are no roads. Everything
has to be hauled through an immense slough. Very
excessive charges for the carriage of the oil have
thereby been entailed. The Atlantic and Great Western
Railway will, I hope, by the time this book appears,
have provided a remedy for this dreadful drawback.
Up to a recent period the line only reached Corry;
but it has now been carried on to Oil City and Pithole,
and, in fact, may be said to reach all the wells. The
railway will also be able, immediately, to provide Railway con-
sufficiently for the requirements of the trade. Hitherto, veyance now
in consequence of a deficient supply of rolling stock, provided.
it has been unable to carry a very large quantity of
the oil with which it has been supplied, and the
consequence has been, that Oil City and other places
have been choked with oil, for which no means
of transport whatever could be found. As the railway
receives no less than 4d. per ton per mile for all the
oil it carries, it has naturally exerted itself to take all

it could; but it has been hitherto impossible to keep down the accumulation. Additional rolling stock is now being most rapidly supplied to the line, and it is hoped that, at no distant date, Oil City may be emptied. In the mean time, it is satisfactory to know that the demand for the article is increasing in every part of the world, and especially in the United States itself.

The shares in petroleum companies, The general use of petroleum in the United States has, perhaps, been fostered by the extent to which the population have embarked in the enterprize of raising oil. At Pittsburg alone there are between thirty-five and forty Oil-Well Companies, some of which have been very successful, and some otherwise. But the extent to which the public have embarked in these Companies is shown by the fact that the favourite shares are not, how divided. as they would be with us, £25, £20, or even £10 shares, but shares *at four shillings and two shillings each !* This would appear very ridiculous in England, which, comparatively, consists of a nation of Capitalists; but it is not at all ridiculous in America, where the capital is so much more distributed, and where there may be said to be hundreds of thousands of provident working men, who prefer the profits of petroleum to the small rates of interest afforded by savings banks.

Speculation in petroleum. It may be urged that these small shares induce speculation. It is questionable whether they do so more injuriously than where the shares of a Company are of higher value. But, be that as it may, it is urged, in America, that the worst part of the speculative mania in petroleum has died out, and that the ventures are now taken out of the hands of mere speculators into

those of substantial Companies, who conduct their risks
on superior systems, and obtain a fair amount of
certain profit. It is claimed, in fact, that petroleum
wells stand, at the present time, on much the same
footing with coal, iron, and other mineral enterprises.

Except the invention of steam, I suppose, that in the
history of commercial and industrial enterprise, there
are few parallels to be found to the history of the
discovery of Petroleum and the development of its
varied uses. Half-a-dozen years covers the whole of
this history. Previous to that period the mineral had
been unnoticed; now, it is an article of trade and of
necessity. Petroleum became known to mankind, as
other supplies have become known, just at the moment
it was needed: at the moment when fish and animal
oils were annually decreasing; whilst the difficulty of
supplying illuminating and lubricating agents was
annually becoming greater. The business is certain to
assume very far larger proportions than at present.
It is interwoven with the necessities of human
existence, and, accordingly, must increase. We want
increasing quantities of oil for the varied purposes of
light in our houses, application to many of our leading
manufactures, and lubrication of machinery. No oil is
so cheap or so efficient for our purposes as that which
springs from natural sources. Every day presents it to
us as an element of increased usefulness; and, as there
is no fear of want of demand, so, happily, there is no
doubt of an abundant supply.

This great natural development made its appearance
at a period when it was of peculiar value to the United
States. At a moment of civil war, when the balance

The benefits and blessings of this discovery,

especially to the United States.

of trade was against the nation, when gold was necessarily going out, and when there was a heavy drain upon the natural resources of the country, petroleum sprung up, from lands previously considered valueless, in quantities sufficient to make a sensible diversion in the national commerce. Nor was that the only benefit it offered. Whilst it assisted the external commerce, it also stimulated the internal industry of the United States. It gave to the railway interest of the country a prospect of large additional profits; it offered employment to capital with every prospect of abundant returns; and it afforded a more than ordinary reward for labour. It is difficult to find a parallel to such a blessing bestowed upon a nation in the hour of her direst necessity.

SECTION V.

COMMERCE.

SECTION V.–COMMERCE.

CHAPTER I.

SHIPPING.

THE people of the United States derive a great advantage from the extent and nature of their sea-board. Their whole Atlantic Coast line from Maine to Florida presents an infinite variety of bays, inlets, river entrances, and harbours. Many of them are capable of accommodating the largest class of vessels. In the whole world there are comparatively few ports which a ship having so great a draught of water as the *Great Eastern* is able to enter, or in which she can lie securely. But she can not only enter the Bay of New York, but can lie close up to the very shore of the city. On the South, the Americans have a number of fine harbours in the Gulf of Mexico; and their Pacific Coast line, though not so well indented as that of the Atlantic, affords, in addition to the great bay of San Francisco, several excellent resorts for shipping,—especially in the Columbia river in Oregon, and in Puget's Sound. Nor can it be said that even on their northern boundary the people of

The Seaboard of the Atlantic.

The Gulf and the Pacific.

P

The Lake
Navigation.
the United States are without a coast line; for the
great lakes which form that boundary afford an extent
of navigation almost equal to that of an ocean, and
are navigated by sailing craft and steamers to an
extent but little inferior to that of the sea-board
itself.

The Naviga-
ble Rivers of
America.
In addition to their coast lines, lakes, and shores,
the country has the great advantage of being per-
meated by a number of most important navigable
rivers. The State of Maine is penetrated by the
Kennebec; Vermont, New Hampshire, Massachusetts,
The Atlantic
Rivers.
and Connecticut by the Connecticut river; New York
by the Hudson and its branches; Pennsylvania by the
Delaware and Schulkyl; Maryland by the Susque-
hana; all flowing from West to East. All the Southern
States, except Florida, which, with a double coast line,
scarcely requires inland navigation, have rivers which
are navigable for larger or smaller craft. Nor is this
great advantage confined to the Northern or Southern
The Missis-
sippi,
States. The great river Mississippi, which takes its
rise in the north of Minnesota, permeates the very
centre of the Continent of America, and by means of
a canal, from the Mississippi to Chicago (which is
about to be enlarged so as to permit the passage of
large shipping), absolutely carries the produce of the
northern lakes directly to the Gulf of Mexico. The
Mississippi, in its course to the ocean, of itself affords
navigation to no less than ten great States,—Minne-
and its
branches.
sota, Wisconsin, Iowa, Illinois, Missouri, Kentucky,
Arkansas, Tennessee, Mississippi, and Louisiana. Its
branches, the Missouri river, the Platte, the Ohio, the
Wabash, the Arkansas river, the Red River, and others

too numerous to particularize, afford opportunities for
navigation even into the most distant regions and
territories of the United States; the most important
of these streams taking their rise in the Rocky mountains, and thus carrying navigation to the very verge
of the rivers which debouch in the Pacific. The
inland navigation of America is indeed quite as important as its coast line : for by it the very heart of the
Continent is touched and vast fields of produce are
brought into direct communication with the sea-board
and the ports of export.

It is something for the people of the United States
to boast of that the whole of these waters are navigated by vessels of their own construction. So far as
their inland navigation is concerned they owe this,
exclusively, to their own industry and enterprize.
With respect, however, to the foreign trade from their
Atlantic sea-ports, they owe still more to political
circumstances. The mercantile marine of the United
States was admittedly built up by the great European
wars at the close of the last and the commencement
of the present century. The United States had no
sooner established their independence, than they found
themselves, as a neutral nation, in a position to conduct, with peculiar advantage, the carrying trade of
the European nations which, in consequence of war,
were ravaging each other's shipping. The condition
of Europe was such that American shipping soon
became, of necessity, the preferable medium through
which to conduct the larger share of the commerce
of the world. The Americans alone could carry, with
safety, the valuable commodities of the nations which

All the American waters navigated by their own Shipping.

The Mercantile Marine of America.

were at war; and having every advantage for ship-building and navigation, they commenced a career which soon became extraordinarily extended and unusually successful.

Its rapid growth and fluctuations

The rapid growth of American shipping and American commerce will be shown by the following account of their tonnage engaged in foreign trade :—

AMERICAN TONNAGE ENGAGED IN FOREIGN TRADE.			
Year.	Tonnage.	Year.	Tonnage.
1789	127,329	1807	1,116,241
1792	414,679	1808	538,749
1795	580,277	1809	605,479
1799	624,839	1810	908,713
1801	849,302	1811	948,247
1802	798,805	1812	668,317
1803	787,424	1813	237,501
1804	821,962	1814	59,786
1805	922,298	1816	877,462

attributable to political occurrences in Europe.

This table illustrates several remarkable facts. It will be observed, in the first place, with what amazing rapidity the American shipping grew immediately after the breaking out of the European war. In twelve years the tonnage had increased from 127,000 to nearly 850,000. Then it will be noticed how instantly the trade sunk on the declaration of the Peace of Amiens in 1802, and how immediately it rose again on the recommencement of the war. After the Treaty of Tilsit, the combination of the great Continental Powers against the trade of Great Britain, exercised a depressing effect on commerce, and we accordingly find the American tonnage in use in foreign trade sink one-half in 1808, and only restore itself by gradual degrees up to 1811. In the following year the Americans themselves put an end to their own navigation and commerce by entering upon war with Great Britain. Our navy swept their vessels from the seas, and two years after the outbreak of this war the Americans had only 59,700 tons of shipping engaged in foreign trade, instead of the 1,100,000 tons employed seven years previously.

Such facts ought to teach both nations how desirable it is for their own interests to keep the peace. If America had not gone to war with Great Britain in 1812 it is probable that she would have retained to this day her great ascendancy in general commerce. For a number of years she had occupied the seas—she had established extensive and profitable lines of trade between countries possessing no commercial marine of their own; as well as with all those commercial states which form the natural and permanent markets for produce. Such advantages would have secured to the United States the bulk of the carrying trade of almost every nation, which did not exclude her by positive legislation; and the increased European consumption of the products of tropical countries would have given her a great advantage. But America lost the great opportunity by inviting war; and she has never recovered it. In 1845 her tonnage engaged in foreign commerce was not greater than in 1807; and although it has since made considerable progress, the carrying trade of the United States cannot be said to be anything like what it might have been; indeed the tonnage of the United

Injury inflicted on the American carrying trade by the War of 1812.

States is employed in the export of American produce rather than in the carrying traffic of the world.

From the form in which the national accounts are published, it is not very easy to arrive at a precise estimate of the number of vessels or the tonnage of the United States engaged at the present time in foreign trade. Their system is to "register" all vessels engaged in foreign commerce, and to "enrol" and "license" vessels engaged in inland navigation and the coasting trade. But a number of vessels appear to be both "registered" and "enrolled," and, consequently, the double entries are numerous. In 1860,

the tonnage was classified as follows :—

Registered Sail Tonnage	2,448,941
„ Steam Tonnage	97,296
Enrolled Sail Tonnage	2,036,990
„ Steam Tonnage	770,641
Total Tonnage	5,353,868

But this total includes not only what we should consider "tonnage," but every class of vessel, even down to fishing smacks and canal boats. The

"registered" tonnage also includes, admittedly, all vessels engaged in the coasting trade, in the whale fishery, and the steamers and ferry boats on the lakes engaged in the trade with Canada.* Moreover, I am by no means clear as to the way in which the Americans measure their tonnage. Until very

---

* " A deduction of at least 600,000 tons from American tonnage should be made for the duplicated tonnage of steam ferryboats, at Buffalo chiefly, in a less degree at Ogdensburg and Cape Vincent." —*Mr. Chase's Report on Foreign and Domestic Commerce,* page 7.

recently, they divided each ton into "95ths," a calculation which it is difficult to understand or follow, and respecting which I have no satisfactory explanation. Within the last year a new system of admeasurement has been introduced; and, from the "Report of the Secretary of the Treasury," just published, it appears that the tonnage which, under "the *old* admeasurement," was computed at one figure, is estimated, "under the *new* admeasurement," at another and a smaller total. Each ton is now divided into "100ths," which, henceforth, no doubt, will greatly facilitate calculations. It will be obvious from all this, that to arrive at a conclusion as to the real amount of the sea-going tonnage of the United States, we must make a large deduction from the total above given.*

Large deductions to be made from this Total.

As to the *progressive* increase of the mercantile shipping of the nation, there can, however, be no doubt. It is exhibited by the following figures, which show the tonnage of the "registered" sailing ships,

Progressive Increase of American Shipping.

* In the Monthly Report of the department of Agriculture, issued from the Government press at Washington in December, 1865, the attention of Congress is especially directed to "the important subject of weights and measures." It is stated that "the different States prescribe their own standards, and change them often," and that "it is most desirable to avoid what the country is fast running into, a change in the weights and measures wherever the boundaries of each State are passed, and as often as the general Assembly of each is convened. The rapid and extensive intercommunication between the States by Railway transportation makes an unchanging and uniform system of weights and measures the more important. It is to be hoped that Congress will not look over the importance of early legislation on this subject."

and of the "enrolled and licensed" steamers for some years :—

Year.	Registered Sail Tonnage.	Enrolled and Licensed Steam Tonnage.
1845	1,088,680	319,527
1846	1,123,999	341,606
1847	1,235,682	399,210
1848	1,344,819	411,823
1849	1,418,072	451,525
1850	1,540,769	481,005
1851	1,663,917	521,217
1852	1,819,744	563,536
1853	2,013,154	574,098
1854	2,238,783	581,571
1855	2,440,091	655,240
1856*	2,401,687	583,362
1857	2,377,094	618,911
1858	2,499,742	651,363
1859	2,414,654	676,005
1860	2,448,941	770,641
1861	2,540,020	774,596

Foreign Trade.

The "Registered Sail Tonnage" of the United States, as given in the first of the foregoing columns, I apprehend to show pretty fairly the annual increase in the tonnage of the country engaged in *foreign* trade. The "Enrolled and Licensed Steam Tonnage," I take to indicate the progress made by the Americans in the navigation of their *inland* waters. To form an estimate of their coasting trade and canal navigation,

Inland Navigation.

* In 1856, all vessels sold to foreigners, lost or condemned, in *previous* years, were struck out of the Register, which reduced the aggregate tonnage in that and the following year by upwards of 680,000 tons.

we must take the " Enrolled and Licensed Sail Ton- Coasting
Trade.
nage," which increased from 1,002,000 tons in 1845
to 2,036,000 tons in 1860. The "total tonnage" of
the United States, in 1845, was returned at 2,417,000 ;
and, in 1860, at 5,145,038 tons ; and although neither
of these figures may represent " tonnage " in our sense
of the word, there can be no doubt that in the interval
between 1845 and 1860 the real tonnage of America,
whether for foreign, coasting, or inland trade, was more
than doubled.

It is probable that the larger proportion of American Character of
the American
Shipping.
vessels are what we denominate " small craft." But,
however this may be, there can be no doubt that
the Americans have gradually enlarged the size of
their sea-going ships, and have constructed them
from finer models. Their sailing vessels also are of
highly increased sailing power. No people build
their ships on better principles. Their skill in
cutting sails, and in applying them to every description of craft, has always struck me as peculiarly
remarkable.

The superior capacity and very fine character of the " Liners " and
" Clipper
Ships."
American merchant ships will be appreciated by all
who remember the beautiful class of sailing vessels
which were formerly on the New York and Liverpool
stations, as what were called " Liners." Those vessels
were the very best vessels of their class, and they no
doubt acquired wide celebrity for American shipping.
They are now superseded by English and other steam
packets ; but the fame of these celebrated vessels has
enabled the Americans not only to possess themselves
of the largest proportion of the emigration trade, but

also to lay on lines of packets between Havre, Marseilles, Hamburg, Rio de Janeiro, Bahia, Panama, the West Indies, and various points both of the Atlantic and Pacific Oceans. They are also about to establish a regular communication with the ports of the Mediterranean, under arrangements with the. Italian Government.

preferred to Steam Vessels for Ocean Navigation.

Some of these lines of communication are conducted by steamers; but generally, except for passenger conveyance, the Americans do not incline to steam in ocean navigation. They have comparatively few ocean steamers amongst their shipping. A few years ago, out of 110 steamers used in the trade of Great Britain with America, only two were American. On the other hand, out of 1,200 sailing vessels in the trade, 960 were American. In 1860, the whole "Registered Steam Tonnage" of the United States (*i.e.* the steam tonnage engaged in foreign trade) only amounted to 97,296 tons. In 1865, on the old admeasurement, it only amounted to 69,500 tons, and on the new admeasurement to 28,400 tons.

Probability of a change in the character of the American Mercantile Fleet.

Recent events, however, may tend considerably to modify the proportion of sailing vessels and steamers in America. During the war, as is well known, the marine of the Republic has severely suffered; so much so that the returns for 1864 show upwards of *a million* less registered sailing tonnage belonging to the United States, than she possessed in 1860. This decrease is only in a small degree owing to captures. It most largely arises from the sales and transfers which American shipowners made of their property during the war, in order to avoid seizure. And not only was a proportion of their sea-going fleet transferred, but shipbuilding, for maritime purposes, excepting of small craft, was almost entirely suspended. At first sight it may appear that this must entail a great disadvantage on the United States, but I am by no means sure that such will be the result. Having got rid of her old stock of sailing ships, she will be likely to apply herself to the construction and acquisition of classes of vessels equal to those of other nations, and I should not be surprised in a few years to find the Americans chiefly employing large steamships in their ocean navigation.

At the recent Detroit Commercial Convention, it was stated by Mr. H. A. Hill, a delegate from Boston, that " at the present time there are twelve Steam Ship " Companies employed in the transit between Europe " and the United States, none of which are American." At the outbreak of the American war, in 1861, there were only two or three American steamers in the European trade. Mr. Hill says that at New York the value of steam shipping is not appreciated as it ought to be. The Boston Board of Trade reports very much to the same effect. They regret the failure of several attempts which have been made to employ steam-vessels in Ocean navigation. They state that, in 1863, an effort was made at Boston to establish a line of American steamers between Boston and Liverpool, and a charter was obtained from the Massachusetts legislature incorporating the company under the designation of the "American Steam Ship Company." The project, however, fell through, from insufficiency of capital, the difficulties of the period, and, above all, from the want of steamers.

Views of the American Merchants respecting Steam Communication.

Report of the Boston Board of Trade, 1865.

Difficulty of obtaining Steamers.

" It was proposed either to purchase or to charter two or more steamers for the principal route; and a Committee of Directors spent much time and thought upon the subject. Correspondence with brokers in England was entered into, with reference to the capacity, adaptation, and value (either for purchase or charter) of vessels in Liverpool and on the Clyde. Careful inquiry was also made on our own coast, with a similar purpose. But the directors failed to find, in this country, steamers suitable to the wants of the service; and, owing to the very high rates of charter at which steamships were held in Europe, there was no opportunity to negociate to advantage there. They prudently declined, therefore, to hazard the ultimate success of the line, by placing upon the route ships which, by any deficiency of speed, size, or earnings, might disappoint the stockholders and the public.

" The difficulties in the way of *building* ships have been found no less perplexing than those which have thus far prevented purchase or charter. With the prices of labour and material much inflated, and with a pressure upon shipbuilders and machinists caused by the demand for governmental and other purposes, it has not been judged advisable to enter into contracts for construction." *

Advantages possessed by Great Britain in Steam Ship construction.

In this question of construction will, probably, be found one main difficulty attending the working of American steam intercourse with Europe. They cannot construct steamships in the United States to the same advantage that we can in Great Britain. Not only are our rates of wages less, but our steam ship-building yards on the Clyde, the Tyne, and the Mersey are situated close to the raw materials, the iron and the coal, required for the purposes of steamship construction. This circumstance must always give Great Britain an advantage over the United States in respect to navigation conducted by steamers. The

---

* Eleventh Annual Report of the Boston Board of Trade. P. 35.

first cost of our steamships always will be less : and the capital invested in them being less, of course they can be worked to advantage at lower rates. In addition to this, we derive, at present, a considerable advantage from the superior quality of the steam-coal with which our ships can be supplied.

The Boston Board of Trade concludes its report upon this subject by intimating its opinion that *" our " foreign trade is not keeping pace with our advance " in other respects."* This opinion appears very generally to prevail in the United States, and if it is so, it is very desirable calmly to investigate the cause. Perhaps it may be found that some other nations have obtained an advantage over America, not from superior enterprise or skill, but from the adoption of different principles in foreign trading. Of late years, there has certainly been, in Europe, great expansion of view, and with that expansion greatly increased liberality in the mode of conducting commercial transactions. It may be doubted if the Americans have, in these respects, altogether advanced in proportion with the other great commercial nations of the world. It would be well that they should see to it. An American writer has well said, that nothing can injure American shipping but restrictions and limitations on American trade. And if the question is candidly examined by the light of their own experience, I think the people of the United States will see that this position is established.

The Foreign Trade of America not sufficiently progressive.

CHAPTER II.

IMPORTS AND EXPORTS.

Extent of the Commerce of America.

WE have seen in the last chapter how the Americans built up and then sacrificed their carrying trade. We have now to see how they have built up their commerce, which at present is only second to our own. The aggregate value of the goods imported and exported from the United States, in 1860, approached $763,000,000, or (say) £152,600,000 sterling. This was an inferior trade to that of Great Britain, which, in the same year, conducted an import and export business, amounting to £375,000,000 sterling—a trade which has since been so much increased as to exceed £500,000,000 sterling. But, except France, there is no other country which approaches the United States in the value of its trade. A very remarkable circumstance is this, having regard to the ages of the nations. The trade of Europe has been the growth of centuries : that of the United States is the growth of less than eighty years, and it already surpasses the trade of every nation but our own.

Rapidity of its growth.

Let us see, in the first place, how this trade has grown up. The following table gives the value of the imports and exports of the United States from 1844 to 1860 :—

IMPORTS AND EXPORTS OF THE UNITED STATES.		
Year.	Imports.	Exports.
1844	$108,435,035	$111,200,046
1845	117,254,564	114,646,606
1846	121,691,797	113,488,516
1847	146,545,638	158,648,622
1848	154,998,928	154,032,131
1849	147,851,439	145,755,820
1850	178,138,318	151,898,720
1851	216,224,932	218,388,011
1852	212,945,442	209,658,366
1853	167,978,647	230,976,157
1854	304,562,381	278,241,064
1855	261,468,520	275,156,846
1856	314,639,942	326,964,908
1857	360,890,141	362,960,682
1858	282,613,150	324,644,421
1859	338,765,130	356,789,462
1860	362,163,941	400,122,296*

* It is quite useless to attempt to give the statistics of the imports and exports of the United States between 1860 and 1866. In consequence of the excessive fluctuations in the values of money during that interval, the declared and estimated values of articles imported and exported were so singularly affected, that no reliable conclusions can be drawn from them. Some attempts have been made to reduce the estimated values of imports and exports to "gold value," so as to arrive at something like a view of the excesses and deficiencies in various branches of commercial business. I am afraid, however, that, from the same cause (the fluctuations in the value of gold at different periods), these calculations can only be approximative. I have, therefore, thought it better, though not without much consideration and considerable regret, to set aside the commercial statistics during the years of the civil war as only calculated to occasion misconception.

Character of
the Trade,
as shown by
these Statis-
tics.
There are two points in this table which must, I think, strike every one who glances at it.

First, That the trade of the United States has been *regularly* and *steadily* progressive.

Second, That the nation has uniformly paid its way: the exports, in almost every year, having exceeded the imports, and the general balance being in favour of America.

It is scarcely necessary to enlarge on these prominent features. The tables, in fact, tell their own tale. They speak of the same progressive prosperity which Great Britain boasts of in years of peace. It will be observed
Expansion of
Trade which
followed the
Gold dis-
coveries.
that the most remarkable rise in *exports* occurred in America in 1851, when that trade increased from $151,000,000 to $218,000,000, or upwards of one-fourth. This is accounted for by the discovery of gold in California, which, in 1851, became, for the first time, an article of considerable export, in the form of bullion and specie. It is observable that the *import* trade of the United States did not altogether rise in correspondence with that export. In 1853, indeed, the imports were less than they had been in either of the three years previous; but after that, the balance of trade being in favour of the nation, and the Californian gold contributing vastly to her wealth, the imports were largely increased. 1854 showed a total of $304,000,000 of imports, or upwards of £60,000,000 sterling, largely paid for in specie, the export of which, in the following year, amounted to nearly $54,000,000, or upwards of £10,000,000 sterling. These figures show the extent to which the discovery of Gold in California affected the development of the trade of the United States.

From 1854 to 1860 the average annual exportation of specie and bullion from America was maintained. It was nearly $54,000,000 in 1854, and it approached $57,000,000 in 1860. In 1857, when the imports rose to their largest amount, the export of native gold was as much as $60,000,000; and it is observable that in 1861, the year of the commencement of the war, the bullion sent in for coinage to the mints of the United States amounted to $83,693,000. But that which is to be regarded as far more satisfactory is, that during these years almost every item of native produce exported had risen in nearly the same proportion with the gold.

Export of Gold from America.

PRODUCTS OF THE UNITED STATES EXPORTED IN SEVERAL YEARS.				
Products of	1847.	1850.	1855.	1860.
	$	$	$	$
The Sea	3,468,033	2,824,818	3,516,894	4,156,480
The Forest	5,996,073	7,442,503	12,603,837	13,738,559
Agriculture...........	68,450,383	26,547,158	42,567,476	48,451,894*
Tobacco................	7,242,086	9,951,023	14,712,468	15,906,547
Cotton.................	53,415,848	112,315,317	88,143,844	191,806,555
Manufactures	10,476,345	20,136,967	28,833,299	39,803,080
Raw Produce	1,526,076	1,437,680	2,373,317	2,279,308
Specie and Bullion...	62,620	18,069,580	53,957,418	56,946,851

Exports of Native productions.

Thus we see the exports of the United States increasing not in gold alone, but in every different description of production. In considering the subject of American resources, nothing could give a more satisfactory view of them than this table. It shows

Progress of American Exports.

---

* The export of grain, as already explained, depends materially, not upon the produce of the country, but upon the state of the crops in other regions of the globe. It amounted to $77,000,000 in 1856. In 1860, the exports of the products of agriculture were low; but in 1861, they rose to $101,655,000, and in 1862 to no less than $124,561,000, or nearly £25,000,000 sterling.

that there is no industrial pursuit in which the people of the United States do not steadily progress, and scarcely any demand for any class of produce which they are not able to supply.

Variety of Articles of Export.

The great variety of the native productions exported, gives assurance of the impossibility of failure in the resources of the nation. If the Americans were limited to a few products, it might be argued that such products might not be in demand, or that their supply might fail, or that other countries might compete successfully with America by producing them in greater abundance and at lower rates. But here we have the products—

Of the SEA—consisting of oil, whalebone, spermaceti, and dried, smoked, and pickled fish.

Of the FOREST—consisting of every description of timber, shingles, staves, lumber, naval stores, and furs.

Of AGRICULTURE—consisting not only of every description of corn and vegetable food, but of the products of animals : beef, pork, tallow, hides, bacon, cheese, butter, wool, lard, hams ; horned cattle, horses, and other animals.

Of the GREAT STAPLES of the Southern States, cotton, tobacco, rice, and sugar.

Of MANUFACTURES—in very great variety.

Of RAW PRODUCE—in increasing quantities; and

Of SPECIE and BULLION—to an extent which has never yet been exceeded.

Security afforded by this variety,

Even then, supposing that the supply or the demand were to fail in respect to any one of these articles of produce, it may be anticipated that any loss in regard to that one item of exportation would be amply compen-

sated for by excess of exportation in some other item.
This occurs with all nations that support an extensive
trade. For example, England, during the civil war in
America, lost a very large proportion of her cotton
trade. For several years she could neither import the
raw material, nor could she export the manufactured
article. Cotton was so important an element of her
trade that, in 1860, "cotton goods" of British and
Irish production constituted upwards of *one-third* of
the whole exportation of the United Kingdom. As we
could not manufacture these goods we could not maintain this export. Yet what occurred? Woollen and
linen goods largely supplied the place of cottons, and
our export trade, so far from being injuriously affected,
rose considerably. In 1860 the declared value of the
domestic produce exported from Great Britain amounted
to £135,842,000; in 1865 it amounted to £165,862,000.
We may take it that whenever one product may fail,
or may be superseded, in a largely producing nation,
its place will be supplied by some other article which
adds equally, if not more largely, to the national wealth.

We may regard it, therefore, as a certainty, now
that peace in America is restored, that the nation will
increase her foreign trade. Not only will the variety of
the native productions tend to this result, but the
variety of the countries to which these productions
are applicable, and the variety of purposes for which
they are required. America trades, as Great Britain
trades, with every nation of the globe. It may be
interesting to examine the character of the trade of the
United States, as shown by her exports to the various
countries of the world.

*(margin note: as exempli-
fied by our
own trade.)*

*(margin note: Wide surface
covered by
American
trade.)*

EXPORTS OF THE PRODUCTS OF THE UNITED STATES TO DIFFERENT COUNTRIES IN 1862.	
Countries.	Value of Exports.
Great Britain	$105,898,554
France	26,014,181
British North America	18,652,012
Hamburg and Bremen	12,672,646
Spanish West Indies	10,626,642
British West Indies	6,928,527
China and Japan	4,328,506
Brazil	3,748,249
British East Indies and Australia	3,520,663
Holland and her Possessions	3,237,022
Belgium	3,192,691
Hayti and San Domingo	3,088,108
New Granada and Venezuela	2,968,871
British Possessions in Mediterranean	1,859,460
Mexico	1,840,720
Italy	1,560,361
Chili	1,010,051
Denmark and Danish West Indies	1,007,667
Liberia and Ports in Africa	994,112
Spain and Canary Isles	990,449
Buenos Ayres and Argentine Republic	974,279
French West Indian Colonies	924,515
Portugal and her Colonies	708,029
Peru	571,652
Sandwich Islands	496,983
Turkey	444,397
Uruguay	290,259
Russia	153,471
Central America	115,640
Pacific Islands	100,414
Sweden and Norway	78,773
Austria	35,615
Total	$213,069,519

I regret being obliged to take this table from the returns for 1862, as it consequently does not represent the full amount or the real value of the exports of the United States to each foreign nation. But it shows sufficiently the diversity and the extent of the trade; and in other respects it is a curious record. It will be seen that no less than *one-half* of the whole export trade of the United States is to Great Britain; and that her third largest trade is with British North America. These facts show the vast importance to both nations of maintaining friendly relations. There is another fact deducible from this table. It shows the current in which the nation principally works. Apart from the commerce which subsists between Great Britain and the United States, British trade is most largely conducted in the old world, and in her own dependencies in India and Australia, whilst this table shows us that a very large proportion of the American trade is directed to countries in her own hemisphere—to British North America, the West India Islands, the Brazils, Hayti, New Granada, Mexico, Chili, Peru, the Sandwich Islands, and the islands of the Pacific Ocean generally. And in some of these cases, America, it should be observed, has the trade almost entirely to herself.

The great bulk of the export trade of the United States is carried on from New York, New Orleans, Boston, Baltimore, Mobile, Charleston, and Philadelphia, in the order in which those cities are respectively named. But it is curious to notice how the trade of San Francisco is developing itself. At the present time, the vessels which enter and clear at that port

Observations on this table of Exports.

Large proportion represented by the trade with Great Britain,

and with countries in the American hemisphere.

Cities from which this trade is conducted.

The trade of San Francisco.

Increasing
trade of California with
China.

number no less than 1,000 per annum, trading with
every part of the Pacific, as well as with other portions
of the world. With China especially, a very large
trade is being developed from San Francisco. Flour,
wheat, lumber, bacon, butter, cheese, lard, wine, and
vegetables, are all exported from San Francisco to
China in increasing quantities. The Chinese who
have settled themselves in California (in spite of the
most determined efforts to exclude them on the part
of a section of the population) have done great service
in teaching their countrymen at home the use and
value of Californian products, and in overcoming their
ancient prejudices to "barbarian" diet. Let this trade
only be fairly inaugurated, and the requirements of
a population almost illimitable will give assurance of
a most important market for the staple products of the
United States at remunerative prices. The enterprize
of the Americans will unquestionably result in making
San Francisco one of the most important of modern
ports. The position of the country, the variety of its
productions, the character of the population, and the
extent of their resources, must all contribute to make
California one of the greatest markets of the world.
And when railway communication shall bring the sea-
board of the Pacific into communication with that of
the Atlantic, it may be anticipated that a very considerable proportion of the trade of Europe with China
and Japan will be conducted through San Francisco.

But I must hasten from this branch of the subject,
in order to consider the imports of the United States.
The principal items are included in the following list
of articles :—

*Commercial
prospects of
California.*

*Imports of
the United
States.*

PRINCIPAL ARTICLES OF AMERICAN IMPORT.		Principal articles of Import.
Buttons.	Oils.	
Beads and Bugles.	Paints.	
Coal.	Paintings.	
Cabinet ware.	Percussion Caps.	
Coffee.	Pickles and Sauces.	
Copper, Manufactures of.	Plated Ware.	
Cottons, and Cotton Goods.	Pins.	
Clothing (not of wool).	Pipes and Pipe Cases.	
Drugs and Dyes.	Plumbago, or Blacklead.	
Embroideries.	Potash and Saltpetre.	
Fruits.	Ribbons.	
Furs.	Saddlery.	
Earthenware and China.	Silks, and Silk-dress Goods.	
Glass, and Glass wares.	Seeds.	
Gloves.	Soda.	
Gums.	Spices.	
Hair, Manufactures of:	Spirits (chiefly Brandy).	
Hemp, and Hempen Manu-	Sugar.	
factures.	Tea.	
Hosiery.	Tin and Tinware.	
Iron, Steel, and Cutlery.	Tobacco, Cigars, and Snuff.	
Lead, and Manufactures of.	Toys and Dolls.	
Leather, Calfskin, &c.	Watches and Watch materials.	
Marble.	Wool, and Woollen Clothing.	
Metals—Platina, Nickel, &c.	Zinc.	
Needles.	Household and Personal Effects	
Nuts.	of Immigrants.	

This list sustains in a very complete manner the observations in a previous section respecting the manufactures of the United States. Of textile fabrics, piece goods of silk, wool, cotton, and linens, carpetings, hosieries, ribbons, and embroideries of all sorts, are the largest classes of goods imported. In metals, cutlery and railroad iron are the largest items; tin, in plates and sheets, and lead, in bars and sheets, following. China, porcelain, and stone-wares amount to a very considerable

Textile Fabrics.

Metals.

Porcelain.

Glass.

Wines.

Fruits.

Spices.

figure, and glass of every description, from polished plate-glass to watch-glasses, forms another large item. Champagne is the largest item in the list of European wines; claret and other red wines (generally of low quality) representing a scarcely less inferior amount. Brandy is the only spirit introduced in any very considerable quantity. Amongst fruits, raisins are the largest item; and amongst spices, black pepper and pimento. Upon the whole, the Americans, judging from their imports, appear to have much the same tastes and requirements as ourselves, though they are exempted from paying the enormous amounts which we pay for imported articles of farinaceous food and general provisions.

Articles of Luxury.

It cannot be said that articles of luxury enter largely into the amount of American importations. Silk dresses and furniture appear to be the two items most largely in demand. But no jewellery is found in the list of imports, and very little plate.

American trade less speculative than is usually supposed.

It is not many weeks since the people of England were cautioned, as many persons thought without due necessity, against entering into largely extended commercial transactions with America. I do not propose to re-open the controversy. But I think the tables given in this chapter will show that the Americans have not been prone to over-trading beyond their means. The American Import trade appears to consist of articles of necessity and utility, for which there is always an abundant market. During the Civil War this trade sunk greatly. In 1860 their imports amounted to $362,000,000; in 1865 they only amounted to $234,000,000, a difference of no less

than $128,000,000. No small credit is due to them
for such an exercise of caution and forbearance; and
now that the war is over, and that largely-increased
prosperity is about to attend the return of a large proportion of the working population to their ordinary
industry, there seems to be no good ground for checking
that supply of articles of consumption which is the
natural consequence of a re-opening of the old accustomed ledgers.

In addition to the increased wealth in process of
development, there is no doubt that the Americans,
during their war, invested largely in the securities of
this country; and we also know that Europeans have
been large buyers of American railway debentures and
State securities. There need be little apprehension,
therefore, either of the balance of trade being unduly
against the United States, or of her being found deficient
in means to pay for whatever she may purchase. From
July, 1865, to the time at which I write (February, 1866),
the price of gold in New York has scarcely fluctuated
5 per cent.,—in singular contrast to the war excitement
of the year before. There has been no export demand
to advance the price; and although gold at present
is from 80 to 83 points below its price at the commencement of 1865 (it was then 227—it is now 145 to 144),
the prices of American securities have not fallen in
proportion. In fact, the commercial men of the nation
rely with confidence on the resources of America.

The capacity of America to purchase in the European markets.

CHAPTER III.

INTERNAL TRADE.

The Internal Trade of the United States.
VERY large as is the export and import trade of the United States, it has been already shown that it is nothing in comparison with her INTERNAL trade. The distances in America are so great, the region of production lies, in many cases, so far from the field of consumption, that the internal trade and traffic of the country must be necessarily a business, not only of vast importance in itself, but of importance enlarging with the rapid increase of population, the still more rapid development of the resources of the country, and the extended and extending field over which the population is spread, and from which those resources are drawn.

Its comprehensive character.
The extent of the territory of the United States implies great diversity of productions. The growths of tropical regions are exchanged for the field crops and forest produce of cooler latitudes; and in another direction the products of the coast and of extreme interior districts are exchanged. Such a trade must necessarily be of a very comprehensive character. In fact, the inland trade of the United States may be

considered almost as various as that of Great Britain with her colonies.*

Principal direction of the traffic.

Whilst the tide of emigration sets from east to west, the tide of commerce flows from west to east. The produce of the country, of whatever description, has all to be conveyed in that direction. The principal routes by which the trade of the West is conducted are those (1) of the Mississippi, which, as already explained, is now chiefly used for home purposes; (2) of the New York canals, formerly of great importance; (3) of the railways penetrating the west and reaching the Atlantic sea-ports; and (4) of the St. Lawrence, and the lakes it empties. By these various routes all the movement of the produce of the country is conducted.

Facilities for conducting it.

Up to a comparatively recent period the river and lake navigation, and the canal navigation which has brought the lakes and rivers into connexion, have supplied the principal facilities for internal trade. The large extent of the "enrolled and licensed" *sail* tonnage of the United States has been referred to in a previous chapter. This tonnage, together with the "enrolled

Tonnage on the Lakes, Rivers, and Canals.

---

* My friend, Mr. W. E. Baxter, the Member for Dundee, in his most valuable book on America, remarks, "It is astonishing to observe the vast quantities of produce in course of transit throughout the country. Huge steamboats on the Mississippi and Alabama are loaded to the water's edge with bales of cotton. Those on the Ohio are burdened with barrels of pork and thousands of hams. 'Propellers,' on the lakes, are filled with the finest wheat from Wisconsin and Michigan. Canal boats in New York and Pennsylvania are deeply laden with flour. Railroad waggons are filled with merchandize, and locomotives struggle, in the western wilds, to drag trains richly freighted with the productions of every country under the sun. The United States reminded me, sometimes, of a great ant-hill, where every member of the community is either busy carrying a burden along a beaten pathway, or hastening away in search of new stores to increase the national prosperity."

and licensed" *steam* tonnage, was computed, in 1860, at nearly 3,000,000 tons. This may be taken as the amount of tonnage, of every description, employed in the internal trade of America, including, of course, the river, lake, canal, and coasting navigation. Such an

The internal trade of America measured by the enrolled and licensed Tonnage.

amount of tonnage shows an immense internal traffic. If we multiply it by ten, we shall not get at more than the average result of the deliveries of goods per annum by vessels employed in navigation of limited duration and extent. And if we take thirty millions of tons per annum as the amount of the river, canal, and coasting trade of America, I think we shall be within the mark. The coasting trade of Great Britain, in 1860, employed, in the aggregate, thirty-four millions of tons of shipping. We have, I apprehend, a much larger coasting trade than America, in consequence of the extent to which our vessels carry coals round our coasts; but to counterbalance this, America has a much greater lake, river, and canal navigation. There are no precise data, that I know of, by which we can measure either the actual amount of tonnage employed in Great Britain and Ireland proportionately with the enrolled and licensed tonnage of the United States; nor, on the other hand, do the American statistics afford us the means of comparing the quantities carried coastwise relatively to our own. But, I think, that we may fairly take the internal and coast traffics of the two countries by water-carriage to be nearly equal, knowing that in our coast trade we employ (say) 34,000,000 of tons annually, whilst in America they have enrolled 3,000,000 tons steam, sailing, and other vessels for employment in the inland and coasting trades.

How far is the amount of tonnage employed in inland intercourse in America adequate to the wants of the country? In considering this point, we have to regard the very great lengths over which traffic has to be carried; and having regard to those distances, no reasonable doubt can be entertained that the inland navigation of America is very inadequate to the wants of the people. It has not, in fact, kept pace with the population and progress of the country; and if it were not for the railroads, the great producing districts of the United States would be at a stand-still for want of means of transport for their produce.

In 1853 the canals between Buffalo and New York carried, annually, 4,247,000 tons. At that time a very small proportion of the Western States were developed. In 1862, with diminished rates and increased appliances, the canals were only able to carry 5,598,000 tons: obviously a very small proportion of what ought to be the great carrying trade between the Atlantic sea-board and the interior, and *vice versâ*. It may be taken as a fact, that the canal navigation of the United States, working at reduced rates, now carries the maximum quantity it is able to convey, and that such is the rapid increase of products in the interior, and so large are the demands of that interior for foreign and other products, that the quantity of goods conveyed by water must be a very small proportion to the whole.

The articles chiefly carried westward in America are groceries, including sugar and molasses, dry goods, hardwares, empty barrels (chiefly carried to the oil wells, and also for packing flour), machinery and castings, soda, pearl and potash, earthenware, boots, shoes, and hats, copper, tin, and lead, drugs, medicines, and dyes, furniture and oilcloth, crockery, green and dried fruits, rolled iron, hemp and cordage, brown sheeting and bagging, marble, cement, lime and plaster, paper, rags and stationery, oysters, nails and spikes, salted meats and fish, tobacco and cigars, and carriages and waggons. The eastward freight consists for the most part of agricultural products, cotton, corn, flour, seeds, live stock, butter and eggs, poultry, pork, beef, and other meats (both fresh and salted), lard and tallow, manure, lumber, malt, petroleum, hides, lead, raw tobacco, and wool and woollen yarn. The miscellaneous freight from the west, which includes a share of manufactured articles, is said to have been recently increasing, but it is still in very small proportion to the bulk of the trade. There is a very considerable local traffic to the large cities and towns in what is denominated "marketing"—*i.e.* garden and orchard produce, hay, grass, &c. This enumeration will serve to show the general character of the interior trade of the United States.

The Lake tonnage of the country has, latterly, been largely on the increase. This has been occasioned by the development of the North-Western States, and the communications required to and from the ports at which the railways have established themselves on the lake shores. The Lake shipping trade has had various alternations of fortune, being sometimes highly profitable, and thereupon stimulated to great development, and at other times suffering under serious depression. An immense business has been done during the last four or five years, beginning with the fall of 1860 ; and

The Eastward freight.
Agricultural products.

Miscellaneous freight.

"Marketing."

The traffic on the Lakes.

the consequence has been a great increase in the
number of vessels of all classes adapted to the trade.
In 1863 the total registered and enrolled tonnage of
United States' vessels at the lake ports was 611,398.
This, however, includes the enrolled tonnage of barges
and boats engaged in the river and canal trade; and it
also includes, perhaps, 50,000 tons of vessels lost or
broken up, and not yet struck off the register. That
there is great development in this trade, is, however,
proved by the fact that every great line of railroad
now employs "propellers" as means of communication
between the various ports at which produce is shipped
on the lakes and its own port of embarcation. There
is also a large amount of Canadian tonnage employed
in this trade; and the shipment of ores on Lake
Superior, estimated at the value of $4,000,000 in
1862, is said to employ not less than 10,000 tons.
The Lake Fisheries are also of much importance to the
Lake Shipping trade. The imports of lake fish at
Buffalo in 1860 amounted to 26,655 barrels; and
although there has been a decrease since that year, it
is said to have resulted from the increased demand
and higher prices obtained for fish at other places.

The lumber and stave trade upon the lakes also
constitutes a large portion of the freight. The eastward movement of lumber usually takes place in mid-
summer, when low rates of transportation rule. The
principal sources of supply are the States of Michigan,
Canada West, Ohio, and Indiana. More than fifty per
cent. of the lumber brought to Buffalo comes from the
State of Michigan. In the northern peninsula of that
State, in and around Saginaw, at Port Huron, on the

Marginal notes:
Tonnage of the Lake Ports.

"Propellers."

Lake Superior.

Lake Fish.

The Lumber Trade.

St. Clair river, are said to be the finest lumber districts of the American North West. In 1862, the number of staves brought into Buffalo was 30,500,000, and the quantity of measured lumber amounted to 125,000,000 feet.

Railroad communications.

The Census Commissioners estimate that of nine million tons of produce, &c., conveyed between East and West, and *vice versâ*, in 1862, six million tons were carried by the railroads; and they argue therefrom, not unjustly, that if these railroads had not been constructed the produce of the West could not have been conveyed to market, and therefore that the population of the West could not have thriven. It is well known that the railroads which penetrated the Western

Their present inadequacy.

districts from the sea-board were quite inadequate, during the whole of the interval between 1853 and 1862, to convey anything like the quantity of goods offered them for carriage. Looking to the fact that during a considerable portion of the year the canals are frozen up, and the navigation of the lakes and rivers of North America similarly interrupted, and regarding also the circumstance that during the entire year the single track lines of the American railways are choked with traffic, it will be readily understood that the provision at present existing for the conduct of the great bulk of the internal trade of the United States is exceedingly inadequate.

Railroads can alone supply the deficiency of the traffic facilities of America.

A development of the railroad system alone can be looked for to cure this defect. We have already seen that the carrying trade of the Mississippi river has been diverted in consequence of the superior advantages offered to the Western States by the commerce of

New York over that of New Orleans. The trade through the lakes and by way of the St. Lawrence must and will be an increasing trade, but it will always be restricted by local circumstances and by the character of the navigation. The canals, as already observed, are supplied with traffic to the full extent of their capacity. Waggon carriage is, of course, out of the question. Railroads, therefore, remain as the only means of affording adequate accommodation for freight from one part of the country to the other.

So much has this been felt in the Great West, that between 1850 and 1860 the five States of Ohio, Indiana, Illinois, Michigan, and Wisconsin, supplied themselves with upwards of 8,000 miles of railroad. Those States had an aggregate of 1,275 miles of road in 1850: they had nearly 10,000 miles in 1860. The consequence was that within those ten years the aggregate cash value of the property in those States was nearly trebled: and in the neighbourhood of lines of railroad it was, of course, increased in very much larger proportions. It cannot be doubted, therefore, that for the development of its great internal traffic what the United States has to look to, is the development of railroads. But I shall have to enlarge upon this subject in another section.

Railroad mileage in the Western States.

I regret that there is comparatively little information at my command respecting the coasting trade of the United States. Before the Civil War there was a great sea-board traffic between North and South, especially between New York and Charleston; indeed a very considerable proportion of the cotton of the Southern States was sent from various cities of the

The Coasting Trade of America.

Cotton.

South to New York for shipment to Europe. Between the Northern and the Southern States there has also been a large coasting trade in lumber. Of course all this trade was interrupted by the war.

Of recent years the most important coasting trade has unquestionably been that of Panama, which the Americans persist in treating as a coasting station in consequence of its being the route at present between

the States of the Atlantic and Pacific. The value of the Panama trade is exhibited in the following table showing the travel and transportation over the Isthmus for the year ending 30th September, 1862 :—

Character of Transport.	Towards the Pacific.	Towards the Atlantic.	Total.
Passengers .... No.	21,456	9,796	31,162
Gold .... Dols.	4,444,268	34,605,467	39,049,736
Silver .... ,,	—	14,286,935	14,285,935
Jewellery............. ,,	578,062	—	578,062
American Mails...... lbs.	232,886	31,964	264,850
English Mails ...... ,,	35,565	10,127	45,692
Extra Baggage ...... ,,	345,547	217,901	536,448
Freight by weight... ,,	54,758,378	20,061,601	74,819,919
Freight by measure . feet	737,684	33,279	770,963

This table is curious not merely as showing the extent and general character of the trade between the Atlantic and Pacific, but as showing its direction. Thus we see that the bulk of the passengers go to California; and, that whilst the bulk of the gold and silver comes from it, the jewellery and the merchandise of every class is, in the largest proportion, directed to the Pacific. It is curious to notice that each traveller from the Pacific returns with a larger *proportionate* weight of baggage than those who go in that direction; and it will also be observed how much heavier are the mails outwards than they are homewards, a circumstance to be accounted for, no doubt, by the greater number of newspapers and other publications forwarded from home.

The total *values* of the trade of Panama are returned as follows :—

Years.	Inward.	Outward.	Total.
1859	$57,679,925	$13,857,000	$71,536,925
1860	53,148,004	17,484,000	70,632,004
1861	64,347,905	12,624,850	76,972,755
1862	57,826,620	24,795,428	82,622,049

Of the trade of 1862, $32,000,000 worth was transacted with Europe, and $40,000,000 with the United States. I am sorry to find Mr. Chase, in his "Report to Congress on Foreign and Domestic Commerce, 1863," urging that because the trade across the Isthmus is thus relatively larger from America than from Europe, it ought therefore to be treated "as a coasting trade to vessels of the United States."

"The magnitude of the trade with the Pacific States," he says, "opens an inviting field to foreign occupation, but its peculiar circumstances have so far protected it. They may continue to do so in a great degree, if the quality of coasting trade and *the laws which preserve it to the United States are rigidly maintained;* but if these were yielded, a very little would suffice to displace United States shipping."

These are very narrow notions, and evince much less faith than a statesman of advanced views ought to entertain in the future of his country. Why should American shipping be displaced if the Panama trade was not

Impolicy of treating the Panama trade as "a Coasting trade."

treated as a coasting trade? Besides the advantage of distance, America must always have advantages over every other country in trading with her own states and with her own citizens. Every country possesses that advantage in so great a degree that, practically, it must carry on its own coasting trade, whether that trade is open or not to other nations. Every description of ruin to British trade and British shipping, was predicted by our protectionists, when it was proposed to throw open the coasting trade of England to foreign competition; but we did it, and the result is, not only that we maintain our own trade, but that it has been a far better trade, since the system of monopoly was abolished than it was whilst it existed. America would lose nothing commercially by altering her present system in regard to this trade : whilst, in the eyes of the world, she would gain much. At the present time, her monopoly of the Panama route is regarded, not so much as a wrong to Europe, as a wrong to those small States of the Pacific, Chili, Peru, Bolivia and Equador, which have quite as much right to the use of the Isthmus as the State of California, or any other State. It is monstrous to exclude the people of those States from the free use of their most direct access to Europe, under the pretext that the trade of the seaboard of the ocean is "a coasting traffic." Such a system is indefensible; and I have no doubt that, in the main, it is also injurious to American commerce and enterprise. Nothing is to be gained by a free people by any restriction upon free intercourse.

It is to be hoped that, with the revival of the South and the introduction of capital and enterprise into those States, the commerce of New Orleans, Savannah, Mobile, Charleston, and the other great ports of the Gulf of Mexico and the Southern Atlantic seaboard of the United States may revive and flourish. There was never any good reason why the South should be forced to send the bulk of its produce to the North for exportation : and if the South is to be regarded and treated as a free country, New York merchants must not attempt to monopolise or control its trade. The South with increased independence and increased resources will probably require increased supplies of European products, and the people ought to be able to obtain them, not through New York, or the other seaports of the North, but under the advantage of a direct trade. Every article in the South has heretofore been increased in price to the consumer by a long and costly transport from New York; but under a better system the South ought to be enabled to save itself this addition to its prices, and to import for itself in return for the articles it exports. It must be for the advantage of both North and South, that the trade of the Southern ports should be developed to the utmost possible extent : and no merely local considerations ought, for one moment, to be permitted to stand in the way of that development. The establishment of a perfectly un-fettered trade at the Southern ports, by promoting the internal intercourse of the whole Southern section of America, would probably do as much as anything else to revive the prosperity of that portion of the United States, and thereby to enable the American people to bear the burden of national taxation.

CHAPTER IV.

For the purposes of the internal trade of the United States, it is obviously of the utmost consequence that there should be the fullest and freest facilities of communication. This subject is found to press itself so much upon the merchants and traders of the interior that, immediately at the close of the Civil War, it was determined to hold a great " Commercial Convention," for the purpose of deliberating upon the business interests of the country. This Convention was held at the city of Detroit, on Lake Michigan, in July last. The commercial and trading bodies of nearly every important town in the north-east and north-west of the United States were represented. Canada, Nova Scotia, and New Brunswick also sent deputations to attend ; but, whilst they took part in the deliberations of the Convention, the British colonial deputations thought it proper to abstain from voting, on the ground that there were many subjects of internal importance connected with the United States, on which it was more proper to allow the citizens of the Union to decide for themselves. The Convention, being organized, deliberated for four days, during which the position of the mercantile community was thoroughly discussed

The Detroit Commercial Convention, July, 1865.

as regarded matters of transit, river and harbour shipment, finance, agriculture, manufactures, and reciprocity. At the conclusion of their deliberations, the Convention took a vote, and unanimously adopted the following important resolution :—

" *Resolved*, That this Convention do respectfully request the President of the United States to enter into negotiations with the Government of Great Britain having in view the execution of a Treaty between the two Countries for Reciprocal Commercial Intercourse between the United States and the several Provinces of British North America, including British Columbia, the Selkirk Settlement and Vancouver's Island, based on principles which shall be just and equitable to all parties, and with reference to the present financial condition of the United States, and which shall also include the free navigation of the St. Lawrence, and the other Rivers of British North America, with such improvements of the Rivers and the enlargement of the Canals as shall render them adeqate for the requirements of the West in communicating with the Ocean."

Nothing can show more clearly than this resolution the tendency and feeling of the commercial classes of America. They want perfect freedom of intercourse, and the most abundant facilities for effecting it. It is deeply to be regretted that anything should occur to deprive the Americans of the advantages they must inevitably derive from the enjoyment of such freedom and facilities. The action recently taken by the United States Government, however, on the subject of the intercourse with British North America, promises, unfortunately, to deprive the people of much of that which they now enjoy.

In the year 1854 a treaty was entered into between Great Britain and the United States for the purpose

between the
United States
and the
British
Provinces
of North
America.
of adjusting old-standing disputes respecting the
fisheries on the American coasts, and also of establishing a reciprocal system of trade between the
United States and the British North American provinces.   Many of the Americans take the view that
this Reciprocity Treaty, as it was called, was more
favourable in its application to the British provinces
than to the United States.   Upon that it may be ob-
Its provisions. served that the Treaty threw open all the British coasts
and bays of the North to American fishermen, thereby
settling the long-vexed questions arising out of the
three-mile limit : that it also gave the Americans the
most perfect freedom in the navigation of the river
St. Lawrence : and that it placed all American manufactures on the same basis as those of British origin
throughout the British possessions in North America.
Its success. These must have been material advantages, and it
is not denied that they have proved so.   The first and
natural results of the treaty were entirely beneficial.
In every department there was not only a sensible
increase but an unexpectedly large augmentation of
trade between the British provinces and the United
States.   No complaints were heard on either side, and
the treaty was confessed to be of public benefit.

Local Taxes
imposed
by the
Canadians.
Some few years since the Canadian Government,
under Mr. Galt, thought it necessary, *for purposes
of internal revenue*, to raise their rates of duty in
Canada upon the importation of certain manufactured
articles.   These increased rates applied equally to the
manufactures of all nations, and therefore could not
be complained of as a peculiar hardship on the Americans.   The same Government, however, also thought

it desirable to assess discriminating rates of toll upon the produce passing through their state canals, with a view, as is believed, of endeavouring to divert the bulk of the trade to the ports of the St. Lawrence.* I must say that I think this latter act was very unwise, and was not at all in accordance with the large spirit and intention of the Reciprocity Treaty.

The effect of this proceeding was to afford an opportunity to the Protectionist party in America of denouncing the treaty. It was to last, I believe, ten years :—at any rate the period at which it expires is the 17th March, 1866. Under the influence of the Hon. Justice Morrill, of Vermont, the great Protectionist leader in the United States Congress, the Washington authorities have given notice that they do not intend to renew this treaty.

Effect upon the United States.

This appears to me to be exceedingly unfortunate for both parties, but particularly so for the people of the United States.

Reasons for maintaining the Treaty.

I. For the purposes of their traffic every outlet is indispensable to the people of America. The St. Lawrence is, without question, the cheapest and the

1. Because its abrogation will prevent Americans from using the St. Lawrence as an outlet for Trade.

---

* The Superintendent of the United States' Census, commenting upon the fears entertained by some persons in that country of a diversion of a portion of the grain trade from New York, observes, with considerable force and justice, that " when it is considered that the production of grain in the North-Western States, increased from 218,500,000 bushels in 1840 to 642,000,000 in 1860, and that of the eight food-producing states west of the lakes, embracing an area of 262,500,000 acres, only about 52,000,000 acres were under cultivation in 1860, *no fear need be entertained that any of the outlets to the ocean will be unoccupied to the extent of their capacity. The only fear,*" he adds, " *is, that we will not keep pace with the increased production by increased facilities of transport.*"

readiest outlet for such produce.* To stop that great outlet will be to raise the cost of transport by every other means of conveyance to the sea-board : a serious injury, it cannot be doubted, to the Western farmer. But by abandoning the treaty the Americans are making sacrifice of all the rights and privileges which it gave them in respect to the St. Lawrence. They are setting the Western States, which want the use of the river, against the Eastern States, which do not require it.

2. Because it will prevent them from using Canadian tonnage.

II. The large American producers on the lakes require freight and tonnage for their produce. This freight and tonnage the people of British North America have been enabled, under the treaty, to supply them with : the treaty having opened to them the right of navigating Lake Michigan and the American waters of Lake Superior. But, inasmuch as the abrogation of the treaty will abrogate the right of the Canadians to navigate those waters, the residents on the American shores of the lakes will be deprived of the advantage of Canadian tonnage, and the consequence will be that the cost of freight for all the produce of their mines, their forests, and their lands, will be proportionately enhanced.

3. Because it will occasion smuggling,

III. The rates of import duties in the United States are, at the present moment, much higher than the

---

* Chicago, the great seat of the corn trade of the North-Western States, is 419 miles nearer to Liverpool, by the St. Lawrence, than by any other route ; and it is proportionately cheaper both in time and money. The difficulty of the grain trade of the St. Lawrence arises from the unsuitableness for ocean navigation of the light draught schooners which are necessarily employed in order to cross the St. Clair flats and pass through the canals. The want of return cargoes is also a serious drawback to the St. Lawrence trade.

rates of duties in any part of British North America. A smuggling trade in all articles of consumption which are lower in price on the one side of the border than they are upon the other is, therefore, inevitable the moment the Reciprocity Treaty is abrogated. At present rates, all this smuggling will be from Canada into the States; and, in order to prevent it, the American Government will have to establish on their frontier not only custom houses at every point which traffic reaches, but a perfect coast-guard upon the shores and the waters of the lakes and northern coasts. I apprehend that this coast-guard will form a source of great expense to the United States Government, and that the duties received will never cover such expenses. Observe what the Secretary of the Treasury, Mr. McCulloch, says upon this subject in a recent report to Congress :— *and thereby largely increase the expenses of the United States.*

"The attempts at smuggling, stimulated by our high rate of duties on imports, have engaged the attention of the department, and such arrangements have been made for its detection and prevention as seemed to be required by circumstance and available for the purpose. *It is quite apparent, however, that with our extensive sea-coasts and inland frontier, it is impracticable entirely to prevent illicit traffic*, though *checks* at the most exposed points have doubtless been put to such practices. Revenue cutters are diligently and carefully employed within limits so defined, as to leave no part of the sea and gulf coasts unvisited. *A similar arrangement will be extended to the Lakes.* . . . There are now in the service twenty-seven steamers and nine sailing-vessels; but in consequence of their large draught of water, they must be principally used as sea-going vessels. They are incapable of navigating the shallow waters which afford the most favourable opportunities for contraband trade. *It is recommended, therefore, that this department be vested with authority to sell these vessels, and expend the proceeds in the purchase of others of a different character and lighter draught,* better fitted to accomplish the purposes of a preventive service, *and which can be kept in commission at a less cost."*

It is obvious from this that the Secretary of the Treasury feels the burden about to be imposed on him, and finds no little difficulty in providing for it.

4. Because it will revive the old disputes respecting Fisheries.

IV. But, beyond all this, there is a difficulty and a danger arising out of the abrogation of this treaty, which may prove even more costly than the protection of the long coast-line of America from smugglers. For nearly forty years, from 1815 to 1854, the fisheries question gave rise to a continuous series of disputes and diplomatic conflicts between England and America. The *Jasseur* case in 1815, the *Argus* case in 1823, the *Dotterel* case in 1824, the *Ringdove* case in 1839, the *Sylph* case in 1844, and a number of other instances of captures of American fishing-boats made in British fishing grounds, by vessels in Her Majesty's service and the service of the Colonies, gave rise to constant disquietudes, alarms, diplomatic correspondence, and threats of retaliation and of war between the countries. The Fisheries Convention adopted by the two nations in 1818 declared that American fishermen should have no right to fish within three miles of the British shores; but the impossibility of defining accurate boundaries and distances at sea, and especially on the foggy shores of Newfoundland and Cape Breton, led to constantly repeated disputes on this point. Such disputes became of more import and significance when it was declared by the law-officers of the Crown that these three miles "must be measured from the headlands or extreme points of land, next to the sea, of the coasts, or of the entrance of the bays." By this declaration (no doubt a correct one) the Americans were limited to fishing-grounds in the open ocean. But the Reciprocity Treaty of 1854 gave them the privilege of fishing on the same grounds as all British fishermen, not only within three miles of the coasts, but in all the bays, and inlets, and inland waters of British North America —a privilege of which the Americans have not been slow to take advantage. They lost millions by being excluded from British fishing grounds; they have acquired millions by being admitted to them. And yet they propose to throw up this advantage, to incur the chance of a renewal of all the squabbles and heart-burnings which attended the working of the Fisheries Convention of 1818, besides the cost and the danger of protecting the fishermen by ships of war, as they were compelled to do for many years previous to the treaty.

The Boston Board of Trade, referring to the proposed abrogation of this treaty, observes :— *Feeling of the Merchants of Boston on this subject.*

"In the place of barred and bolted ports, the people of the United States and of the Colonies, now, and under the 'Reciprocity Treaty,' deal with one another at will—exchange without customs, even, the 'wealth of the seas' and the principal raw staples of the soil—mingle, as if of the same nation, on all the fishing grounds ; and, as if of the same nation, too, use the St. Lawrence and the canals which connect it with the great lakes and with the ocean. True, in this happy condition of things, there are some grave evils to lament and to correct; yet we are still to rejoice that the inhuman restrictions which existed for nearly half a century, have been removed. And, now ! are the misunderstandings of a moment to be cherished, and to terminate in utter alienation

and hatred? Is retaliatory legislation to be revived on both
sides? . . . We had supposed that in commercial freedom,
and of consequence in the promotion of human brotherhood,
there was no recession. Is the case before us to prove an
exception to the rule?"

Every right-thinking and right-minded man, of whatever nation, must echo these observations.

Mr. Morrill's
arguments in
opposition to
the Treaty
examined.The abrogation of this treaty has been urged by
Mr. Morrill and the Protectionist party in Congress on
two principal grounds :—

First, That the ancient laws of trade are subverted
by this treaty.

Second, That, under its operation, the balance of
trade has proved to be against the United States.

The first position is, I am sorry to say, supported
by Mr. McCulloch, in his recent report to Congress.

" There are grave doubts whether treaties of this character
do not interfere with the legislative power of Congress, and
especially with the constitutional power of the House of
Representatives, to originate revenue bills ; and whether such
treaties are not in conflict with the spirit of the usual clause
contained in most of our commercial treaties, to treat each
nation on the same footing as the most favoured nation."

The
Reciprocity
Treaty not
opposed to
the Laws of
the United
States.Such an argument can scarcely be regarded as conclusive. If the legislative power of Congress is required
to give effect to a commercial treaty, surely the power
can be obtained. In Great Britain, the government
make treaties and submit them to Parliament ; and it
is in the power of Parliament to condemn them should
Parliament see fit. I apprehend the same system prevails in the United States ; but I have not heard that
Congress, after the Reciprocity Treaty was adopted in

1854, in any way disapproved of it. The treaty, be it observed, was not concocted in the dark. It was a measure for which some of the greatest statesmen of both nations took credit. It was negociated, on behalf of England, by the Earl of Elgin, and on the part of America, by Mr. Webster, Mr. Marcy, President Fillmore, and Mr. Everett, all distinguished names. It is not to be supposed that any of these great men, some of them great constitutional lawyers, would have attempted to give effect to a document which "interfered with the legislative powers of Congress;" and if they did, it is not to be supposed that in a free nation like America, such an attempt to usurp the authority of the great council of the nation would have passed unnoticed and unchecked.

But perhaps Mr. McCulloch's real meaning is better explained by a passage which follows :— The Treaty "a financial embarrassment"

"In the arrangement of *our complex system of revenue*, through the tariff and internal duties, this treaty has been the subject of no little embarrassment. The subject of the revenue should not be embarrassed by treaty stipulations, but Congress should be left to act upon it freely and independently."

That is to say, that having adopted, in time of peace, a system of free trade, and a treaty giving effect to that system very much to their advantage, the American Government, having adopted "a complex system of revenue" [involving an almost prohibitory tariff] in a period of necessity arising out of war, chooses, at the close of that war, to adhere to its "complex system," and to throw over the more simple, or free trade, system, as a "subject of no little embarrassment." Mr. McCulloch evidently does not suppose, to the adoption of a prohibitory policy.

with the Boston Board of Trade, that "in the history of commercial freedom there is no recession."

But, as to Mr. Morrill's second point :—

The balance of Trade not opposed to the United States.

"Our exports to Canada," he told the Congress, "which formerly largely exceeded our imports, are now greatly less. They sell to us, to go elsewhere to buy."

Even if this were so, it would be a very bad reason for abrogating the treaty. It would be a bad reason in point of honour and morality : it would be even a worse reason in point of commercial policy, knowledge, and discretion. For it is by no means certain that the nation which has what is called " the balance of trade" in its favour, is the nation which profits most largely by the trade which leads to that balance. For example, Canada, and the other British North American colonies, send to the United States large quantities of their raw produce : corn, timber, ores, &c. The Americans manufacture and export those raw productions, carrying them long distances through their own territory, and exporting them in their own shipping. The Americans, we will assume, pay for those raw materials in gold ; the " balance of trade" is consequently against them. But who pockets the largest profit : the producer of the raw material, or the importer, manufacturer, and exporter of it ?

Evidence on this point.

Let us see what some of the manufacturers of America themselves think of the effect of the treaty on their trade. Two gentlemen largely engaged in the woollen business recently reported to the Boston Board of Trade as follows :—

" Considerable investments have been made in machinery for the manufacture of worsted goods, of which we now import from Great Britain alone about 50,000,000 yards. These could all be made in this country, if we had a supply of wool suitable for them. *At present we depend mainly upon those grown in Canada*, whence we import from 3,000,000 to 4,000,000 lb., *which supply we shall be deprived of if the Reciprocity Treaty is abrogated.* The wool we import from Canada does not compete with that raised in this country, but the drain we make upon the Canadian supply sends the manufacturers of that country into our market to buy the fine wools of the United States, which they can purchase for less money than they obtain for their coarser grades."

It appears, therefore, that the reciprocity is perfect, and materially beneficial to both countries.

If Mr. Morrill was right in fact, therefore, he would be entirely wrong in principle and theory. But he is not only wrong in theory, but wrong in practice and in fact. It is not true that the "balance of trade" is in favour of Canada. On the contrary, official returns show that during the ten years ending with 1863, the exports of the United States to Canada amounted to $170,635,000, whilst the imports from Canada were of the value of $152,051,000, so that the "balance of trade" was in favour of the United States to the extent of $18,584,000. Upon this state of facts, the Boston Board of Trade asks :— *The Evidence of the Official Returns of the United States.*

"What becomes of Mr. Morrill's assertion that the Canadians 'sell to us to go elsewhere to buy?' The truth is, that under reciprocity, and until the rebellion, *Canada bought more of the United States than of all the rest of the world besides!* *Evidence of the Boston Board of Trade.*

"From 1855 to 1860 (both years included) her total imports from every country were $215,982,776, of which $114,259,345 were from American ports, showing a balance in our favour against all other nations in those six years of $12,535,914, *or more than two millions of dollars annually!*"

S

How unfairly Mr. Morrill has dealt with the facts is shown by one illustration. He told Congress that the amount of *gold* sent out of the United States to Canada in 1863 amounted to $3,502,180. That was the truth, but not the whole truth. The accounts of the American Secretary of the Treasury for 1863, show that the importations of the *precious metals* from Canada amounted to $4,892,195 ; being a balance in favour of the United States of $1,390,015 in that one year !

During the years over which the treaty has extended, it is estimated that the balance of trade has been in favour of America to the extent of nearly $56,000,000. But, as has been eloquently said, " in the presence of " the great benefits conferred on both countries by this " measure, it is a waste of time to chaffer over their " distribution. In the interests of peace and honest " industry, we should thank Providence for the bless- " ing, and confidently rely upon the wisdom of our " statesmen to see that it is preserved."

The inhabitants of British North America, as a body, have behaved very well about this treaty. In its origin it was a compromise, and in its provisions they did not originally think it advantageous to them. They complained that the right of trading coastwise, fully conceded by the British to the Americans, was not conceded by America in reciprocity ; that the right of registering their colonial vessels for trade from America to foreign ports, was not permitted them ; that no equivalent whatever was given for the free navigation of the rivers and canals of British America ; that the concession of the right of fishing and curing fish within the bays, and harbours, and in-shore fisheries of the maritime provinces was given without equivalent. Again, when the Civil War broke out, one half of the sea-board of the United States was blockaded, and all the advantages of the Reciprocity Treaty were lost to the provinces, so far as regarded the consumption of many millions of the American population.

At the same time, the British Americans have been desirous to maintain the treaty, as a measure of peace and national fraternity. It has, they say, secured to both countries freedom from disputes and heart-burnings. "There have been no intrusions, warnings, captures—no rival squadrons guarding boundaries impossible to define." Had no other good been accomplished, he would be no friend to either country who would desire to open again the old field of controversy. The trade between the British provinces and America, previously feeble, restricted, slow of growth, and, in many respects, vexatious, has been annually swollen by mutual interchanges and honourable competition, until it has come to be represented by a grand total of $456,350,000 in about nine years; or upwards of £91,000,000! If this wise adjustment of interests is not disturbed, who can estimate what this trade will amount to in the next decade?

What are the consequences of the policy of the American government, in relation to this treaty? The Canadians, having for the past ten years enjoyed the advantages and sweets of commerce, are now endeavouring to seek outlets for it elsewhere. Having raised products for the American market, which the Americans will no longer take, and having built

They have desired to maintain the Treaty.

Their good feeling towards America.

Antagonistic feeling of American protectionists.

shipping for their service which the American government will no longer allow their citizens to employ, the inhabitants of British North America are endeavouring to form treaties of commerce with Brazil, Mexico, the West India islands, and other countries, where it is not thought so essentially necessary to refuse to conclude commercial arrangements on the ground that they ought to be the subject of direct legislative provision. The Americans, in fact, have created the Canadians into commercial competitors. On the whole continent, as long as the people of the United States and of British North America were united in trade under the Reciprocity Treaty, there was no one to compete with their joint trading. But the action of the Washington Government, in addition to all the other disadvantages which must result from such bad policy, will create a trading competition with the United States of America from their own continent.

Detrimental effects on American commerce.

The commercial men of the United States, and a large section of its press, are still pressing upon the American Government not to forego the existing advantages derived by America under this treaty, but to consent to postpone its termination in order to enter into some more permanent arrangement for carrying out its general provisions. Some Americans may say that in the present state of the revenue and expenditure of the United States, it is impossible to renew the Reciprocity Treaty without modifications which will favour their revenue. The people of the provinces do not fail to recognise the duty of the American Government to sustain the credit of their country, and

Feeling of commercial men and of the American press upon this subject.

Desirability of a compromise.

to discharge its obligations. One of them, speaking at the Detroit Convention, said,—

" If you do not, we should share in the disgrace ; we should feel, as a part of the British family, that when you had issued your bonds, and sent them largely into other countries, we should be disgraced, as well as you, if you did not sustain them. But," he added, " the RESOURCES of your country are so vast and varied, and the development of its industry is so rapid and extensive, that I believe you will be able to master the debt, maintain your credit, *and deal with your neighbours in good faith besides.*"—(*Speech of the Hon. Joseph Howe, of Nova Scotia.*)

SECTION VI.

RAILROADS.

SECTION VI.—RAILROADS.

CHAPTER I.

EXISTING LINES.

RAILROADS in the United States may be said to be cotemporaneous with those in England. Before steam power was applied to railway lines in America, iron tracks, on which vehicles were drawn by horse-power, were in use from granite and coal quarries to ports of debarcation. In Quincey, Massachusetts, one of these, terminating at the quarries with a self-acting inclined plane, was begun in 1826 and opened in 1827, and in the latter year similar lines were constructed in Pennsylvania. I apprehend, however, that these were very imperfect constructions. The first locomotive which was ever seen in America was imported from Mr. Stephenson's locomotive engine factory at Newcastle-upon-Tyne, in 1829, and was for some time exhibited, as a curiosity, in New York. The first locomotive engine, which appears to have been used in the United States, was constructed by Messrs. Foster, Rastrick,

Early American Railroads,

and Locomotive Engines.

and Co. of Stourbridge, and was introduced in the latter part of the same year. In 1830, no doubt from these models, a locomotive engine was made in New York, by the Americans themselves. The American Cyclopædia states that " it was a small four-wheeled engine, with an upright boiler and water flues close at the bottom, and the flame circulating round them," and that " it worked successfully for about two years, when it exploded."

The first American Railroad for Passenger traffic.

Of the more considerable railway enterprizes of the country, the first which appears to have been commenced was a portion of the now Baltimore and Ohio Railroad, the first stone of which was laid (or as we should say, probably with more propriety, the first sod of which was cut,) on the 4th of July, 1828.* This road, as I understand, was originally planned for a horse track only; but the introduction of steam locomotives from England encouraged the attempt to run them on the line; and in 1830, a small engine, constructed at Baltimore, was put upon the road, which still exists, and is preserved in the Company's workshops at Baltimore, as a very interesting relic. Although the traffic was great, the engine appears to have been only partially worked, the trains having also been moved by horses.

"This road was constructed of longitudinal rails pinned down to wooden or cross-stone ties, imbedded in the ground ; and upon the rails were fastened flat bars of iron, $\frac{1}{2}$ inch and $\frac{5}{8}$ inch thick, and $2\frac{1}{2}$ to $4\frac{1}{4}$ inches wide, by spikes, their

---

* The "*Fourth of July*," the anniversary of the day on which the Declaration of American Independence was signed, is a public holiday throughout the States.

heads countersunk in the iron. This method, which was generally adopted upon the early American railroads, from considerations of economy, and with a view of extending the lines to the utmost limit of the capital provided, was soon found to involve great danger and consequent expense. The ends of the rails became loose; and, starting up, were occasionally caught by the wheels, and thrust up through the bottoms of the cars. It was found necessary to run the trains with great caution upon the roads thus constructed, and the passenger traffic was seriously diverted from those lines that acquired a notoriety for snake-heads."—*New American Cyclopædia*, vol. xiii. p. 729.

In 1830 the "Hudson and Mohawk Railroad," from Albany to Schenectady was commenced. In October, 1831, the number of passengers on it was stated at 387 a day, and in 1832 a locomotive " with a load of eight tons, travelled on it at the rate of thirty miles an hour." " In 1831, twelve different railroad companies were incorporated ;" and " from this time railroad enterprizes were multiplied with great rapidity."

Rapid increase of Passenger lines.

" In Pennsylvania, it is stated, sixty-seven railroads were in operation in 1832 ; and in that year were commenced the most important lines of Massachusetts and New Jersey. They have, however, been planned and constructed, in great measure, independently of each other, without regard to any great system ; and as the charters were granted by each State for the roads in its own territory, a single State has sometimes, by refusing to authorize the construction of a proposed road, succeeded in preventing the establishment of an important line, the opening of which might injuriously affect the whole or an important part of such State. This want of system is perceived, and its evils are experienced in the various gauges adopted by different roads, rendering necessary frequent transhipment of passengers and freight." — *New American Cyclopædia*, vol. xiii. p. 730.

It cannot be doubted that the original construction

Imperfections of these roads. of the American railroads was very imperfect, and I am afraid I must add that many of them remain so to this day. But when we speak of the imperfections of American railroads, we must not be unmindful of the element of comparison. When we commenced our construction of railroads in Great Britain, we were at what may be considered the very perfection of turnpike roads. Such was the excellence of our public ways in England and in Wales that the Holyhead mail was able to traverse the whole road from London to one of the most distant parts of North Wales, through what was then, in a great degree, a barren country, at the rate of twelve or thirteen miles an hour. In Scotland and Ireland, the roads, which were less traversed, and which were originally constructed by military engineers for military purposes, were even superior to those in England. But, in America, as in all new countries, all was different. Many of the highways were mere sloughs : the best roads were extremely rough, and very ill-adapted for rapid locomotion. In such a country the most rudely-constructed road on which a locomotive engine could be worked must have been comparatively luxurious, and an English friend who travelled over some of the earliest railways in America, those for instance from Philadelphia to New York (the Camden and Amboy line) and the Hudson and Mohawk Railway from Albany to Schenectady, soon after they were opened for passenger traffic, tells me that he thought them, in those days, very nearly perfect.

There are points, moreover, about the construction

of railroads in America which contrast very favourably with the system under which, in those early days, we instituted the railway system of Great Britain. If railroads were important to the United States because their highways for traffic were exceedingly inferior, they were equally important to England, on account of the enormous traffic we had to pass over our roads, and the large comparative cost of keeping those roads in effective order. But whilst the Americans recognized immediately the importance of constructing railroads through their comparatively sparsely populated country, it was our misfortune in England that we could only develop our lines, for the purposes of much larger traffic and accommodation, with infinitely greater difficulty. From the first the American people favoured railroad construction, and afforded every possible facility for it. In England, on the other hand, we had to go through all the difficulties of landowners' oppositions and parliamentary conflicts, which immensely burdened the cost of every line of road that was permitted to be constructed for the accommodation of the public and the advantage of the locality it penetrated. It will be remembered that Oxford, Northampton, and other large towns forced the railways to take routes at a distance from them, and now, seeing their former error, in some cases too late, have been trying in vain to remedy the very lamentable results of their former mistake.

The system upon which we have been compelled to construct lines in England has involved extreme difficulty. That on which railroads have been permitted to be constructed in America has been one of great

Early encouragement given to Railroad construction in America.

Anxiety of
the Ameri-
cans to facili-
tate the con-
struction of
Railroads.

simplicity. Here we have had to go through all
the difficult and expensive ordeals of parliamentary
notices, oppositions, contentions, claims for residen-
tiary damages, severances of lands, and every variety
of litigation that could add to the expense of constituting a railroad. In America, on the other hand,
every one in the country has felt, from the first, what
every Englishman has experienced at last, that the
construction of a railroad through his property, or to
the city, town, or village he inhabited, was a source
of prosperity and wealth, not only to the district
in which he resided, but to himself personally. In
England, in fact, we have treated railroads as things
to be discouraged; whilst in America they have regarded them as sources of wealth and of convenience,
and have given every encouragement and facility for
their extension.

Ease with
which
" Charters "
are obtained
for making
lines.

As a rule, nothing has been easier than to obtain
from the legislative authority of a State in America
a concession, or as it is there styled, a " charter," to
lay down a road.* The land in many cases, especially

---

* Mr. William Lance, the railway actuary, of 26, Throgmorton-
street, London, who has written on the subject of American railways
with great knowledge and experience, says, in a little pamphlet
published some years since :—

" Nothing can be more simple, expeditious, and cheap, than the
means of obtaining an Act for the establishment of a railway company in America. A public meeting is held, at which the project
is discussed, and when adopted, a deputation is appointed to apply
to the Legislature, which grants the Act without expense, delay, or
official difficulty. The principle of competition is not brought into
play, as in France, nor is there any investigation as to the expe-
diency of the project with reference to future profit or loss, as in
England. No other guarantee or security is required from the
company than the payment of a certain amount by the shareholders,

where it belonged to the public, has been freely given Land Grants. for the line; in other cases, where landed proprietors were affected, comparatively small compensations have sufficed to satisfy their claims. The citizens residing in the towns and populous places of the different districts, have hailed the approach of a railroad as a blessing. Under certain regulations, lines have been Towns permitted to be traversed. permitted to be laid down in the main streets and thoroughfares of the cities, so that the trains may traverse them at prescribed speeds, and so that goods may be put upon trucks at the very doors of the warehouses and shops. Whilst most people in our country have, in fact, repelled the railroads from their localities, the people of the United States have invited them to their very streets and doors.

The outlay upon the American lines, has been from Comparative cost of construction. £8,700 up to £15,000 per mile, whilst the average cost in Great Britain has been nearly £40,000 per mile. In this estimate of cost, we have, of course, to consider the relative character of the lines. The American lines are almost invariably single, whilst the English railroads are mostly double lines. In other respects the American railroads are, as a rule, very inferior to ours. A railroad has been defined to consist of earthworks, sleepers, and rails. The earthworks of

----

constituting the first call. In some States the non-payment of a call is followed by the confiscation of the previous payments; in others a fine is imposed on the shareholders; in others the share is sold, and if the produce be less than the price at which it was delivered, the surplus can be recovered from the shareholder by process of law. In all cases, the Act creating a company fixes a time within which the work must be completed, under penalty of forfeiture. The traffic in shares before the definite constitution of the company, is prohibited."

the American railroads are, for the most part, of a very
simple character.　From the generally level surfaces
through which their lines are made, (in the Prairie districts especially) little has been required but to lay out
the track, and I am afraid that the proper preparation
of the road-bed has not always been as well attended
to as it should have been.　The timber for the
sleepers has been obtained from the roadside, or from
the woods in the immediate neighbourhoods.　The
supply has usually been abundant : and it has immensely contributed to the economic construction of
the road, enabling the constructors to lay down sleepers
at much more frequent intervals than we usually find
them in Europe.　The rails have been usually obtained
from England, Wales, or Scotland, and I believe that
in many cases the cost of the iron has formed, in
America, the largest proportion of the cost of the
construction of the lines.　The rails are generally too
light.

With regard to some other points of American railroad construction, no comparison can be instituted
between the arrangements on the other side of the
Atlantic and those which prevail amongst ourselves.
There are scarcely any artificial drains.　The ballasting
of their lines is often very imperfect ; indeed, I believe
it has not been thought necessary generally to ballast
a line at all until after it has been opened, and the
consequence, it need scarcely be said, has been very
imperfect working and serious detriment to the rails
until the road-bed is drained and ballast is complete.
The railway stations in America are also very inferior.
For the most part, they are mere wooden erections of

a temporary character, although, it should be observed, the land on which they are erected has been generally freely given by parties who well understand the greatly-enhanced value which a railway station brings to every adjacent property. On the more important lines, however, the stations are gradually rebuilt, substantially and in every respect suitably, from the income of the road.

I observed very little tunnelling on the American railways. Most of their bridges and viaducts are constructed on wooden piling in a very inexpensive manner. *Tunnels, Bridges, and Viaducts.*

The influence of railroads on the value of real estates along their lines, and in the cities in which they terminate, is so well understood in America, as to have afforded important financial facilities to their construction. It is not the public who are invited in America to take railway shares; they are subscribed for in a wholly different manner. In order to promote the construction of a line, not only does the State which it traverses frequently afford it facilities with respect to land, but pecuniary facilities are often given by the cities and towns giving securities for certain amounts on their Municipal Bonds. The cities in which it is to have its termini also agree to subscribe for portions of its share capital, and so do the inhabitants of the towns and villages through which it is to pass. This is a very important feature of the American railway system, inasmuch as it gives the inhabitants of each district which a railway traverses a direct local and individual interest in the promotion and well-working of the line. Every one, in fact, is interested in contributing traffic to his own railway. *The Capital of a Railroad frequently subscribed for by the State traversed and the Cities served.*

T

Cost of construction largely thrown on the Revenue of the lines.

Not only the whole cost of maintaining the roads, but a very considerable proportion of the cost of their construction, has, in the case of the majority of the lines in America, been thrown *upon revenue.* I am afraid that the consequence of this has been injurious to public confidence in the American rail-

Effect on public confidence,

ways as commercial securities. Where lines are imperfectly constructed in the first instance—where they have to bear all the effects of climate and of wear and tear, whilst in indifferent condition, it is quite obvious that the cost of reparations, even in the very early stages of their working, must be a serious burden. And where all this is thrown, at once, on revenue,

and upon Shareholders.

adequate dividends cannot be expected. Yet many shareholders in American railways, constructed with such limited amounts of capital as to make it obvious that they must have large debits which could only be liquidated from their resources, have never ceased to complain that they have not received dividends out of receipts, which have been necessarily appropriated to perfecting construction, and making good deficiencies which ought originally to have been provided for out of capital.

Fish Jointing.

Another great deficiency in America arises from the absence of the simple system of "Fish Jointing," which appears scarcely to have been introduced at all into the States. Of all things for such a country, and for such a climate as that of America, and for railroads constructed as theirs are, on transverse sleepers, sufficiently close together, but not very well imbedded, fish-joints are especially desirable—I might say absolutely requisite. It is owing to the absence of fish-jointing that those accidents, so common from what is termed technically " the engine mounting," occur. Such accidents are not possible where the ends of the joints are securely " fished " by plates bolted on each side of the ends of the rails, rendering them a part of the continuous line. The adoption of this system would altogether obviate the cause from which six out of every eight railway accidents in America arises, as shown by the reports ; and I hold it to be the worst possible economy not to introduce this system, especially on lines where rails of light weight are used, or where heavy trains or high speeds are common.

The progress of railways in America has been rapid. The following table will show the number of miles completed in periods of two years, from 1838 to 1860 :—

The absence of fish joints a frequent source of accident.

Progress of Railroads

RAILROAD MILEAGE IN THE UNITED STATES.			
Year.	Miles.	Year.	Miles.
1838	1,843	1850	8,827
1840	2,167	1852	12,841
1842	3,863	1854	19,195
1844	4,285	1856	23,724
1846	4,828	1858	27,158
1848	6,491	1860	31,185

from 1838 to 1860.

The railways in America are almost universally *single track* lines, and this fact has to be regarded in estimating the amount of railroad accommodation provided for the United States in comparison with that of other countries. It is a common thing to hear the American railroads spoken of as exceeding in

The Railroads of America are single tracks.

T 2

length those of all the rest of the world put together. But those who speak in this way do not appear conscious of the fact that the greater proportion of the English and French lines are double lines; and that when we speak, for example, in England, of 10,500 miles of railway open in 1860, that estimate of mileage does not include duplicate, and even in some cases triplicate, lines of communication.

No. of miles open, 1860.

The number of miles of railroad open in each State in 1860 is shown in the following table :—

NUMBER OF MILES OPEN IN EACH STATE.			
State.	Miles Open.	State.	Miles Open.
Ohio...............	3057	New Hampshire.	658
Pennsylvania ...	2943	Alabama	643
Illinois............	2925	Connecticut	608
New York	2809	Vermont	575
Indiana............	2058	Iowa..............	549
Virginia...........	1805	Kentucky.........	531
Georgia...........	1401	Maine	476
Massachusetts ...	1314	Maryland.........	406
Tennessee.........	1283	Louisiana.........	328
South Carolina...	978	Florida............	326
Wisconsin........	937	Texas	294
North Carolina...	887	Delaware	137
Missouri	813	Rhode Island ...	104
Michigan	807	California.........	70
Mississippi	798	Arkansas	38
New Jersey	627		

Railroad development in the North Western States.

This table will illustrate the extent to which railway enterprize has been developed in the North-Western States, especially in Ohio, Illinois and Indiana. The Illinois Central Railroad, which passes through 706 miles of that State, was endowed with *alternate* sections of land for a width of three miles on each side of its track, the State reserving each other section. It thus acquired 2,595,000 acres in an excellent farming region; and from the sale of these lands the expenses of construction, &c., have been or will be met. The effect of this policy in the development of the State has already been referred to.

Most of the American lines were originally made in short lengths, as lines of communication between different towns in the same State; and without regard to any general system of communication for the nation. It follows, that even in the cases of lines which are now united and brought under a single management, much diversity of construction and a great want of unity of system is observable. One of the great deficiencies of the American railroad system is, in fact, the absence of a general policy of management. Scarcely any attempts are made to render the working of lines convenient to travellers by working the trains of one company in conjunction with another; and this gives rise to complaints on the part of the public, which may, some day or other, be made to afford a ground of excuse for governmental interference. Nothing can be more desirable for the success of American railroad enterprizes than well considered general arrangements for the working and interchange of traffic. *Want of uniformity in construction and working.*

Remarkable as has been the rapidity with which the American railroads have been constructed, and great as is the total mileage already made, the railroad accommodation of the United States is not to be *Insufficiency of the existing railroads.*

regarded as by any means meeting the requirements
of the country. The rapid growth of the system
has only been co-equal with the rapid growth of the
population : the extent of mileage is attributable to
the vast extent of territory settled, and the great
distances between the seats of population.

Insufficiency
of the Rail-
ways in the
South,

In many parts of the States, indeed, the existing
railways are quite insufficient. In the South, the
system is very imperfectly developed. Whilst slaves
existed, there was a determined hostility in the
Southern States to the expansion of any general
railway system, arising from the apprehension that
it would be used for the escape of slaves. Any one
who glances at a railroad map of the United States,
will observe, that whilst the Northern States are
covered with lines, the Southern have only a few main
trunk roads, and that the greatest care has been taken
to prevent those lines from communicating with the
Free States. It will be necessary to correct all this,
and to bring the South into much more intimate
communication with the North than she stands at
present.

and in the
West.

From West to East, also, the present railways are
quite insufficient for the growing traffic. The lines of
communication from the West by canal, &c., which
existed previously to railways, have not been affected
by their construction. The produce of the Western
States has, in fact, increased faster than the means of
transport, and additional facilities for the conveyance
of goods are urgently required. It is of the utmost importance to the development of the West that no time
should be lost in making this additional provision.

The extent of the traffic of a railway depends upon its
capacity to convey produce, and, consequently, the extent of that produce is limited to the capacity of the
line and the certainty of delivery within reasonable
periods. An inadequate railroad provision, and a corresponding uncertainty as to conveyance and delivery
of freights, must have the effect of checking production
in the West, and consequently of checking the capital
of the East from seeking employment in the West.
Railway facilities are now the measure of the prosperity of the country.

The capital invested in railroads in the United States,
in January, 1861, amounted to $1,177,994,828, or
(say) £235,600,000. This amount represented the
" cost and equipments" of 31,168 miles. But, for
reasons already adverted to, we cannot judge of the
cost of American railways from the capital subscribed
for their construction ; and I incline to agree with a
writer in the New American Cyclopædia, who says,
" While the English roads exhibit an extraordinary
amount of first cost, it does not appear that the expenditures for actual construction have been in much
larger proportion than in the United States." I
incline to think that, considering all the amounts
abstracted from revenue, to complete, repair, renew,
and maintain the roads, to add to the originally
imperfect rolling stock, double the tracks and sidings,
construct station accommodation, &c., the cost of the
American railroads has been quite equal to ours,
especially considering the large proportion of English
capital expended in preliminary expenses.

Importance of adequate Railroad provision for Western development.

Capital invested in American Railroads.

CHAPTER II.

RAILWAY MANAGEMENT.

Comparative cost of maintenance in America and England.

IN one of his valuable " Letters on American Railways" published in the present year, 1866,* Mr. Lance has given a synopsis of the cost of maintaining six leading railways in England and America for one year. The result comes out as follows per train mile run :—

	COST OF WORKING PER TRAIN MILE.		
	Expenditure on	America.	England.
1	Maintenance of Way.....	18·87905	5·36424
2	Locomotive Power	21·59805	8·04043
3	Rolling Stock — repairs and renewals..........	10·03886	2·39016
4	Transportation Expenses	12·77770	10·28949
5	General Charges	2·04185	1·42394
6	Special Charges..........	6·57710	3·69964
	Pence.........	71·91261	31·20790

These results

It thus appears that the cost of working on the American lines is considerably more than double that of working in England, being at the rate of nearly 72d. or 6s. per train mile, against 31d. or 2s. 7d.

Now if we come to examine the items included in

---

* Letter No. 2, on "The New York Central." By William Lance, Railway Actuary, 26, Throgmorton Street, London, 1866.

the expenditure under these six heads, we shall arrive, I think, at a tolerably correct conclusion as to the main defects and advantages of the American system of railway management.

1. Under the head of "MAINTENANCE of WAY," we find the principal charge to be for "repairs of road and buildings." These items in America average nearly 17*d*. per train mile, against 3½*d*. in England. This illustrates the position on which I enlarged in the last chapter : that a large proportion of the cost of construction in America was thrown not upon capital, but on revenue account. Nothing, in my opinion, can be more erroneous. The shareholders of a line are entitled to its earnings ; and it is as great a misappropriation of income to make it supply the means of increasing the value of capital, as it is a misappropriation of capital to employ it for the purpose of providing dividends. We are constantly hearing complaints in England from some dissatisfied shareholder, or some one on the Stock Exchange, anxious to "*bear*" railway property, that, in particular cases, "Dividends have been paid out of capital account;" but, in America, we find no less than 1*s*. 5*d*. per train mile, or nearly a quarter of the entire cost of working, spent in what in reality is an expenditure due exclusively to capital account. In cases where money is applied, in this way, those who have embarked in a company on the faith of low estimates for cost of construction do not get their own. They have invested their money in expectation of a return ; but instead of obtaining it, when fairly earned, they find the profit applied to making good deficiencies. In some of the

railway companies of America, enormous sums have been received and applied to the reduction of bond capital, without any benefit to the existing shareholders, except in the form of a contingent reversionary interest. It is not often that we find railways earning more than they distribute ; but this does occur in America. The earnings are agreeable to contemplate, but their non-distribution is very much to be objected to.

Locomotive
Power.

II.   Under the head of " LOCOMOTIVE POWER," we find that "repairs" amount to 7*d*. per train mile in America, and to $3\frac{1}{2}d$. in England. The actual "working" costs above $3\frac{1}{2}d$. in America, and under 2*d*. per train mile in England.   The "fuel and stores" are 9*d*. per train mile in America, and $2\frac{1}{4}d$. in England.   I apprehend these excesses in the United States arise for the most part from the inferior quality of the fuel, and from the deficient number of engines.   In consequence of the locomotives being more severely worked than they are in England, they require more frequent repairs and renewals, and these repairs and renewals are rendered the more necessary, in consequence of sulphuretted coal more speedily injuring the works. It no doubt also occurs, that the locomotives are more frequently thrown out of repair and are more rapidly worn out by the indifferent condition of the roads, and also the accidents thereby occasioned.

Rolling
Stock.

III.   This seems the more probable from the very heavy relative charge for "repairs and renewals of rolling stock." The "rolling stock" costs 10*d*. per train mile in America, to $2\frac{1}{4}d$. in England, and it is all "renewals and repairs." The quantity of rolling stock in America no doubt is insufficient. It does not suffice for, nor will it bear, the work it is required to perform. The consequence is, that the equipments of a line having been, from the first, imperfect, revenue is made to pay an undue and excessive proportion for repairs, renewals, and additions to the rolling stock, and the wear of the rolling stock is more rapid by reason of the imperfect state of the road.

IV. The expenses of "transport" are also generally more than in England; wages, which constitute the larger proportion of this item being higher in America. But there is one figure under the head of "transport" in which the cost in England is much greater than the cost in America. I refer to the item for "collection and delivery." The whole system of collecting and delivering the goods carried by railway differs in America from the system in England; and I am bound to say that I think the English system much the best.

The rule of English companies is to undertake all the various duties involved in removing goods from the premises of the consignor and delivering them into the premises of the consignee. Convenient arrangements exist in every town of even second or third-rate importance in England, under which the service of collection and delivery of goods is performed by the staff of the railway companies at moderate and fixed rates; and these charges are not uncommonly embraced in the railway freight.

In the chief ports, London, Liverpool, Hull, Newcastle, Glasgow, &c., goods are carried by the companies direct to the docks and shipping, and the public are thus secured a certain and punctual performance

Marginal notes:
Transportation charges.

Collection and Delivery,

performed in England by the Railway Companies.

of transport under one responsibility, and fixed payments, which are at once reasonable and ascertainable beforehand.

The American system of Collection and Delivery by "Express Companies."

This system gives the English companies a more intimate acquaintance with the necessities of traders ; and promotes a more direct interest between the companies and their customers. It is, besides, a source of profit directly and indirectly ; for carriers, and what are called in America, " express companies," who conduct their business over railways, not only impose all sorts of arbitrary and petty charges upon the public, according to their opportunities ; but they deprive the companies of the profit to which they are legitimately entitled, by packing parcels together, and so getting them conveyed at a less charge—by falsely declaring goods, both as regards class and weight, and by other well-known contrivances for evading proper payments.

The inconvenience and expense thereby occasioned.

It is clearly the interest and duty of railway companies to take upon themselves *all* the duties of carriers of goods ; and not as they do in America, only that part of them which embraces the conveyance from one railway station to another ; thus leaving the public exposed to the inconvenience and extra expense they must incur by having to engage the services of town carters or others, to remove their goods to and from the railway.

Evil effects

I am afraid that this system of collecting and delivering goods by means of Express Companies is fraught with evil in another way. The proprietors and managers of many of these companies are, I am told, the directors and officers of railways ; who are consequently obtaining for themselves a revenue which we in England should consider ought to belong to the line they serve, and who, besides this, acquire, by means of these companies, a power and authority over the railway which cannot but be prejudicial to its independent working. In many cases the negotiation of rates is entirely taken out of the hands of the railway management by the action of the "Express" companies; who, in their turn, are very apt to insist on the railway companies entering into contracts with themselves at lower prices than those at which they serve the public. Thus both parties suffer—the railway companies, and the public whose goods they convey. *on the Railroad Companies,* *and on the Public.*

V. In the General Expenses, including the direction, management, office expenses, law expenses, and contingencies, there is not a material difference between the cost in England and America. The office expenses are largest in America: the law expenses are largest in England. The entire expenditure on all these charges is 2*d.* per train mile in America to about 1½*d.* in England. *General Expenses.*

VI. The special charges of America which appear to be nearly double those of England, arise from the heavy taxation imposed on railways during the war, and also from the condition of the currency. These are charges from which it may be hoped that the railway companies of America will be speedily relieved. It will be remembered that the President of the United States, in his last Message to Congress, thus wisely expressed himself :— *Special Charges.*

"It is of the first necessity for the maintenance of the Union, that COMMERCE SHOULD BE FREE AND UNOBSTRUCTED.

No State can be justified in any device to tax the transit of travel and commerce between States. The position of many States is such that, if they were allowed to take advantage of it for purposes of local revenue, the commerce between States might be injuriously burdened, or even virtually prohibited. It is best, while the country is still young, and while the tendency to dangerous monopolies of this kind is still feeble, to use the power of Congress so as to prevent any selfish impediment to the free circulation of men and merchandise. *A tax on travel and merchandise, in their transit, constitutes one of the worst forms of monopoly,* and the evil is increased if coupled with a denial of the choice of route. When the vast extent of our country is considered, it is plain that every obstacle to the free circulation of commerce between the States ought to be sternly guarded against by appropriate legislation, within the limits of the Constitution."

Working Expenses in relation to Earnings.

But there is another form in which to look at these items. Mr. Lance renders them in proportion to the relative train mileage run. But let us look at them as they relate to the earnings. In America, the receipts of the six railways whose expenditure has been thus dissected, amounted to 109·4 pence per train mile: in England the receipts of the six lines were only 64·3 pence per train mile. The American lines,

Large Earnings of American Lines.

therefore, were able to bear a larger proportion of cost of working than the English lines; and if the expenditure had been properly apportioned they would have paid much larger dividends.

Dividends.

As it is, let me observe, that the dividends of American railroads can not be generally considered unsatisfactory. I have before me a "table, compiled " from the New York Share Lists, of the financial de- " tails of all the dividend-paying railroad companies " of the United States during 1865," and whilst I find the Camden and Amboy paying 35 per cent., some Ohio and Pennsylvania lines paying 25 to 30 per cent., and many others paying 20, 19, 18, 16, 15, 14, 12, 11, and 10 per cent., I find only four on the list that pay less than 5 per cent., and only one of those is of any importance.   Despite every drawback, therefore, the first-class American railroads are better investments than our own.

The rates in America are generally low, both for passengers and goods, and yet there are differences of opinion whether they are low enough.   The New York Central, perhaps one of the most important of the American lines, is restricted by law to a charge at the rate of *two cents* per passenger per mile.   This is a most successful railroad, paying a steady dividend of 9 per cent. on a capital exceeding $42,000,000— (£8,500,000) : yet the company assert that the rate for passengers involves a loss instead of a gain, and the Legislature has been appealed to for authority to increase the rates.   On the other hand, it is said that American railroads would make much larger profits were they to adopt a system of " second-class " cars ; thereby affording travellers the opportunity of consulting their convenience and their pockets, by travelling either expensively or cheaply as they thought proper.

The present car-system is bad, both for the public and the companies, in an economic point of view. Uniformity of class, means uniformity of rate : and whilst some American companies are precluded under the powers of their charters from accepting what the more opulent class of travellers would willingly pay for superior accommodation, they must of neces-

Rates.

Passenger Traffic.

Uniformity of class.

sity keep up the price to the more needy classes, who would be quite ready to set diminished charges against moderate comfort, and any supposed admission of social inferiority involved in travelling in a cheaper class. It may be well worthy the consideration of the American railway administration whether they should not adopt at least two classes of carriage in their trains: and obtain powers where necessary to make higher charges than they are at present authorized to do, to those who elect to travel with superior comfort.

Second Class carriages recommended.

Whilst upon this subject of carriages, let me add some observations as to the conveniences provided for travellers in America.

Conveniences provided for Travellers.

The great distances over which it is necessary for Americans to travel has induced more attention on the part of the railway administration to the conveniences for long journeys, than is found in England : and some of the English companies, especially those running night trains, would do well to emulate their transatlantic brethren, by adopting thsoe conveniences in such a modified form as would be suitable to the habits and requirements of English travellers. For instance, the chief American lines have attached to their night trains "sleeping cars," which are so arranged, that while serving the purpose of a comfortable railway carriage in the day time, they can at night be converted into as comfortable sleeping chambers. Good beds are made up by the train attendant, and the occupants can traverse from 160 to 240 miles of their journey, insensible to all the inconveniences of a night journey on Eng-

"Sleeping Cars."

lish lines. In the morning they rise refreshed, and
without that sense of weariness which every one expe-
riences after a night's journey in England. Washing-
rooms and other essentials of a long journey are also Washing-
provided in the " sleeping cars," so that the passengers
can make their toilet independent of the stoppages of
the train. All this valuable additional accommodation
is furnished for a small extra payment of from 5s. to
7s. 6d. for the journey ; which payment is recognized,
and gives the passenger the right to the occupation of
his bed. The public are therefore not under the necessity of bribing the guards to secure them a compartment : nor, having paid, are they subject to be
dispossessed, as not unfrequently happens on this
side of the water.*

"High speeds" are not generally in favour on Speeds.
American lines; indeed, as a rule their condition

---

* I add a description of a "Sleeping Car " which can be used
also by ingenious arrangements as a Day Car, and is now running
between New York and St. Louis.—" The car will accommodate
about forty-eight persons. The partitions usual to sleeping cars
are entirely excluded, and the only things substituted for them are
columns of German silver, which improvements give the car a
cheerful appearance, and allow a free ventilation from end to end.
The windows of the state rooms are of plate glass. The seats are
covered, and the floor carpeted. The car is provided with washing
facilities, tables, and the other appurtenances pertaining to an hotel,
parlour, or bedroom. The curtains in front of the berths are of buff
brocatelle, bordered with blue and trimmed with silver lace. The
windows of the car are of fine cut glass, with tastefully executed
designs. The car will be lighted by three large lamps, the globes
of which are of fine cut glass. The car is heated by means of
stoves at each end, so constructed as to allow the hot air to pass
along the whole length of the car."

U

does not admit of high speeds. The rates of the Express trains between New York and Boston do not exceed 29½ miles per hour, which is about the average of the leading lines. As regards loads, their goods trains (or freight trains, as they are called in America) are, as a rule, heavier than those in England; but they are drawn generally by lighter engines, which accounts for the deficiency of speed. Although the Americans are great travellers, there are no such things as "Excursion Trains," or at any rate they are very rare. It would be worth while trying the experiment. The Americans appear much more generally to accustom themselves to long journeys. The experience of the New York Central, the Erie, and the Pennsylvania Central Railways shows that the through traffic is 65 per cent. of the whole.

I must not omit to refer to the manner in which the goods traffic is worked upon some of the lines. The American railroads, as already noticed, rarely afford more than one pair of rails. The trains pass each other at certain stations on the road, when the first which arrives is compelled to wait until the other, coming from the opposite direction, may pass it. This could hardly work if the trains were very numerous; but as a rule in America they are not numerous: certainly not so numerous as they ought to be. There are, however, instances where the traffic has got far beyond the capacity of a single line of rails, and the difficulty has been to arrange for it without laying down a second track, or doubling the line. On the Baltimore and Ohio Railway this has been very ingeniously accomplished. That rail-

Express trains.

Goods trains.

Excursion trains.

Through traffic.

Mode of working single lines,

way has a very large coal and a very considerable
goods traffic. It is obliged also to run three passenger trains each way a day. The way the trade
is conducted is this. A passenger train is started
early in the morning. In succession to it there is
started "a convoy" of trains, consisting of as many
as fifteen goods trains following each other at five
minutes intervals. Some hours after another passenger train is started, followed again by "a convoy"
of goods trains. And so on with a third passenger train, and a third "convoy" of coal or goods
trains. By this arrangement the passenger trains are
kept entirely clear of the goods trains; and of course
the arrangements are so made that the convoys from
each end pass each other without difficulty. Thus
forty-five goods trains and three passenger trains are
taken each way each day on one pair of rails. This
struck me as being a very ingenious arrangement for
meeting a great difficulty.

CHAPTER III.

THE RAILWAY FUTURE OF AMERICA.

Great advantages conferred by American railroads IN speaking of the railroads of America, we must not forget to look at the immense positive advantage they have conferred upon the country. It is to railways, that America owes its recent development. Its rivers and lakes afford, no doubt, great actual opportunities on the whole nation, for internal communication ; but the lands of America are so wide-spread, that the more distant territories could scarcely have been reached, or, if reached, could never have been cultivated to profit, without a means of rapidly communicating with the seats of population. The Commissioner of Census of 1860 de- and especially on the Western States, clares, that so great are the benefits railroads have conferred on all departments of agriculture, " that, " *if the entire cost of the railroads between the* " *Atlantic and Western States had been levied on* " *the farmers of the Central West, they could have* " *paid it, and been immensely the gainers.*" This proposition, adds the writer, becomes evident, if we look at the mode in which railways have become which could not have been cultivated to profit beneficial. They effect that which could not have been done without them : they secure to the pro- ducer very nearly the price of the Atlantic markets, which is greatly in advance of what could be obtained on his farm; they enable the producer to dispose of his products at all times, and consequently at the best prices; and they increase rapidly the settlement and production of the interior States, which must be beneficial to the entire nation.

Forty years ago, the surplus products of Ohio had accumulated beyond the means of transport, and wheat sold in the interior at 37 cents per bushel, and Indian corn at 10 cents. Then the Erie Canal was opened, and soon after the Ohio Canal, and prices were raised more than 50 per cent. Now that the means of transport have been increased, the price of flour at Cincinnati is nearly double its price in 1826, the price of Indian corn four times, and the price of pork three times as great. On the other hand, the prices of corn and meat on the seaboard have not been reduced in the least. It is therefore evident that the bulk of the gain obtained by the increased facility of transport, has gone to the producer.

Nor is this all. Not only have railroads cheapened the transport of the produce, but also the cost of the transport of every article of manufacture required by the producer. They have brought him labour and machinery, and articles of foreign growth, with which he could scarcely have been supplied without railways. Sugar and coffee were no dearer at Cincinnati in 1860 than in 1835, although the population of the Western States in that interval had increased in the enormous proportions already mentioned. During that interval, also, the lands of Illinois, Indiana, Michigan, Wisconsin, Minnesota, and other States, had become of substantial

without facilities for transport.

Gain to the producer by

increased prices for produce;

without increase in the price of labour, &c.

Consequent enhancement of the value of Land.

value.* Between 1850 and 1860, the value of the farms throughout the West had doubled; which would have been impossible had there not been the facilities afforded by railroads for conveying the produce of those farms to markets.

Insufficiency of the existing railroads,

But it is to be added, that even now these facilities are by no means sufficient for the West. We have seen that the Atlantic and Great Western railroad has as yet been unable to convey from the oil wells anything beyond a small proportion of their prolific and increasing supply. The traffic of the wonderful coal fields which it traverses has been scarcely touched; its cattle traffic has not been commenced. In the same way, the corn-producers of the Western States are quite unable to find sufficient means of conveyance for their produce, because the railroads from west to east are choked with traffic.

and evils occasioned thereby.

The existing railroad requirements of the West are, in fact, insufficient. The main arteries of communication are the great railroads known as the "New York Central" Railway, the "Erie" Railway, with the "Atlantic and Great Western" Railway, the "Pennsylvania Central Railway," and the "Baltimore and Ohio" Railway. But to ensure what is needed in America, these lines ought to be doubled, and no time ought to be lost in doing it. At present, because they cannot carry the produce, the whole traffic of the country is subject to two gigantic evils, arising, first,

* "The best lands in Illinois were worth but $1. 25 an acre prior to the construction of railroads. They are now worth $20."— *Report of the Commissioner of Census*, p. clxix.

from uncertainty of conveyance ; and second, from uncertainty of charge.

Out of about 9,000,000 tons of produce annually conveyed from west to east, it is estimated that the canals carry one-third : the railways the remainder. But there is a period of the year when the canals are frozen up. The whole task of conveyance then falls upon the railways ; and the consequence is, not only an immediate rise in their rates, but absolute inability to conduct the traffic. The results are often most disastrous. I know one case, in which 40,000 barrels of flour were detained at Toledo (nearly half-way between Chicago and New York) for several months, in consequence of want of carriage. A vast mass of produce is yearly destroyed, from the inability of the carriers to forward it. The owners are ruined, and parties in the Eastern States who advance money on this produce charge excessive rates to cover the risks of delay.

Injurious consequences of want of carriage,

Now, what is the effect of this ? The producer, the merchant, the railway company, and the consumer, are all directly injured : but the indirect injury extends far beyond those interests. The whole produce of the West, and consequently the entire cultivation of America, is affected. If the produce cannot be carried, it can only find local markets. If it only finds local markets, prices must abate. If prices abate, the stimulus to the cultivation of land is lost. If the land is not required for cultivation, in the same proportion it necessarily diminishes in value. The prosperity of the West, the value of its produce, the value of its land, and the extent of land cultivated—all depend, therefore, upon increased facilities for the convey-

and the indirect injury inflicted on the whole country.

ance of produce ; and those facilities railroads must afford.

Policy which should govern American railroads.

The Atlantic and Great Western Railroad, of which I am Chairman of the London Board of Control, and which I went to the United States to inspect, is in communication with the other main arteries I have mentioned. By means of them it will connect, when complete, the whole Atlantic sea-board with all the great depôts of produce in the Western and South Western States. It will unite New York, Philadelphia, Baltimore, and Washington with Cincinnati, St. Louis, Chicago, Cleveland, and Knoxville, and by the International Bridge at Buffalo it will connect the whole Canadian System with the United States System of Railways. I look forward to the time when the Atlantic and Great Western system will tend more than anything else to a complete development of the country. But it must be accompanied by a large, a liberal, and a progressive policy. The railway system, in fact, must go hand in hand with the advance of national prosperity. *The American public ought never to be satisfied until they are able to calculate on fixed moderate prices for freight, and fixed periods for its delivery.*

Without obtruding my views in connexion with any particular railway, I think I am entitled to propound

Moderate rates:

the principles on which I consider the railway arrangements in America ought to be conducted. And my first principle is, that those arrangements ought to be such as will secure ample accommodation. The public

Certainty of communication:

are entitled under the Railway system to certainty of communication ; they ought also to be ensured uni-

formity of rates, subject to needful and beneficial alte- Uniformity of working.
rations, generally in the direction of reduction. In the
conduct of our Railways in England this is, unquestionably, the principle by which we are influenced.
Our policy is almost invariably in favour of low fares
for passengers, and reduced rates for goods. It appears
to me that, consistently with the policy of the country,
it ought to be so in the United States. If it has not
been altogether so, up to the present time, I am
entitled to say that it has been no fault of those with
whom I have the pleasure to be associated. The
fact is, as I have already indicated, that the American
railways have been made, and are conducted, too
much in detached portions, and too little on a large
and liberal system of co-operation. The wide extent,
the enlarged resources, the rapid development of the
territory, accounts, very much, for this. Where railways are made in short lengths, for the purposes of
local traffic, they cannot be expected to supply the
wants of rapidly increasing communities, extending
over wide spaces. But I desire to see this original The Railways should be worked as one great system.
error corrected. I want the American railways to be
worked as one great system. I am convinced that
this will subserve the benefit of all the Companies as
well as of the public. It may be accomplished by
substituting for a system of jealousy, rivalry, and
opposition, one of common understanding, compromise, alliance, friendship, mutuality, and interchange :
each line acting as a part of one great entire whole :
the railways, in fact, considering themselves not a
system of States, but a system of United States. I
do not recommend this system as a theory : there

Advantage of a uniform system of working illustrated.

are practical proofs of the advantages resulting from it. Some years ago, the London and North Western Railway, which now brings Scotland, Ireland, and Wales, into communication under one united system,

The London and North Western Railway,

with Liverpool, Manchester, Birmingham, the whole of the Midland district and the Metropolis of England, consisted of a series of lines, made by different companies, with different objects, very many of them merely local. The system of that railway, and of the other lines which it has now amalgamated, was one of opposition. It proved an unprofitable system : costly in its working : entailing vast expenses as the consequence of competition : injurious to its own prosperity, and most disastrous to many who were placed in antagonism to it. Of late years, all this has been altered. The various competing lines have been brought into combination with the one great

before and after the adoption of a policy of Amalgamation.

system on equally advantageous terms. What has been the consequence? No increase of rates : no diminution of train accommodation : no detraction from the conveniences afforded to the public. On the contrary, the system of the one great line, and of all its branches and ramifications, has received immense development. It is the one line, of our country, of which we never hear complaints. Its trains are unequalled for speed, security, regularity, and, I believe I may add, for cheapness. It sets the great example to the other railways of Great Britain, whether as regards punctuality, speed, accommodation, or economy. With a road unequalled in its character, and chiefly laid with the most costly metals (steel rails, manufactured at great expense, being laid over the most frequented portions of the line), it is enabled to sustain a traffic, which is conducted on almost every portion of the district, through every hour of the night and day. By the use of an ample supply of the best locomotives, with an abundant rolling stock, it is able to carry on a trade, vast and heavy, consisting not only of passengers, for short and long distances, but of goods and of the heaviest minerals, with the most perfect despatch and punctuality. Despite all the vicissitude of storm at sea or on shore, it delivers the mails between Dublin and London with greater punctuality than the Post-office can deliver them between one portion of London and another. Its express trains travel at the rate of nearly sixty miles an hour, and are rarely, if ever, delayed. Upon the delivery of its goods, the merchant and the manufacturer can depend. The markets are supplied by it, with such regularity, that I know of no cases in which complaints are brought before the courts for losses sustained in consequence of its default. Its rates afford such facilities for the trade of England, that although it necessarily conducts the larger part of the business of this empire, it economizes, instead of increasing, the burden of our trade. There is no facility which it does not afford *without competition*. And how is this accomplished? By an united system, which looks for profit to the development of commerce: by a system of co-operation, good understanding, and mutual interchange; by a system which has been brought to perfection by a determination to develop the resources of the nation; by a resolve to meet the demands of the customers of the line, at the most

[margin: Its traffic and its rates.]

[margin: Their influence on the Commerce of the United Kingdom.]

reasonable rates, and to perfect for them the science of reception, conveyance, and delivery, so that each and all shall be brought to the highest point of railway perfection.

The same system required in America.

Now, so far as I and my friends are connected with the railway system of America, I say that we shall not be contented—that we will never rest contented—until we see the same system developed between St. Louis, Chicago, and Cincinnati, in the west, and New York, Philadelphia, Baltimore, and Boston, in the east of the United States, which prevails between Dublin, Belfast, Edinburgh, and Glasgow in the north, and Manchester, Liverpool, Birmingham, and London, in our own country. I only regret to think that it is not now done in the United States as it is with us; but, so far as we are concerned, it is intended to be done, and in the interests of America, I may add the expression of my conviction, that, at whatever expense or trouble, it must be accomplished.

Certain effects of an improved Railway system on American development.

I have already shown that, without railways, the States of the great West would have been nothing. With railways they are—what they are. With a proper development of the railway system, they may be ten times—nay, a hundred times greater than they are. With us, in England, railways can only reach and bring together developed fields of wealth, agricultural, manufacturing, and commercial. But wherever a railway penetrates in America, it reaches some field of unopened productiveness and enterprize. The railways which reach the Western States cannot at present convey their produce. The line I am especially connected with has been unable to carry the

abundance of oil which has been offered for its conveyance from one very small portion of the district
which it professes to serve. People in London are
astonished when they hear that the returns of the
"Atlantic and Great Western Railway" are every
month as great as those of the leading English
railways. It is difficult to bring them to realize the
fact that that line, with many sources of profitable
traffic not yet touched, is earning almost as large
a sum per mile per week as the London and North
Western Railway itself.* But there is nothing surprising in the fact, when we consider the character of
the produce of the country—its great variety—the
wide field over which it extends — the breadth of
country interested in the traffic. The London and

Immense
fields of pro-
ductiveness
and wealth
developed by
American
railroads.

---

* The extent of the railway traffic in America is remarkably
shown by the following statement of the rapidly increasing monthly
traffic returns of the Atlantic and Great Western Railway :—

The Atlantic
and Great
Western
traffic.

1865.	Miles open.	Passengers, Mails, &c.	Freight.	Total.	
				1865.	1864.
		$	$	$	$
January........	322	111,751	249,379	301,130	207,298
February......	,,	109,718	277,930	387,648	229,041
March.........	,,	113,412	336,403	449,815	226,733
April	,,	117,691	288,989	406,680	197,267
May	,,	135,434	324,988	460,442	214,679
June..........	,,	163,733	350,289	514,022	314,521
July..........	490	162,655	432,868	595,523	332,098
August........	,,	213,469	525,059	738,528	406,076
September	,,	210,914	466,711	677,625	446,044
October........	,,	207,861	512,050	719,911	396,847
November.....	,,	180,428	550,842	731,270	381,810
December.....	,,	157,499	442,763	600,262	357,566

Its extent
and rapid
increase.

Distances over which traffic is carried in America.

North Western carries goods between Liverpool and Manchester (30 miles), and between Manchester and Birmingham (90 miles), and between Liverpool and Manchester and London (say 200 miles) : here are its great traffics. But the American railways carry over spaces of more than 1,000 miles. St. Louis is distant from New York 1,200 miles ; Cincinnati and Chicago are distant from Philadelphia and Baltimore 850 miles. To these ports of shipment, therefore, the mileage from the producing districts in America is far greater than it is in England.

The effect on the receipts of American lines.

And when it is considered that every train on the main lines of America is over-laden with freight, and that they have, indeed, far more than they can carry, I do not think there is any reason for surprise at their accumulating and increasing profits. *

What is required for the future well-working of the existing system.

The great means of developing the system is co-operation. A system which will place the various great lines of railway in a position to carry any amount of freight which may be offered with certainty, regularity, and despatch, at fixed reasonable and economical rates of charge, is not only needed for the advantage of the railways themselves but for the prosperity and advancement of the country.

---

* It is due to my friend Mr. James McHenry, that I should state that his countrymen are indebted for this great system of railways entirely to his energy and foresight. In the midst of the Civil War the greater part of the Atlantic and Great Western system was constructed by funds supplied to him by friends having confidence in him and in his country ; and though the line has now passed into the hands of a corporation, with Directors both in America and England, the policy I have stated, as to its management and future, is the policy he again and again impressed on those conducting its affairs.

The value of the produce depends upon it : and consequently the success of the cultivator and the value of the land. On all these depend the immigration to the West, and the flow of capital which will be sent there to promote its cultivation and development. The future of the West depends upon its means of communication with the East : and the success of its means of communication with the East is, I believe, expressed in a few words, such as " PROMPT AND ECONOMICAL DELIVERY—IN A FIXED TIME AND AT A FIXED PRICE." *

I think I have said all I need say on this part of the subject. The first object of those who are interested in American railroads should be a combination for the due development of the traffic of the North. Next to that, it appears to me that the great object to be accomplished is to bring the immense chainwork of Northern railroads into closer communication with the Southern system, so that the whole South, its vast produce and its great resources, may be duly and advantageously developed. The importance of this connexion can scarcely be exaggerated. It must be borne in mind that the products of the South and of the North are entirely dissimilar, that the South is fed by Northern produce, whilst the commerce of the

New Railway systems needed.

The Northern system should be connected more closely with the Southern.

* Since writing this, I observe a bill brought into the New York Legislature compelling railways, under a penalty of one per cent. per diem on the value, to forward freight *not later than ten days after its receipt.* It may be questioned, however, whether the effect of such a measure would not be merely to cause the railroad companies *to refuse to receive* freights, or to *raise the rates* so as to cover the possible penalty. But the necessity of such a law proves the existence of sad mismanagement.

North is largely supplied by Southern productions. Hitherto the greater amount of the trade between North and South has been carried on coastwise, on the seaboard of the Atlantic, or by steamers down the Mississippi.

A link of less than 200 miles of railway, connecting the lines at Cincinnati, would place the whole network of railways in the North and in the South in such intercommunication that the necessity for all the varied shipments and transhipments incidental to a seaboard service would be rendered needless. The late President of the United States recognised the

importance, and was most anxious for the construction, of such a line, and mentioned it in more than one of his Messages; and now that the great cause for keeping one system of railways distinct from another is entirely removed, there can be no reason why this link should not be made, over which must pass the traffic of two regions equally dependant on each other.

I have already referred to the apprehensions of Railroad communications entertained in the Southern States during the existence of slavery. I cannot better illustrate the extent to which this feeling prevailed, than by quoting from an account of one of the most important railways in America.

" This railroad," writes the author, " is, to all intents and purposes, a Southern improvement, identified with Southern interests, and built by Southern capital. This fact gives it an enduring advantage over the rival lines of Pennsylvania and New York, and their connexions on non-slaveholding soil. This is, in fact, the only route by which Southerners can reach the Atlantic cities, *with their servants*, unmolested by the wily 'underground' interferences of crazy abolitionists, now swarming along all the great lines of travel in the States of Illinois, Ohio, and New York. When a few miles of intermediate railway are added, the population of the whole Southern country may reach Baltimore or Washington from Louisville without setting foot on a single inch of *inhospitable* ground. The road, therefore, without appealing to the feelings or interests of one class more than another, is, nevertheless, entitled from its geographical position, to all the preferences which the vast amount of Southern travel may confer."

Another extension of the railway system is felt by all the people of the United States to be most essential. Every one appreciates the importance of establishing railway intercourse across the continent from the shores of the Atlantic to those of the Pacific. Four different routes have been projected in different parts of the continent, and eventually, there can be little doubt, they will all be made. I shall not discuss the relative merits of the projected lines, only one of which is at present constructing. The great object, of course, is to connect San Francisco with New York. The effect of that connexion, politically, upon the Union, cannot be regarded as of too deep importance. If only for political purposes, the line *must* be made : and the nation must afford every possible encouragement to its early construction. But apart from political objects, there are other requirements which such a railway will supply. The mining interest of the United States alone can maintain such a railway. California and New York support, already, lines of packets from the one port to the other, by the circuitous route of Panama, occupying not less than twenty-two to twenty-eight days in the transit, and requiring several transhipments. A direct railway route, occupying only five or six days, and requiring no transhipments,

A line to the Pacific,

Connecting San Francisco and New York.

Its political necessity.

Certainty of the commercial success of a Pacific Railroad.

X

would, obviously, be attended with such superior advantages, that it would engross all the traffic. The Pacific Railway will, moreover, penetrate the new mining districts, especially those of Nevada and Colorado, and will bring to the Atlantic, by a direct conveyance, all the precious freight, which now reaches a market with great risk and at extreme cost. The effect of this railway, not only on the Pacific States, but on the Union, and on the world at large, cannot be over estimated.   Links in the chain of this great communication are in course of construction ; but this railway ought to be regarded *by the State as a whole.* It ought not to be permitted to be worked in a disjointed manner.   The public ought to have the benefit of such a line under an united system.   For the development of the resources of America, nothing can be more important ; and nothing ought to stand in the way of a policy which should lead to the perfect accomplishment of the object.*

If constructed and worked as a whole.

Since my return from America, many persons have asked my opinion of American railroads as securities.

American Railroads as securities.

---

* At present, six companies are engaged in the work of construction. The connexion with the existing American lines will be made at St. Louis on the Mississippi. From thence to the eastern slope of the Sierra Nevada, there are no particular obstacles ; and it appears that the passage across the chain, which involves two tunnels near the summit, will be effected by the people of California, who are reported to have 3,000 labourers at work upon the road. They expect to reach Salt Lake City, in Utah, where they will join the Eastern section, in 1868. The *New York Tribune* anticipates that "not very young men will see the day when Calcutta and Pekin, and Melbourne and London, will make their exchanges on the New York Broadway."

Now, the value of any railroad as a security depends on the qualifications of that railroad :—

First, as to its extent : its mileage must be sufficient to embrace places and districts sufficient for its requirements.

Second, as to its position : it must be so situated as to connect a great producing district with its natural market.

Third, as to its management : it must have the confidence of its customers, and it must fully develop the district which it serves ; and

Fourth, as to its officers : it must have honest and intelligent men in its councils, who have no interest save in its prosperity.

Wherever a railroad exists which combines these elements, I cannot doubt that it offers excellent security ; and if I am asked if there are such railroads in America, I unhesitatingly reply in the affirmative.

SECTION VII.

THE SOUTH.

SECTION VII.—THE SOUTH.

CHAPTER I.

POPULATION AND PROPERTY.

In the earliest section of this volume, I have considered the numbers and position of the population of the United States as a whole. In considering specially the resources of the Southern States, it will be necessary to bear in mind the wide distinction between the States of the North, which have been mainly peopled by immigration, and the States of the South, which have not had that advantage.

In the history of the United States, no State has *declined* in population. Some of the smaller and older States, such as Maine, New Hampshire, and Vermont, may be said to be 'filled up:' the number of their inhabitants being 26·26 to the square mile. Nevertheless, they go on increasing in population with considerable rapidity. But the Southern States show nothing like the same increase. South Carolina, between 1850 and 1860, only increased its entire popu-

The Southern States,

without Immigration,

have been nearly stationary

in respect of population.

lation from 668,000 to 703,000, or by about 35,000 inhabitants, equal to 5¼ per cent.; and this State made slower progress, in respect of population, during that decade, than any other State of the Union, having advanced only from 27·28 to 28·72 inhabitants to the square mile. Tennessee made but the moderate gain of 10·68 for all classes, and the rich country of Virginia only showed an aggregate increase of 12·29 per cent., of which the slave population only gained 3·88 per cent. Missouri was the only Slave State of 1850 that largely increased its population between that period and 1860. In 1861 Missouri declared for the Union, and deposed its anti-Union Governor; and in 1863 it passed an ordinance for the Emancipation of its Slaves.

Relative increase of population Let us look at the relative increase of population in the Southern and the Northern States.

The fifteen Slaveholding States of America contained, according to the census of 1860, 12,240,000 inhabitants. Of these 8,039,000 were whites, 251,000 in the South, free coloured, and 3,950,000 were slaves. The actual gain of the whole population of these States, from 1850 to 1860, was 2,627,000, equal to 27·33 per cent. The slaves during the same period advanced in numbers 749,931, or 23·44 per cent.

and in the North. Contrast this with the Free States. The nineteen Free States and the seven Territories of America, together with the Federal District of Columbia, contained 19,203,000 persons, of whom 18,920,771 were whites, 237,283 free coloured, and 41,725 civilized Indians. The increase was 5,624,101, or 41·24 per cent.

The marked disproportion between the increase in

the Northern and the Southern States is due, as I have already argued, to immigration. But what is it that has induced immigrants to settle almost exclusively in the North? Obviously, superior inducements. What were those inducements? No doubt the opportunities affording of settling on lands, where free labour was respected.

Let us next see what has been the position of the population of the South with reference to slavery. The following table shows—

THE NUMBER OF SLAVEHOLDERS AND SLAVES IN THE UNITED STATES IN 1860.

State.	Number of Slaveholders.	Number of Slaves.
Virginia	52,128	490,865
Georgia	41,084	462,198
Kentucky	38,645	225,483
Tennessee	36,844	275,719
North Carolina	34,658	331,059
Alabama	33,730	435,080
Mississippi	30,943	436,631
South Carolina	26,701	402,406
Missouri	24,320	114,931
Louisiana	22,033	331,726
Texas	21,878	182,566
Maryland	13,783	87,189
Florida	5,152	61,745
Arkansas	1,149	111,115
Delaware	587	1,798
Total	383,637	3,950,513

We thus see that out of a population of 12,000,000 the slaves numbered nearly 4,000,000, whilst the whites numbered more than 8,000,000. But of the 8,000,000 whites, only 383,000 were slaveholders. There was, therefore, an immense proportion of free whites who were, to a large extent, practically excluded from the cultivation of the Southern soil, and compelled to earn their livelihood in other occupations.

Three other points appear to be shown by this table ; first, that the number of Slaveholders in the United States was distributed over an immense territory ; second, that the whole number bore a very small proportion indeed to the aggregate population of the United States ; and, third, that the average number of slaves held by each master was little more than ten. Upon the last point the following table will show that the number of owners holding more than 20 slaves was not more than 45,000 out of the whole 383,637.

The Slave system examined.

Large proportion of Slaves held by small holders.

SLAVES HELD BY SLAVEHOLDERS.				
Holding	1 Slave			76,670
,,	2 Slaves			45,934
,,	3	,,		34,747
,,	4	,,		28,907
,,	5	,,		24,225
,,	6	,,		20,600
,,	7	,,		17,235
,,	8	,,		14,852
,,	9	,,		12,511
,,	10	,, and under	15	40,367
,,	15	,, ,,	20	21,315
,,	20	,, ,,	30	20,789
,,	30	,, ,,	40	9,648
,,	40	,, ,,	50	5,179
,,	50	,, ,,	70	5,217
,,	70	,, ,,	100	3,149
,,	100	,, ,,	200	1,980
,,	200	,, ,,	300	224
,,	300	,, ,,	500	74
,,	500	,, ,,	1,000	13
	1,000 and over			1
	Total			383,637

Wherever the Slaves were held in small numbers, we may take it for granted that they were held for domestic purposes: a large proportion of them, no doubt, being household servants in the cities and towns. It is only where they were held in numbers of 10 and upwards that they were held for plantation and field work, and these, it will be seen, constituted not much more than one-third of the whole.

Large proportion of Slaves employed in domestic service.

Small proportion engaged in field work.

Now, the deduction is, that the great proportion of the land in the Southern States has been heretofore held by a few very large proprietors ; that a very large proportion of the cultivable soil has not been tilled at all ; that the bulk of the white population in the South has been extremely poor ; and that a very considerable proportion of them have not been Slaveowners.

Deductions.

The deductions thus arrived at throw much light upon the condition of the South. The Slave population has, evidently, been insufficient to develop its resources : the whites have been precluded from applying themselves to the cultivation of the country : and the consequence has not only been disastrous to the land but disastrous to the great bulk of the settlers.

Results that may be expected from the abolition of slavery.

The whites, who have been prevented from applying themselves to the cultivation of the country, in consequence of slavery, have formed a separate and a depressed class, in strange contrast with their brethren in those States where no slave labour existed. The result of the abolition of slavery must inevitably be to place these " mean whites," as they have been termed, on a new footing. They will be able, without disgrace or disparagement, to enter upon the cultivation of the country. They will acquire little farms

The " mean whites " enabled to acquire homesteads,

and homesteads, as the people in the North have done; and will make their own labour and the labour of all around them valued and respected—as valued and as respected as the labour of the population of the North.

Let me here observe that in the North there is very often what the Americans themselves call "big-talk" about free labour. We hear it spoken of as "respected," "regarded," and "esteemed;" and some persons in England have been led to imagine that this is a sort of reflection upon our labour, and that it is intended to imply that labour is not only more valued, but more respected in America than it is in other countries. Naturally, it is more valued, because labour of every sort obtains higher wages; but it is very questionable whether, in the proper sense of the phrase, it is more respected or more esteemed. I question whether the American expression is properly understood in Europe. The distinction they have desired to draw is not so much between the relative respect paid to labour in Europe and in the free States of America, as to the relative respect paid to labour in the free States and in the slave States.

Labour has presented itself to the Americans in two aspects: as the labour of free men and the labour of slaves, and it is in these aspects that the material distinction has been drawn. Labour, amongst the slaves, has not been respected or esteemed. Hitherto, the slave, in the freest country of the world, has been admitted to no social privilege whatever. On the other hand, in the Northern States, the poorest person from Europe has been admitted to the rights and privileges of citizenship,

Margin notes:

and to become cultivators.

The "respect" paid to labour in America.

an implied distinction between free labour and slave labour.

Different aspects in which different descriptions of labour have been regarded.

has been permitted to settle himself upon lands belonging to the State, and has been esteemed and respected in proportion to the extent to which he cultivated and raised produce from them. The Americans in the North have seen this principle answer. The great West has been built up by giving to the immigrant, irrespective of his nationality, his creed, or his degree, equal privileges with every citizen. They have, therefore, naturally drawn a wide distinction between free labour and slave labour; and they have spoken of it in terms and in senses which have been misunderstood in Great Britain and elsewhere— terms which do not imply an invidious distinction between European free labour and American free labour, but terms which were intended to mark the distinction between the rewarded free labour of the North, and the unrequited slave labour of other localities.

Misapprehensions as to this phrase in Great Britain.

I am not anxious, however, to enter into the controversies about free labour and slave labour. Happily for the United States, and for the world at large, these disputes and controversies have terminated. Practically, slave labour no longer exists. I believe it will be ultimately found that its suppression will greatly add to the national advancement of all the States in which it existed. In justice to the Southern States of America, I ought to say that, to use the national expression, I believe slave labour was more respected in America than it was amongst any other slaveholding population. It was more respected than it was at any time in the colonies of Spain, where the slaves were

Treatment of the slaves in the South.

treated as mere utensils. It was more respected than
in any of our own West India Colonies, especially
Jamaica, where the black and coloured population
have frequently been much abused. It was more
so than even in the colonies of France, where a
milder system of slave treatment has prevailed —
where the household slaves (who have everywhere the
greatest influence) have, according to the French
system of manners, been often treated not merely as
domestic servants, but even as companions and familiar
friends.

Probable
results of free
labour,

But Slavery has been put an end to ; and what we
have to consider is the prospect of the development
of the resources of the South, under the system now
existing. Now I cannot doubt for a single moment,
that the South will prosper much better under a
system of free labour, than under a system of slave
labour. For the purpose of this argument let us take
a short review.

upon the
property,

In respect of POPULATION we have seen that the
increase of the Southern States has been in very small
relative proportion to the North. But let us consider
how this has affected PROPERTY. Hitherto the whole
capital of the South has been invested in "planting."
The investment in "planting" was only another and a
less disagreeable form of expressing investment in
slaves. It was not by increase of population, or by
increase of capital applied to land, but by increase of
capital invested in slave labour that the South was
built up. The labourer, in fact, was made the sole

upon the
capital,

representative of capital. But under this system,
capital has, in reality, been prevented from flowing

to the South. No doubt the nominal capital of the South increased, but the cause of that is easily explained. Inasmuch as free labour could not go there, the value of the slave labour existing there became enhanced. But all this was unreal. In no one respect have the slave States, since the Union, made anything approaching to an equality with the advances made by the free States. Nor has this been owing to the absence of superior advantages. On the contrary, the advantages of situation, soil, and climate have, for the most part, been on the side of the South, as I shall hereafter show.

and on the progress of the South.

Under the Slave system, the plantation business, virtually and practically, was a monopoly. No one could go into it who could not acquire large numbers of slaves; and, as we have seen, the price of these was continuously increasing — the supply being unequal to the demand. The plantation trade was therefore shut up in the hands of a few rich capitalist proprietors.

The Monopoly existing under the Slave system.

And this led to the great distinction existing in the South between the rich slaveholders and the large class who were denominated "mean whites." Inasmuch as labour was regarded as the work of the slaves, any of the white population, who were inclined to employ themselves in industrious pursuits, were regarded as "mean" and low, and unfit to be associated with by the better classes of their fellow-countrymen.* The consequence was that, being with-

The consequences of that Monopoly.

---

* The same feeling prevailed in our West India islands before emancipation. Any white man who could not keep a horse, who did not own some slaves, or who worked with his own hands on

out capital and prevented from exercising industrious pursuits, a very considerable class of the white population fell into a condition worse than that of the slaves themselves, by whom, it may be added, they were held in much contempt.

The " Mean Whites " of South Carolina.

The author of the "Story of the Great March" of General Sherman (who served with the General as aide de camp, and whose graphic narrative of all he observed has passed, I believe, through nearly twenty editions) gives the following description of the Mean Whites in South Carolina :—

" The peasantry of France are uneducated, but they are usually cleanly in their habits. The serfs of Russia are ignorant, but they are semi-barbarians, and have, until lately, been slaves. A large proportion of the working classes in England are debased, but they work. But the people I have seen and talked to for several days past are not only disgustingly filthy in their persons, but are so provokingly lazy, or 'shiftless,' as Mrs. Stowe has it, that they appear more like corpses recalled to a momentary existence than like human beings, and I have felt like applying a galvanic battery, to see if they could be made to move. Even the inroads of our foragers do not start them into life; they loll about like stalks, and barely find energy enough to utter a whining lamentation that they will starve.

" During this campaign, I have seen terrible instances of the horrors of slavery. I have seen men and women as white as the purest type of the Anglo-Saxon race in our army, who had been bought and sold like animals. I have looked upon the mutilated forms of black men who had suffered torture at the caprice of their cruel masters, and I have heard tales of woe too horrible for belief; but in all

his own property, was *universally* despised. As he was despised by the proprietors and overseers, so he was despised by the negroes, in imitation of their masters.

these cases I have never been so impressed with the de-
grading, demoralizing influence of this curse of slavery as in
the presence of these South Carolinians. The higher classes
represent the scum, and the lower the dregs of civilization.
They are South Carolinians, not Americans."

The consequence of such a state of things as this
upon the property of the Slave States is very obvious.
Inasmuch as the institution of slavery forbade free
labour in the South, the land could only be cultivated in proportion as the slave population of the
South increased. And, as that increase was trifling,
hundreds of thousands of square miles of land in the
Southern States have been lying uncultivated, under
the most superior advantages of climate and of sunshine.

It is remarkable to contrast the small quantities of
land in the Southern States which are "improved,"
in farms, with those which are "unimproved," though
owned. Observe the proportions, as shown in the
following table :—

Extent of uncultivated land in the South.

Large proportion of the "Unimproved" to the "Improved" lands.

ACREAGE IN THE *SLAVE* STATES, "IMPROVED" AND "UNIMPROVED," 1860.		
State.	Improved.	Unimproved.
Alabama	6,385,724	12,718,821
Arkansas	1,983,313	7,590,393
Florida	654,213	2,266,015
Georgia	8,062,758	18,587,732
Kentucky	7,644,208	11,519,053
Louisiana	2,707,108	6,591,468
Mississippi	5,065,755	10,773,929
North Carolina	6,517,284	17,245,685
South Carolina	4,572,060	11,623,859
Tennessee	6,795,337	13,873,828
Virginia	11,437,821	19,679,215

Y

These returns contrasted with the returns of Free States.

This disproportion is very great; and yet some of these are amongst the oldest States of the Union. Let me observe, that there are nothing like such disproportions in the Free States, whether old States or newly settled. On the contrary, the proportions are, for the most part, largely the other way. Take the following instances, which I give as fairly illustrating how the case stands, both in old States and in new :—

ACREAGE IN THE *FREE* STATES, " IMPROVED " AND " UNIMPROVED," 1860.		
State.	Improved.	Unimproved.
California......................	2,468,034	6,262,000
Illinois........................	13,096,374	7,815,615
Indiana........................	8,242,183	8,146,109
Massachusetts	2,155,512	1,183,212
Michigan......................	3,476,296	3,554,538
New Hampshire..............	2,367,034	1,377,591
New York	14,358,403	6,616,555
Ohio..........................	12,625,394	7,846,747
Pennsylvania	10,463,296	6,548,844
Rhode Island	335,128	186,096
Vermont	2,823,157	1,451,257
Wisconsin	3,746,167	4,147,420

The proportions.

As a whole, I believe it may be taken that in the Free States they have about 112 acres of uncultivated to about 100 of cultivated land, whilst in the Slave States the proportions are 130 of uncultivated to about 60 cultivated. Such facts show at once the comparative absence of labour and of industry in the South.

Conclusion

The conclusion is that, under a system of free labour, industry will become stimulated in the

Southern States, and that emigrants, tempted by the riches of those most prolific districts, will resort to the South when free labour is established, almost as largely as they have done to the North. " Do you " suppose," said Mr. Bright, in one of his speeches on America, " that those beautiful States of the South " —those regions, than which the whole earth offers " nothing more fertile or more lovely—are shunned " by the enterprizing population of the north, be- " cause they prefer the rigours of a northern winter " and the changeableness of northern seasons ? " Once abolish slavery in the South, and the whole " country will be opened to enterprize and industry. " More than that ;—when you hear of 4,000 emi- " grants from the United Kingdom being landed in " one day at New York, do you suppose that they " will all go to the north and to the west, if other " fields are open to them ? Do you not believe that " some of them will turn their faces towards the " south, where they will find a soil more fertile, " rivers more abundant, and everything that nature " offers more profusely and bountifully afforded ? "

that the South will prosper under Free Labour.

With freedom, I believe, there will be a gradual filling up of the Southern States, as there has been of the Northern. We shall find there, hereafter, popu- lation, and capital, and industry, and railroads, and schools (now so sadly wanting), together with all else that can tend to produce progress, prosperity, and wealth.

CHAPTER II.

The Products of the South,

HAVING in the last chapter examined the population and property of the South, I now proceed to inquire into the PRODUCTS of the Slave States. From a table in the Census Report (vol. Agriculture, p. 129) I am able to compile the following statistics, showing the amounts of the principal agricultural products, in the Southern States, in proportion to population, in 1860; and it may help the consideration of the subject to contrast the productions of the Southern with those of the Western States.

in proportion to population,

AMOUNT OF AGRICULTURAL PRODUCTS TO EACH INHABITANT, 1860.		
Products.	Southern States.	Western States.
Wheat	3·49	9·75
Indian Corn.................	30·83	45·27
Barley	0·02	0·43
Rye	0·24	0·49
Oats	2·18	6·51
Buckwheat	0·05	0·41
Peas and Beans	1·26	0·10
Irish Potatoes	6·72	3·55
Butter	6·58	16·13
Cheese	0·08	2·97

It will thus be seen that, with respect to every item of produce for human consumption, except potatoes (for the cow pea, as already stated, is used in the South for cattle and manure), the Southern States stood, in 1860, at a considerable disadvantage in comparison with the much younger district of the West. All their produce was in less proportion to their population, although, between 1850 and 1860, their population had shown a very far less relative increase. *far inferior to those of the Western States.*

Now, if these facts stood alone, the argument might, not improperly, be regarded as imperfect : because it might be urged, that whilst the Western States applied themselves specially to the growth of agricultural produce, the South was engaged in the development of other products.

But these facts do not stand alone. Not only were the Southern States relatively far behind the West in 1860, but as regards all the principal items of agricultural produce in the South, *the production of* 1860 *was absolutely less than in* 1850 : a fact which does not apply to any other section of America, where, as I have shown in previous pages, the increase of production has been so rapidly progressive. *The production of the South a diminishing production.*

Let us take Indian corn, which is the principal item of human subsistence in the South. Formerly, Tennessee, Kentucky, and Virginia stood at the head of the list of the corn-producing States. They have now been entirely superseded by Illinois, Missouri, Ohio, and Indiana. Tennessee, indeed, produced less Indian corn in 1860, than she did in 1850. So did South Carolina ; and Georgia remained almost stationary. The whole produce of Indian corn in the *Indian Corn.* *Its production in the South*

does not keep
pace with
population.
Southern States was only 282,626,778 bushels, in 1860,
against 238,209,743 bushels in 1850. Comparatively
small as was the increase of the Southern population,
the increased production of corn did not keep pace
with it. In 1840, the Southern States produced over
33 bushels to each inhabitant; in 1850, 32¾ bushels;
and in 1860, less than 31 bushels.

Oats,
Next to Indian corn, Oats was the largest cereal
crop grown in the Southern States in 1850. In 1860,
the oat crop of those States had fallen off upwards
of one-third. In 1850, they produced 33,566,913
bushels; in 1860, only 12,906,032 bushels. It is re-
a declining
crop in every
Southern
State.
marked in the Census returns that, "with the ex-
"ception of Texas and Virginia (where it was almost
"stationary), the oat crop had declined in every
"Southern State." In Alabama, the crop fell from
nearly 3,000,000 bushels in 1850 to 682,000 bushels
in 1860. Mississippi fell from 1,503,000 bushels to
221,000, and other States to an equal extent. In fact,
says the Report, "the rapid decrease of the production of oats in the Slave States is quite curious."
Whilst they produced nearly four and a half bushels
to each inhabitant in 1850, they produced only two
bushels in 1860.

Sweet Pota-
toes.
Take Sweet Potatoes,—so much more largely produced in the Southern than in any of the other States,
that, up to the commencement of the war, they may be
said to have been an exclusively Southern produce.
The production of this prolific root scarcely showed any
increase between 1850 and 1860, and in some of the
largest of the Southern States it showed an absolute
decrease. In the aggregate, the Southern States

raised 4·87 bushels to each inhabitant in 1850, to 4·16 bushels in 1860. On the other hand, the free State of Illinois doubled her production.

In the article of Wool, the Southern States showed an increase between 1850 and 1860; but this was exclusively owing to the increased production of Texas. In Virginia, Georgia, and both the Carolinas, there was a very large deficiency, although Virginia has heretofore been amongst the largest wool-producing States of the Union. In Flax, for the production of which some of the Southern States are peculiarly fitted, the product fell from nearly 2,000,000 lb. in 1850 to 876,336 lb. in 1860. In 1850, Kentucky and Virginia were the two largest flax-producing States of the Union. Mark the contrast exhibited in the following account :—

(margin: Wool.)

(margin: Flax.)

(margin: Contrast between the Flax production of)

Flax produced.	1850.	1860.
Kentucky...............lb.	2,100,116	728,234
Virginia	1,000,150	487,808
New York	940,577	1,518,025
Ohio..........................	446,932	882,423

(margin: Slave States

and

Free States.)

Swine have been bred in the Southern States so largely that in 1850 there were no less than 215 swine to every 100 inhabitants. But, in 1860, the number of swine had decreased to an average of 175 to each 100 inhabitants, and there were less swine by nearly 250,000 head in those States than there were ten years previously. This is the more remarkable, considering the prolific character of the animal.

(margin: Swine.)

But the fact is, that the same principle enters into

All Southern productions have diminished.

almost every article of southern produce, except that one article to which slave labour is especially directed. Having seen the decline in those productions which are not peculiar to the Slave States, let us now look at the condition of the staples which are peculiar to those States.

The Rice

The cultivation of RICE is limited to a very few Slave States. South Carolina and Georgia produced, in 1860, 171,000,000 lb. out of the total produce of all the States, which amounted to 187,000,000 lb.

and

In 1850 South Carolina and Georgia produced 198,881,000 lb. and the total product of the States in that year exceeded 215,000,000 lb. Rice, therefore, which, in America, is a product peculiar to the Slave States, is a declining cultivation.

Sugar, cultivations both declining.

The cultivation of the SUGAR CANE in America is almost wholly confined to the State of Louisiana. The produce of 1850 was 236,814 hogsheads; in 1860, it was 230,982 hogsheads: showing a decrease of another product exclusively produced by slave labour. Since the commencement of the war the

Cane Sugar, grown by Slave labour, largely superseded by Maple and Sorghum Sugars.

cane sugar has been almost entirely superseded in the North by the sugar extracted by free labour from the maple; and also by the produce of the Sorghum sugar plant, recently introduced from China, and which has spread with immense rapidity throughout the States.

The extent to which maple sugar is made in the North, and the character of the manufacture, has been thus described:—

The Manufacture of

"Making maple sugar in this region of country (Pennsylvania) may be said to comprise one of the characteristic employments of the people. The quantity of the sugar, raised in the western counties of Pennsylvania, averages something like two million and a half pounds per annum, so that it will be observed that it is by no means an inconsiderable item of domestic trade. Indeed, we have no doubt but that this amount, large as it seems, might readily be trebled and quadrupled, with profit, were the manufacture reduced to the basis of a regular and systematic business. Immense districts, otherwise unproductive, might be timbered with these sugar-bearing trees, and large sums annually realized from their productions, without in the least depreciating the value of the trees for timber. If we are not greatly deceived, this sugar-maple business will ultimately become important:—that is, it will enter the market in such quantity as to offer a determined competition to the products of the sugar-cane.

"The sugar-maple is a beautiful tree, reaching the height of seventy or eighty feet, the body straight, for a long distance free from limbs, and three or four feet in diameter at the base. It grows in colder climates, between latitude forty-two and forty-eight, and on the Alleghanies, to their southern termination, extending westward beyond Lake Superior. The wood is nearly equal to hickory for fuel, and is used for building, for ships, and various manufactures. When tapped, as the winter gives place to spring, a tree, in a few weeks, will produce five or six pailfuls of sap, which is sweet and pleasant as a drink, and when boiled down will make about half as many pounds of sugar. The manufacturer, selecting a spot central among his trees, erects a temporary shelter, suspends his kettles over a smart fire, and at the close of a day or two will have fifty or a hundred pounds of sugar, which is equal to the common West India sugar, and, when refined, equals the finest in flavour and in beauty. When the sap has been boiled to a syrup, and is turning to molasses, then to candy, and then graining into sugar, its flavour is delightful, especially when the candy is cooled on the snow."

TOBACCO is a weed which grows rank and wild over every part of the United States. There is no State which does not grow more or less of it, although hitherto Virginia and Kentucky have produced by far the largest quantities.* Once planted, the production of this weed cannot be stopped. The labour expended on it is trifling, and only applies to picking and curing the leaves. It is, therefore, not surprising to find an increase in the production of tobacco, even in the Slave States; but it is remarkable to find that, with their peculiar advantages of climate, the relative progress of the tobacco produce is less in the Slave States than it is in the Free. Thus, New York produced 83,000 lb. of tobacco in 1850, and 5,765,000 lb. in 1860. Massachusetts produced 138,000 lb. in 1850, and 3,233,000 lb. in 1860. Connecticut produced 1,267,000 lb. in 1850, and 6,000,000 lb. in 1860. Pennsylvania produced 912,000 lb. in 1850, and 3,181,000 lb. in 1860. † These were enormous increases; and what is observable is, that they were much larger than any increases in the Southern States, although, during the decade, the amount of tobacco raised in those States was doubled.

It will be seen then, as regards three out of the four staples of the South, the production of rice declined, whilst that of sugar remained stationary, during the decade previous to the last census. The tobacco

The Tobacco produce of the Free States

enormously increasing.

---

* An American writer has characterized tobacco as "the bane of the Old Dominion." It prevents, he argues, the proper cultivation of the soil. There is no doubt that shallow ploughing and want of manure are the banes of every Slave State; but there is reason to think that the real "bane of the Old Dominion" is rather the want of labour properly to cultivate the soil than the growth of the tobacco-plant which overspreads it.

† *Vide* "Agriculture of the United States, compiled under the direction of the Secretary of the Interior," pp. 185-189.

production increased largely, but not in proportion with its increase in States which had the benefit of free labour. During the same period, every other article of production, but one, in these States decreased largely. The one remaining item, however, exhibited a vast increase : that item is COTTON. Cotton.

The amount of ginned cotton raised in the United States, in 1850, was 2,445,793 bales ; in 1860, the official returns present the total as 5,387,052 bales : or more than double the amount produced in 1850.* The amount raised,

In 1860, Mississippi produced more cotton than any other State. She raised nearly a million and a quarter bales, or half the amount of the produce of the whole of the United States, in 1850. Alabama comes next. She produced nearly a million bales, or nearly double the amount she produced in 1850. Louisiana, in 1860 produced 777,000 bales ; having produced only 178,000 bales in 1850. Georgia produced 700,000 bales ; having produced 500,000 in 1850. These four In Mississippi, Alabama, Louisiana, and Georgia.

---

* The Cotton produce of the United States in 1860 is said by many persons to be incorrectly reported in the Census tables; and my attention has been especially directed to the "Annual Circular of the Liverpool Cotton Brokers' Association," issued on the 30th December, 1865, in which the growth of America is stated at 4,675,770 bales in 1859-60, or 711,222 bales less than the produce shown by the official records. But I do not know the sources from which the "Liverpool Cotton Brokers' Association" derive their information as to the American crop, or whether they may have included the produce of all the States, or of all the qualities of cotton, or at what average weights they have calculated their bales. Whatever the causes of the difference between their estimate and those of the United States Commissioners of Census, it appears to me that I am bound to rely upon the latter and more official account.

States,—Mississippi, Alabama, Louisiana, and Georgia,
—produced 3,672,000, whilst all the other States produced only 1,715,000 bales.

The whole
Slave power
thrown into
this cultiva-
tion,

It is clear from these facts, that the whole force of
slavery and of the slave power, was thrown, between
1850 and 1860, into the production of cotton.   There
was, indeed, good reason for this.   The price of cotton
in Europe had largely increased in the interval.   Between 1856 and 1860 every pound of cotton in Liverpool fetched 20 per cent. more than it did from 1840
to 1845.   The demand for raw cotton, had, in fact, ex-

which was
nevertheless
inadequate,

ceeded the supply.   But why was this?   Not because
there was not land enough; for the uncultivated lands
in hand, as we saw in the last chapter, far exceeded
the quantity of land brought under cultivation.   Then,

in conse-
quence of
want of
labour.

what was it that rendered the supply insufficient in the
face of high prices and large profits to the producer?
It was solely and simply the want of labour.

Number of
Slaves en-
gaged in the
Cotton culti-
vation.

There were nearly 4,000,000 Slaves in the United
States.   Of these, as we have seen, a large proportion
were employed in domestic servitude and business
occupations in the towns.   Others were engaged in
rice-growing, sugar-production, and tobacco-growing.
It is computed that 1,000,000 slaves, or about a quarter
of the whole, were engaged in the cultivation of the
cotton plant.

Proof that
their labour
was insuf-
ficient

Now, the cotton production of America progressed
from 2,400,000 bales in 1850, to 5,387,000 in 1860:
a very large increase.   But that was insufficient.
Large as was the supply, it was outstripped by the
demand.   The very extent of the increase shows
that it was in consequence of the paucity of labour

alone that the production was inadequate. There are some remarkable facts with reference to cotton-cultivation in the United States between 1850 and 1860. We have seen that the great bulk of the cotton was produced in four States. But, when the rapidly-increasing price of cotton stimulated culture, other States began to enter upon its cultivation, especially the new States of Arkansas and Texas. In 1850, Arkansas only produced 65,000 bales of cotton, but in 1860 she grew 367,000. In 1850 Texas only grew 58,000 bales, but in 1860 she grew 432,000. Besides the land lying uncultivated in the old States, there were abundant and wide fields in the new, applicable to cotton-cultivation if labour could have been found for them : but the slave system prevented immigration to those States, prevented the application of free labour to those lands, prevented, of consequence, the cultivation of those lands, and prevented the supply of cotton from equalling the demand.

to cultivate the extent of land required for a sufficient cotton product.

The inference is, that the slave system has been the bane of the Southern States of America. Under that system the land could not be peopled, and the slaves alone were insufficient for its cultivation. In point of fact, whilst everything in Southern America has been sacrificed to slavery, slavery has sacrificed all else to itself. The cultivation of cotton—and the cultivation of cotton alone—has made progress in the Southern States ; and the supply of that article has not kept pace with the demand for it. The logical inference is, that slavery in the United States has proved a failure, and that the sooner it is superseded by another system the better for the nation and the world.

Conclusion that the Slave system has been the bane of the South.

and that the
South will be
far more
prosperous
under Free-
dom.

In support of this argument I cannot, however, do better than quote a passage from the recent Message of the President of the United States—a document that does equal honour to his heart and to his head :—

" Now that slavery is at an end, or near its end, the greatness of its evil, in the point of view of public economy, becomes more and more apparent. Slavery was essentially a monopoly of labour, and as such locked the States where it prevailed against the incoming of free industry. Where labour was the property of the capitalist, the white man was excluded from employment, or had but the second-best chance of finding it ; and the foreign emigrant turned away from the region where his condition would be so precarious. With the destruction of the monopoly, free labour will hasten from all parts of the civilized world to assist in developing various and immeasurable resources which have hitherto lain dormant. The eight or nine States nearest the Gulf of Mexico have a soil of exuberant fertility, a climate friendly to long life, and can sustain a denser population than is found, as yet, in any part of our country. And the future influx of population to them will be mainly from the North, or from the most cultivated nations in Europe. From the sufferings that have attended them during our late struggle, let us look away to the future, which is sure to be laden for them with greater prosperity than has ever before been known. The removal of the monopoly of slave labour is a pledge that those regions will be peopled by a numerous and enterprising population, which will vie with any in the Union in compactness, inventive genius, wealth, and industry."

CHAPTER III.

THE FUTURE OF THE SOUTH.

I THINK there will be a general agreement that the treatment of the South, at the conclusion of the war, was dictated by a wise, humane, and generous policy. The whole country was in the possession of the Northern armies, and they might have held the seceding States as conquered territory under military authority. But the Government at Washington determined to regard the States of the South as restored, by the cessation of open warfare, to their place in the common nationality. As regarded individuals, the President of the United States resolved to exercise, to its fullest extent, his power of pardon. No executions for treason, no confiscations, and few arrests have followed the defeat of the revolutionists. As respects Mr. Jefferson Davis, many persons in the United States, no doubt, consider that it would have been better that he should have escaped : but having been taken, I do not see what else could have been done with him than has been done. He has been kept in confinement to await trial, but that trial has not been pressed forward with a view of convicting him at a period when the people

The treatment of the South at the conclusion of the War, wise, humane, and generous.

were still excited : on the contrary, it has been post-
poned until peace and tranquillity may be restored
throughout the Union, and until the ordinary tribunals
of the law resume their functions in the districts
which were subject to disturbance.   The probabilities
are that the late Confederate President will never be
tried at all.

Policy of the President.   The exposition which the President of the United
States made of his policy in his recent Message, appears
to me to do him great honour.   He explains why he
refused to subject the South to military rule :—

He refuses to subject the South to Military rule.   " Military Governments, established for an indefinite
period, would have offered no security for the early sup-
pression of discontent ; would have divided the people into
the vanquishers and the vanquished ; and would have en-
venomed hatred, rather than have restored affection.   Once
established, no precise limit to their continuance was con-
ceivable.   They would have occasioned an incalculable and
exhausting expense.   Peaceful emigration to and from that
portion of the country is one of the best means that can be
thought of for the restoration of harmony ; and that emigration would have been prevented ; for what emigrant from
abroad, what industrious citizen at home, would place himself
willingly under military rule ?   The chief persons who would
have followed in the train of the army would have been
dependents on the General Government, or men who expected
profit from the miseries of their erring fellow-citizens.   The
wilful use of such powers, if continued through a period of
years, would have endangered the purity of the general administration, and the liberties of the States which remained
loyal.

" Besides, the policy of military rule over a conquered
territory would have implied that the States whose inhabitants may have taken part in the rebellion had, by the act of
those inhabitants, ceased to exist.   But the true theory is,
that all pretended acts of secession were, from the beginning,

null and void. The States attempting to secede placed themselves in a condition where their vitality was impaired, but not extinguished—their functions suspended, but not destroyed."

The next step was to restore the constitutional relations of the States, by inviting the South to participation in the amendment of the Constitution. The war had terminated slavery, but it was desirable, for the future maintenance of the Union, that that result should be confirmed by such an amendment of the Constitution as would provide for the abolition of slavery for ever within the limits of the country.

He seeks to restore the Constitutional relations of the States.

" This," said the President, "is the measure which will efface the sad memory of the past; this is the measure which will most certainly call population, and capital, and security to those parts of the Union that need them most. Indeed, it is not too much to ask of the States which are now resuming their places in the family of the Union, to give this pledge of perpetual loyalty and peace. Until it is done, the past, however much we may desire it, will not be forgotten. The adoption of the amendment reunites us beyond all power of disruption. It heals the wound that is still imperfectly closed; it removes the element which has so long perplexed and divided the country; it makes of us once more a united people, renewed and strengthened, bound more than ever to mutual affection and support."

The relations of the Government towards the four millions of inhabitants called into freedom, was the next important point for consideration; and here I think it will also be allowed that the policy of the North has been very temperate and judicious. The President refused to declare these new freemen to be citizens and electors by proclamation; he determined that, constitutionally, it must be left to each State to

Policy of the President as to the Freedmen.

Their Admission to the Elective Franchise left to the several States.

decide for itself the conditions for the enjoyment of the elective franchise. He had no right, he said, to create new classes of voters. That would have been an assumption of power by the President, warranted neither by the Constitution nor the laws. The proper course, and the best course, was to refer the question to the several States.

Measures for the security of their liberties and property,

" But while I have no doubt that it is not competent for the General Government to extend the elective franchise in the several States, it is equally clear that good faith requires the security of the freedmen in their liberty and their property, their right to labour, and their right to claim the just return of their labour. I cannot too strongly urge a dispassionate treatment of this subject, which should be carefully kept aloof from all party strife. We must equally avoid hasty assumptions of any natural impossibility for the two races to live side by side, in a state of mutual benefit and good will. The country is in need of labour, and the freedmen

for the encouragement of their industry,

are in need of employment, culture, and protection. Let us encourage them to honourable and useful industry, where it may be beneficial to themselves, and to the country; and, instead of hasty anticipations of the certainty of failure, let there be nothing wanting to the fair trial of the experiment. The change in their condition is the substitution of labour by contract for the status of slavery. The freedman cannot

and the payment of their wages.

fairly be accused of unwillingness to work, so long as a doubt remains about his freedom of choice in his pursuits, and the certainty of his recovering his stipulated wages. In this the interests of the employer and the employed coincide. The employer desires in his workmen spirit and alacrity, and these can be permanently secured in no other way. And if the one ought to be able to enforce the contract, so ought the other. The public interest will be best promoted, if the several States will provide adequate protection and remedies for the freedmen. Until this is in some way accomplished, there is no chance for the advantageous use of their labour; and the blame of ill-success will not rest on them.

"I know that sincere philanthropy is earnest for the immediate realization of its remotest aims; but time is always an element in reform. It is one of the greatest acts on record to have brought four millions of people into freedom. The career of free industry must be fairly opened to them; and then their future prosperity and condition must, after all, rest mainly on themselves. If they fail, and so perish away, let us be careful that the failure shall not be attributable to any denial of justice."

The career of free industry to be fairly opened to them.

How much may be expected from this career for free industry, and how little the Slave system contributed to the advantage of the Southern States has been shown by my friend the Hon. Robert Walker, in the important comparisons he has instituted between the progress of the Free States and the Slave States. He shows, by the contrast, how largely the Free States have progressed in proportion to those in which slavery has been perpetuated. His first comparison is between Maryland and Massachusetts; and he says he specially selects those States because, whilst they are about of equal age, Maryland has great natural advantages over Massachusetts, in area, soil, climate, hydraulic power, shore-line, bays, sounds, and rivers, and other circumstances which affect the advance of wealth and population.

Contrast between the progress of the Slave States and the Free States since the Union.

Maryland and Massachusetts contrasted.

"As to area, Maryland exceeds Massachusetts by 43 per cent.; as to shore-line, that of Maryland is nearly double that of Massachusetts. As to climate, that of Maryland is by far the most salubrious, and therefore ought to have attracted most immigration. . . . The area of Maryland fit for profitable culture is more than double that of Massachusetts, the soil much more fertile, its mines of coal and iron rich and inexhaustible; whereas Massachusetts has no coal and no valuable mines of iron. The hydraulic power of Maryland also exceeds that of Massachusetts."

Natural advantages Mary¹

Great proportional development of Massachusetts.

Such are the vast natural advantages of the Slave State over the Free. Now let us look at the results :—

	MASSACHUSETTS. (Free State.)	MARYLAND. (Slave State.)
Area in square miles	7,800	11,124
Population in 1790	378,717	319,728
„ in 1860	1,231,066	687,049
Products in 1859	$287,000,000	$66,000,000
„ per capita...........	$235	$96
Railroads in miles	1,340	380
„ cost of	$61,857,203	$21,387,157
Freight in 1860	$500,524,201	$101,111,348
Shipping built—tons........	34,460	7,789
Bank Capital in 1860........	$64,519,200	$12,568,962
Imports and Exports in 1860	$58,190,816	$18,786,323
Value of Property in „	$815,237,433	$376,919,944
Newspapers circulated	102,000,760	20,723,472
Pupils at Public Schools.....	176,475	33,254
Volumes in Public Libraries.	684,015	125,042
Churches, value of...........	$10,206,000	$3,947,884

No cause for this but the existence of Slavery in Maryland.

No cause except slavery can be assigned for these wonderful differences. The original colonists of Maryland were distinguished for education, intelligence, and gentle culture. Lord Baltimore, under whose patronage and personal influence the State was settled, was a statesman and a philanthropist. His colony, from the first, was a free representative government, and it has produced many of the most eminent soldiers, statesmen, and clergymen of America. Yet, in relation to other States, the progress of Maryland in power, wealth, and population has been deplorably small.

The relative positions of Maryland and Massachusetts

Massachusetts, it may be said, is a manufacturing State. But she only became so after the year 1824, when Congress first adopted a protective policy.

Massachusetts was previously a commercial State ; and was far more injured than any other State by the effects of the war with England in 1813. But whether commercial, manufacturing, or agricultural, Massachusetts has always outstripped Maryland ; and this has to be accounted for by those who would adopt any other theory than that Maryland has suffered from her institutions. Maryland might have become commercial and manufacturing equally with Massachusetts ; she ought to have become so. Having better harbours, a longer shore-line, and, in the bay of the Chesapeake, a deep, tranquil, and protected basin, far more advantageously adapted for commerce than the rock-bound coast of Massachusetts, Maryland ought even to have outstripped Massachusetts in commerce. Having iron and coal in abundance, she ought, also, to have outstripped her in manufactures ; but the foregoing table shows that, in every respect, she has relatively declined.

To take, however, the instance of a single State might be regarded as unfair, or, at any rate, as not affording conclusive proof upon this question. Let us then examine the relative progress of some other States. Governor Walker contrasts the position of Virginia with that of New York and of Pennsylvania.

In 1790, the population of Virginia was more than double that of New York : in 1860, the population of New York was more than double that of Virginia ! The natural advantages of Virginia far exceed those of New York : Virginia has the larger area, a superior shore-line, her harbours are more numerous and deeper, and much nearer the great valley of the Ohio and the Mississippi. She has also a great advantage in her interior navigable streams. The James river flowing into the Chesapeake, cuts the range of the Blue Mountains, and the Kanawha, a confluent of the Ohio, cuts the Alleghanies, thus opening an easy and practicable route either for canals or railroads from the eastern to the western waters. Virginia possesses vast mines of coal and iron; New York has none. Her hydraulic power very far exceeds that of New York, and the milder climate of Virginia renders this power available for a greater portion of the year.

Relative progress of the three States,

Such being the resources of Virginia—the "old dominion"—the State to which America owes WASHINGTON, JEFFERSON, MADISON, and, it may be said, all the great men of her early age,—let us see how this State, which retained slavery to the last, has progressed, in comparison with the Free States of New York and Pennsylvania.

New York, Pennsylvania, and Virginia.

	NEW YORK. (Free State.)	PENNSYLVANIA. (Free State.)	VIRGINIA. (Slave State.)
Area in square miles ...	47,000	46,000	61,352
Population in 1790	340,120	434,373	748,308
,, in 1860	3,880,735	2,900,115	1,596,318
Products of 1859	$606,000,000	$399,600,000	$120,000,000
,, per capita......	$156	$138	$75
Value per acre of Farm Lands.................	$38·26	$38·91	$11·91
Railroads, miles	2,842	2,690	1,771
,, cost of.........	$138,395,055	$147,483,410	$64,958,807
Canals, miles	1,038	1,250	178
,, cost of...........	$67,567,972	$42,015,000	$7,817,000
Tonnage built, 1860.....	31,936	21,615	4,372
Bank Capital..............	$111,441,320	$25,565,582	$16,005,166
Exports and imports....	$394,045,326	$20,262,608	$7,184,273
Newspapers circulated..	320,980,884	116,094,480	26,772,518
Pupils at Schools........	675,221	413,706	67,428
Vols. in public Libraries	1,760,820	363,300	88,462
Value of Churches	$21,539,561	$11,853,291	$2,002,220
Percentage of Free Population unable to read or write.	1·87	——	19·90

There is *nothing* to account for this but SLAVERY ! The Virginians themselves, in point of fact, admit it. They say Virginia has cultivated the tobacco plant, and hence her decline in other cultivations. But the tobacco cultivation is the emanation from and the result of slavery : that enervating system, which reduced industry to its minimum by inculcating the superior advantages of indolence.

Slavery the sole cause of these disproportions.

Governor Walker estimates that the additional value of the lands in the Slave States, if they were brought up to the value of the lands of the Free States, would be no less than $5,859,246,616—or say £1,172,000,000. Arguing from the relative agricultural products of those States, he contends that the crops of the Slave States would be much greater if their farms were cultivated by free labour ; that slave culture, in fact, has exhausted and reduced in value their most fertile lands, and that, of consequence, the system of Slavery is attended with ruinous effects.

Estimate of the additional value of the Lands of the South under Free labour.

In the following table he shows what the Slave States of 1790 were in relation to the Free—and what the same Free States of 1860 are, in relation to the Slave. The comparison is remarkable.

Contrast between the Free States and Slave States of 1790,

	Free States of 1790.	Slave States of 1790.
Area in square miles.........	169,668	300,580
Population in 1790	1,968,455	1,961,372
„ in 1860	10,594,168	7,414,684
Pop. per square mile in 1790	11·60	6 50
Pop. per square mile in 1860	62·44	24·60
Increase of ditto...........	50·84	18·11

	Free States of 1860.	Slave States of 1860.
Area in square miles.........	835,631	888,591
Farm Lands, acres............	161,462,000	248,721,062
„ value of........	$4,067,947,286	$2,570,466,935
„ value per acre	$25·19	$10·46
Total product of 1859	$4,150,000,000	$1,140,000,000
„ per capita..	$217	$93
Total Agricultural product..	$2,527,676,000	$862,324,000
„ „ per capita	$131·48	$70·56
„ „ per acre	$15·65	$3·58
Copies of Press issued	760,034,360	167,917,188
Ratio of White Inhabitants unable to read or write, 1850	4·12	17·23
Ratio of White Inhabitants unable to read or write, 1860	3·21	17·03

and the Free States and Slave States of 1860.

Immense development of Southern resources anticipated.

I think, then, that we are justified in arriving at the conclusion, that the Southern States are capable of immense development; and that this extensive and naturally wealthy region only requires the introduction of capital and free labour to become equal in point of production to the rest of the United States. If this point is admitted—and I do not think it will be denied by any one who understands the condition of the nation—we shall find in the Southern States, immediately after their peaceful return into the Union, an immense additional field from whence America will be able to draw resources for the liquidation of her liabilities and for future progress. In the earliest years of that restoration there will be, necessarily, a somewhat diminished production of the staples; but that diminished production will be satisfied by enhanced prices, which will be borne by the consumers. But this state of things will last only for a brief period. Except tobacco, there is no product of agriculture which expands so rapidly as cotton. In the five years between 1855 and 1860 the Southern States doubled their cotton product. Now that the war is concluded, it can be restored in a less period, and advanced upon in an increased ratio. It is to be borne in mind, that there are not fewer labourers to-day in the Southern States than when the war commenced. Whatever of injury has fallen upon those States in consequence of the war has not fallen upon the labouring class. Mr. Tobey, in a speech delivered before the Boston Board of Trade on the 27th November of last year, declared, with emphasis, that "nearly the same working population which raised the five million bales of cotton and other products in 1860, is now there to plant and raise the crops of 1866." All that is wanted is capital and enterprise to stimulate that labour: and that capital and enterprise will be afforded. Whilst I was visiting the North, I was invited to spend some hours with a family of the highest distinction. One of the young ladies of that family introduced me to her brother, and I inquired was he the only brother? "Oh no!" was the reply, "we had two other brothers in the war. They were in the army of General Sherman; but so delighted were they with what they saw of the South, and so impressed were they with its advantages, that on the return of peace they begged to be allowed to go and settle there, and our father having provided them with funds, they have gone down South to purchase property and cultivate estates." This is an illustration of what is occurring amongst the families of capitalists throughout the North; and now that the Southern lands are open to free labour, I have no doubt that emigration from the North to the South will be stimulated to an extent of which there has been no previous precedent.

The abolition of slavery has disburdened the Southern States of an incubus. Those States have at command all the resources that soil and climate can afford. They lack nothing but the stimulant afforded by free institutions to bring them to a condition of prosperity equal with the most advanced States of the Union. The Americans know and acknowledge this. They understand that the commercial and financial interests of their country depend very largely upon the organization and development of Southern industry. They are prepared to throw capital and enterprize into the Southern States, for the purpose of producing results on which the prosperity of the whole nation is acknowledged largely to depend. The Government, no doubt, so far as lies within its legitimate province, will encourage and support those efforts. And what will be the consequence? Mr. Bright, in a speech delivered in the House of Commons in 1863,* said—

" I was speaking the other day to a gentleman from Mississippi : I believe no man in America or in England is more acquainted with the facts of this case. He has been for many years a senator of the State of Mississippi ; and he said to me, ' I have no doubt whatever that, in ten years after the freedom of the South, the production of cotton will be *doubled*, and cotton will be forwarded to the consumers of the world at a much less price than they have had it for many years.' "

---

* Speech on Mr. Roebuck's motion for the recognition of the Southern Confederacy, 30th June, 1863.

I am inclined to take even a more sanguine view than that of the Senator of Mississippi. Looking at the rapid growth of the cotton-plant—at the enormous extent of the lands capable of its cultivation, which have hitherto never been brought into it—and looking also at the capital and labour which, under the free system, is flowing, and which will continue to flow into the Southern States—I do not believe I am over-sanguine in predicting—that, within *five years* from the present time, the cotton production of America will be doubled, and that the consumers of the world will have the article at a less price than they ever had it before. Southern prospects.

Let me observe, in conclusion, that this has a most important bearing on the RESOURCES OF AMERICA. If due facilities are afforded for bringing to market the bread-stuffs of the North, and if the product of the cotton-plant in the South is restored and increased, not only will America bear, with ease, all the burden of her debt, and pay it, but she will immediately commence a career of commercial prosperity unexampled in the experience of nations. Important bearing of this question on the American future.

SECTION VIII.

FINANCE.

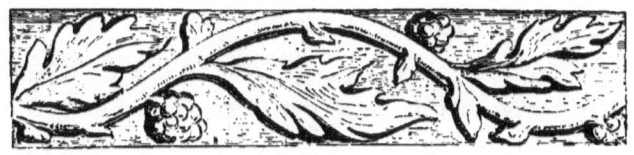

SECTION VIII.—FINANCE.

CHAPTER I.

REVENUE AND EXPENDITURE.

IN examining the financial position of the United States, the first and most striking feature is the comparatively small amount of the ordinary national expenditure. Whilst the expenditure of Great Britain and Ireland, in 1860, amounted to upwards of £68,000,000, the expenditure of the United States, in that year, was only £15,500,000; and this amount included a payment of about $14,000,000 dollars, or (say) £2,800,000, on account of the principal of the public debt then owing by the nation. The entire interest of the Public Debt at that time amounted to $3,144,620 or (say) £650,000; an amount which shows a very limited liability on account of the nation.

The items of the expenditure of the United States in 1860 are shown in the following table :—

Expenditure of the United States in 1860.

EXPENDITURE OF THE UNITED STATES GOVERNMENT, 1860.	
1. Civil List	$6,077,003
2. Foreign Intercourse	1,146,143
3. Navy	11,514,649
4. War	16,472,202
5. Pensions	1,100,802
6. Indians	2,991,131
7. Miscellaneous	20,708,183
Total Ordinary............	60,010,113
8. Interest on Debt	3,144,620
9. Principal of Debt	13,900,392
	17,045,012
Grand Total..............	$77,055,125

The expenditure of America contrasted with that of other nations.

In proportion to population, the United States, in 1860, had, I apprehend, the smallest expenditure and the smallest national debt of any country in the world. Let us look at the expenditure and liabilities of the greater European nations.

Nation.		Population.	Expenditure.	Debt.
			£	£
Austria............	(1860)	35,000,000	36,660,033	225,000,000
France	,,	37,000,000	82,620,301	389,000,000
Great Britain ...	,,	30,000,000	69,502,289	802,000,000
Italy..............	(1862)	22,000,000	38,973,896	200,000,000
Prussia............	,,	18,500,000	19,031,041	40,000,000
Russia	,,	74,000,000	44,374,248	60,000,000
Spain	,,	16,000,000	20,366,183	107,000,000

It will be seen that the United States, with a population of nearly 31,000,000, had a much smaller expenditure than any of these, whilst her debt was little more than nominal.

This contrast is very striking, if we regard it only as it relates to the population. But if we come to look at the expenditure of America in relation to the extent of her territory, the abundance and variety of her products, the value of her mineral resources, the industry of her population, her manufactures, her commerce, and the accumulated and rapidly-increasing wealth of her people, the contrast presented is even more remarkable. For, with the exception of Great Britain, no nation approaches the United States in any one of these respects; and yet every one of the nations, with less resources, had to bear, up to 1860, a heavier burden of expenditure. *The force of this contrast.*

The whole revenue of the United States, in 1860, was raised from Customs duties and sales of land. For a long series of previous years there can scarcely have been said to have been any direct internal taxation for national purposes in America. At the outbreak of the war of 1812, the expenditure of the United States was only $13,500,000, or £2,700,000 a year, the whole of which was met by light and easy Customs duties. The war of 1812 raised the expenditure from $13,000,000 to $22,000,000, $39,000,000, and $48,000,000; and direct taxes were then obliged to be levied. But about the year 1818, a surplus, amounting, I believe, to nearly $40,000,000, being found in the Exchequer, the burden of direct taxation was removed, and the internal taxes became of merely nominal amount up to 1836, when they ceased entirely. In addition, therefore, to having the smallest proportionate expenditure of any nation, the people of the United States, during the greatest part of the present *The American Revenue, how raised.* *Very small amount of the American taxation.*

century, have enjoyed the remarkable advantage of being the most lightly taxed people of the world. If we except the enhanced prices of certain classes of manufactures, caused by Customs duties, imposed for the purpose of protection, the people of the United States may be said to have, practically, paid no taxes for national objects.

Effect of the Civil War on the national expenditure.

But the breaking out of the Civil War in 1861, altered the whole condition of the expenditure and revenue of the United States. The total expenditure, which was $77,000,000 in 1860, rose to $85,000,000 in 1861, to $571,000 in 1862, to 715,000,000 in 1863, and to no less than $1,897,000,000 in 1865 ; or from £15,500,000 to nearly £380,000,000 in five years. The bulk of this enormous expenditure went for purposes of war. Out of the $1,897,000,000, the army and navy absorbed $1,153,000,000, or nearly two-thirds of the whole. The interest on the debt rose from $3,000,000 in 1860 to $77,000,000 in 1864 : or to as much as the sum-total of the national expenditure five years previous.

Direct Taxation levied.

To meet this large expenditure, not only were the Customs duties largely enhanced, but direct and internal taxes of large amounts were levied, and largely augmented in each successive year. They produced as follows :—

Amount of the direct taxes.

PRODUCE OF DIRECT TAXATION IN AMERICA.	
Year.	Amount.
1862	$1,795,332
1863	41,003,192
1864	116,850,672
1865	211,129,529

Thus upwards of £42,000,000 sterling was levied in the form of direct internal taxation during the last year of the war.

I think it is worth observing what the Commissioner of Internal Revenue says in his last report upon this levy of taxation :— *This heavy taxation patiently borne.*

" It is a matter of sincere congratulation that, thus far, the people of this country have so patiently borne the burden which has been put upon them, and have so freely contributed of their substance to fill the national treasury. With few exceptions, the demand of the tax-collector has been met promptly and willingly. And when it is recollected that the present generation only know by tradition, or by reference to obsolete statutes, that taxes have ever been imposed in this country upon articles of their own manufacture, and the objects of internal traffic, or upon the various crafts or professions in which they are employed; and when, too, it is considered that the revenue thus collected for the single year ending June 30th, 1865, amounts to a sum nearly or quite equal to all the receipts of this Government from whatever sources, except loans and treasury notes, from its organization to the war of 1812; and when it is further considered that this amount was contributed at a time when the commercial marine of the country had been nearly destroyed, and more than a million of hardy men were withdrawn from the productive pursuits of life, we may not only be justly proud that the material strength has been fully equal to the burden imposed, but that it has been borne so quietly and so willingly."

Even in the darkest hours of the war there appears to have been no shirking amongst the people of the North. They were prepared to submit to any outlay —to any burden of taxation possible to be borne—in order to bring the war to a conclusion, and to preserve the Union. Estimates were made by well-informed *Confidence of the people in the resources of the country.*

statists, that, even should the Union not be preserved, and even should the Southern States succeed in forming a separate Confederacy, the North alone was well able to bear the burden of taxation which the war would inevitably entail.* But when the war was brought to a termination, and the South once again came under the peaceful and undisputed control of the general Government, it seems to have been felt that no ground for alarm or distrust remained ; and that, once brought back to the prosperity which they enjoyed previous to to the war, the South would in due time contribute largely to the liquidation of the public debt, and would thereby vastly relieve the general pressure of the burden of taxation.

The Debt incurred.

I desire now to consider what the extent of that burden is, and how it is to be met by the revenue of the country.

Its Amount.

It has been already estimated that the total debt of the United States is $3,000,000,000.† It is taken at this amount by the Secretary of the Treasury in his Report to Congress, who says, that "it is safe to assume that the debt incurred will not exceed that amount." Now the annual interest upon $3,000,000,000 at 5½ per cent. per annum, would be $165,000,000 ; at 5 per cent it would be $150,000,000, or £30,000,000 of our money.

---

* *Vide,* in especial, Dr. William Elder's "Debt and Resources of the United States," Philadelphia, 1863 ; "Our Burden and Our Strength," by David A. Wells, published by the Loyal Publication Society of New York, 1864 ; and the several pamphlets of the Honourable R. J. Walker, published by Ridgway, Piccadilly, London.

† *Vide ante,* p. 7.

Now, I do not suppose it will be possible for the
Government of the United States at once to reduce its
war expenditure to the rate of the expenditure before
the outbreak—(say) £15,000,000 per annum. Provision
has to be made for increased establishments, which
cannot at once be reduced ; for pensions which have
become entailed upon the nation by the war ; for
differences arising from the condition of the currency ;
and for the necessary expenses entailed by the re-
settlement of the country. Giving the Government
credit for every possible anxiety to reduce the establishments of the country to a peace standard, and making
due allowance for the peculiar opportunities they have
of doing so, yet it is difficult to suppose but that,
for several years to come, there must be an enhanced
provision for increased establishments. It is so after
every war. The Continental wars of the early portion
of the present century were commenced by Great
Britain at a period when her annual expenditure did
not exceed £20,000,000, and since that period our
expenditure has never been less in any one year
than £45,000,000. The war of the United States in
1812 was commenced when her total annual expenditure was as little as $13,600,000 (£2,720,000) ; but,
although she very speedily paid off the debt occasioned by it, her annual outlay never fell again to
that amount. In 1823 it was, indeed, reduced as
low as $15,314,000, but it speedily rose again to
much larger amounts.

The President of the United States mentions, in his
Message, that there were 530 armed vessels in commission at the commencement of 1865, manned by 51,000

Marginal notes:

Estimate as to future national expenditure.

Increased establishments to be supported.

Large reductions in the Navy

men, and that at the close of that year the number had been reduced to 117 vessels, manned by 12,128 men. " By this prompt reduction," he says, " the expenses of the Government have been largely diminished." On

and Army.

the 1st May, 1865, the national military force numbered 1,000,516 men. By November last this force was reduced " by the discharge from the service of over 800,000 troops, and the war department is proceeding rapidly in the work of further reduction. The war estimates are reduced from $516,240,131 to $33,814,461, which amount, in the opinion of the department, is adequate for a peace establishment."*

This shows the anxiety of the Government to restore its establishments to an economical footing : but still I apprehend that it must be many years before the estimates of 1860 are again reached ; if, indeed, it is possible that they should ever be reduced to that amount.

Estimated Total Revenue and Expenditure of future years.

We will assume, then, that the total ordinary annual expenditure of the United States will be necessarily augmented for some years to come from £15,000,000 to (say) £20,000,000 sterling ($100,000,000). To this has to be added the £30,000,000 sterling, or $150,000,000, required for the payment of the interest upon the debt at 5 per cent. per annum. Here, then, we have the total indebtedness of the United States. The expenditure of the country is raised to an average of $250,000,000, or £50,000,000 a year. By reference to the table at the commencement of this chapter, it will be seen what proportion that amount bears to the annual expenditure of other nations.

* President Johnson's Message, 14th December, 1865.

The Secretary of the Treasury (Mr. McCulloch) puts the result as follows :—

Mr. McCulloch's proposal to pay off the Debt

" If," he says, " $200,000,000 per annum shall be applied, in half-yearly instalments of $100,000,000 each, in payment of the accruing interest and in reduction of the principal funded at the higher rate of 5½ per cent., the debt would be entirely paid in 32⅛ years. At 5 per cent per annum, it would be extinguished by the like application of $100,000,000 every six months, in a little over twenty-eight years. . . . After careful reflection, the Secretary concludes that no Act of Congress would be more acceptable to the people, or better calculated to strengthen the national credit, than one which should provide that $200,000,000, commencing with the next financial year, should be annually applied to the payment of the interest and principal of the national debt."

This would be practically an addition of $50,000,000 annually to the taxation of the country, for the purpose of redeeming the whole debt incurred by the War, in a period of about thirty years ; and the simple question is, whether $300,000,000, or £60,000,000 a year, is a burden of taxation which the American people are unable or unwilling to bear for (say) thirty years to come ? It is, no doubt, a large increase on the amount of revenue and expenditure in 1860. The payment also involves that which the people were not accustomed to prior to 1861, direct and internal taxes. Are the Americans willing to bear the burden ? Are they capable of bearing it ? The facts appear to answer both questions in the affirmative.

in thirty years.

First, as to their willingness.

The President of the United States observes :—

Willingness of the Americans to bear the burden.

" Our debt is doubly secure—first, in the actual wealth and still greater undeveloped resources of the country, and next, in the character of our institutions. Political economists have not failed to remark, that the public debt of a country is safe in proportion as its people are free; that the debt of a republic is the safest of all. Our history confirms and establishes the theory, and is, I firmly believe, destined to give it a still more signal illustration. The secret of this superiority springs not merely from the fact that, in a republic, the national obligations are distributed more widely through countless numbers in all classes of society; it has its root in the character of our laws. Here all men contribute to the public welfare, and bear their fair share of the public burdens. During the war, under the impulses of patriotism, the men of the great body of the people, without regard to their own comparative want of wealth, thronged to our armies and filled our fleets of war, and held themselves ready to offer their lives for the public good. Now, in their turn, the property and income of the country should bear their just proportion of the burden of taxation; while in our impost system, through means of which increased vitality is incidentally imparted to all the industrial interests of the nation, the duties should be so adjusted as to fall most heavily on articles of luxury, leaving the necessaries of life as free from taxation as the absolute wants of the Government, economically administered, will justify. No favoured class should demand freedom from assessment, and the taxes should be so distributed as not to fall unduly on the poor, but rather on the accumulated wealth of the country. We should look at the national debt just as it is—not as a national blessing, but as a heavy burden on the industry of the country, to be discharged without unnecessary delay.

"It is estimated by the Secretary of the Treasury, that the expenditures for the fiscal year ending the 30th of June, 1866, will exceed the receipts $112,194,947. It is gratifying, however, to state that it is also estimated that the revenue for the year ending the 30th of June, 1867, will exceed the expenditures in the sum of $111,682,818. This amount, or so much as may be deemed sufficient for the purpose, may be applied to the reduction of the public debt. Every reduction will diminish the total amount of interest to be paid, and so enlarge the means of still further reductions, until the

whole shall be liquidated; and this, as will be seen from
the estimates of the Secretary of the Treasury, may be accomplished by annual payments even within a period not
exceeding thirty years. I have faith that we shall do all
this within a reasonable time; that, as we have amazed the
world by the suppression of a civil war which was thought
to be beyond the control of any Government, so we shall
equally show the superiority of our institutions by the prompt
and faithful discharge of our national obligations."

We have already seen how willingly the burden of
heavily increased and rapidly increasing taxation was
borne throughout the War. It had then to be borne
under the most unfavourable circumstances. The
great bulk of the labour power of the nation was
withdrawn from the ordinary pursuits of agriculture
and commerce. The nation itself was divided, and the
people of one section of the country alone had to bear
the burden. Everything was opposed to the levy of
taxation to such an extent and under such circumstances. The taxes themselves were framed under
circumstances of pressing necessity, with little regard
to the principles which ought to govern the true levy
of taxation. Nevertheless, these charges were cheerfully met. Is it then, to be doubted that under a
reconstruction of the Union, with the people restored
to their accustomed industrial pursuits, and with re-
vised legislation by which taxation will be equably
and justly apportioned, the people who cheerfully paid
during the War will make any difficulty in bearing
the burden during Peace?

Is there any question as to their ability to bear the
burden? I shall have written these pages to very little
purpose, if those who have followed me through them

*Ability of the
Americans to
pay the debt.*

doubt the ability of the American people to bear sixty millions of taxes, either at the present time, or during the thirty years next to come. So far from there being any reasonable doubt on that head, the doubt seems rather to be whether, after peace is fully and entirely restored, the nation will not be able to bear a far heavier levy of taxation than that which she is at present called on to endure. Let us examine this part of the question by the light of the past.

Value of real and personal estate in America.

It appears from the Census tables, that the total value of real and personal estate in the United States was—

In 1850 .... $7,135,780,228
In 1860 .... $16,159,616,068

Estimate of its increased value in 1870.

or an increase of 126 per cent in ten years. At the same rate of increase, the value of real and personal estate in 1870 would be $36,593,450,585. But suppose that, in consequence of the Civil War and the position of the South, we estimate the increase at the end of the next decade at one half only of the rate of increment during the last decade. That will give nearly $27,000,000,000 as the aggregate property of the United States in 1870. In proportion to this capital

Proportion of the debt and annual taxation to these values

the whole debt of $3,000,000,000 stands in the relation of one in nine, and the annual taxation of $300,000,000 only in the ratio of one in ninety.

The Secretary of the Treasury offers these facts to our consideration in another form. He says :—

" Taking the increase of wealth in the loyal States in the ten years from 1860 to 1870, at 125 per cent., we have, as their capital in 1870, $24,111,000,000; and if we put the wealth of the other States at the same figure as in 1860, without allowing anything for increase, we have a capital, for

1870, of $27,000,578,000. This sum gives us the product of the year at $6,000,894,500, upon which a payment on the debt of two hundred millions is 2·9 per cent.

"If we add but 25 per cent. to the wealth of 1860 for the States lately in insurrection as their probable valuation in 1870, the charge of two hundred millions upon the products of that year will be 2·81 per cent. But, allowing all that can be claimed in this respect, and taking the lowest estimate for 1870 as the basis for calculating the wealth and products of the year 1880, 125 per cent. increase in this period gives a capital of sixty-two thousand and fifty millions, and a product of fifteen thousand five hundred and twelve millions, upon which sum a charge of two hundred millions falls to 1·29 per cent."

The burden of the debt and the taxation of the United States is, therefore, in comparison with that of other nations, still an easy burden. It is a very much easier burden than that which we have to bear in Great Britain, with a debt one-fourth larger, with ordinary expenses of more than double the amount of those in the United States and with, in many respects, less wealth-producing power. "The Government charges for all expenditures fifty years ago," says Mr. McCulloch, "took one pound in six of the products of Great Britain, but those charges have now fallen to one pound in nine. We commence our National burden with resources that, in the very first year, will be required to bear an aggregate of less than five per cent., or $1 in $20." *The burden light in comparison with that of other nations.*

But it is especially necessary, in order that this taxation may be willingly and ably borne, that it should be equally assessed. At present, the whole system of the levy of taxation in America is crude and ill arranged. I propose to consider, in the next Chapter, how the public burdens may be better apportioned. *Necessity of a proper apportionment of taxation.*

CHAPTER II

The present system of American taxation only temporary.

THE system of taxation at present existing in the United States can only be regarded as a temporary system, framed under circumstances of pressing necessity, for the sole object of raising revenue to meet great emergencies. In principle, as well as in practice, nothing can be worse than some of the taxes at present imposed. Not only is every individual taxed, but almost every article, not only of luxury and convenience, but also of commerce and necessity, is, in some form or other, made to bear the burden of taxation. Exemption from taxation is the exception, not the rule : indeed, the very diffuseness of the system is one of the greatest possible objections to it. Were it perpetuated, there can be no doubt that the system would exercise a most injurious influence on the commerce and industry of the country.

Steps already taken to revise the system.

But I am happy to say that this taxation is not to be perpetuated. The Americans are too far-sighted to allow it to be continued a moment longer than can be avoided. Immediately at the conclusion of the Civil War a Commission was appointed, consisting of Mr. D. A. Wells, of New York ; Mr. Stephen Colwell, of

Pennsylvania ; and Mr. Hayes, of Illinois, " to inquire and report upon the best and most efficient mode of raising revenue by taxation." Few commissioners were ever charged with a more important task, or ever had offered to them a greater opportunity. By the light of the improved principles of taxation prevailing in other nations, this Commission has the opportunity of laying down for the United States a sound and permanent basis of taxation, sufficient for the provision of the required revenue, and at the same time calculated, in the least degree, to shackle the trade and commerce of the country. America, in fact, has the opportunity presented to her of setting, in respect of her taxation, an example to the world.

The principal items of the direct taxation levied during the war, have been derived from banks, income-tax, licenses, railroads, Insurance Companies, taxes on salaries, stamps, iron, petroleum, tobacco, spirits, fermented liquors, legacies and successions. Besides these, however, there have been latterly imposed a number of duties of various descriptions, many of which have been of a very vexatious, inquisitorial, and obnoxious character. Taxes have been levied, under one schedule, upon all wagons, carriages, harness, watches, pianos, plate, yachts, and other articles, all of which were treated as articles of luxury. Another tax was imposed upon *the repairs* of all engines, cars, carriages, ships, pianos, furniture, &c. Another tax was levied upon the manufacture of articles of wearing apparel—a tax designed to reach large wholesale manufacturers, but which, practically, operated with most severity on a number of small operatives—such as

The principal War Assessments.

Minor Taxes

on articles of Luxury,

Repairs,

Wearing Apparel,

milliners, dressmakers, knitters, shoemakers, &c. An-
Books, other tax has been recently levied on printed books,
magazines, &c., the effect of which has been to induce
the printers of New York, in many cases, to send their
books out of the country to be printed, inasmuch as the
Customs duty on foreign publications was not so heavy
as the aggregate of the internal duties upon printed
books. A tax in the form of a stamp-duty has
Photographs, been levied upon "photographs" and "match-boxes,"
Matches. and, curiously enough, the tax on the last-mentioned
article has been found eminently profitable. It is a
small tax, of one cent per box or bunch of one
hundred matches ; and for the fiscal year 1865, the
"match-stamp" brought the revenue about $1,000,000.
From the large quantity of matches manufactured in
anticipation of the tax (which only took effect 1st
August, 1864), it is believed that, up to the present
time, the Government has not received from this
article its legitimate revenue, and that in 1866 it will
produce nearly $3,500,000.

Duplication One of the great evils complained of under this
of Taxation. system is the duplication of taxation, and the consequent increase of price of the article to an amount
disproportioned to its value. An illustration of this is
given in an account of the taxation applied to an
umbrella. If the supporting-rod is of iron or steel, or
foreign wood, it is subject to a tax. The handles of
carved wood, ivory, or bone, are subject to another tax.
The brass runners, the tips, the elastic bands, the silk
tassels, the buttons, and the cover, whether of silk,
gingham, or alpaca, are each and all taxed as distinct
products of manufacture. The umbrella having thus

contributed to the revenue at the rate of 6 per cent. *ad valorem*, in respect of every one of its constituent parts, is subjected, when made up, to another duty of 6 per cent. *ad valorem*, as a whole. From 12 to 15 per cent. is thus directly added to the cost of the article, and as the manufacturer of each product comprised in the umbrella has to make an addition to cost price, by reason of his special outlay in respect of the tax which applies to his department, it may be computed that the cost-price of an umbrella is raised from 20 to 25 per cent. above its value, although only charged with a direct tax of 6 per cent. Again, in the case of books and pamphlets, it is said that every separate item which enters into the composition of a book—paper, boards, cloth, glue, thread, gold leaf, leather, and type materials—are all charged with duties of from 3 to 6 per cent. in the first instance, and then 5 per cent. *on the selling price* of the book in addition. Such a system as this obviously violates all the fundamental principles of taxation. Such taxes are neither definite in amount, nor equal in application ; and they ought to be repealed at the earliest moment.

The principle which ought to be laid down in dealing with the question of taxation in America, is to *concentrate* the system ; to levy the taxes in the form which is the most simple, the least vexatious and inquisitorial, the least calculated to impede industry or to provoke fraud. The taxes permanently imposed should be such as can be most surely and satisfactorily collected, and they should be direct, comprehensive, and sufficing. That these views are understood and appreciated in the United States, cannot be better shown than by the

Concentration of Taxation needed.

Mr. Secretary McCulloch following extract from the recent Report of Mr. Secretary McCulloch :—

on the future Taxation of America. "The present system of internal revenue is one of the results of the war. It was framed under circumstances of pressing necessity, affording little opportunity for careful and accurate investigation of the sources of revenue. With the restoration of peace, industry is returning again to its former channels, and a revision of the system now becomes important to accommodate it to the changed and changing condition of the country.

"Every complicated system of taxation opens the way to mistakes, abuses, and deceptions. Temptations to dishonesty and fraud are placed before the revenue officers and the tax-payers, and both are often thereby demoralized. Honest men, who pay their taxes in full, are injured, if not ruined, by the ingenuity of those who successfully evade their share of the public burdens.

"The multiplicity of objects at present subject to taxation is one of the most serious objections to the present system. Many of these yield little revenue, while its collection is troublesome to the collector, and irritating and offensive to the tax-payers. This multiplicity also involves as many temptations to fraud, and as many difficult questions for decision, as the objects from which large revenue is derived.

"To impose taxes judiciously, so as to obtain revenue without repressing industry, is one of the highest and most difficult duties devolved upon Congress. Taxation which in one year may be scarcely felt, may the next year be oppressive; and that which may not be burdensome to those who are well established in business may be fatal to those just commencing. Every branch of industry has its infancy, and ought to be encouraged by liberal legislation. Whatever of industry or enterprise is destroyed, by injudicious taxation or otherwise, is a damage to the national welfare.

"Heavy taxation may drive capital from our shores, or prevent its employment in the manner most advantageous to the country, and thus prevent that demand for labour which is the best security for its proper reward."

Inclined as they are to face the difficulties of their
position, I can have little doubt myself that a comprehensive tax upon the property and income of the
country is the first to which the Americans should
look for revenue. The products of America—in other
words, the property and income of the country—
increase in a far more rapid ratio than the population;
and in a few years hence they may be expected to be
so great, that any tax now levied on them will fall
very lightly. It would be far better, I think, for
the Americans, to face a stern reality than a petty
taxation. Let them have one large tax levied upon
property and income, and have done with it. Under
such a tax every class will bear the great burden of
taxation proportionately to their means of bearing it,
and no class would have to chafe under petty and
irritating personal assessments.

Taxation of Property and Income.

In some of the cities of America, at the present
time, the assessments for purposes of local improvements and public works are extremely heavy. The
citizens of New York pay more than three millions
sterling in the shape of local taxes : a sum greater than
the entire taxation of Canada. All this taxation is
direct taxation—assessed upon house property, &c.,
according to value. The payments are made without
difficulty, and in most cases uncomplainingly. In
England, perhaps, we should think it would be right,
in the face of a heavy burden of taxation for national
purposes, to restrain, as far as possible, the expenditure
for local purposes. I am by no means sure that the
Americans would require this. They are very proud of
their local improvements, and in most cases very cheer-

*Local assess-
ments upon
property.*

fully respond to the calls made on them to meet their cost. These taxes stand in substitution of the large amounts we pay, in Poor's-rates and Police-rates, to maintain our paupers and suppress our criminals. The large amounts the American people contribute, by direct taxation, to their local assessments, show how well they are capable of bearing the burden of direct national taxation.

Spirit duties.

Next to the tax on property and income, I should look to a tax on the products of distillation as the best tax for purposes of revenue. In order to render this tax effective, the honest distiller must, however, be supported against illicit manufacture. I think this should be done. The policy of every country is in favour of taxing spirits to the maximum amount which is consistent with the development of revenue. In Great Britain, a uniform duty of 10s. per gallon does not check consumption, nor is it found to stimulate illicit manufacture. I think the United States can bear an equally high rate of duty on this article. The revenue demands its imposition; and in justice to themselves, the people, having decided what is the best system of taxation, should be invoked to assist in the enforcement of the law. I appreciate so highly the American character, that I believe, if it were decided to levy a high rate of duty upon spirits as a source of revenue, the people of the country would demand and see to the enforcement of the law.

Duties on Manu-factured Tobacco.

I am the more inclined to this opinion from finding that the tax upon cigars and manufactured tobacco, first imposed in 1863, has been very productive. Last year no less than $11,387,799 was paid by the North alone in the form of duties on cigars, snuff, and chewing and smoking tobacco. I understand that this amount would have been much greater, but for disturbing causes, arising from a large supply of Southern tobacco being brought for sale to Northern markets, under defective revenue regulations, and also from large quantities being brought into consumption which had paid duty at the lower rates of previous years. But in a country where tobacco may be said to grow in every garden, it appears very remarkable that so large a revenue should be received from the article. The present tax on cigars is $10 per thousand, or one cent on each cigar; the duty on fine-cut and plug tobacco (so largely consumed in America) is 40 cents per lb. These duties, under the circumstances of the country, do not appear excessive. I think it would be advisable to continue them, and I believe that when the causes which disturbed the trade last year are removed, the revenue from this source will be nearly doubled.

A true financial policy cannot admit of duties upon raw materials. There is a party in America which advocates the imposition of a duty on raw cotton, resin, and other products of the South. I confess that I require much better arguments than any which have yet reached me to justify such taxation. The South is on the eve of recovering from a great depression: it is therefore bad policy to do anything calculated still further to depress her. She is about to re-enter a market, over which she has lost the command, and to re-enter it as a competitor with other nations for the sale of her staples. At such

Duties on raw materials.

Their policy considered,

in relation to the South,

a moment it would surely be unwise to levy a tax
upon those staples. Besides this, a tax upon raw
cotton, nearly the whole of which is exported from

in their
effects on
Exports.

America, would be tantamount to a tax on exports,
which is not only opposed to the law but opposed
to the very policy and genius of American commerce.
The people of the United States, from the days of
Washington, have been taught to regard all duties
with apprehension, but export duties with especial
dislike. Nor is it to be doubted that a duty upon
exports is, of all duties, the most disadvantageous
to a nation. Under all circumstances such duties
are erroneous in principle and injurious in operation.
A duty upon cotton in America would be a premium
to the producer of cotton elsewhere. Some years ago,

Sir R. Peel's
Export duty
on British
Coal.

Sir Robert Peel, with a view to raise revenue, imposed
a duty upon the export of coal from Great Britain.
The imposition of this duty was strongly opposed by
the Free Traders, but was defended by the protectionists upon the ground that foreigners were using
our coal in their own manufactories, and thereby
competing with British manufactures by the employment of her own raw material. The duty lasted
three years, and then Sir Robert Peel came down to
Parliament and abandoned it.* It had had the effect,

Its injurious
results on
trade and
commerce.

he said, of rapidly checking our foreign coal trade.
The revenue raised under the duty was insignificant;
and the tax had only operated to reduce the profits
of the British coal-shipper and induce activity in

* I hope I shall not be charged with egotism in quoting as to
these facts from a previous publication of my own. Vide "*Taxation: its Levy and Expenditure*," by Sir Morton Peto, page 65.

working mines for coal in foreign countries. Under this duty, in fact, our trade in coal with France passed into other hands. France developed coal mines of her own, and also coal fields in Belgium, on her immediate frontier; and England, which can supply the largest quantities of coal at the cheapest price, instead of regulating the French market, was reduced to the condition of affording France only one-twelfth part of the coal required for her consumption.

It appears to me that the two cases are quite analogous. Cotton is the principal staple of the South, as Coal may be said to be the principal staple of the British isles. Any tax which may partially act as an export duty upon either commodity cannot fail to check trade, and stimulate production in other countries. I believe that, at the present moment, no worse tax could be devised for America than a duty upon cotton.

Analogy between the cases of Coal and Cotton.

It may be argued, that in consequence of the prices obtained for the article at the present time in foreign markets the raw cotton of the United States can bear the imposition of a small duty. But this is an argument not to be relied on. Markets fluctuate with supply and demand. Those who favour a small duty upon raw cotton look to obtain a large revenue from an abundant supply. But it is to be remembered that an abundant supply will depress the price of the article: and the more the price of the article is depressed the heavier will be the weight of this duty on the producer.

Arguments in favour of the duty considered.

It is curious that those who contend the most vigorously in America for a duty upon cotton, are those who contend the most vigorously for the removal of every duty on native manufactures, as injurious to native industry. But surely if a manufactured article cannot bear the burden of taxation, the raw product from which it is made cannot be expected to bear it.

Feelings under which the duty on Cotton is sought to be imposed.

It is much to be feared that the feelings which enter into the consideration of this question are far from pure. It is not any mere question of revenue or taxation that is thought of, so much as a means of shifting the burden from one portion of the country to another. But I put it to the people of the United States, if higher and nobler feelings ought not to prevail in the adjustment of this great question ? I put it to them, whether the prosperity of the nation, as a whole, is not the object to be regarded ? The national taxation should not be adjusted by a conflict of interests, but by a fair and equable apportionment of burdens. A property and income-tax, a tax on spirits and fermented liquors, a duty on manufactured tobacco, would fall on all ; but taxes on cotton or resin, levied on the producer, would fall on one class only, and that class the least capable at the present time of bearing it. Justice and policy alike demand that the products of the South should not be subjected to taxation.

The duties on Iron, Coal, and Petroleum.

On the same principle that I condemn the application of taxation to the raw products of the South, I would contend for the removal of duties on the raw products of the North. The duties now levied on mineral products,—iron, coal, and petroleum,—ought immediately to be removed. These articles all lie at the basis of industry, and it is for the advantage of every interest of America that their production and sale should be, in the largest degree, increased and cheapened. It is quite clear that if the production of native coal and iron is to be stimulated, which I think so possible and so desirable, the object cannot be accomplished in the face of duties on the raw material. As regards petroleum, of which the supply is, at present, so largely in excess of the demand, it is obvious that to levy a heavy duty on that article in its original and crude state is merely to throw on those, who enter into enterprizes for its development, a tax to which their skill and industry ought not to expose them.

Next to the taxes upon raw materials, those upon trade require to be dealt with. These involve general licenses to traders and taxes upon banks and monetary operations. Almost every one who carries on an important business in the United States needs to be licensed, as the following table shews :— *Taxes on Trades.*

Apothecaries.	Butchers.	*Traders licensed.*
Auctioneers.	Distillers.	
Bankers.	Hotel Keepers.	
Billiard-table Keepers.	Lawyers.	
Brokers.	Lottery-ticket Dealers.	
Bowling-alley Keepers.	Manufacturers.	
Cattle Brokers.	Peddlers.	
Commission Brokers.	Photographers.	
Produce Brokers.	Physicians and Surgeons.	
Pawnbrokers.	Retail Dealers.	
Stockbrokers.	Wholesale Dealers.	
Builders and Contractors.		

The payments on account of these licences amounted, in 1865, to $12,613,478, equal to more than 2,500,000*l.* annually.

The principal amounts received for these licences are taken from wholesale dealers, retail dealers (especially the dealers in liquors), hotel-keepers, bankers, and brokers. If it is considered necessary, for existing purposes, to continue for any period this sort of taxation, it ought to be apportioned upon these traders, as to a certain extent is done with ourselves in England. We have a system of licences to auctioneers, attorneys, bankers, brokers, brewers, and other dealers, which is not complained of, but which, on the contrary, is regarded as useful and discriminating, by many of those who follow such pursuits. But care should be taken in America, as with ourselves, that trade and traffic is not prejudiced by the manner in which such duties are applied. If assessed at heavy rates, such taxes fall very detrimentally on the young and struggling. They prevent enterprizing young men from following trades and professions in which they might often be usefully employed; and such duties are, consequently, apt to create monopolies. If they are to be continued for a time, all these license duties should therefore be levied with as light a hand as possible, so as not to deter any one from entering into any of the various occupations they affect. Wherever these licences are found to produce very small amounts to revenue, they should be at once removed; and in all cases they should be reduced, with a view to ultimate removal as soon as possible.

In the same way with regard to banks and banking. The original idea in America was to levy a duty upon the dividends derived from what we should call the dividends on joint-stock banking operations. To this, as a source of income, there can be no valid objection. But the tax on banks has been applied to their capital, to their circulation, to their deposits, and in March, 1865, it was even extended to the deposits placed in savings banks having no capital stock. All these duties ought to be abandoned at the earliest practicable period. They are taxes, not on wealth, but on the industry employed in its accumulation. To tax the deposits in banks is merely to check deposits; and the effect of that must be, not merely to check circulation but to limit every enterprize throughout the community. Nothing could be more fatal to the people of the United States, dependent as they are on enterprize. In the same way with the tax upon insurances. It has been levied not only on the dividends and capital of insurance companies, but on premiums and assessments. A worse system could scarcely have been devised. A tax on insurance is a tax not only upon industry but upon providence and frugality. And the American system seems to be far worse than that of which we have been so long complaining in Great Britain in respect of fire insurance, and which, by such complaints, we have recently compelled our Government to a large extent to forego.

Tax upon Insurances.

The taxes on transit, chiefly paid by railroad companies, will, I apprehend, after their denunciation in the Message of the President, be immediately removed. In a country like America, where everything depends on facilities of transport, a tax on those facilities must be most injurious. These taxes were originally intended to reach the dividends and profits of carrying companies, but they have gone far beyond that object.

Taxes on Transit.

They are now, practically, impediments to transport, and in this light it is essential to the prosperity of the nation that they should be entirely removed. Such has been the power and influence of the "Express Companies," that those monopolists, although far more capable than other carriers of bearing the burden of this taxation, have never been taxed to the same extent as other companies. I am far from recommending that the tax to which they are at present exposed should be increased. However much I may think that such companies are detrimental to the interests of railroads and of the public, I believe that the true interest of the nation is to repeal altogether every duty which directly or indirectly affects the intercommunication of the nation.

Stamp
duties.

The duties derived from stamps appear to have been very willingly borne in the United States, to have been collected with care, with small expense, and with a comparative absence of attempts at fraud. I would not, therefore, recommend any discontinuance of these items of taxation at present. Under a proper system the stamp duties may, probably, be made increasingly available and lucrative. There are certain difficulties, I know, respecting the application of these duties. The proceedings of some of the Courts of law, from neglect to affix or cancel the requisite stamps on written and other legal processes, have been rendered practically abortive. And, in the South, difficulties have arisen in consequence of Acts of Congress not having been operative during the Civil War, and conveyances and other processes not having been, in those districts, duly subjected to stamp duties. But these, as it seems to me, are temporary inconveniences, for which proper provisions may be made. The amount received from the stamp duties is very large; it is likely greatly to increase, and I should not recommend any disturbance of those duties beyond such as is likely to facilitate the general application of the law.

Duties on Sales by Auction or Commission.

I am afraid that the duties on sales by brokers and by auctioneers must remain as they are at present: and the duties on legacies and successions ought, I think, also to be continued, with a view to test their ultimate effect. All the other direct taxes recently enforced in the United States, ought in my opinion to be forthwith removed. The petty and vexatious applications of taxation to umbrellas and parasols, repairs, watches, piano-fortes, passports, theatres, circuses, and to pickles, confectionary, glue, pins, pottery, and, above all, to "animals slaughtered," (whereby a direct tax is levied upon the food of the people,) ought all to be swept away, as unworthy of a great nation, and injurious to the freedom of its internal trade. Anything is better than that a great people should attempt to meet a great emergency by petty duties. They entail disproportionate cost in collection; unnecessary vexations to those who are assessed; numberless attempts at fraud and evasion, most injurious to the moral bearing of the people: and in their result they only in a small degree mitigate the weight of the burden to be borne. Far better in every respect, that the people of the United States should face the difficulty and pay one heavy impost, than that they should submit to countless petty burdens, encumbering their businesses, entailing endless incon-

Petty Taxes.

venience and annoyance, and calculated to excite impatience of taxation.

Customs Duties.

The same principle should be applied to the levy of duties upon foreign articles of import under the Customs Acts. There are certain Customs duties, such as those imposed upon silks, spices, sugar, tea, coffee, drugs, fruits, and a variety of articles of luxury, and even of general necessity, that produce large amounts to the general revenue, and that it is desirable, at any rate at present, not to discontinue. But all petty charges should be abandoned, and the duties concentrated on as small a number of items as possible. In Great Britain, in 1841, we had Customs duties on no less than 1163 articles; in 1862, we levied such duties on only 44. And whilst the gross produce of our duties on the 1163 articles, in 1841, was £21,900,000, in 1862, upon only 44 articles, and at reduced rates on most of those, it was £24,036,000! This shows what is to be gained by unshackling commerce. Our policy has been to remit every duty that offered an obstacle to the extension of trade; it has proved the true policy in our case, and America ought to profit by our example.

Collection of Customs Duties.

I am afraid, from what I heard in America, that a very great reform is required in the system under which the Customs duties of the United States are, at the present time, collected. Tales are very widely spread (for which, however, I have no better authority than general belief) of a most imperfect, not to say irregular system, prevailing in that department. It is asserted that the national exchequer receives but a limited proportion of the revenue which it ought to derive from duties upon imports. " Undervaluations " of invoices, and great laxity in the mode of " refunding " duties, paid or alleged to have been paid in excess, are said to be fruitful sources of what amounts to fraud on the revenue. A laxity in the system of levying revenue must be equivalent to increased taxation, and it is, therefore, most desirable in the present state of American finance, that these complaints should be investigated and the evil removed, if it exists.

With regard to the department of Internal Revenue, it is also said that, having been recently organized on a very imperfect basis, it is at present utterly incompetent to discharge the multifarious and onerous duties which devolve on it. It is stated that a late Commissioner of Internal Revenue declared that " if the law, as it now stands, could be fully and effectually executed, the receipts from that branch of taxation would not fall short of $500,000,000 annually," or double the amount received in 1865 from these sources of revenue. In order to carry out a better system of finance, it is obvious that one of the first objects must be to place the establishments for the collection of the revenue on a proper footing. I fear that from England we cannot offer America any model for the accomplishment of this object; but I have no doubt the people of the United States will be able to devise an efficient system for themselves.

In conclusion :—there is not the slightest cause to doubt that, under a simple and efficient system of taxation, the Government of the United States will find ample funds to meet every national requirement. In the last chapter, I have estimated the expenditure

The Inland Revenue department.

of the country for the next ten years, at an average of $300,000,000 per annum. A paper very recently laid before Congress by the Secretary of the Treasury, affords assurance that the income for the year ending 30th June, 1866, will not be less than that amount. I do not think that it admits of doubt, that under a revised system of general taxation, carefully and faithfully administered, it is possible to raise this aggregate to $400,000,000. In either case a large margin is left, either for the immediate reduction of the taxation of the people, or for the defrayment of the principal of the debt. Some may incline to the opinion that it is best at once to get rid of a portion of the burden for which taxation is imposed; whilst others may think that it is more desirable to afford the fullest opportunity for that complete development of those resources, which will lead to an earlier removal of the encumbrance than even a payment by instalments. To other nations, it is immaterial which course the people of the United States think it the better to adopt. As it concerns themselves, it will be satisfactory to them to know that those who have investigated the sources of their wealth and prosperity, feel assured that they are fully competent to the discharge of all the liabilities which the war has entailed upon them; and that, if properly and judiciously apportioned, the burden of taxation will not press unduly on their means.

SECTION IX.

CONCLUSION.

SECTION IX.

CONCLUSION.

THE Hon. R. J. Walker, in one of his letters on America, observes :—

"In view of the fact that the people of the United Kingdom, and of the United States, are mainly of the same race, speak the same language, have the same literature, ancestry, and common law, with the same history for centuries, and a reciprocal commerce exceeding that of all the rest of the world, it is amazing how little is known in each country of the other.

"This condition of affairs is most unfavourable to the continuance of peace and good-will between two great and kindred nations. It causes constant misapprehension by each party of the acts and motives of the other, arrests the development of friendly feeling, and retards the advance of commercial freedom. It excites almost daily rumours of impending war, disturbing the course of trade, causing large mercantile losses, and great unnecessary Government expenditures. If war has not ensued, it has led to angry controversy and bitter recrimination. It is sowing broadcast, in both countries, the seeds of hatred."

C C

It has been my endeavour, in the foregoing pages, to inform my fellow-countrymen as to the condition of the population, the agriculture, the manufactures, the mineral resources, and the commerce of the United States. I have treated of those facilities of communication which are so essential to the prosperity of the country. I have considered the present position and future prospects of the South: and the financial condition of America with reference especially to the revenue, expenditure, and taxation of the nation. But before bringing to a conclusion this account of the resources and prospects of the country, there are some other features of America with which it is scarcely less important that the British public should be made familiar.

On their return from the United States, travellers are not unfrequently asked what feature struck them most forcibly in their journey through the country. Looking to the territory, I should certainly answer to such a question, its wide expanse and its abundant resources: but looking to the people, I should say, *the absence of pauperism.* Nothing is more striking to a European than the universal respectability of appearance of all classes in America. You see no rags, you meet no beggars. In London the painful scenes, whether of real or of fictitious woe, that are encountered at every turning are in the highest degree distressing. Pauperism pursues the passenger on every pavement. It is to me one of the most distressing reflections of existence, that our great and thriving nation goes on, year after year, increasing the numbers of those who are dependent upon charity for

---

Marginal notes:

Features of America examined in these pages.

Remaining topics.

Absence of Pauperism in America.

daily food. Why are we not able to afford employment to the population of these realms? Why is it
that one out of every twenty of our entire population
is a pauper? How comes it that our union work-
houses, our hospitals and asylums, and charitable
institutions of every class, are so full of objects of
benevolence, and that yet there is such a super-
abundance of beggary thronging our streets? Our
population does not increase in anything approaching
the ratio of the increase of population in the United
States; and yet, with us, every branch of labour and
business is so overcharged, that the introduction of
a new hand can only be accomplished by the dis-
placement of an old one. In America, on the contrary, every addition to the population and labour
of the country is hailed with satisfaction, as an addition to its wealth; no one is without employment,
and every one has the means before him of improving
his position.

Contrast between England and America.

It was observed the other day in the House of
Commons, that Parliament would do well if it devoted
an entire session to the consideration of the state of
Ireland. Another session might be equally well employed in the exclusive consideration of the condition
of our poor. After having seen the state of society
in America, I feel quite convinced, that it is impossible we can go on much longer on the present
system. We fill our statute-books with poor-laws;
we annually increase our rates for the relief of the
poor to such an extent that many parishes become
quite unable to bear them, and call aloud for a
national assessment; our tables are covered with

The increase of pauperism in Great Britain,

appeals for donations to charitable institutions, until
people become perplexed and hardened by the very
number of the applications; we enact new laws to
provide accommodation for the casual and home-
less poor; the emigration from our shores to America
and Australia is so enormous as to people those con-

a subject which requires grave consideration

tinents; and yet, whilst our trade and commerce
increases beyond any parellel, the pauperism of the
country increases also. Here is, indeed, a problem
requiring solution, and to which the best statesmen
might advantageously apply themselves. Let it be
considered by the light which the condition of American society reflects on it—where there is no beggary,
and only such poverty as arises from causes beyond
the control of human nature.

The diffusion of wealth in America.

The equal distribution of wealth in the United
States is, certainly, a very marked feature of the
nation. Whilst there may be said to be no poor,
the number is also comparatively few of those whom
we should class as very rich. As I write these
lines I read in the daily papers of the death of a
London merchant, whose personal property is sworn
in the Court of Probate, at £2,995,000, a sum which
approaches $15,000,000. Such fortunes, amassed in a
single life-time, are not common amongst us: though
we no doubt have many great merchant princes,
capitalists, bankers, and landowners, whose individual
wealth equals the amount. But in America there are
very few people indeed who can be considered "mil-
lionaires." Three or four well-known cases of great
wealth will occur to every one acquainted with commercial circles in New York and Boston: but exces-

sive accumulations do not extend beyond a very
limited number of individuals. In a word, the wealth
of America is *diffused*. You find few inordinately
rich, but you find every one able to meet the demands
that can be justly made on him.

And this has an important bearing on the political
position and action of the nation. I do not think
that we at all comprehend, in England, what is
implied by universal suffrage. Universal suffrage is
regarded by the largest portion of our population as
utterly unsuited to the condition of Great Britain,
and as calculated to lead to political confusion. And,
no doubt, it would be utterly unsuited to the present condition of society in this country. But it is
another thing in its application to America. Where
every man has his proportionate share of the good
things of this world, all feel entitled to claim a
fair share in the administration of the affairs of the
nation. "Equality," as it is construed with us, "is
the reduction of the competent to a level with the
incompetent." But "Equality," as it is construed
in America, "implies neither the degradation nor the
elevation of any one class at the expense of another.
All are equal amongst equals : citizens—not subjects. We are accustomed to believe that a man
is solely measured in America by his wealth. I
doubt if that idea does not prevail in Europe in
an exaggerated degree. Wealth undoubtedly has
great influence in America : it has influence everywhere ; nowhere, perhaps, has it more influence than
amongst ourselves. Those who pursue trade and commerce always have regarded, and I suppose always

The Ame-
rican Suffrage

unsuited to
Great Britain,

but well
adapted to a
nation

where
Equality
implies Citi-
zenship.

The influence
of wealth ;

In England ; will look up with the highest admiration to those who
make the largest profits in the occupations, trades,
professions, and pursuits which they respectively fol-

In America. low. That sort of feeling prevails on both sides of
the Atlantic. But I greatly doubt if men are measured by their wealth by the people of the United

The dis- States at large. Everything appears to indicate the
tinction. contrary. It is not the very rich, or even the
wealthier class, who are elected to state offices, or
to Congress, or to the Senate, or the Presidency.

President Abraham Lincoln was not a rich man, or even a
Lincoln. powerful man : on the contrary, he was a very
humble man—one who had raised himself from the
smallest beginnings, by the energy of his character,
and by his ability, address, sound judgment, transparent honesty, and great discretion. His position
in life, when he was elected president, was very
moderate. I have before me, as I write, a picture of
his house at Springfield, Illinois, a neat, modest, little
wooden tenement, such as we should allot to a half-

The homage pay officer in the country. It is, in my opinion, not
paid in Ame- so much a man's wealth which the American people
rica to the
energy and recognise and to which they pay their homage, as
ability which the energy and ability which may turn wealth to
produces account. Equality and brotherhood they regard, not
wealth. in theory only (as the idea of mammon worship would
imply), but in truth and in reality, as of the essence
of the Constitution under which they live and of their
social well-being and existence.

The exercise It is from this point of view that the suffrage comes
and results of to be regarded in America not only as a right common
the suffrage
in America, to all, but as a primary necessity. What is there to be

said against its universal employment? Has universal
suffrage been abused in the United States; or has it
led to results beneficial to the nation? Here again I
am forced to a contrast between Great Britain and and in Great
America. When I see our tenant farmers in England Britain,
driven to the poll by undue influence: when I see the
priests in Ireland selling their flocks, and leading them
to vote under the symbol of the Cross; when I see
the abominable system of attorney intimidation which
is practised over voters in many of our smaller boroughs,
and the venality which in some form or other is attendant upon almost every contested election, I must
say that I think our restricted suffrage has nothing to not in favour
boast of over the more universal system of the United of our system.
States. And if we judge by the results, I think the
Americans may point to the Statute Books, and demand of us which nation has perpetuated and enacted
the most bad laws.

England, I have said, does not appreciate the feeling Our estimate
of America upon this question of Universal Suffrage— of America
which lies at the basis of all her institutions. It is, unfortunately, not the only point on which we do not
understand America. We have not appreciated the entirely in-
American character as we should have done: its energy, adequate.
its enterprise, its independent spirit. Look at the industry of the country and its results as developed in
the foregoing pages. Where do we find such results
in the old world? Take the great nations of Europe—
Spain, Italy, Austria, Russia, Germany, France—where
do we find such advances in material progress, as those
which have been developed within the last few years
in America? Even under all the effects of Civil War

—with a population diverted from her labour fields, with her commerce impeded, and the country labouring under a burden of taxation, rendered the more onerous, because it could only be applied to a section of the population—even under all these disadvantages, America is shown to have progressed. I have already observed that there is nothing to correspond with this in the records of history. The occurrence is indeed without a parallel, and it ought to teach us a great lesson with regard to the resources of America.

America a field of peaceful enterprize,

How little we have appreciated America is, I think, conclusively shown by a single fact. Whilst the Civil War was pending, British capital was almost wholly diverted from the North. In London we made loans for Austria, for Greece, for Turkey, and for Egypt,—we even offered loans to Spain: in fact, there is no country in Europe which might not have drawn more or less on our finances. In Liverpool they even lent money, I believe, under the name of a Confederate loan, for the purposes of the South. All these advances were for the purposes of warfare, or for the defrayment of debts incurred by war, or at least for the support and maintenance of military establishments. How comes it that the cautious and careful and far-seeing capitalists of Great Britain think it so much more advantageous to lend money to nations to expend for purposes of war, than to make advances for the development of peaceful enterprises? Is there not a great mistake in this policy? What can Austria and Italy pay us, supporting as they are enormous military establishments in hostility and antagonism, and as a standing menace to each other, compared with what America can pay

whilst European nations maintain standing armies in menace to each other.

us, where, in the course of a few months, the army has been restored to a peace establishment, and the navy has been converted into a commercial marine? If we have money to lend beyond what is required for the development of our own internal and external progress, would it not be far better to invest it in the securities of a country which is at peace, than in those of nations which are perpetually threatening their neighbours, and which, at a cost beyond their means, persist in maintaining large military forces for the mere purposes of menace?

It is the more singular that we should not have seen this, because the Germans saw and appreciated it. Whilst the Civil War in America was raging, the Bourses of Frankfort and of Hamburg were open to the enterprises of the North. Large sums of money were advanced by German capitalists on account of enterprises and works of industry in the United States. Great pecuniary advantages have resulted to Germany therefrom. The moment the War closed, the securities upon which the Germans had made advances rose largely in value.

Superior appreciation of America by the Germans.

All this comes from the want of a proper understanding in this country respecting America and her resources—an absence of knowledge which I hope that this volume may, in some degree, tend to remove. Let me say, however, that whilst I blame my own countrymen for their want of knowledge and appreciation of America, I cannot acquit the Americans of a like error. Mr. Walker, in the passage from which I have quoted at the commencement of this chapter, refers to the error as mutual. I agree with

American misapprehension of English sentiment.

him, that the Americans understand England and the English people as little as we understand America and the Americans. It has been the fashion of late years for the Americans to travel much on the European continent; in fact, they have overrun it. It is most remarkable that the result of this travelling has not been to afford them a better knowledge of the character of the country from which they derive their origin. The fact appears to be, that to a very great extent they have merely made passages through England and Ireland on their way to continental scenes and climates; and that when they have stopped, it has rather been to rest from the fatigues of voyage or of travel than to cultivate a knowledge of and an acquaintance with our people. I think this is very much to be regretted. I think it would be very desirable both for America and for England, that the Americans who visit our country should take every opportunity of investigating the resources and prospects of the country, cultivating acquaintanceships, and endeavouring to ascertain, from personal observation and investigation, the real condition and position of the people. They would have every opportunity. They may rest assured that they would meet, in English society, with the same hospitality they themselves show to our countrymen who travel in America. The Englishman is often thought frigid towards a stranger at first. I have heard that some of the Americans call us " proud." But, if frigid at first, the moment the ice is broken—and it is not difficult to break it—the hospitality and friendliness of English society, especially towards foreigners, is universal and unbounded.

American travellers in England.

The superficial character of their investigations.

Perhaps, if it comes to be closely examined, it will be found that there is more real frigidity in the American character than in our own. I think this is especially observable in commercial and trading circles, and I am not at a loss to attribute it to a cause. It will be universally found, that wherever people with comparatively small means enter into large operations, their views and ideas of results are restricted. Immediate, though comparatively small, profits are desired, instead of those large, ultimate results, which are looked for by larger capitalists. Now, in great operations, great results are not immediately to be expected. It is necessary to wait for their due development. And calculations have to be made proportioned to the time required for those developments. The Americans have accustomed themselves to this in a far less degree than we have. The immense successes arising from their grand developments render them impatient of delays. But it has given, no doubt, a character to their trading reputation, which, according to our ideas, is not favourable. They are "fast," where we are willing to wait. They demand results where we only look to progress. Their enterprises are, consequently, directed to the more immediate, whilst ours incline to the more certain, consequences. It is, probably, in consequence of this difference, that we have come in Great Britain to look on American investments as less secure. I could instance the case of some of their railway enterprizes, in which the ultimate results were large and certain, but into which discouragement is introduced, because such results were not unexampled and immediate. Life in America, as every

The frigidity of social intercourse between the countries.

The results of this frigidity.

American will tell you, is led at a rapid pace : commerce is advanced at a pace still faster. With ourselves, we expect the development with greater certainty, and we find that it comes in increased proportions. We examine and inquire carefully, and lay our foundations accordingly. The Americans lay their foundations on too great immediate expectations.

American views of Europe and of Europeans.

Americans condemn us very much, and not altogether without some degree of justice, for the way in which English travellers have spoken of their institutions. But, on the other hand, no one who reads American journals of European travel but must be struck with the phase in which Europe is regarded by those who visit us from the other side of the Atlantic. If we take two or three of the most intelligent American writers on Europe, what do we find ?

The American view of our agricultural

One who travels, by railway, through the length of England, observes especially on the *finished state* of our nation. Everthing, this writer observes, is so complete. The observation is, no doubt, very just, from an American point of view. They have none of those hedges and ditches which divide our lands, or of that finished agriculture by which they are cultivated, or of those smiling hamlets and villages which overtop the scenery. The results, however, as regards the crops, are less ; and the income, as it affects the cultivation of the soil, is in far inferior proportion. I wish the Americans stopped with us to inquire more fully into

and mining districts.

this. Another American traveller observes on the country he passes through in the neighbourhood of Birmingham. It is one vast plain, he observes, of calcined soil. The people are the dirtiest objects it is

possible to behold. The fires at night remind him of
a pandemonium. Nothing can be more wretched or in-
tolerable. He passes through a district of smoke and
dirt, and enters into a city which seems to be the
metropolis of both. He should stay, however, to
inquire as to the real character of this district. He
should investigate its resources and its wealth. He
should see that herein lies the great central iron and
coal field of England, in which we produce the great
essentials of national prosperity.

*Their mis-
appre-
hensions.*

Now, we know with what different views and objects, and with what widely different imaginations
and results, various parties will visit different portions of the world. Perhaps critics in America, re-
viewing this volume, may enunciate a *" tu quoque."*
You, also, they may say, went through some parts of
our country too hastily, and formed judgments upon
it with too little reflection and consideration. I shall
not object to such criticism. I wish time and opportunity had been afforded me of seeing more of the
United States, and of associating to a greater degree
with every class of a people whom I learned to like and
to respect. But, in anticipation of such criticism, I
must be allowed to make one or two remarks. I went
to America with the avowed intention of studying its
resources and its prospects. I lost no opportunity,
whilst I journeyed there, of making myself acquainted
with them. I was assisted in my investigations, inquiries, and observations, by some of the most talented,
able, and experienced persons in the country. I
derived my information from the highest and most
authentic sources. My observation is my own; my

*The " Tu
quoque "*

*and the
rejoinder.*

*My own
conclusions.*

conclusions are my own. I may, in many respects, be wrong in those observations and conclusions. I may have been misled or misguided (though I do not believe I have been) in the premisses on which I have arrived at them ; but this I do claim, that what I have herein set down, whether for or against the country, and the national character, has been the result of a judgment arrived at, impartially, without fear or favour, and has been reported with a sincere regard to truth, and with a perfect disregard as to the way in which prejudice, whether American or European, may interpret it.

And having said so much, I would add an expression of my earnest hope, that what I have further to express as my views upon the future of the United States may be received on both sides with due consideration. I do not profess to pay compliments to either Great Britain or America : I only seek to enunciate views that may be ultimately advantageous to both.

The mistakes of the Americans.

First, as regards America. I am convinced that considerable mistakes are being made in that country in endeavouring to force its artificial instead of its natural progress. The resources of America are not merely abundant—they are *super-abundant.* The great aim of the nation should be to endeavour to develop those resources, and that can only be effected by entire acquiescence in the laws of nature, which gives to every nation its peculiar advantages, if un-trammelled by artificial restrictions. It is a singular fact, that from the time of WASHINGTON to a comparatively recent date, the people of the United States have insisted upon the importance of observing these natural laws. The whole policy of the country, from the earliest period, was one of free trade as opposed to restriction ; and, considering all the circumstances of this progressive country, it certainly does seem the height of folly that any portion of its people should now desire to change that policy. One cannot but feel the utmost surprise that any section should incline to substitute a policy of restriction for a policy of free trade, at the moment when all the great nations of the world have seen the importance and the material advantage of adopting the policy of which America, in the earlier period of her national existence, was the only exponent. That any party, in a country of exports, should desire a system of duties, whether upon imports, exports, or raw materials, is an hallucination beyond every reasonable and sensible comprehension. It can only be accounted for by the idea that one section of the community has grown so rich, under a temporary system, that it wishes to perpetuate that system to the disadvantage of every other section.

Yet, looking at the fearful experience which America has just encountered, may we not tremble at the consequences which it is possible that such a policy may entail ? America has just issued from a civil war, occasioned by the determination of one part of the Union to resist the perpetuation, in another part, of a system to which it, no doubt, justly, wisely, and humanely objected. Does it not occur to the people of the United States, that another civil war may be occasioned, if one section of the Union endeavours, whether directly or indirectly, to levy taxation upon the staple products of another part, and to make the

price of either corn or cotton subservient to the unnatural task of increasing the prices of manufactured
products? If I feel assured of one thing more than
another with regard to the future of America, it is that
that future can only be successful by a prosecution of
that policy which has contributed to her present position—I mean a policy of free intercourse with every
nation of the world.

Effect of a policy of restriction on the nation.

I trust I may be excused, if, in my anxiety to
exhibit this to the American people, I again advert
to their statistics. In 1860 the total value of their
exports was $373,189,274. Of this their cotton pro-
duce was nearly $192,000,000; their agricultural
produce $48,500,000; their manufacturing produce
only $39,803,000. In 1862, when the export of
cotton was interrupted by the war, the aggregate of
the exports of the North amounted to $213,000,000,
of which amount the products of agriculture consisted of $125,000,000 (or more than one-half), and
the products of manufacturing industry of only
$27,000,000, or less than three-fourths of the exports
of two years previous. Do not these facts prove (if,
indeed, proof was needed) that it is on corn and
cotton, and not on manufactures, that America has
to place dependence? And if so, can another word
be wanted to show, that the imposition of duties
which protect manufactures at the cost of corn and
cotton, must be injurious to the internal trade as well
as to the external commerce of the nation?

Its effect on cultivation and on revenue.

Look at the unsettled territories. A considerable
proportion of the national revenue of the United
States, and, which is of even greater importance,

the development of its lands, depends, entirely, upon
the extent to which those lands are settled. The
extent to which they are settled must, necessarily, depend upon the extent to which they can be cultivated
to a profit. Their profitable cultivation must, in its
turn, depend upon the advantage to which the cultivators can sell their produce. Let taxes be imposed
which diminish that advantage, and the lands will
not be cultivated, settled, or sold. The consequences
will be disastrous, both on the settlement of the
country and on the national revenue—the two great
elements of American prosperity.

Look at the commerce of the country. It has been
already shown that the great bulk of the sea-going
tonnage of the United States is primarily employed
in the export of its own produce. It is in the highest
degree desirable, at the present moment, to afford
every opportunity for the revival and encouragement
of that commerce. How is this to be done if the
export trade of the country is abated by enactments
which have a tendency to raise the prices of the
products to be exported ? Is the whole commerce
of the United States to be prejudiced, in order to
afford some fancied advantages to native industry ?
The idea seems so repugnant to all American policy,
that I cannot believe it will be entertained.

Its effect on Foreign Commerce.

Regard the question in another point of view.
America has suffered greatly in the eyes of the world
by the filibustering enterprizes of some of her citizens.
We believe that those enterprizes, whether directed
to Cuba, to Mexico, or to Canada, have mainly origi-
nated amongst the unemployed populations of the

*Its effect on the popu-
lation of the
Union.*

South; and that the Government and people of the United States, so far as they are disassociated from the South, have given them no encouragement, and are desirous of repudiating and preventing them. But what is the true way of preventing them? It is clearly by affording such opportunities for cultivation, trade, and commerce, as shall keep the population of the nation in active employment, and afford them no excuse for taking up arms in illegitimate and piratical enterprizes. When great armies are disbanded, it is naturally to be supposed that some portions of those who have been engaged in those armies, thrown out of the avocations in which they have been for a long period employed, will seek to find occupations for themselves in kindred though irregular pursuits. Germany, after the forty years' war, was overrun with disbanded musketeers who preyed upon the people. More recently Italy has been infested with brigands, the off-scourings of the Neapolitan, Papal, and other armies, whom it has been difficult to eradicate from the fastnesses of the country. When General Sherman entered into communication with the leaders of the Confederate forces, he tells us, himself, that his primary object was to prevent the Southern States of America from being overrun by troops of desperate and starving soldiers who had no means of subsistence, save by plundering the people. We must not be surprised, therefore, if we hear of filibusterers, however contemptible, from the American armies. Some of these have visited Ireland, and have been caught in their toils, and will probably suffer punishment for their folly and temerity. But what is the

Ordinary consequences of the disbandment of great armies.

American apprehensions of disbandment.

true means of preventing this? Surely that which
led to the absorption of the MILLION OF MEN who
returned to their homes and occupations on the disbandment of the armies of America. The most sanguine supporters of the war did not conceal from
themselves some misgivings as to the future of the
great armies raised in the United States. So long as
they were subjected to military authority, they were
merely instruments of war; but it was feared that
the lessons with which war might familiarize them,
might be repeated when they were free from the control of leaders. But of the hundreds of thousands of
gallant men who arrayed themselves in the army, and
passed like a storm-cloud over the nation, presaging
destruction more direful than anything resulting from
any natural commotion, not one in a thousand remains
a soldier. "The cloud has broken, and this aggre-
gation of violence and of power has sunk into the
earth, like so much sweet and grateful rain, to freshen
and strengthen, and send forth harvests, and manufactures, and wealth, homes made happy, virtue, peace,
and rest." *

The absorp-
tion of their
armies.

---

* A New York paper says :—

"One of our military leaders is now in charge of a machine for
patent pumping; another is building a railway through the oil
country. One of the first soldiers of the army of the Potomac is
in the pistol business; another keeps a retail grocery store; while
one of Sherman's most trusted lieutenants is a claim-agent. One
major-general prints a weekly journal in Baltimore. Some of
our officers have drifted into Congress; others are on their way
to distant Courts to represent the honour of a nation they did
so much to sustain. These starred and belted gentlemen go
down from the command of cohorts to become agents and part-
ners, and dealers, perhaps, with the orderly who stood before their
tents, or the private who held their stirrup. So with the gene-
rals of the rebellion. The greatest of them all is now a teacher of

How was it, that the men composing that great army, returned in this easy manner to their several occupations instead of overrunning the country? *It was because their several occupations afforded them superior rewards for their labour.* When I was in Chicago I visited a printing establishment conducted by a gentleman (The Hon. Charles L. Wilson) who some years ago was Secretary to the American Legation in London. Speaking to him respecting the war, he told me that no less than forty-seven of the compositors in his office had been soldiers. "That man," he said, "was a major, the next to him a captain, the third a lieutenant, another a sergeant in our armies." They were all at work as hard as if they had never left the compositor's desk. I asked if they had willingly returned to their original pursuits? "Undoubtedly," was the reply: "they receive four dollars here for every dollar they received in the army, and they were only too happy to return to situations

---

mathematics in a university. Sherman's great antagonists are in the express and railroad business. The once-dreaded Beauregard will sell you a ticket from New Orleans to Jackson; and, if you want to send a couple of hams to a friend in Richmond, Joe Johnston, once commander of great armies, will carry them. The man whose works Grant moved upon at Donelson edits an indifferent newspaper in New Orleans, while the commander of the Rebel cavalry at Corinth is his local reporter. Marshall practices law in New Orleans; Forrest is running a saw-mill; Dick Taylor is now having a good time in New York; Roger A. Pryor is a daily practitioner at our courts; and so with the rest of this bold, vindictive, and ambitious race of men. The Government against which they warred is now their friend and protector. The people whom they opposed are their daily friends and companions. Rebellion is a dream. They only think of it as of an aspiration that once was possible, but is now gone for ever. As for our soldiers, victors, and masters, they have lain down the sword, and said, 'Now that blood is no longer shed in anger, it shall not be shed in revenge.'"

which I had given them an undertaking, when they left me, that I would retain open for them." *   This was the means by which a reign of terror from disbanded soldiers was prevented in America at the conclusion of the Civil War. If there had been no employment for the people, there would have been anarchy throughout the country ; but inasmuch as there was ample employment for the people, every man returned to the work which afforded him that employment, and anarchy was prevented. How entirely inconsistent all this with our European notions of the consequences of military success ! In Europe we see a military commander rising to the government of an empire as the reward of a successful battle-field : in America we see him returning to his farm, his university, or his printing press, and asking nothing more from his country than the privilege of resuming his daily occupation.

But if employment is lessened, if commerce is checked, if cultivation is impeded, if the people, whether of North or South, find it more profitable to engage in filibustering than in business occupations,

The national interests involved in the disbanded armies.

* Next to the absorption of the army in the ordinary occupations of the country, perhaps the most remarkable feature of the War was the alacrity which all classes in the North showed in joining the army. Skilled mechanics of every sort left lucrative employments, without the smallest hesitation, to fight as common soldiers. I met with an English engineer at Meadville, who had given up an appointment at £4 4s. a week to enlist in the army for three years. He said " he thought it was better to settle the war right off." The Society of Friends in America lamented " that almost all their young people should have gone into war," and recommended that they should be " treated with Christian consideration " on their return from the battle-field.

the Government of the United States will find it difficult to put down such a system ; and if it is unable to do so it will find itself at discord and issue with all the governments of the world. Every European nation is interested, not less than America itself, in checking filibustering outrages. It is necessary that they should be stopped for the peace of the world and for the interests of the United States. The best mode of stopping them is not by a combination of European Powers—such as England, France, Belgium, Austria, Spain, and other countries—to represent to the Government of Washington the necessity of the suppression, and to require it,—but the best way is for the Government of Washington to place itself in a position to say to the population of the United States : " Here we afford you abundant opportunity of agricultural, commercial, and manufacturing employment, profitable to yourselves and useful to your country—come and do your duty, or consider yourselves no longer citizens to whom we will afford protection."

The fate of the South dependent on Free Trade.

Again : with reference to the future of the South, it is in the highest degree desirable that nothing should be done to impede free trade. The World unquestionably looks to the Government of the United States to deal justly, and even liberally, by the States restored to the Union. By their sufferings they have paid a heavy penalty to justice. It is a fine feature in the character of the President of the United States, that he knew how to forget and forgive ; and that at the conclusion of the War, despite all the irritation and excitement amid which it closed, he held out his free pardon to the en-

tire people of the South, on the one sole condition that
they abandoned slavery. But, "disciplined by woe,"
the people of the Southern States should now be treated
with peculiar kindness. The North asks of them, as
the price of re-admitting them into the Union, what
is considered a severe sacrifice—the manumission of
their slaves. To secure the accomplishment of that
object with advantage to the different races peculiarly
requires that the position of both should be put on a
sound basis. How is this to be accomplished if cultivation is impeded, and if the reward of labour is, thereby,
prejudiced? I have no fear for the future of the freedmen unless they are driven by harsh enactments to
array themselves against the whites. In the North
we are told that such enactments can only proceed
from State legislation in the South; but let not the
North give the South a pretext for saying, that, in
consequence of taxation on its products, it was compelled to prescribe a price for labour,—which would
be only another mode of controlling the condition of
the emancipated race.

The fate of the Freed-men also dependent on a just national policy.

Let justice, however, be done to the working classes
of the South, and the whole of that part of the nation
must speedily become largely contributory to the
national revenue:—far more largely than from any
taxation levied on its staple productions. There is
nothing that the South cannot grow; and I do most
heartily concur with those who believe that, as the
result of the emancipation of the slaves, such new life,
energy, and vigour will be introduced into the cultivation of those States, as will render them far more productive than they ever have been heretofore. Many

Anticipations as to the future of the South.

Present con-
dition of the
Southern
States.

people in England seem to fancy that the South has
been absolutely devastated by the War, and that such
injury has been done to her by hostile armaments,
that it will be very many years before she can recover
her position. I do not participate in any such apprehensions, nor do I believe them to be well founded.
Sherman's army, in its long march through Georgia
and the Carolinas, no doubt carried devastation with
it; but the march of Sherman's army was only on a
track at the utmost of not more than sixty miles in
breadth. And when we come to measure on the map
that track with the great spaces of the States which
were penetrated, it is sufficiently obvious that it was
only a certain district which suffered from military
violence, and that the greater portion of the South
remains entirely intact.*

Advantages
resulting
to the nation
from the
War.

For all America, indeed, I think that the War, (apart,
of course, from the bloodshed and misery it has occasioned,) may be considered an advantageous occurrence.
It has cleared the atmosphere of the great cloud which
so long overhung and threatened everything in the
country. The result relieves the nation of its one

---

* The narratives which have appeared in the English newspapers
of the deplorable condition in which the War has left the South
have been chiefly written, it is to be remarked, from Richmond,
the very scene of the principal campaign, by writers whose especial
business it was to visit and describe the battle-fields. Those who
suppose that such accounts give a fair view of the condition of the
South would have pictured the state of the whole of Belgium, after
Waterloo, from a view of the road from Brussels to Hogoumont,
and an inspection of the field of battle. Individuals, engaged in
the agriculture and trade of the South, who visit New York for
purposes of commerce, give a very different description of the condition of their country.

great difficulty.   Apart from bloodshed, it was worth any sacrifice to America, to be rid of slavery.   Whilst that system existed, it was impossible that the nation could have a settled, firm, or united administration. No public legislation could be attempted which in a greater or less degree was not affected by that absorbing question.   In consequence of the jealousies it occasioned, new States could not be brought into Union, new territories could not be developed, the enterprize of America could not properly be pursued. Look at what occurred even during the progress of the War.   Oregon, the new Washington territory, Idaho, Dakotah, Utah, Colorado, New Mexico, and Arizona, have all been more or less opened out to settlement and enterprize.   Besides their vast mineral riches, these territories are estimated to contain eight hundred millions of acres of fertile land, through which it is only needed that railroads should be constructed, in order to induce cultivation.   The nation, moreover, will henceforward be consolidated.   Orators have been accustomed to speak of America as extending "from the Lakes to the Gulf, and from the shores of the Atlantic to those of the Pacific."   But the idea was unreal until the conclusion of the War.   Now, for the first time in American history, it can be said, with truth, that the nationality of the United States does extend from the Lakes to the Gulf, and from one ocean to the other.   And I believe that all that is now needed to give absolute reality to so vast an empire, is that development of intercommunication which I have recommended.

When such communications are completed, when the

Political consequences.

New Territories.

The vast field for settlement and enterprize.

The Union, not only preserved, but consolidated.

South is effectually united with the North, and when the whole continent is traversed by one great trunk railway, worked as a united whole from the Atlantic direct to San Francisco, we shall be called upon to

Future prosperity and greatness of the Union.

regard America as the greatest nation of the world. She will be entitled to take that rank by reason of her extent, her diversity of soil and climate, the character of her communications, the variety of her resources, her vast mineral riches, and the abundant field which she presents for labour and for the employment of capital and enterprize. Many amongst us are accustomed to smile when we hear the Americans speak of the United States, in their accustomed manner, as " a great nation." But there is no mere boast in that description. Emphatically, America is " a great nation." Where can we find her equal in geographical and natural advantages, in material progress or in general prosperity? As a united people, the Americans present to the world a spectacle that must excite general admiration. Regarding them as of the same race and ancestry with ourselves, as a people using our language, governed by our laws, united by the same religion, influenced by kindred sentiments, their progress is a spectacle which should kindle our admiration and enthusiasm. It is a great thing to boast of, that from the shores of our own land, there has gone forth a nation which is able to reflect so many advantages upon the country from which it started, and which has before it so grand a future. It should be our object here in England, to form a more familiar acquaintance with America, to prompt and promote larger and closer intercourse with her, and to ask her to enter with us into that large field which is open to us in common, for the development of the commerce and civilization of the world. It is the duty of both nations to bury all jealousies and discords, to settle irritating questions by mutual concessions and harmonious co-operation, and to endeavour to emulate each other in the development of those arts which tend to universal happiness, and which are based on the promotion of AMITY, and the preservation of PEACE.

INDEX.

INDEX.

416

Index.

Animals slaughtered, value of, 67.
Anthracite, first use of, 183; its supply to towns, 184; quantity raised in Pennsylvania, 185.
Apprentices, number of, 35.
Arizona, precious metals found in, 170.
Arkansas, State of, its population, 20; gold discovered in the river, 167.
Army, large reductions in the, 358; ordinary consequences of its disbandment, 402, 403; the various occupations resorted to by the disbanded soldiers, 403 n.
Asses, bred as substitutes for horses, 80.
Atlantic, seaboard of the, 209.
Atlantic and Great Western Railway, extent and rapid increase of its traffic, 301 n.
Auriferous territories of America, insufficiency of our information respecting, 172; probability of large emigration to the, 173.
Austria, cotton spindles employed in, 115.

B.

BACON AND HAMS, curing of, 94.
Bakers, number of, 35.
Baltimore, population of, 20.
Banjos, manufacture of, 152.
Banking operations, a tax on, 376.
Bankers, number of, 35.
Bar-keepers, number of, 35.
Barley, production of, 69; used for malting purposes, ib.; growth of in California, ib.; the "volunteer crop," 70.
Beans, production of, 70.
Belgium, cotton spindles employed in, 115.
Blacksmiths, number of, 35.
Boarding-house keepers, number of, 35.
Boatmen, number of, 36.
Books, taxes on, 366.
Boot and shoe manufacturers, 144; worked by steam power, 145; the invention introduced by Sir M. I. Brunel, ib.; details of the machinery, 146; state of the trade, ib.; caution respecting, 147.
Boston, population of, 20.
Boston Board of Trade, their report on steam communication, 219; their evidence on the Reciprocity Treaty, 257.
Bread stuffs, export of, 56; (see GRAIN TRADE).
Bricklayers, number of, 35.
Brickmakers, number of, 35.
Bridges and viaducts of railroads, 273.

British provinces, trade with the, 246—249.
Brooklyn (N. Y.), population of, 20.
Brunel's inventions for the manufacture of boots and shoes used in America, 145.
Buck-wheat, production of, 70.
Buffalo (N. Y.), population of, 21.
Buffon, Count, his opinion of Merino sheep, 85, 86 et n.
Butchers, number of, 35.
Butter, produce of, 71.

C.

CABINET MANUFACTURE exported from the United States, 149; character of, ib.
Cabinet-makers, number of, 35.
California, State of, its population, 20; added to the Union, 27; grand trade of, 61; a wheat exporting country, 62; the future granary of the Pacific, ib.; her exportation in proportion to her product, ib.; growth of barley in, 69; number of horses in, 79; gold discovered in, 161, 162, 164; agricultural progress of, 163; favourable prospects of emigration to, ib.; native gold brought from, 165, 166; the gold discoveries a main cause of the recent development and progress of the United States, 173, 174; quicksilver found in, 181; increasing trade of, 330; commercial prospects of, ib.
Campbell, Mr., of Vermont, his Merino sheep, 83, 84.
Canada, local taxes imposed by, 248; position of the British colonists, 258; desirous of maintaining the Reciprocity Treaty, 259; good feeling of towards America, ib.
Canal traffic, limited capacity of, 237.
Cane, Sugar, of the South, 328.
Capital, probable results of free labour upon, 318.
Carolina, North, its population, 20.
Carolina, South, its population, 20.
Carpenters, number of, 35.
Carpets, manufacture of, 121.
Carters, number of, 35.
Cattle, number and value of the, 77; a breed of short-horns originally imported from the valley of the Tees, 82 n.
Census of 1860, population of the, 20.
Cereals, quantity produced, 66.
Charleston, population of, 21.
Chase, Mr., his financial policy, 9; his description of the Pacific gold-fields, 162.

pete with the European manufactures
in American markets, 117; vast importations of from Europe, *ib.*;
absurdity of attempting to protect
it, 118.

Cotton trade of the South, 241.

Cow-pea, production of the, 70.

Cows, number of, 81.

Credit, sustentation of during the Civil
War historically unexampled, and
attributable to the resources of America, 5; the national debt, and its
rapid increase, 6, 7; Mr. Chase's
financial policy, 9; the nation able to
support it, 11.

Customs' duties, 380; collection of, *ib.*

Cutting machines for boots and shoes,
146.

D.

DACOTAH TERRITORY, gold and silver of
the, 172.

Dahlonega in Georgia, manufacture of
coinage at, 161 *et n.*

Dairy produce, 71.

Davis, Mr. Jefferson, kept in confinement to await his trial, 335.

Debt (*see* NATIONAL DEBT).

Denver, the capital of Colorado, 167.

Detroit (Michigan) population of, 21;
commercial convention, 246, 247.

Dividends of railways, 286.

Drivers, number of, 35.

Druggists, number of, 35.

E.

EASTERN STATES, increased demand for
wheat to supply the, 52.

Edge tools, manufacture of, 140.

Egan Canon Mines, 169.

Empire Well, 193.

Engineering manufactures of great
magnitude, 139, 140.

England, the people of, imperfectly informed of the American character,
385; contrast between her and America, 387; increase of pauperism in,
ib.; universal suffrage unsuited to,
389, 391; influence of wealth in, 390;
her estimate of America entirely inadequate, 391.

English, the States in which the greatest
number reside, 22.

Erie Canal, the development of the
grain trade consequent on opening
the, 58; opening of the, 293.

Excursion trains, speed of, 289.

Exhibition of 1851 in Hyde Park, 102,
128; its effects on implement manu-

facture, 102; Commissioner Riddle's
report on, 128, 129; articles exhibited by Russia and America, 129.

Expenditure, 351, (*see* FINANCE *and*
REVENUE).

Export grain trade, 56 *et seq.* (*see* GRAIN
TRADE).

Exports of gold, 225; of native products, *ib.*; progress of, *ib.*; great
variety of, 226, 227; of Great Britain,
227; to different countries in 1862,
228, 229; to the United States from
Great Britain, 43, (*see* IMPORTS).

Express trains, speed of, 289.

F.

FACTORY HANDS, number of, 41.

Farell Well, 195.

Farmers and farm labourers, number
of, 35.

Farms, increase and the numbers of,
49; nature of the holdings, *ib.*; their
size, *ib.*; the increased value of throughout the West, 294.

Files, manufacture of, 140.

Financial policy of Mr. Chase, 9.

Finance, revenue, and expenditure, 351
et seq.

Fish, production of, 152.

Fish-jointing on railways, 274, 275.

Fisheries, disputes respecting the, 252,
253.

Fishermen, number of, 34.

Flax of the Southern States, 327; contrast between the production of
Slave States and Free States, *ib.*

Flax and hemp, cultivation of, 74.

Flour and meal, one of the principal
products of American manufacturing
industry, 37.

Foreign population, proportion of, in
the Northern and Southern States,
19, 20.

Foreign trade, 216; not sufficiently
progressive, 221.

Fort Wayne, town of, 28; M'Culloch's
description of, *ib.*

France, cotton spindles employed in,
115.

Free labour, probable results of, 318;
the South will prosper under, 323.

Free States, acreage of the, "improved"
and "unimproved," 322; contrasted
with the Slave States in 1760 and
1790, 339, 340.

Free trade, system of not fully adopted
in the United States, 96; increased
traffic and advantages arising from,
126; fate of the South dependent on,
406.

Freedmen, the President's policy re-